Blue Rodeo

ALSO BY JO-ANN MAPSON

Hank & Chloe
Fault Line (stories)

Blue Rodeo

A N O V E L

Jo-Ann Mapson

HarperCollins*Publishers*

Grateful acknowledgment is made to the following for permission to quote from copyrighted material:

T. Jefferson Parker for the use of Cat Bagley Parker's song "Blue Rodeo." © T. Jefferson Parker. All rights reserved.

Meridel Le Sueur for "Making the Earth Bright and Thanks." © Meridel Le Sueur. Used by permission. All rights reserved.

Robert Bly for excerpt from "After Working," reprinted from *Silence in the Snowy Fields* (Wesleyan University Press, 1962), © 1962. Reprinted by permission of the author.

HarperCollins books may be purchased for educational, business, or sales promotional use. For information please write: Special Markets Department, HarperCollins Publishers, Inc., 10 East 53rd Street, New York, NY 10022.

FIRST EDITION

Designed by Alma Hochhauser Orenstein

Library of Congress Cataloging-in-Publication Data

Mapson, Jo-Ann.
    Blue rodeo: a novel/by Jo-Ann Mapson.—1st ed.
      p.   cm.
    ISBN 0-06-016944-3
    1. Man-woman relationships—New Mexico—Fiction.   2. Mothers and sons—New Mexico—Fiction.   3. Women artists—New Mexico—Fiction. I. Title.
    PS3563.A62B58   1994
    813'.54—dc20   93-46453

94 95 96 97 98 ❖/HC 10 9 8 7 6 5 4 3 2 1

for Jack:
listen up

Perhaps all the dragons of our lives
are princesses who are only waiting to
see us once, beautiful and brave.
Perhaps everything terrible is in
its deepest being something
that needs our love.

RAINER MARIA RILKE

Heartfelt gratitude to Terry Bennan; everyone at the California School for the Deaf; Craig Candelaria; Gil Carrillo; Mark Chapman; audiologist Renee Dobkin; the Farmington, New Mexico, Chamber of Commerce; Earlene Fowler; Stuart Johnstone; Rich Linder; C. J. Mapson, for keeping me current on everything Western; Martin Nava, my language expert; T. Jefferson Parker, who lent me Cat's inspiring song; Tracy Robert; and to Camp Pine: Clark Hepworth, Patrick Kersey, Marilyn Shultz, Alexis Taylor, and Amanda Wray.

Very special thanks to my agent, Deborah Schneider, and to my editor, Janet Goldstein, and her associate, Peternelle Van Arsdale, for their continued friendship, support, encouragement, and wisdom.

■　■　■

Blue Dog, New Mexico, and all of its inhabitants are products of the author's imagination, as are the Riverwall School for the Deaf, its faculty, students, and the town in which it is located.

Blue Dog

A man's work is nothing but a slow trek to rediscover, through the detours of art, those one or two things in whose presence his heart first opened.

ALBERT CAMUS

T O OWEN GARRETT'S KEEN SHEEPHERDER'S EYES, IT APPEARED
entirely likely that the woman in the blue shirt and red
panties running back and forth between the water faucet
and the two copulating dogs was the Californian. First off, the red
panties were the itty-bitty lace variety. You didn't come by those
easily in a town like Blue Dog unless you ordered off one of those
fancy color catalogs. If you did, the folks who worked at the post
office got to know your weakness, and before long everyone from
Shiprock to Silver City would hear about it. From the way she
ran—high up on the balls of her feet—he figured probably she
was a jogger. When they weren't driving convertibles, Californians ran everywhere, pumping arms and legs and inhaling diesel
fumes from Mercedes, all in the name of health. Every time she
banked and turned from the water faucet and raced toward the
dogs—hands cupped in front of her, making good time but not
good enough to keep hold of the water—he could see those
panties strain for all they were worth, a deep Comstock cherry-
pie red that graced the tops of the longest legs he'd seen all at one

stretch in maybe fifteen years. It was common knowledge they all dressed like that out there, you know, certified members of a nation of crazy people. Women who never wore brassieres except as outerwear, doing aerobic exercises twenty-four hours a day in neon-colored girdles. The men, too. What kind of man was it who voluntarily put on tights and went out among them? True, they had to exercise, because they never did any hard work aside from pushing a computer button now and again or sending one another a fax. And in the state of California it was a sin to be soft. Little wonder they all got skin cancer and had nervous break-downs every fifteen minutes. Good Lord, had she come to Blue Dog to get over one? She might also be one of those New Age crystal-rubbers searching for a cure-all to the kind of depression that came from idleness and too much money.

As Owen pondered these questions, he sat straight atop Red-Bow, his twelve-year-old quarter horse, an animal with just enough mustang thrown in to keep things exciting. Together they surveyed the woman's lack of progress. Hopeful, Owen's three-legged blue Queensland heeler, was locked up tight to the Californian's sorrel bitch, one of those tall skinny dogs that probably cost two months' salary and was too nervous to finish a meal. Long Legs wasn't having much luck breaking them up, though with handfuls of water she was managing to sprinkle them in a pretty kind of way. It brought to mind old Father Morales down at the reservation with his holy-water rattle and the Easter group baptism.

Might even be that the dogs appreciated the water. It was a warm day, somewhere in the high eighties, could hit ninety before noon. He could see she was about to give up now that it was clear the dogs were set on following nature's urgings. He watched her stamp her long, bare foot and give out a holler of frustration. She had powerful lungs, and the yelling indicated she was plenty angry, probably about something or other that happened long before the dogs got into it.

Owen Garrett knew about anger. How it could turn you to a chunk of crumbling asphalt, all tarred up, just stinking in the sun. Anger could change your whole life. It had his. He hoped it wasn't like that for this woman. She was built lean, not too heavy up top—a characteristic that caused most men he knew to stammer and beg like fools. Owen himself didn't care for that kind of breast on a woman. As his father used to say: *More than a mouthful's just being greedy.* Though Owen wasn't clear about the greed part, he knew he liked his women trim but not rib-showing skinny. She was five ten or so, he figured, close to his own height, but at least thirty or forty pounds lighter. Nice little slope to her tummy—he liked a tummy on a woman—it usually meant she took a relaxed view of things. Her curly hair, all messed up, had a healthy red glow to it in the sunshine. It looked like she'd just woken up. And wasn't that a handsome thing! Some women were at their best in the morning, smiling at you over the coffeepot, reliving what you two had done the night before. Others were downright beastly until they'd poured half that pot of coffee on down their stringy throats and had a firm hold of your paycheck. On God's own earth it came down to basically those two types of women, whether you were in the country or the city. Ones who wouldn't flinch reaching up inside a laboring ewe to yank out a turned lamb, and the rest, who didn't want to do anything but shop, listen to the radio, and put on layer after layer of pink nail polish—like Sheila.

Half a day's drive northeast, in the skyscraper- and smog-filled city of Denver, Owen's ex-wife rode around Larimer Square in her little black 600 SL. Small as a wind-up toy, costing more than any house should, the car was a gift from Sheila's current husband, Hal, the real estate magnate. Old Hal, who could do no wrong. Owen and Sheila's daughter, Sara Kay, had turned twenty years old this last spring. Living at the university, she was studying on something that she assured him "would damn straight keep me from ending up like either one of my parents." Well, as much as Sara Kay wanted that statement to wound her daddy, he recognized it as ambition, and Owen Garrett was the first man to applaud aspirations, having come to his own so late in life.

■ ■ ■

You name it, he'd worked it. Offshore oil-drilling rigs in Texas; pumping gas, peddling shocks and tires in Flagstaff, Arizona, to road-weary families stopping off at the Grand Canyon and then later that same day heading east on their way to Meteor Crater for a six-dollar disappointment. He'd even done a short stint at UNM, where all he had to do was dress up in his cowboy clothes, pose for art students, and they got him twenty-five dollars an hour.

He wasn't uneducated. He'd finished high school, just barely, because when you fed the superintendent's cows at dawn, he was more than glad to give you a ride on down the hill with him. He kept up. He read books he traded back and forth with his Navajo friend, Joe Yazzi. Growing up on working ranches had given him a solitary nature and supplied him with an overload of patience, which certainly helped out with Sara Kay, who took after her momma.

Patience had given him the courage to quit all that and change his life after that sorry night in southern Colorado. Once a day he forced himself to think about it, to give it a full ten minutes by his eighteen-dollar Timex, to assess the pros and cons of continuing to live his life piecemeal or driving north to the nearest sheriff's office to confess his part in what happened.

After that, he'd made a deal with himself. He wasn't allowed to think about it anymore until the sun had gone all the way down and come back up again. A man could drive himself mad just thinking. Too much thinking turned your nights to enemies.

He'd tried following the Big Book, going to AA meetings and working his twelve-step program, but after awhile those people started to get on his nerves with their chain-smoking and holier-than-thou attitudes. Step eight stalled him: *Made a list of all persons we had harmed, and became willing to make amends to them all.* Did you go clear back to breaking your brother's toys, or even further, to being born to your momma at a time when she should have been done with mothering, had put in her hard time rearing four other children? To this day he still puzzled over it. Certainly you could make restitution up to a point—right most wrongs—

and what he'd done was about as wrong as they came, but chasing after sainthood twenty-seven hours a day swung things just as far out of balance as too much drinking did.

Just because he'd quit didn't erase his status of being a drunk. That much he did buy. He accepted the fact that he was, for all time, a drunk who no longer drank. He amended those twelve steps and lived by them as best he could, offering his insurmountable worries to his Higher Power. There were times he even went back to AA—when a job took him to a new town or the guilts steeped him in a terrible brew of self-pity—he'd search out a meeting in one of the churches or American Legion halls, and listen, both ears open, to what other folks had to say. Saying the words of greeting always started out the same—a confession that stuck in his throat like too-sweet cake: *Hello. My name is Owen, and I'm an alcoholic.* The rush of kindly voices that came charging back: *Hi, Owen!* never failed to cheer him, to reassure him he could blend into the background of whatever small town he'd landed in. And for ten full minutes each day, each minute a considerable chunk of time when you weighed them against one another, he forced himself to recall one particular day seven years back, in as much detail as he could summon.

He was a forty-five-year-old drunk cowboy, tanked up on bullheadedness and wounded pride, who had let his anger get the best of him. Owen had been working cattle on the Watson ranches that summer, and came into town after four straight weeks only to receive Sheila's message: *I can't take it anymore. You gone all the time and me here with no more than two nickels to rub together. I'm taking Sara Kay and going with Mickey. He loves me and that's that.*

Before he could cry himself to sleep in a fifth of blended whiskey, he got into a pointless fight with a young man in a goofy straw Shepler's hat. Rattlesnake hatband, complete with fanged mouth agape in the center and painted chicken feathers collaring the unlucky reptile like a Vegas showgirl—he could still see the thing, clear as unwanted ice on a cattle tank. He remembered a skinny guy who couldn't have been more than nineteen or twenty, one of those types with a mouth as big as his rodeo belt buckle. After Owen accidentally bumped his arm at the pool table, spilling just a little of his beer, the fellow began needling him, calling him Pops, making fun of his duct-taped boots and soiled Wranglers, his battered hat with the cattleman's crease. Owen remembered leaning his face into the young man's personal space and giving him a chuck under the chin. *See here, I'll buy you another two inches of beer, but I've heard about enough, son.* Then nothing specific, just the blind rush of anger and so much motion, the guy coming at him with a pool cue. The cue bounced off his hand and the lighter half of it flew against three men standing at the bar. It was the year of all those terrible fires. Ranchers were going broke hauling water. The fight arced through the bar crowd the way one of those fires went about creating its own wind, crossing boundaries randomly, eating whatever lay in its path. Liquor spilled into it like gasoline. Tired-out strangers who'd been sharing drinks and listening to Ernest Tubbs "walk the floor" on the jukebox suddenly were raising their voices and clenching fists, letting go a year's frustration. At the sound of the first shattering bottle, Owen brought his fist down on the smart-mouthed knucklehead who wouldn't let up.

Oh, certainly, now he knew the psychology of the incident. He was more hurt than angry. It was Sheila he wanted to go after. The idea that Mickey the stereo salesman probably had her on her back as she hooked her legs over his shoulders was killing him. He couldn't shake the image of the idiot jackhammering her with all six of his cheap-suit-and-jasper-bola-tie inches. A man didn't need a headshrinker to figure that out—but instead of telling his wife what he thought of her judgment, this unknown bigmouth became the recipient of his mixed-up sorrow. Blindly, he swung. When he next looked up, there was blood running out the man's ear and his smart mouth was quietly sagging to the left. In his left hand Owen was holding the weighted end of the pool cue. He couldn't remember anything after the first punch. His own teeth felt loose. He tasted blood. His knuckles were ripped open, exposing tendon, and a warm liquid was running down his left cheek. He reached up to wipe it away and his fingers came back bloody. A quart of whiskey under his belt, he experienced a sober moment of perfect clarity. He knew that the man under his fist was dead, and in all likelihood he had delivered the telling blow. He let go of the man's shirt, picked up his own hat, and exited the bar through the front door, still holding the pool cue he would later burn out by the dam. In all the chaos no one noticed him leaving. He could not afford to look back. After a night out by the dam, he sent Sheila a five-hundred-dollar money order for Sara Kay's birthday, bought an old pickup and horse trailer at the New Mexico border, drove straight through to El Paso, and took a summer job breaking horses for a wealthy heart doctor who owned four hundred acres.

Looks like whoever gave you that scar was after your eye. You mind if I ask how it happened?

Car wreck.

I've done my share of stitching. I'd say knife wound—am I close?

Owen had kept his face immobile, though his lies felt like they were crawling all over him. *Your fences look like they could use some tending, doctor. I'm handy with fences.*

Only the next winter did he find out the stereo salesman was history. Sara Kay'd been in the hospital with a ruptured appendix, destroyed that her father hadn't even called to see how she'd fared under the scalpel. That was the end of her loving him as that larger-than-life daddy, and maybe that was for the best. They wrote letters every once in awhile. She told him how many A's she'd racked up on her report card, the colors of the ribbons she'd garnered in the last gymkhana. But there was only so much you could tell a child on paper. Sara needed new heroes, and Sheila gave her plenty between that stereo salesman and the real estate king she finally married. Well, a change of pasture made for a fatter calf. Hal certainly could provide in the money department better than Owen, who felt like he was always trying to keep the wolf from delivering pups on his front step.

Sometimes he missed Sara Kay so bad his heart felt herni-ated. His feisty little girl, the one who rode out the bucks and shot a rifle as easily as she tied bows in her braids. At thirteen she'd been a champion barrel racer, once breaking seventeen sec-onds. *Ladies and gentlemen, first place to Sara Kay . . . !* She won a silver buckle, but it might well have turned to gold next to her face-splitting smile. Whenever he felt the urge to take inventory, Sara Kay emerged as the one good act he had done on this earth. He hoped she had kept up with her riding. She was a woman now, complete with her own set of bitternesses tucked away inside her, festering.

He checked his watch—nine minutes, forty-three seconds. The dogs were still at it. The woman was sitting down in the dirt, arms folded over her knees, head resting there, all done yelling, watching. RedBow sighed beneath Owen. Owen sighed too. *Come on, wrap it up, Hope, we got sheep to tend.*

He'd drunk himself into memory loss for six months after the fight, solving nothing when it started to take more and more liquor to keep things comfortably hazy. When he poured his last bottle down a motel sink, half his problems disappeared, but remembering the fight clearly had taken a year. After his last job ended, as close as it was to the Colorado border, he said okay to the town of Blue Dog and caretaking this farm. Tybolt and Phyllis Starr, the elderly couple who owned it, didn't care if he raised hot pink llamas, they were so happy not to see the land lying idle. They set him up in the bunkhouse. Owen liked small-town life. People weren't overly friendly. They'd leave you alone if that was what you wanted, but if one of your animals was in trouble, they were there to offer help.

He'd made a few friends among the Navajo who'd moved to town from the reservation. Good people, they worked harder than half the white men he knew. He felt a kind of ease alongside them. They had a different way of looking at transgressions. They saw punishment as *naayéé'*, the gods delivering justice in their own way, with a wisdom often as humorous as it was fair. For example, a *yeibechai* dancer might pop right up in the pasture one day and shake his turtle rattle in Owen's face, rendering him impotent, or just as casually change him into a stalk of tall blond yucca. The People believed in the old stories. To them it wasn't so much a matter of faith as it was listening to and thinking about what you heard, then relating the story to your own life. Back in Colorado such talk had been called "spinning windies," and elsewhere, lying. But here, if a story felt right, there was no reason why you couldn't accept it as true.

His friend, Joe, a fellow recovering alcoholic, had once told him, *Take that scar on your face, Owen. No knife did that. Eagle talon, maybe. Fork of lightning. Whatever it was, it's all part of* hozho, *the natural cycle.*

Owen had listened and smiled, wishing it were that simple. Joe's army pension didn't quite make up for him losing six feet of intestine, or cover the surgeries to fit back what shrapnel had rearranged, but the money allowed him to live simply and time to indulge his theories. Every morning, shaving, the finger-thick scar beneath his own left eye reminded Owen that the truth was he had taken a life. He'd never gone to get the wound properly stitched. He'd gritted his teeth and washed the two halves of the cut with a small bar of motel Camay and tap water, then doused it with equine bloodstop powder from his tack box. When the bleeding slowed to a manageable trickle, he taped it shut with small strips of adhesive. Initially a raised rope of purple scar tissue, over time it had receded into a flesh-colored line that gave his eye a permanent tendency to wink. He marked the passage of time by that scar, tallying up his losses. In seven years: Sheila, Sara Kay's respect, a house to call home, money in the bank. On the credit side: RedBow, his dog, Hope, the bunkhouse on this farm, and a few ragged sheep who might turn a profit to keep him going another season.

So what if sheep were maggots at the bottom of the manure pile to cowboys—animals Indians and fools tended and neither made a dime off? Owen no longer cared what cowboys said about him. He liked having animals around, and cattle took more time, space, and money than he had available. He ran two dozen sheep on three acres of grazing land, though sometimes as few as five or six, if he'd gotten a good price and people were in the market for rams. Presently he had ten, a handful so small most would call it a hobby flock.

Forage in northwestern New Mexico was fit for little else, and by selling young rams for breeding, a few Suffolk for mutton, and the Merino crosses he kept just for wool to trade to the weavers, he stayed flush. Of course, with the environmentalists yapping about desertification, overgrazing, and the loss of different species of native grasses and the government imposing all kinds of stipulations, who knew how long it would last? The feud between cattlemen and shepherds was still alive, too, breathing shallowly, a centuries-old conflict that wouldn't die, at least not in Owen's lifetime.

Fifteen minutes now—the dog was being downright greedy.

He legged Red to a trot and headed toward the farmhouse. He'd heard from Big Lulu Mantooth at the trading post that the Starrs were looking to rent the big house. If this woman had signed a lease, the farmhouse, at the farthest end of the property, was now officially occupied. Some nights Owen had let himself dream what it might be like to move in, to climb the stairs to the second floor, to soak in the old clawfoot tub, cook his meals in a real oven, not just over a hotplate burner, to have a dryer to dry his clothes in so they came out warm and fluffy, people in the rooms to talk to besides himself. The Starrs used to come up for summers, but they were getting frail with old folks' complaints, and they liked staying in Albuquerque, where the weather was easier on old bones. Whether his neighbor lasted the winter or turned tail for Santa Fe opera season next July was a question not to be answered for some time yet, but whatever happened, Owen Garrett knew he had a front-row seat.

"Excuse me, ma'am." He tipped his hat. "I don't mean to intrude on your morning."

She looked up from studying the panting dogs. "Where did you come from?"

He could see she'd been crying. Her eyes were puffy, the piercing clean-sky kind of blue that shows up best when you wash it over with tears. The dogs were in the awkward part of things now, trying to disengage, falling over each other, all legs and confusion. "Over there, by the river. I can see you're none too pleased with what's happened here."

"Did you expect me to start in writing birth announcements?" She pulled the now-buttoned shirt down and sat there like it was normal to be outdoors without your britches. The red panties that had first caught his eye were concealed beneath the long shirttails. "I tried throwing water on them."

He smiled gently. "But they weren't thirsty."

She got to her feet and swatted at the dirt that had collected on her bottom and thighs. With each swat, the shirt lifted and revealed flesh. She abandoned the dirt chase and folded her arms across her chest. "Listen, I don't know whose dog that is, but he shouldn't be running around loose if he isn't neutered."

"He's my dog, ma'am. He break a window and kidnap your bitch?"

"Of course not. I . . . she. . . ." She let her words trail off and frowned. "Look. I pay rent. This is private property. It's fenced."

"Can't argue with you there."

"Then this dog—and you—have no business here."

The plains cottonwoods shifted their heart-shaped leaves in the warm breeze, and Owen could hear the lowing of neighboring cattle across the Animas River. She was as handsome up close as she had been from a distance, but guarded, wary.

He pointed across the acreage to his bunkhouse, eighteen by twenty-four feet of lapped logs and newly patched roof. "That's my place," he said. "I'm your neighbor. I've lived here a little over two years, and those white dots in the far pasture are my sheep."

"Sheep?"

"Yes, ma'am. Suffolk and a few Merinos. Brought them down off the mountain last week. They wouldn't win any honors at the state fair, but I'm working toward a decent strain, even if it takes until I'm toes-up." He reached down into his saddlebag, retrieved his stainless-steel thermos of coffee, and held it out to her. "Go on, take it. Hot coffee won't bite you. Have a little."

"Mrs. Mantooth didn't say anything about sheep." She unscrewed the thermos, poured coffee into the cup lid, and took a drink.

"Sheep won't bother you. I move them in and out so fast you'll hardly know they're here."

"This is good coffee."

"I worked a stint or two as Cookie on a couple of ranches. You learn to make coffee or you move along."

She eyed him, drank some more, and set the cup down in the dirt. "There's no electricity in the house yet, and I was going to drive to town for some convenience store coffee." She shuddered. "That's what kept me driving from California all the way here. Those sixty-nine-cent coffees in the Styrofoam cups."

"No electric?"

She shook her head. "It was supposed to be turned on before I got here."

"Got your phone hooked up?"

She sighed, and he watched the rise and fall of her broad shoulders. "I don't really care about the phone."

A woman without a phone? Well, now, that was a new one. The nervous breakdown theory was looking more and more like a sure bet. Possibly she'd had her fill of telephone salesmen. He let the comment pass. "Likely they'll be by today to get you hooked up on the electric. Maybe they confused the days, or some emergency came up. Meanwhile, you're welcome to keep that thermos and the coffee in it."

"Thanks." She tried to smile, but apparently her face muscles had made some kind of pact not to engage in such activity. The dogs were separated now. The bitch had her tail between her legs and was looking up guiltily at the woman.

She made a face at the skinny dog. "Stop trying to look penitent, you little hussy."

Owen chuckled. "Now don't insult her. Your dog's just following the natural order. Her first heat?"

"I don't know. Do they get them every month?"

He smiled. "No. She looks young, so maybe she won't catch. But if she does, you just let me know, and I'll assume responsibility for the litter."

"She's my son's dog."

"You have a boy?"

"Fifteen. But he doesn't live with me."

Owen dismounted and held Red's reins in his left hand. "Well, that can be hard on a dog, not to mention a mother."

She put out a hand toward the dog, who nosed in her direction, then turned and fled toward Owen. He knelt to meet the dog at her own level. She sniffed him all over, then gave him a lick on the cheek. He took her into his lap and scratched her behind the ears.

The woman's face softened. "Do all dogs come to you like that?"

"Some of them, anyway." He set the dog down. "Owen Garrett, ma'am. Your neighbor. Give a holler if you get into trouble. I'll come by, see what I can do."

"Thanks for the offer, but I'm sure I'll be fine as soon as I get power."

Power—so many women seemed to be after that. "Well, then." Owen put one foot in the stirrup, and the three-legged heeler hopped to his side. "Come along, Hope."

"How did your dog lose the leg?"

"A fondness for chasing cars. Cured him but quick." He slung himself the rest of the way up, turned his horse and started out for the south pasture the long way, just to have a moment to collect his thoughts. Behind him he heard the slamming of the screen door at the Starr farmhouse. His own momma had taught him to be polite. You get to your feet when a lady enters the room. You don't wear your hat into a restaurant. When someone introduces herself, you shake hands and you say your name back.

He saw her take off for town about ten o'clock that morning, down the gravel road that ran parallel to the pasture. She drove an older Toyota Land Cruiser, nice car, well cared for, a faded blue-gray color with white trim. It bore a California license plate. Be for the best if she got that taken care of right away, the way some people could get around here. New Mexicans didn't care much for the Texans, and it wasn't the Texans alone who had it in for Californians—they were fair game for all. The sight of those white license plates struck terror into most hearts. The Californians seemed to be trying to buy up all the land to build themselves getaway places. Not her, though. She was renting. *I pay rent. This is private property.* Seemed like out there in California they grew up believing every square inch of land could be bought, and they took the idea with them out of state, didn't they, locking doors and fencing up what was once pretty, uncluttered country. She drove around the curve of road way too fast, like all Californians, spraying gravel that would nick her nice car in places that would be sure to rust come winter, and then she was gone, out of his sight.

Below him, his sheep grazed, giving out that funny huff of breath that was part of their dining process. They looked silly, half-grown out from the last shearing, but when the autumn nights started lowering the temperatures, they would wool out quickly.

Sheep were simple enough to tend that Owen could work afternoons three days a week in Rabbott's Hardware and Lumber. He put on his green vest with the dual waist pockets and checked stock against the yellow packing slips. Next he replaced fast-moving items on the floor—screws, ballcocks for toilets, keychains that lighted up when you squeezed them around the middle. They stocked housewares as well—Libby glasses with orange slices painted on the sides, oil lamps, and kitchen gadgets like shiny aluminum garlic presses and even a stainless-steel melon baller. They had steady customers, and lumber sales kept them flush, but a week might go by without a significant sale in hardware, since here in Blue Dog most folks didn't have the necessary cash to get things fixed right away. Dave Rabbott carried a few accounts; he was in no danger of dying a wealthy man. He sat in his office and licked the tip of his pencil, tallying up long columns of figures, answering the telephone, and sometimes calling Owen over to check for a certain part for a customer.

There was a good deal of shoplifting in the store, which vexed Dave something terrible. All kinds of people thought it was okay to steal a seventy-four-cent screw, but the most blatant cases by far were the young Indian children, who couldn't seem to keep their hands off the shiny copper piping and the cut glass salt-and-pepper shakers.

Goddamn hunter-gatherers, Rabbott called them, as if there were some shoplifting encoding built into their DNA. True enough, the Navajo were descended from hunter-gatherers who once made their way across the land surviving on what the earth offered up as bounty. No crime there. New things glittered on the shelves—it was as natural for little kids to pick up a gadget and want it for their own as it was for the tourists to finger their silver jewelry. Owen came up with the idea of setting out baskets of penny toys at small-hands level. At first Dave shook his head at what he saw as a waste of twenty-five dollars a month, supplying Indian children with whistles and plastic race cars. The shoplifting dropped by 50, then 75 percent. Dave gave Owen a twenty-five-cent raise. "Just don't go after making me manager," Owen said. "I'm busy building my herd."

His neighbor came into the store around three-thirty that afternoon. She loaded up her cart. An expensive drip coffeemaker, pack of a hundred filters for it, corkscrew, clothespins, a small flashlight, and a six-pack of some of those copper-top batteries. Then she wandered every aisle, standing by the art supplies for the longest time, studying the pastel chalk assortment, the paints, and the sketch pads. Sometimes tourists bought markers for their kids, but mostly the stuff sat there, yellowing. She put two cheap pads into her basket, took them out again, and set them back on the shelf. She turned to wheel her cart away, then returned and picked up the pads again. Once more she set them down. Dave Rabbott came in from his coffee break and stood with Owen, watching her.

"Seems to be having a little trouble making up her mind," Owen observed.

"Want to bet on whether she buys them or not?"

Dave was a gambler the same way Owen was an alcoholic, testing himself on a daily basis, but Owen wasn't buying into today's review. "Not a fair bet, Dave. She'll buy them, if not today, then another day."

"You think she's one of those obsessive-compulsives like Enid was telling me about on the Oprah Winfrey show?"

"I kind of doubt that."

"I'm telling you, Owen, you never can tell what regular-looking people are up to behind their own curtains." Dave lit a cigar and walked up the stairs to his office.

Owen took his Sharpie marker out and marked $4.59 on some brass couplings before he set them into the wire bin. That was a lot of money for so small a piece of metal. Every now and then he looked up from his work to see his neighbor going through this agonizing routine of yes to the sketch pads, no to the sketch pads. His heart went out to her. Eventually she loaded up her basket with two of the cheapest pads, recycled newsprint. She turned once and caught him looking at her; then, recognizing him, she turned quickly away. But it had been long enough for him to glimpse the depth of her fear of those art supplies. She bought the big box of colored pencils, the small pastel set, an old, marked-down tube assortment of watercolors and three sable brushes, one of which Owen knew for a fact cost eleven dollars. Minnie Youngcloud checked her out, leaving her register to take the check to Dave for approval. After she'd left the store, Owen went to Minnie.

"How's your old momma doing?" he asked.

Minnie rolled her eyes behind the thick lenses of her glasses. Tucked into the arms of the frames were tan hearing aids that made sense on an older woman, not a girl still in her twenties. "Driving me crazy. She finished another Storm Pattern last night, a beautiful rug, Owen, all reds and grays with just a little white in it. The best wools. Now she'll take it to the trading post and get maybe a third of what it'll eventually sell for, so of course then I got the big lecture on carrying on the weaver's tradition, how if I don't learn to weave then the craft will die, like the whole Navajo race depends on whether or not Minnie Youngcloud makes rugs to sell to tourists whose dogs probably puke all over them. Mama says that someday I'll get snapping-turtle lips if I don't show respect. Other than that, she's fine." She gave his shoulder a little swat. "You should go see her. She asks about you every night."

"Maybe I'll try to get over there this weekend. She going to have something in the Blue Dog auction?"

"A Burntwater, I think."

"Well, I'll be sure and buy me a raffle ticket then. Listen, can you give me change for a dollar so I can get a Dr Pepper?"

Minnie smiled. "Owen, if you want to see that lady's check so you can get her name, just ask me." She pressed No Sale and reached under the till box for the checks and set them on the counter.

Embarrassed, but thankful for the year-round tan that hid his blushing, he took the check from Minnie. *Margaret R. Yearwood, P.O. Box 1187, Blue Dog, New Mexico, 87401.* Sixty-seven dollars and ninety-two cents drawn on the Bank of New Mexico, Santa Fe branch, check number 103. She had good handwriting and used a blue fountain pen.

He handed the check back to a smirking Minnie. "You know something?"

"What?"

"Your old momma's right, Miss Turtle Lips."

2

FOR THE FIRST TIME IN SIX MONTHS, MARGARET YEARWOOD HAD company in bed. Sometime during the night, Echo had crawled in beside her, wormed her way between the pillow and her chest, and lain so still Margaret hadn't noticed she was embracing a dog. She awoke with her arms cast around the skinny brown body, the funky aroma of canine tickling her nose. Add stealth to her sins, right after promiscuity. In her mind's eye Margaret pictured that strange blue dog taking advantage of Echo, his cowboy master tipping his hat and saying a big Western "ma'am."

Welcome to New Mexico, where the first thing we do is knock up your dog. All I need is a litter of puppies to send me over the edge, she thought. I'll make a few calls, take her to the nearest veterinarian, have her spayed, won't even mention this fracas to Peter. That's the responsible thing to do, just have her fixed and quit worrying. She sighed. God knew how long she'd slept like that, but it was bliss to once again feel a warm body against her own. "You slept like this with Peter, didn't you?" she whispered to his dog, who stretched lazily and gave one of those funny mystery-mutt noises, a sound halfway between a growl and singing, then tunneled deeper beneath the sheets on the old iron bed that came with the rented house.

She pulled the covers up over the hump of dog body, remembering how Peter's "made" bed had looked the same way back home—a place neither of them lived any longer. A hundred and forty miles south, in the town of Riverwall, her son was settled into the boys' dormitory at the School for the Deaf.

She could have pictured Pete at age fifteen a lot of different places, ranging from a varsity water polo meet to juvenile hall, but never there, or so far away.

The administration took into consideration his "special circumstances," meaning his newly acquired deafness following the meningitis. Initially they indicated they might be able to "umbrella" Peter in under his father's gene pool. Ray was one-quarter Cherokee, just barely qualifying his son as Native American. But it turned out one-eighth Cherokee blood wasn't enough. Margaret could sense the paper shuffling, the committee about to say no, when she offered them herself in exchange. If she moved from California to New Mexico, providing proof Peter was establishing residency, they would keep her son. She agreed, on the stipulation that they kept this information from Peter. That last thing she wanted from her angry son was gratitude based on guilt.

At his birthday party he'd made it clear he wanted to live with a foster family; that if he had to be deaf, he might as well live with other deaf people. He was still a minor, and the divorce had awarded her custody. She knew she could have reeled him back in and forced him to stay with her—if she wanted to play dirty, she could have gotten his father on her side as well. Or, this one time, she could set aside her own desires and give him his wish. Sure there were other schools for the deaf, good ones; three in Southern California alone, but Riverwall was the nearest one with a foster family program. Family—as if she could define what that word meant anymore. Her own parents were dead, she wasn't speaking to her sister, Nori, and a month ago her divorce from Raymond had grown its legs and begun walking out into the world. The therapist supported Peter's wish. She thought placing Peter with a deaf couple was a great idea, and a way to "defuse" the explosive situation their fractured family had become. Maybe so, but letting Peter go made her feel branded with the words *parental failure*. Logically, there was wisdom in allowing everyone a corner in which to heal. In her heart, however, logic made a weak opponent.

In order to submerge Peter fully into the deaf culture, he would have to learn American Sign Language by immersion—what place more logical than a residential school? But on the weekends, when other kids went home to their families, Peter would take the bus not to his mother in this three-bedroom farm-house, but to Santa Fe, to the Hidalgos, a deaf couple who had raised two deaf children of their own. *Just like an exchange student*, the therapist said. *A whole different culture*. As she said the words, Margaret had focused on the therapist's desk, where a framed photo showed two sunny-faced toddlers, both no doubt in pos-session of all their faculties, both not yet capable of hating their mother. That, too, comprised a different culture.

With Peter in his school, weekending with foster parents, where did that leave his mother? Literally, without purpose or plan in Blue Dog, New Mexico, paired with a mixed-breed dog who as of yesterday was no longer a virgin. If she drove ten miles over the speed limit, Four Corners was one hour away. Closer to town, trading posts offered a variety of attraction from mass-produced San Ildefonso–type pottery to museum pieces secured under glass. Scattered on the nearby reservations, weavers pulled woolen yarn through their hand-built looms, creating painstaking patterns in the old tradition. But right now, what Margaret knew of Blue Dog was this house, the hardware store, and the market. It was a town she'd chosen for reasons nearly as faded as the once-green T-shirt in which she slept.

As she dressed in the previous day's jeans and a clean blouse, Margaret imagined her son walking into the classroom in his new school. Pete always had a hard time starting out. He'd project this deliberately sullen exterior to keep everyone distant; he wasn't easy with others. Someone else always had to make the first move. Maybe they'd place him with the perfect roommate, someone with a similar background who would take him under his wing. More likely, though, he'd lock himself up inside and fit in nowhere. This is separation anxiety, she told herself, trying to ignore the adrenaline tingles cramping her empty stomach and causing the hair on the back of her neck to lift. Whether your son succeeds or fails, whatever happens this year, Margaret Yearwood, your job is to stand back and watch. If she said it enough times, she might begin to believe it.

Downstairs, she set out kibble for the dog and made herself a piece of toast. Washing the butter knife and putting it away at once, she realized she was trying to bond with the old house, impart familiarity into those gaping spaces by opening drawers and cupboards, surveying her meager belongings, all newly purchased, items without history. She'd left behind her Limoges china; the everyday dishes, too, Blue Mesa from Dansk. After Peter's illness, everything she touched felt like detritus, the accumulation of twenty years of a failed marriage. Most of the furniture stayed with the house as part of the rental agreement. Everything else went to the thrift shop. The only things she'd salvaged were her most comfortable clothing and a secondhand Navajo rug Ray liked to make fun of—*Come take a look at Margaret's little relic*, he'd say. *My wife, the junk-store pack rat.*

She thought Ray might want a lamp or two, a painting; he'd chosen most of them, insisting they buy only the best because, by God, they could afford it. But neither his son nor his wife ever held his interest like the pages in his typewriter or those Hollywood women, ambitious, ready to shinny up to whatever body might land them one step closer to the fame game—women like the one he'd left her for, the one who was going to have his baby, in the not-too-distant future, actually. If I could have, I would have given him more babies, Margaret thought. If I'd had more than one to practice on, I might have done a better job at motherhood.

I don't want to live with either one of you, Peter'd said on his birthday. After a raging scene, though it was clear his father had no intention of making space for Peter in his new life, Ray had driven off, leaving Peter in tears. That was the moment I really lost him, Margaret thought. Right then he was on his way to New Mexico, even if it meant he had to hitchhike to get here. It was up to her to hold herself together, drive Peter and his duffel bag to the airport, watch him board the white America West jet with the other passengers as casually as if he were going off on a hiking trip with friends. Pete was fair at reading lips of people he knew, a quick study when it came to speech reading. But how would he communicate with the stewardess if he needed something more complicated than a Coke? Sure, he still had command of his voice, and though he'd initially resisted, in the past two months he had mastered finger spelling, but how many people in airports knew the rudiments of sign language? The therapist suggested that he carry a note pad and pen at all times. He might use them. But things happened, people panicked. And it wasn't just children who could be cruel. Adults had more practice.

He'd had to change planes in Phoenix for Albuquerque. She worried the entire duration of the flight, allowed him two hours for claiming luggage and the bus ride, then worried some more. At six, right on the hour they'd promised, the secretary called and told her Peter had arrived safely. He was fine, he would write soon. They had TDDs—telephone services for the deaf. Margaret had the system installed herself as soon as she knew he was coming home, the awful coma business in the past. But it wasn't lack of hearing that kept Peter distant.

Before his illness he wore his clothing like garments for battle: Def Leppard T-shirts, torn black jeans, the shin-high combat boots with long red laces. When they were a family, Peter polished them every Sunday on the deck on folded newspaper, making certain they were in full view of his father, just to let Ray know that he was buying his shoes at Army-Navy surplus. His vocabulary seemed limited to as-few-syllable communiqués as he could muster: "Later"; "No way"; the occasional "Cool."

There were times she had no idea where he was or who he was with. He kept his parents at arm's length. To recall life before meningitis felt like sifting though the wreckage of some train disaster, but there'd been occasions during that time when she and Peter could talk. They'd taken drives together, circling through the canyons and watching the hillsides change color. In Southern California that meant two shades: vivid green in winter, flammable dry yellow in summer. She remembered one day two years ago they'd stopped across from a crumbling stables to feed their lunch apples to pasture horses, some of them so thin and poorly kept their ribs showed clear as barrel staves. At Peter's request Margaret had taken his notebook paper and sketched the horses. Until she'd taken it down to pack away, the drawing had been tacked above his computer in his room. Unless Peter begged her to, she didn't really *draw* anymore, except for doodles on her shopping list, cartoons to liven up notes reminding him to clean his room. The horses in her sketch had four legs and all the other expected horse accoutrements, but horses were meant to be represented the way Da Vinci had drawn them, lovingly painted into the landscape like Caravaggio, or sculpted life-size in marble by Bernini's chisels.

The day of that drive, Peter was at his best. His long fingers stroking the neck of a gray gelding, his low voice wooing the animal toward the fence and the apple, he'd turned to her and said, "You know, you really are pretty, Mom," then blushed and turned back to the horse, a much easier companion. On his birthday, with just as much eloquence, he'd called her a bitch.

A husband could leave you if he felt like it. So, too, a son. But how did you go about leaving yourself? Did you just pick up and leave behind your waterfront house, your friends, the old Margaret who dropped off everyone's dry cleaning, remembered the gardener's birthday, learned three different ways to make ratatouille? Could you simply rent a new life among these yellow summer flowers in northern New Mexico, foregoing people for a place? Somehow, without thought to what leaving meant, she'd done just that.

. . .

Peter's aversions couldn't keep her from driving *by* the school.
After the dry heat and traffic of I-44, a left turn onto 25 deposited
her into the rarefied air of Santa Fe. From there it was surface
streets all the way to the town of Riverwall. For exploration along
the way, there were art galleries by the score, museums that
shamed Los Angeles, jewelry so finely crafted it belonged in private collections that would someday reflect history, instead of tar-
nishing on tourists' necks. The state capital was so small a town
and so artfully clustered together it seemed an unlikely place to
conduct anything but a sleepy kind of government. The Santa Fe
River ran through the center of downtown, narrowed to a trickle
of water easily traversed by a bridge, barely a hint of what it
would become in wintertime. Once Margaret got past the glitzy
Plaza hotels and the shops off Palace Avenue, the town grew
tough looking, calloused. In winter enough snow accumulated to
transform the small streets and roadways into narrow, icy path-
ways. Perhaps that was what rusted out cars and turned people
who lived here so inward and guarded.

Despite the whimsical chili pepper lights strung in the shop
windows, there was evidence that wind and rain worked on a
daily basis to erode adobe, chiseling its way into the smooth,
thick walls. Sober-faced workmen troweled and painted right
alongside the tourists, unnoticed. The shopkeepers were sullen
and businesslike. The Indian women selling jewelry in the Plaza
stared vacantly into space, inured by continual rejection, flatly
stating, "Necklace," if Margaret so much as hesitated as she
passed.

Yet the tourists were upscale, anxiously toting three or four
shopping bags apiece, hurrying into shops for another pricey
treasure. If they weren't trying to bargain with the Indians over
turquoise, they were charging art on their credit cards.

She stopped for a cup of coffee at an outdoor café down the
block from the Hurd Galleries, where one of the Helga paintings
sat pedestaled beneath a column of carefully directed light. The
face took hold of her momentarily, and she thought that Helga—

chin downward, left braid starting to unravel over her naked shoulder—looked slightly ashamed of herself, possibly even guilty for causing such a furor in the art world. She wanted to visit all the galleries; someday, if Peter would agree to it, together. They could walk side by side through the exhibits of folk art without speaking, absorbing the energy of the paintings and sculptures, creating a kind of temporary bond between them. Art might be eternal, but right now, looking at it alone hurt.

The town of Riverwall lay five miles to the west of Santa Fe. The school for the deaf was on a busy two-lane thoroughfare, a cluster of pale yellow adobe-style two-story buildings framed by dark brown beams. Empty on the weekend, it resembled an abandoned fortress. No one came out to meet her; no one swung on the swing sets or was there to pledge allegiance to the three flags in the raised platform in the entryway. Trees lined the grounds, several generations of tall junipers; hardy, redolent pines; and something that looked like chokecherry. She explored the circular driveway at ten miles an hour, her driver's-side window rolled all the way down. Magpies called to one another so loudly that they seemed almost to be barking rather than singing. Passing trucks periodically assaulted her ears, but whether the noises here were birds, cars, or alien starships didn't really matter. The students wouldn't hear them.

Ullman Hall, the dormitory visible from the school front, was festooned with hand-painted shields that looked faintly Indian. Uneven lightning slashes and crude animal fetishes in primary colors decorated white paper circles. Next door to the school, surrounded by a chain-link fence, was one of those old grave-yards—*Madrone Cemetery*—the kind with marble and granite slabs of inscribed headstones, thick old cottonwoods, and over-grown grasses that took away any potential spookiness. They'd buried her mother, Colleen, in such a place, in Massachusetts, just south of their hometown of Deerfield. Everyone stood out in a light rain, ruining their good black dresses. She knew her sister, Nori, was equally relieved that Colleen was dead, but neither of them was able to acknowledge that to the other. Soberly they watched the polished casket being lowered into the rocky earth. Her mother had spent the last six months angry at everyone, trying hard to drive them away, bewildered when they retreated. Her father would follow in less than a year. In California cemeteries were called "memorial parks," kept as well trimmed as a golf course green, squeaky-clean and somehow terrifying down to each individually clipped grass stem. There, despite the attention to cleanliness and manicured grounds, the undeniable stench of death filtered through the sunshine, thumbing its nose at the well-manicured perfection. Here, in this weedy graveyard, death felt like a medium, a process that accepted worn-out human beings and, in return, gave back seasonal wildflowers. The surrounding trees patiently oversaw each generation's exit.

She parked. If Peter were here, he wouldn't know the car. She'd bought it only a few weeks ago. She entered the courtyard and wandered through the headstones, finding whole families of Garcias, Sandovals, and Estradas. Both wives of the school's founder, Louise and Gyda, were buried on either side of their husband, the man to whom they'd each borne deaf children.

Farther down the rows, the headstones were haphazardly placed, carved out of crumbling red stone, the names on them well into the process of erosion. On one headstone after another, each no larger than a dinner plate, she read the legacy of the Gutierrez family. Baby girl, three months; baby boy, one day. After that they quit giving the ages of the children. Margaret fingered a strand of New Mexico fleabane, growing rampant over the cemetery grounds. The flowers resembled miniature daisies, needle-thin petals and a tuft of yellow center smaller than the moon on her little fingernail. She let the spindly stem go and watched it bounce back toward neighboring grasses.

When they were first married, she and Ray planned to fill their house with children. She got pregnant the first month they tried. Ray sent her a bouquet of pink sweetheart roses. When she miscarried that baby at four months, she thought they had used up their quotient of bad luck, that it would never happen again. But luck had nothing to do with biology.

There were wild roses weaving in and out of the chain-link,

obscuring traffic. A creamy white-and-red-violet color, the petals fragile on stems. Pretty to look at, but if you so much as touched them, wild roses dismantled.

Come on, Maggie. What's tying you here? her friend Deeter had said to her when Ray left. *Get Pete through school and then take off. Travel. Move somewhere pretty. Do whatever it was you were going to do before Ray stepped in and rewrote your life.* Deeter made sense when they sat on the deck, drinking themselves jittery on coffee, the bay water lapping sleepily at their feet. At forty Deeter had retired from working, sold his house, bought the sailboat Ray had been foolish enough to register in Margaret's name. When he talked about sailing to Hawaii or Mexico, changing lives seemed viable. Deeter had time to be there for her when Pete was in the hospital. He walked Echo, attended the mail, trimmed back the bushes, and refinished the dock he moored the boat to.

When she came home leaden from sitting outside the ICU, certain Peter would never wake up, it was Deet who rubbed her shoulders and made her tea with a shot of Johnnie Walker so she could fall asleep. On that grim day when Peter's doctor called in the specialist, he'd held her in the hospital corridor, brushed his lips across her cheek, cried with her, kissed her mouth. Before she could fully comprehend what it meant, Nori arrived, Peter came out of the coma, and they discovered his deafness, diminishing all else to low-priority concerns. But along the periphery of her conscious mind, Deeter's kiss and his kindness grew layers, until Margaret thought it might be a good idea to try it again, to see what happened.

Whether it was a fringed suede jacket back in high school or cutting her long hair short in one of those spiky styles, Nori was the first to try it. Her height and jutting hipbones made her look glamorous in a way her sister could admire only from a distance. It seemed like Nori always grabbed the things Margaret wanted, even before she realized she wanted them. Let her sister fall into bed with whomever she pleased, no matter if Margaret's friendship with Deeter crumbled as a result. She didn't need a sister or a husband, and friends like Deeter—well, maybe they were only a check in the mail every month after all.

She had followed the lines on the map, every inch equal to ten miles, and at the end of all those ten-mile increments was Blue Dog, the trading post, that two-inch advertisement on the bulletin board for the Starr farmhouse, now hers by lease, a field of yellow summer flowers—some distant relation to peace from which she thought she could resurrect a self.

At the horizon she could make out the Sangre de Cristo Mountains, fog shrouding the peaks even this late in summer. As she left the cemetery behind to complete her walking tour, staying to the outside of the school's perimeter, she stopped at a long curving wall decorated with handmade earth-colored tiles. Running the length of the top edge of the wall, a V-shaped piece of copper directed a stream of water down toward a reflecting pool, where it fell in droplets. *Fountain of Thanks: made by the maintenance crew and the students, 4/3/92, Riverwall, New Mexico*, read the incised words in the right-hand corner of the wall. Each tile held a stamped word, and each word contributed to the whole of the poem:

> *I am making the sacred smoke*
> *that all the people may behold it*
> *We are passing with great power over the prairie*
> *the light is upon our people making the earth bright*
> *feathers of sage and cedar upon our breasts*
> *shaking on wrists, ankles,*
> *the tail of the red fox lighting us*
> *We are crying for a vision*
> *behold one that my people may live*
> *Our people are generous*
> *this is our day*
> *your ancestors have all arrived*
> *the past has arrived, behold!*
> *Behold, listen, all is established here*
> *We are relatives this planet earth is in our hands,*
> *let it fly bird of earth and light*
> *all that moves well, rejoice, hey a hey a hey!*
> *Approach in a beautiful manner*

Approach in your best buckskin
Thanks, all the people are crying
grandmother of the earth,'
Thanks

Each drop of falling water sounded a lutelike plunk as it hit the surface, beneath which carp swam through murky shallows. This was Peter's world now, composed of people she didn't know involved in learning things she could never completely understand.

Back in Santa Fe, before she tackled the freeway, she spent an hour in the Red Cloud Café, drinking diner coffee, feeling the odd and sudden absence of tears, ignoring the sweet roll she'd ordered so she wouldn't feel guilty taking up a table. On her third pass, the waitress patted her arm and said, "Sugar, you don't have to say one word. Just sit there and drink your coffee, and I'll keep out of your way."

Days later, Margaret stood washing her face at the pedestal basin. Every room in the Starr farmhouse was high ceilinged, spare of windows, plastered by hand. She could see places where the trowel had swooped and circled, leaving uneven surfaces, and imagine the hard work necessary to build up such thicknesses. Underfoot smooth pine floors dipped in areas that had taken the most traffic, cool on her bare feet. The walls were painted a pale yellow—not one of her favorite colors—but when sunlight filled the house, the yellow reflected a warmth that she imagined brightening the snowiest day of a long winter. Twenty-two years ago, B.A. in hand, she'd left winter behind in Massachusetts, forsaking the pleasure of leaves changing color in the fall and flowers blooming in spring for graduate school in California's single balmy season. She'd left graduate school to marry Ray. In the early years it hadn't been that bad a partnership. Ray worked hard to finish school. She loved driving into Los Angeles every day, earning her assistant curator's salary, writing diplomatic letters of rejection to artists who didn't quite pass the committee's standards. When Ray got his first job staff writing for a television series, their future looked like it was lit with neon. He was a good writer, a hard worker, and they would have handsome children who would thrive in the year-round sunshine. She never imagined that twenty years later she'd have to start all over again, buying long underwear, finding a heavy coat, ordering lined boots—the East Coast essentials. No matter what happened with Pete, she'd made up her mind to stay through to the following summer, just for a chance to see the wildflowers bloom again by the roadside. A one-year lease, during which time her ex-husband and his new wife would produce their first baby, her son would learn his new language, and everything else would unfold in whatever mysterious plan it chose.

Between Deeter's payments on the sailboat and the temporary settlement, she had enough to live on if she lived carefully, without looking for a job just yet. She had no plans beyond staying; day to day was how she intended to proceed. Let everything heal.

The Starrs were just names on her rental agreement—Phyllis and Tybolt—she'd never met them and she didn't expect to. Lulu Mantooth, real estate agent/trading-post clerk/town historian, had given her a brief history.

"That Phyllis Starr is Blue Dog's own angel. When the city started talking about shutting the library down to save money, she gave the down payment to build our own library downtown, right next door to Rabbott's Hardware, even come up with the plan to fill it with books by charging folks ten dollar a year to use it. She never could have no children, so her man Ty just babied her something awful. Whatever Phyllis wanted, Ty would hop bob-wire fences to get it. He let her run the show. Now, Mrs. Yearwood, some people will tell you that's henpecked, but they are the only couple I ever knew who still kissed in public after forty-five years of married life, hungry-for-each-other kisses, you know the kind I mean. A long time ago, I remember that way of wanting a man. I guess that kind of sugar's only meant for the young and childless. But look at me, a good job, a pickup truck, what do I need a man for? I got me seven babies with babies of their own. Sometimes I think a man is like a pair of beautiful heavy silver earrings, see right here in the display case? Oh, they look good on you, sure they do, and folks will notice you wearing them, think you're rich, but the minute you get home you can't wait to take them off and stick them in a drawer where they won't bother you no more."

Lulu Mantooth, over two hundred pounds in her blue velveteen skirt and matching blouse, a rope of museum-quality tooled silver beads resting on her heavy breasts—but her fingers bore no wedding rings and her earlobes were bare. She was old, Margaret could tell, but how old? All the Navajos seemed to have weathered skin, and Lulu's long hair done up in a fat bun was still black.

If it hadn't been for Owen Garrett yesterday morning, riding over on his red horse to fetch his randy three-legged mutt, she could have answered truthfully that she'd successfully avoided prolonged contact with the male species altogether since the evening of Peter's birthday fiasco. Now, whether she liked it or not, she had a neighbor, Owen Garrett, and she had to return his thermos or wait for him to come and fetch it.

A latter-day cowboy was more Nori's speed than hers, but after her one-night fling with Deet, and her hand in Peter's leaving—well, Nori was a big part of the reason Margaret didn't want a telephone. With Lulu Mantooth's permission, she gave the trading post telephone number to the school via a letter. If there was some massive emergency, let them call Ray. She sighed, rubbed her face dry with a towel, and went downstairs to feed the dog.

Margaret drove into downtown Blue Dog to find a pay phone to call a veterinarian. The area's two vets, she learned, also practiced large-animal medicine. One was out in the field assisting an equine delivery, the other was in surgery on somebody's prize cow, but she could leave a message and he'd try to get back to her next week. After a few minutes of frustrating chatter, she came to an agreement with the receptionist. She could bring Echo by tomorrow and someone qualified to do so would administer a "morning after" shot. Even this alternative sounded grim. Margaret hung up the phone outside the liquor store and sighed. How long were dogs in gestation? A month? Three? Did they get morning sickness? How did you ascertain a dog's pregnancy? She tried to imagine asking the pharmacist for a canine home-pregnancy test; further, obtaining a sample of dog pee to perform it. To her right three elderly Navajo men leaned against the building's sign—NO SALES AFTER 2:00 P.M. SUNDAYS—dressed in baseball caps, flannel shirts, and jeans, despite the high temperatures. They wore sunglasses with mirrored lenses and didn't answer when she said a tentative hello. She bought some small red apples out of a basket by the register and bottled water from the cooler case, glanced at her Triple A map, and turned the Toyota left onto the highway, in the direction of the Navajo reservation and the town of Shiprock.

She passed two more trading posts, both featuring hand-painted signs advertising Navajo and Chimayo weavings. Part of her wanted to veer off the highway and touch the genuine articles that had interested her years ago, before Peter, before Ray, when she thought she might actually complete her master's thesis. She'd been approved by the committee to pursue early American weaving techniques, which had turned out to be as dull as it sounded. Then the library had mistakenly delivered *Weavings and Posts*, a book on Navajo rugs. Before returning it, she'd glanced through the pages, studied the known designs: Two Gray Hills, Ganado Red, Chief's Blanket Third Phase, Storm Pattern. These hand-loomed weavings had been the unraveling of her thesis. She read everything the library had on the weavers, bought a tour book on the Southwest, and drove out Easter week to see for herself what this magical Four Corners was all about. There was still snow on the ground, but those red rocks grounded her in a way she'd never felt before. In May she'd met Raymond, and that, coupled with the idea of starting her research all over again, was the end of graduate school. But now she was in Blue Dog, and there was plenty of time for taking up loose threads.

First she wanted to see nearby Shiprock, to explore the

intriguing red blur seen years ago at eighty miles an hour, as she raced her old Ford toward home via Flagstaff's steam-heat motels and overpriced gas stations. Shiprock lay beyond the town of Farmington, whose center was the Holiday Inn, painted peach stucco, trying its best to blend into the surroundings. A handful of cheap, circa-1950 motels had their vacancy signs lit. Wasn't it funny how after the war ended, in a time of such economic promise, the buildings they built reflected none of that implied hope? Instead blocky, quickly assembled structures and gaudy neon signs were the rage. YOU'LL REST RIGHT PEACEFUL AT THE RED-WOOD LODGE! Architecture ranged from Victorian to utilitarian. "Señor Mouse" offered six tacos for two dollars, or you could dine on burgers at one of several "Chat 'n Chew's," while the inevitable "big" smiling white man in overalls topping the auto parts supply loomed over you, authoritatively grasping a six-foot socket wrench. There were a handful of stores, a tiny movie house, evidence of a past mining industry, the small airport off to her left, and the nearby racetrack. According to her guidebook three rivers flowed here: the Animas, which coursed one farm across from the Starr place, the San Juan, and the La Plata, irrigating farmlands, but none of them were visible from the road. It was the tail end of haying season; she could see fat bales of hay rolled into circles in the field.

Soon the long stretches of asphalt led onto the reservation land, where dozens of red woodframe houses shouldered together, uncomfortably close to the highway. A yellow shepherd mix trotted along the arroyo, his nose lifting skyward as Margaret's car passed. He looked underfed to the point of starvation, but wise to the road. Clotheslines with brightly colored laundry wafted in the wind. She saw a horse blanket tacked up in the doorway of one house, and a dark-haired little girl holding onto the edge of it. Forget the cozy hogans and charming pueblos depicted in public television specials, these houses looked desperate and empty.

Shiprock monument was miles away from the highway. Disappointingly, no signs indicated where to turn. No entrances claimed a fee and a way to view the monument up close. Margaret drove past it, then circled back. Wire fences met her at every bend. She found two fire roads with open gates, and took the first one. The Toyota bumped along the dirt and potholes, past the no trespassing signs and scattering a few hardy rabbits from rarely disturbed hollows. Discarded empty beer cans were faded to a chalky white. She stopped three miles down the road and shut the engine down. Outside her car, the silence was absolute. Grasshoppers leapt from the road along the desert floor. Birds cast larger-than-life shadows on the hard ground. The rocks beneath her feet were as red as brick, some chipped in the vague shape of arrowheads. She bent to pick one up, thought about pocketing it, then set it down. This wasn't the Petrified National Forest, but the same feel met her fingertips. To disturb anything was to dismantle a part of the natural cathedral. In the distance, Shiprock rose from the earth, a vast boulder with such odd spires and contours she was reminded of Peter's childhood drip-sand-castles, when on the beachfront he'd dribble wet sand from his hands to fashion a fantasy castle. In her Triple A guide, the Navajo legend alluded to Shiprock as being the great bird on whose back the *Diné* rode into Four Corners, populating the land. It seemed as likely an explanation as any creation myth, or the mystery of human evolution. To the left of the monument, a long wall of basaltic rock jutted from the earth, forming a twenty-foot-high ridge. Hawks circled and lit on the crags, giving the rock the appearance of a decaying castle wall, a last bastion, decomposing over centuries in the elements. The sun hit the cracks and gaps, exposing great blooms of pure light.

She opened her passenger-side door for the camera, but her sketch pads, having bounced from the seat to the floor, fell out instead. The paper felt as perfect as baby's skin. She felt herself begin to tremble ever so slightly, her sure hands suddenly become blocky, useless chunks of wood. *Loosen the chalk, Margaret. It isn't going to give you precision just because you squeeze it to death. . . .* Professor Brownwyn was long retired by now, maybe even dead. She could crumple up anything she drew, burn it in the fireplace, or shred it and leave it for the desert animals to use as bedding.

Her first mark on the paper—brick-colored Conté crayon in a slight arc—wavered. She made a sound of disgust and turned the page. *See inside the object; re-create the shape from the inside outward.* She remembered Peter, sitting in her lap: *Now draw a picture of Spiderman, Mom. Now a hedgehog. Make a fireman rescuing a boy from a burning building. . . .*

The nervous trembling, having no exit, backed up and seemed to charge into her center. Humming began in her brain, a mildly orgasmic buzz she recalled from hours logged in at the easel. One of the small benefits of the work was this pleasant physical sensation. "Work for the work," was Brownwyn's credo, borrowed, she'd discovered years later, from the *Bhagavad Gita.* He had believed in her. What art demanded of you was blind courage, that you "look" with other faculties than just eyes and mere vision. The vision came from shutting your eyes, opening your heart, and lifting the pencil.

For Brownwyn she would draw Shiprock if it meant she sat here all night. Okay. I'm a failure as a mother, she thought, and I couldn't keep my husband. I still probably can't draw a hedgehog to save my life, but I'm here, where I want to be, right now, and I am going to sit here until the sun goes down and draw the best damn rock New Mexico has ever seen.

3

DEAR LORD, I'M STANDING HERE WITH AN ARMFUL OF SOPPING WET Wranglers and all five pairs of threadbare briefs, and not fifty feet away in the east pasture is that woman with the longest legs I've ever seen, hanging out her wash. Suppose if I had me an Indian name, it'd have to be Likes Tall Women. Go on, look for yourself, she's your design. Her legs are pale and smooth, like those stripped ironwood Spirit Ladders the Navs use to climb down into the Great Kiva. Now I don't claim to be any kind of expert, but I'm reasonably certain a man could climb up those legs and find himself a little bit of heaven. She is hanging out her underthings now. All colors, and that unholy white that hurts my eyes even to look. There is only so much a mortal man, even a confessed sinner like myself, can take without breaking down. Think you could send me something to help me get by? This wash sure won't dry in my hands. And I can't seem to stop thinking about those legs. As bad an idea as it is, I'm sure you'll agree a drink is in order.

Owen set the damp laundry back down in the washtub, waiting for his bargain to be addressed. His Higher Power was being his usual inscrutable self—no ready answers forthcoming to such silly questions, no signs, just the same hard steps over familiar rocky ground. This white man's religion was an unforgiving business. Maybe that's what they meant by blind faith. The Navajos had a much better deal. Changing Woman placed her grain of guidance into your skull at birth. That small chip could cause you to go the way of good, but it was fickle. One strong wind of desire might blow by and veer you toward the other side. Owen's evil side had won out many times. Underwear, even the lacy kind, was just another piece of clothing. Ladies wore it to keep their behinds from chafing. That was all there was to it. You had to keep after weakness or eventually it would get the better of you. She rented the farmhouse and the immediate yard around it; he had the bunkhouse and the pastures. It wasn't much of an imposition to allow her to use his clothesline. Probably she didn't even know he'd gone to the trouble of stringing it. Her lights were on, so she had electric now, but with her mad-on for the telephone, it was entirely possible she had a prejudice against clothes dryers to boot. Maybe her cat had come to a bad end napping in one, or maybe one had shrunk her best dress. She didn't look like the dress type of woman, though. More blue jeans and the occasional silk blouse. He wondered what she had drawn inside those newsprint sketch pads she bought down at Rabbott's. Wildflowers? Indian children's faces? Crazy designs no one could make head or tails of? Not that last one, he hoped.

He took down his farrier's tools to finish shoeing Red. An early life of team-roping had nearly ruined the horse. His feet required corrective shoeing as a result of all that running hard and turning left, and even in semiretirement he had a lot of built-in prejudices when it came to any man touching his legs. Owen worked patiently. He had gained Red's trust, on alternate Thursdays, during turquoise-blue moons, when he remembered to recite the magic words—which changed every time you said them, sometimes in the very act. Red held an especially large grudge against shoeing, no doubt having had it executed upon him in a manner that caused him undeserved pain, so Owen performed the job in stages: Pull the old shoes first, then give him a break to think about things. Trim and file, then let him scrub a bucket with some Four-Way, alfalfa, and molasses. Fit and nail in four phases, and step lively throughout that part, because there was nothing Red liked better than stamping down a newly shod hoof when you weren't paying attention.

"Give it here now, Red. We're taking you to Kinney's today, and I don't want to hear another word about it." He fitted the left rear hoof between his knees. Some folks favored foot-stands, but Owen had seen a lot of wrecks come out of that time-saver, and others swore by knee straps or hobbling. That would work once with Red, but the next time his feet needed work, it would be the Fourth of July with equine fireworks. He freed the last shoe with his clinch cutter. "You're about done in on these old ones, aren't you, boy?"

The horse huffed his sweet breath and nuzzled Owen's back pocket, looking for treats. Once, about six months back, Owen had some penny candy tucked in back there, and Red had sniffed it out and kept on hoping for a repeat episode. Owen kept a red handkerchief knotted through his belt loop and tucked into the pocket, and Red made do with that, pulling it out by inches. Horses communicated by touch, and this mouthing and blowing was about as close to a love song as old Red could sing. Owen set the hoof down, reached into his tack box, and tucked a dozen horseshoe nails into the upturned cuff of his Wranglers. Long ago, he'd learned that holding them in your mouth made for emergency X-rays and an unpleasant natural course of events. He sent Red off to think about his last bare hoof.

The sheep were penned in the far pasture, all accounted for, the babies growing fat off the summer grasses, almost ready for the auction. He needed the vet to see to the oldest ewe; she was broken mouthed, and this might be the last season he could use her for breeding unless he got all her teeth pulled and set her on easy grass. He'd read in a magazine down at the Blue Dog library that a dentist could make false choppers for sheep. Did some folks actually have so much spare cash they could afford animal dentures? Old Ruby, the six-year-old pure Merino he kept for her wool, had the bad mouth. Likely he'd hand-feed her a season, get one last set of twins out of her, and that would be all for her.

He hauled Red back as he seemed to be milling around, thinking more about biting on fence posts than shoeing, and retied him to the hitching post. He leaned to the right to pick up his nippers, and the horse brought his hoof down hard—one thousand pounds of horseflesh separated from the human foot by only a quarter inch of twice-resoled Dan Post bootleather. He gave Red a shove and he moved off the foot, which sang out in a mighty burst of pain. Over at the laundry line his neighbor was singing too. But for a different reason. He could hear isolated scraps of song, but his foot hurt so much he couldn't catch it all. He shook his head to clear the pain, picked up the nippers, and set them back in the toolbox. She wasn't about to put old Kitty Wells out of business, but a woman's unabashed voice, singing for no apparent reason—that was worth taking time to listen to. She reached for the high notes, didn't always make it, but sure enough never gave up trying.

Owen found a clean corner of his red bandanna and wiped his brow. His smarting foot kept up rhythm as he tapped the last horseshoe nail into Red's hoof. Without giving him his usual break, he clipped the excess, tamped each one smooth, and the job was done, not the best but hardly the worst work he was capable of doing. "Enough of that," he said, and turned his grateful horse loose to graze in the pasture.

It hadn't rained today. Like summer itself, the rainy season was passing. The last few weeks of summer could get stiflingly hot, but soon enough fall would be here. The teenagers who raced down the gravel road in their parents' pickups would head on back to school. The tourists would finish up their vacations and drive off in those space-age, slant-windowed minivans. Then the town of Blue Dog would have its annual celebration, Blue Dog Days—a welcome distraction from the heat—and whoop it up hard before getting down to the business of trudging through another winter. Much to be done before the snow came—get the sheep ready for sale, stockpile hay, reinforce fences, wrap the

Starrs' pipes. There was never enough time to get to everything, but today was all he had to live through, and today was going along all right, save for the now-sore foot and a place to hang his laundry. His singing neighbor seemed to be having a better time of things, which was no reason for getting a "rise in your Levi's," as his friend Joe Yazzi so aptly described the phenomenon Owen was surprised to find himself experiencing. Not that he found it so terribly unpleasant—it was just that after all this time, it came as somewhat of a wonder. He had pretty much stayed clear of women after Sheila, though every now and again, he'd bed one down and endure the mutual embarrassment of the next morning. But he'd kept them distant. It wasn't safe. Not sexual diseases, though, mind you, they alone were sufficient reason to make you second-think your inclination, but a woman was God's hungriest animal, never satisfied with your body alone. She wanted to know your past, present, future, and every thought that fluttered sideways across your mind. He couldn't exactly explain away a thing like accidental murder while basking in the afterglow and not expect consequences.

He watched her finish hanging the laundry, looping bras over the clothesline when she ran out of pins. She sure had a pile of clothes, didn't she, and a good portion of them were intended not to be seen.

Owen met Joe for supper at Embers, one of three local cafés in Farmington offering all-you-can-eat enchilada nights twice weekly, competing for one another's business. Joe favored the cheese enchilada smothered in red sauce; at fifty-two Owen no longer had the stomach for more than an occasional one set alongside a combination dinner plate. While waiting for Joe, he ordered them both a basket of *sopaipillas*, the delicate pillows of frybread no sane man could resist, extra salsa for the complimentary tortilla chips, and a bowl of tortilla soup for himself, managing to stay within his budget of five dollars.

"Ice water," he said, when the waitress asked him if he wanted something to drink. Some of the Navajos came off the reservation, which was "dry," into Farmington just to have the option of drinking beer. Owen watched them lift the tall-necked brown bottles and laugh quietly among themselves. It sounded prejudiced to say so, but even Joe agreed it was a fact that the Navajos weren't built for processing alcohol. Centuries of a feast-to-famine dietary regime had blessed them with the ability to live on little food for long periods of time. But alcohol quickly turned to sugar in the body, and when you couldn't handle the excess, you ended up not only alcoholic but often diabetic to boot. You couldn't beat alcohol for sterilizing your castrating knife, but that was about it. It had set a heavy burden on the Native Americans. Now, beer went all the way back to the Egyptians—or so one of Sara Kay's little school projects had informed him—but that's where the problem was born. You couldn't turn on the radio without hearing how much fun beer would bring you. Owen could still remember how well it quenched thirst when dust rattled in his throat. They made a fake beer now, and he'd thought of trying it but didn't trust himself to stop when memory and taste met up and shook hands.

"Here you go." His waitress left a pitcher of water on the table and sent his order to the kitchen. Joe Yazzi came in the side door.

"*Ya hey*," Joe said, "You keeping sober?"

Owen checked his watch. "The last hour anyway, brother. You?"

Joe nodded and turned his hat upside down on the seat. His waist-length hair was thick and black, shiny as a woman's, and Owen knew women envied it as much as loved to run their hands through it. The imprint where his cowboy hat had rested remained pressed into his seamless forehead like an intaglio. All the women in the restaurant had to take a look at this man, and Joe was used to that kind of treatment.

"You made the Police Log in today's paper again."

Joe put on a shocked face. "All us Navs look alike. Might have been any other Indian. Even a Hopi."

Owen picked up the newspaper from the seat beside him.

"'Local authorities spent an hour chasing a white dually Ford pickup traveling in excess of seventy miles per hour, but were unable to track its progress after it turned down Great Kiva road.'"

"Lots of white pickups around. This here's pickup country."

"Not so many that can outrun a Taurus cop car."

"Blame Ford." Joe leaned back in the red Naugahyde booth. "Some people like to fish. They spend all their money on fake bugs and fishing line, just to throw 'em back in the water. Seems like a waste of time, but some people call it a sport."

Owen stuck one finger in his ear and wiggled it. "Why do I get the feeling that somehow the philosophy of fly-fishing is going to link up with you racing the Police Department?"

"If they catch me, sooner or later, they got to throw me back, too." Joe dipped a tortilla chip into the bowl of salsa. "This looks pretty good. Maybe they're making it fresh again, instead of buying it in the big cans. Hope so. I like a fresh salsa."

"Me, too, friend. Now, about those cops."

"Could be we got too many cops with nothing to do getting paid a lot of money and not enough for Indians to do and them're all broke."

"Views like that, you could write a letter to the newspaper, run for public office." Owen waited for Joe to eat his salsa-loaded chip. "What I want to know is, where is it you go, Yazzi? How come they're always after you but you never get caught?"

"Trickster takes many forms, brother. Don't piss him off asking questions. Hey, you order my enchiladas?"

"Hold on there, Trickster. I only just got my *agua*."

The bell on the door jangled, and both men turned to see the woman walk in. Margaret Yearwood. She was dressed in a red work shirt, her jeans rolled up above her Reebok tennies. Owen could see her pretty, slim ankles, that same pale flesh. Up close she had more freckles than he remembered, something he'd missed in the glare of the sun that first day. His imagination was running, making all kinds of reckless guesses. He thought about that one horse on the doctor's ranch that wouldn't tame down, who never came to trust his rider. The doctor said it was worth the price of feed just to watch him run off bullheaded at the sight of a halter.

"Whoa—who's that Amazon?" Joe asked. "She has a fine butt."

Owen laughed. "Blue Dog's newest resident. Out of California. Also my neighbor. Hope had his way with her mutt."

Joe Yazzi smiled, exposing a silver-capped eyetooth. "Looks like Hope ain't the only one interested in having his way."

"Order your enchiladas, pal. You aren't Dr. Joyce Bother Me, and I came here to eat my supper in peace."

"Dr. Joyce can bother me anytime. I like that old-time blond hairdo. Bet she's a wildcat in the tipi."

"Like to see you try and find out."

Joe licked both his thumbs and smoothed down his eyebrows. "Bring her on, this skin is ready."

It was like any other Thursday night. They tanked up on discount food, joked with the pretty young waitresses, killed time until they would go back to Joe's and play cards or amble into the Trough to listen to whatever country-and-western band was passing through on their way to Denver. Owen ate his *sopas*, getting honey all over his fingers. The waitress was kind enough to bring him a damp towel and offer a refill on his soup, which he accepted and finished happily. He and Joe emptied two bowls of tortilla chips, mopping up the last of the salsa. They talked about a number of things no one else would find interesting except two sheepmen who worked second-class livestock. But never once could Owen shake the feeling of Margaret Yearwood's presence two booths away. Even with the food smells coming at him, the cigarette smoke from the other tables, and the yeasty essence of beer in the air, he swore he could smell Margaret Yearwood just the same as he had the morning they met—citrusy female sweat—a woman who would have some bite to her. When he and Joe got up to leave, he nodded to Margaret, whose menu choice, he noticed, was the bean tostada. Was she one of them bean-and-caterpillar health food eaters?

"Ma'am," he said, and she looked up, her fork halfway to her mouth. "My dog hasn't been bothering your bitch again, has he?"

"No, things have been pretty quiet."

"Good to hear. Well, enjoy your supper."

She smiled politely. "I am."

Joe elbowed Owen, demanding an introduction.

"This is Mr. Joe Yazzi," he said. "Past vice-president of the Navajo Sheepherders Association, a twice-decorated vet, and a man who has little interest in fishing but much in the way of sport. Joe, my new neighbor." He stopped there, because although he knew her name from the check at the hardware store, they hadn't been formally introduced, which made proceeding any further awkward.

She set her fork down. "Margaret Yearwood, Mr. Yazzi."

Mr. Yazzi grinned, showing his silver. "You honor this town with your beauty," he said. "Will you be blooming with us through the long white winter?"

Please, Owen thought, but the smirk that passed quickly over her face faded into a patient smile.

"Oh, I expect so." She pointed to a poster-covered wall near the register. "If I make it through Blue Dog Days, how tough can a New Mexico winter be?"

"You've heard our town's legend, then?"

"No, but I've had my mailbox stuffed and my car plastered with flyers. What is the legend?"

Joe winked. "Come to the powwow and find out."

She took a sip of water. "It must be quite a legend if it rates a festival."

"Oh, big-time parade. They shut down Main Street. Fancy dancers and competition for open drum. Barbecue, games, and rodeo, where the only event you got to watch is team-roping. And"—Joe's eyes sparkled as he said this—"even the Blue Dog himself sometimes shows up."

She looked away from Joe to Owen, who felt his mouth gone rubbery and stupid next to charming Joe. "Well, I've already had one blue dog make an appearance in my yard. I wasn't that impressed, truthfully."

Owen put his hands into his pockets and touched his quarters and dimes. "Ma'am, you've probably hurt Hopeful's feelings, but not his reputation. Again, should the bitch catch from that unfortunate incident, my offer stands."

She smiled at Owen. Straight-ahead blue eyes looking right into his own. His sore foot chose that moment to give a king-size throb. "Don't worry. If she's pregnant, I *will* call you."

"How can you, with no phone?"

"I know where you live. I'll hike over and fetch you."

Joe nudged him again. "Ma'am. Enjoy your supper now, and we both hope to see you at the powwow."

Owen pondered that idea of "fetching" all the way back to Joe's cabin, which was constructed out of aging chicken wire, stray boards, roofing paper, and earth, cottonwood limbs acting as beams. The government had relocated most of his people to two-bedroom dwellings. They weren't quite refined enough to call houses. Off the highway just west of Shiprock, they made up the reservation. Joe, like a few old-timers, refused to follow suit. Why should he change his lifestyle so that the government could ease its guilty conscience? Being labeled a resister made you automatically suspect in the eyes of the law, but Joe didn't care. He stayed in his small place with his few belongings and paid no bills for electric or gas. He drank the same water his sheep did, hauled it from the river when the creek was down, and in the three years they'd known one another, Owen never once heard him complain.

This August night Owen lost four straight hands of gin, playing distractedly. He turned his cards over on the telephone cable spool that functioned as Joe's game table. Forty-six points plus twenty-five for gin—a new record for Joe, who usually lost the majority of the games.

"Your mind is somewhere else, brother," Joe observed. "You draw three tens, then one by one, throw them back like fingerling trout. The ten not a big enough card for you?"

"You cast some Indian spell on me just so you could weasel me out of my last five bucks. You're buying supper next week."

Joe tipped his mended chair back and grinned. The arms were worn down from the turquoise paint to a colorless wood. "Maybe that good-looking tall lady took your attention home with her."

"For all your ribbing, I sure don't see any women around here."

"Women hold the power, Owen. A man has to be in excellent condition to handle one. See, I'm still in training. I'm in no hurry. Maybe this neighbor of yours, maybe she'll be my next woman."

Owen gave him the eye. "Maybe so."

"Maybe yours."

The thought didn't sit well, and he had to respond. "Look, just because she lives down the pasture doesn't mean we're going to end up tugging sheets."

Joe's face grew serious. "Up from the earth comes the first sprouting and you grow together, off the same stalk, like tall sweet corn. Sha, it happened to a cousin of mine. He let this woman make him supper, and all of a sudden he has twelve daughters and a great big wife."

Owen shook his head. "Red trampled my foot today. I can't hardly concentrate when I'm craving aspirin."

"Woman hooves are sharper."

"Won't argue with you there. Got a scar or two to prove it."

"Let me fix some herbs to take your pain away. Some rub-on arnica."

"No thanks. The last time I let you talk me into that meadow tea, I got a week-long case of the runs."

"Got herbs for that, too."

"Well, I don't want them. What I need is a good night's sleep and a couple of those Advil tablets, and my five bucks back."

"A little late for that, brother. But I'll see what I can do in the way of nice tea for you. Let me check the pharmacy."

The pharmacy consisted of several shoeboxes filled with paper envelopes of dried plants. Joe fancied himself a kind of herbalist and had learned a great deal about medicinal plants from his mother and grandmother. As hokey as they sounded, the teas often worked. Owen had seen him doctor one young ewe who'd hemorrhaged her first time lambing with *bellota de sabina*, a remedy made from the juniper mistletoe, with obvious success and little fanfare. He'd made Owen a lemongrass poultice now and then, for a bruise or sprain, and the treatment had hurried the healing process along. On cold winter days Joe fixed *yerba buena* teas that sent heat into the far corners of his body. He watched his friend hold the envelopes up to the kerosene lamp-light and identify them by their tiny peculiarities. Hopeful was asleep on the hearth, his three legs stretched out in front of him, soaking up the heat of the small fire. Atop the jutting mantel leaned a single homemade arrow, flint pointed skyward. Joe wasn't a bow-and-arrow hunter; in fact, Owen had never seen him use any kind of weapon, save for a small curved knife for castrating lambs. He'd served in Vietnam, come home medaled and wounded, and after the parades and newspaper articles, had his nervous breakdown very quietly, only going so far as to see the enemy in out-of-the-way places, and most frequently in the bottom of bottles. At AA meetings Joe would say his name and only one other thing: *I'm thankful to be here with brothers and sisters who've seen it, too*, as if they all were privy to the same monster they drank to escape. They couldn't be. Owen knew two things: Joe had tried to drown himself, and Owen had too. They might have worn different colored skins, but they spoke the same language: recovering alcoholic. It was more than enough to base a friendship on, and a sober friendship was an interesting thing. The doctors at the Indian Health Institute had Joe on medication to keep him even, and everything went along just fine when he remembered to take it. But sometimes he forgot the pills, or his checks didn't arrive in time and the pills ran out, or he worked up enough courage in his mind to believe he didn't need them anymore. During those times there was no telling where you might find Joe Yazzi—wandering the Bisti Badlands in his over-coat, walking the centerline of the highway toward Gallup, or sitting in his old painted blue chair, here in the cabin, sunk so deep inside himself that he wouldn't hear a word you spoke. Owen watched out for him. He told Joe he should get a dog, that a dog kept you current. When it didn't get fed, it sure enough let you know what day it was. But Joe had seen unspeakable things happen to dogs in Viet Nam, and his own white dog had come to what he referred to only as a "bad end." Maybe so. Owen didn't press.

Hopeful stretched, seeming to soak up the last of the fire, which was in danger of dying out if Joe, busy taking a twig of this dried grass and that powdery berry, didn't feed it a stick.

"Here," Joe said, pressing the completed packet of herbs into Owen's hand. "Steep this in hot water for fifteen minutes, and drink it before you go to bed."

Owen took a sniff of the herbs. "Smells like licorice."

"That's star anise. Now the star anise makes a wonderful cure. Just the one to take for a nervous midnight bellyache. Be sure you thank Grandmother Earth for her gifts, or you might insult her. You don't want that. She might give your ewes hoof rot."

Owen tucked the packet into his shirt pocket. "This isn't going to make me have 'visions,' is it?"

Joe adjusted the envelopes and replaced the lids on his shoeboxes. He set them on one of his few rickety shelves alongside a yellow coyote skull. Owen could see the hole where the bullet had entered, right above the left eye socket. "The herbs for encouraging visions ain't for white boys, Owen. Any visions you come up with you probably can blame on Margaret Yearlegs." He laughed and ducked comically, as if his words might cause Owen to throw him a retaliatory punch.

"Right." Owen adjusted his hat on his head and found his keys. "Come along, Hope. Time for us to get gone."

The heeler jumped up from his resting place on Owen's hearth and followed his master to the truck. Outside the moon was full, a yellow thumbprint in the inky sky, shining down, filling animals' heads with notions that would cause them to misbehave in most peculiar ways and dousing the humans in a kind of daze as well. Joe Yazzi stood out front of his ramshackle house with the old truck tires holding down the roof to keep it from blowing away. He pointed to the moon, chuckling as if it were some colossal omen for their future. Owen waved and drove the truck down the dirt road to the highway and through town in silence.

Long ago, before he owned the truck, someone had ripped the radio out. He didn't need music. The truck was helpful when he needed to go somewhere or feed animals. He had covered long distances on Red in silence, too, including a trek from Durango through the woods and camping by the Navajo dam. He'd heard the story of the Coloradans moving the entire town of Arbolejes north of the New Mexico border because it lay in the floodpath. Moving a house was one thing, but they had gone so far as to move an entire graveyard so that their ancestors might rest high and dry, with only the manageable rain and normal snowfall touching their graves. Moving the dead—it sent a chill down his back, causing him to pull his collar up. Foolish old moon. When it was full, a man had trouble sleeping. It made his friends talk in mysterious stories. At least Hope was behaving. Owen checked the rearview mirror just to touch base, and caught sight of the pointed ears.

They made the turn down the gravel road past the yellow-tipped rabbit brush to the Starr farmhouse. Her bedroom light was on, light coming through the window. Though she wasn't conveniently silhouetted in the window, he could see every inch of her in his mind. He unloaded the dog, who propped his front end up on the rear tire and peed. It was a constant marvel, the dog's ability to adapt to life without his fourth leg and still maintain dignity. Owen checked Red, who, backlit by moonlight, stood out in the pasture like a paper-doll horse. In a month or two the horse would gladly come into the barn at night, but for now he preferred the wide-open spaces. Inside the bunkhouse he switched on the radio, tuned it to an all-night request station out of Albuquerque.

"Are you crying, loving, or leaving?" the disc jockey asked a female caller.

"Crying," she answered, her voice low and dull. "I want to

hear 'Desperado,' the Ronstadt version, and you can dedicate it to Keith, or even better, the entire male race."

"One of the finest songs ever written," the disc jockey said, and cut directly to the music.

Why don't you come to your senses. . . . Owen listened carefully to all the words Linda threw her heart so deeply into singing. *You been out riding fences for so long. . . .* Well, Linda, truth of things was, sometimes there wasn't much else for a man to ride.

He made his tea from Joe's herbs, but before he drank it, he went outside and hung up two pair of damp jeans and flannel shirts in the moonlight. His briefs he laid over a chair inside the bunkhouse. Some things a man needed to keep private.

The herbs delivered him dreams. He stroked his way to wakefulness feeling that he'd spent his sleep like carnival dimes, a flash of silver thrown recklessly into the air, winning fragile glass adventure in exchange. He was a boy again, learning to cut cattle alongside his brothers, smelling the scared animals' excrement, the meaty aroma of trailside slaughter for the unlucky cow who'd shattered a leg, the bawling of her orphan calf nearby, desperate to mother up to something familiar. Then he was in a bed covered in roses—it was summer and there were enough roses around him for a funeral. He smelled Sheila's hand cream, pink goo she always overdid, trying to keep her callused work hands city-smooth. Her pinched face loomed over him with accusations he knew he deserved. *You son of a bitch you're drunk again, and the landlord's asking me where the rent money is. . . .* It dissolved into alcohol and shattering glass. His young friend with the rattlesnake hat, that same punch moving as inevitably as a train toward his face, but this time rising up, his broken bottle taking Owen's eye out easy as an ice cream scoop. Maybe it had happened that way, and Owen was the one who died that afternoon, and this living he'd done since was some kind of lengthy trek through purgatory. He sat in his bed, drenched in the sweat of fear, teeth chattering, his bedsheets damp, as tired as if he hadn't slept at all. There was a knock at the door. It was morning. He was alone. Sometime in the night Hopeful must have gone out the window. He was an agile dog, what you might call stealthy.

The knocking persisted.

He got up and hitched his jeans over his lower half. He had his fly halfway buttoned when the door opened.

"Oh, I'm sorry. I thought no one was home. I brought your thermos back," Margaret Yearwood said. "I took the liberty of filling it with coffee. Don't worry, it's not some fancy blend, it's plain old Maxwell House. Good God, did I wake you up?"

He tore a flannel shirt from the closet and pulled it over his bare shoulders. "Don't worry about it."

She stood in the doorway, sunlight coming over her shoulder, fingering its way through her hair. "Sorry. I thought you were an early riser."

He ran his hand over his thinning hair, trying to smooth it down, and looked around desperately for his hat. "I am. What time is it?"

"Little after nine."

"Nine?" He inhaled sharply. "Well, I guess I've got some hungry horses waiting on me."

"Horses?"

"I feed the Dofflemyers' animals from late August through spring. Pasture across from the river on the west side. They're summer people, teachers down in the Duke City. Nine o'clock. I hate like heck to get animals off schedule."

He could see her looking at his underwear, spread out over the chairback and sides, then politely pretending to be admiring his solitary painting, a thrift-store-find, second-rate oil of a cowboy napping against a cloud, a cloud horse flying by, the Bar-4-Y brand on its ample flank.

"Interesting painting. I could give you a hand catching up."

"With what?"

"Feeding the horses. What did you think I meant?"

He buttoned his shirt. "I don't know. Sleeping late has me all goofed up."

She pointed toward his shirt. "You're one button off, Mr. Garrett. That won't get you through the day. Better start over."

He looked down at his shirt, the buttons and holes all kitty-wampus. The woman stood before him, watching his fingers work. He felt his shallow breath catch in his throat as he redid the buttons. Hat, hat—where was that brain bucket when you needed it most? Now was when he could use a drink. Higher Power still in bed, or off attending to someone with a bigger problem. Drink something else. "Would you like some of your own coffee, Mrs. Yearwood?"

"No Mrs. and no more ma'am's, please. I keep looking up, expecting my mother in her church clothes and white gloves. Margaret's fine. Coffee sounds good, but I'll bet it could wait until after we get those horses their breakfast."

He brightened. Patience was a wonderful thing to discover in another human being and seemed to be a rare quality in a woman. "Can you drive a column shift?"

"Is that the one like an H on the steering wheel?"

"That's it."

"Well, it's not my strongest point, but lately I'm learning to adapt."

He found his socks and boots and put them on. "And how's that going?"

"Let's just say it's going."

Hat—as mysterious as Joe, it suddenly appeared over there on the ladderback chair, upside down, the way he'd learned to set it so the brim didn't break. The other way was supposed to bring bad luck. Gratefully he put it on. "Okay then."

They took his pickup, loaded up with hay. At the Dofflemyers' pasture, she drove while Owen knelt in the bed of the truck, tossing flakes out to six nervous mares who began claiming their hay piles with snapping teeth and short kicks. Hopeful went out after them, his three legs moving him swiftly if bumpily over the fence gate. Idiot dog. Owen whistled him back. Inside the truck he could hear Margaret laughing, and it was Margaret the dog went to, not Owen. A first, because up until now Hope had seemed to be a one-person animal. Owen got in the truck cab and let Margaret drive the rest of the way home, the heeler between them like a canine chaperon.

"Thanks," he said when they paused at the road to let a Jeep pass. "If you're looking for a job, you'd make a good hand."

"Not at present, but I'll keep it in mind. And you're welcome."

Red came trotting up as they returned, wanting his own breakfast. At the barn door Margaret killed the engine and opened the driver's door. Red squealed from the fence.

Owen said, "I've kept him fed eight years, but the horse still can't quite believe regular meals."

"I remember when my son was like that. Then he turned thirteen."

"That's a hard age, all right."

"Yes, it is. Fifteen's even more—" she hesitated a moment "—challenging."

Owen studied her face. From the smile at Red's behavior it journeyed a thousand miles back to California, where it met up with whatever trouble had driven her here. "Well, this big baby," Owen said, "he's easy enough to please. A slice of apple, a palmful of brown sugar, he'll hop this fence and find a way into your kitchen."

She had to squint and shade her blue eyes in the bright sunlight. "I'll remember that if I get lonely."

"Remember you have a neighbor, too."

The smile came slowly back.

Overhead, clouds moved, casting shadows on the pasture. Far in the distance the sheep traveled in a small pack, their rounded backs moving together like animated, dusty hummocks. Owen's stomach felt like an empty suitcase, hollow, but remembering being packed up full for previous trips. He thought maybe he should ask her to breakfast, to thank her for helping with the horses. The only women he ever ate with were Verbena and Minnie Youngcloud, and breakfast with them was coffee and hot, fresh bread, interspersed with grandchildren coming and going, hens being shooed outdoors, great fables of Verbena's distant love life. "You probably already had your breakfast, didn't you?"

She shook her head. "I ate so much last night I didn't get

hungry yet. Up here I can eat when I feel like it. No one else to cook for."

"I know a great place for eggs."

"I'm not keeping you from your work?"

"You woke me up for it, and I'm grateful. Just sit tight, I'll bring the coffee out here in the sunshine."

He squirreled the underwear away in his clothes box and cracked six eggs into a bowl, adding a little milk. No one to cook for—a boy fifteen divorce—that little gift that frequently accompanies the forties. While the bottom half of the omelet fried, he chopped up a tomato and two sweet chiles, grated the last of his cheese into a bowl, then folded it inside the eggs. He salted and peppered the top, dumped salsa on that, eased it onto his one good clay plate and brought out two forks. Margaret sat on the end of the truck bed, Hopeful alongside her, studying her, allowing her to scratch his neck.

"Your blue dog here. How many generations has he fathered?"

He stood at the end of the truck bed, handing Margaret the plate. "Despite his lack of standard equipment in the leg department, he's in demand as a stud. People around here use the Queensland for working cattle and sheep. I let him throw a few litters every couple years. Your dog's probably some fancy breed I never heard of, probably twice as valuable as Hope here."

She shook her head no. "A bona fide mutt. My son bought her for four dollars outside a health food store near where we used to live. In his words, 'Some junkie was trying to sell her so he could afford another hit.'"

"That's a shame. Your son get involved in drugs?"

She bristled. "Of course not. He's just away at school. That's all. I'm keeping the dog. This is all temporary." She took a bite of the eggs. "I can't believe you made these so quick. They're wonderful."

He accepted her compliment in silence, watching her eat, noting how she seemed to release the tension of his question with every measured breath. Boarding school meant money or a decent settlement. Temporary could also mean custody battle. But why run all the way to a hole-in-the-wall like Blue Dog? His dog liked her before he brought out the eggs, and eggs were Hope's weakness, though he preferred them raw. He sat down next to her and felt the distance between them vibrate with interest. "Well," he said. "Draw a line down the middle and leave half, Margaret. I'm hungry, too."

4

RELUCTANTLY MARGARET HANDED OWEN BACK THE PLATE WITH his half of the omelette—perhaps her newfound appetite came from helping to load the old green pickup truck with flakes of hay, or from watching Owen hotfoot it back to the safety of the truck while a dozen nervous brown horses charged across a field to their belated breakfasts. She could get fat eating like this, but did that matter if there was no one left to stay thin for and food made this comfortable a Band-Aid? Owen Garrett, she noticed, ate his eggs like a gentleman, small bites, chewing with a closed mouth, blotting his lips with a napkin. She loved the painting on the wall inside his house: If someone mined far-off Salvation Armies and found a gallery willing to take a chance, thrift-store art would make a wonderful retrospective.

"Watch," he said, and set the plate down on the truck bed, holding a forkful of omelette out toward his three-legged dog. The dog stayed put, mesmerized. Owen set the egg down on the dog's nose, balancing it on the long snout. For one long minute, it seemed as if the dog's eyes would cross permanently as he studied that egg.

"Go on, Hope," Owen said, and with a quick snapping motion, the egg disappeared into the dog's mouth and was on the way to his stomach.

Margaret laughed. "Does he even taste it?"

"He might catch a whiff on the way down, but I won't swear to it."

"You couldn't get Echo to do that. She's the only canine I've ever met who actually picks at her food."

"That's rare in a dog."

"Tricks are beneath her dignity, I'm afraid. She spends most of her time sleeping in the laundry basket."

"Well, don't write her off yet. We have a lot of down time here in the north when it gets to be winter. Maybe she'll change. Come November, Hope starts getting a little like a posthole that ain't been filled up. If food's available, he'd climb trees to get to it."

"You're selling him short. That dog could go on David Letterman. The only thing mine would do on command is mess on the rug."

"Dave Letterman?"

"You know, that late-night talk-show guy."

"Afraid not. Don't get much chance to watch television when you're working sheep."

"Well, you're not missing much. But once he had a border collie herd sheep into a New York City taxi."

"That I'd have liked to see. Don't be so hard on your dog, Margaret. She's got four legs, and she'll fit in your lap."

"How did Hopeful lose his leg again?"

"Nerve damage when a car clipped him. Cured him of that desire in a hurry. He went around with a limp for a month, then started looking so poor I took him to the vet. Even tried a chiropractor, anything anybody could think of to save it. Look how well he gets on without it, though. Now that's about his best trick."

They were quiet a moment. Margaret considered telling him the story of Echo's singular accomplishment. But to speak of that, she had to explain about Peter—relive the weeks he lay in the hospital, where he was now, why he wasn't with her, offer the reasons she'd left California. The last thing she wanted was to revive her tired-out life story with all its disappointing curves and dead ends for a stranger. But it was rude not to make conversation when someone went to the trouble of making you breakfast.

"Echo's been in the newspaper."

"Which part? Not the Police Log, I hope."

She smiled. "No. I think they call it 'human interest.' The story even got picked up by the wire service and was syndicated across the country. Her brief fifteen minutes of fame. Not bad for a mutt."

"Well, I'll bite. Fill me in."

"It's the kind of thing that happens once in a lifetime, I guess. There isn't a day goes by I don't feel grateful down to my heart. She deserves a medal, really. My son got very ill and lapsed into a coma. For weeks he just lay there, not getting better and no one knew why. After the doctors had pretty much given up, Echo was the one who brought him back."

Owen turned to look at her face. No smirk of disbelief, no feigned interest there; he was listening. "Is that so?"

Saying the words caused the memories to surface in Margaret's chest. One after another, the pictures of Peter's illness clicked into view, the accompanying emotions as sharp and astringent as the smell of new paint. The physical therapist rotating his wrists and ankles, for all the good mobile joints did Peter. The IVs in his arms keeping her son hydrated and seminourished, but they hadn't kept his hair from falling out. Three different monitors spewing out sophisticated information hourly, none of them explaining why this boy slept on so long after his fever was gone. That night at home after surely the longest day ever humanly endured, she lay tossing in her bed. The dog had come down the hallway to her, toenails clicking on the tile floor. Tentatively a tongue licked Margaret's hand, seeking who it was she should transfer her affection to. Echo, barely out of puppyhood, missed Peter as much as she did. What she'd done by sneaking the dog into Peter's room inside a straw beach bag she'd bought at

Albertson's had been an act of desperation. She hadn't taken the time to weigh the ramifications. Screw their rules, the sterile procedures that kept Peter antiseptic but comatose. Stripped of hope, nearly as angry as she was afraid, she'd deposited the dog on Peter's bed just after dawn. She remembered the dog's excited squeals of recognition, the tail wagging a hundred miles an hour, almost as if she were saying, "So *that's* where you've been!" and Peter's grunts, the vocalizations she no longer got excited over or took for anything more than incidental noise he made in the coma. Then, as the dog nuzzled his face, licked inside his ears, he spoke the first words he'd said in weeks: "Go 'way."

On your basic miracle scale, what started out as a three, in the space of a week, worked into the perfect ten. Peter came back. It was so. He was awake and he was with them, but he was never going to be the same. Finally she answered Owen's question. "Yes."

Owen put his right cowboy boot on the rusting chrome bumper of the truck. "Margaret, now, I realize we don't know each other too well, and you might find it hard to trust a stranger, even one who's your egg-cooking neighbor, but you can't just drop a bead of information like that and not follow up. Be fair. This might have to last me until Thursday night."

"What happens on Thursday night?"

"Seven o'clock I'm picking you up for the opening ceremonies of Blue Dog Days."

"You are not 'picking me up.'"

"Oh yes I am. Might even sweep out my truck if I'm feeling ambitious."

"Thanks for the thought, but I'm not much for parties or parades, Owen. I think you'd better take someone else."

"You'll like this. I promise. Folks dress up, turn all out for the Blue Dog. Good food, dancing, even a rodeo."

"I gave every dress I had to the Goodwill back in California."

"Then wear your bathrobe if you like. People are tolerant in this town." He picked up the plate and fork and took them into the bunkhouse.

Margaret followed, lining up all her good reasons for saying no. She stood by the sink as he scrubbed the plate and utensils. With his hat tilted forward, shadowing his face from the thinly bridged nose to the fine whiskers he hadn't yet had a chance to shave, he was hardly more than a mysterious profile, forearm-deep in sudsy dishwater. She couldn't go out with this man—not with any man. He filled the frying pan with hot water to let it soak, then he dried his hands on a plain white towel and turned to face her.

"When are you going to tell me about your son?"

She looked down at the cement floor, swept so clean it was hard to believe a man who worked with livestock lived here. Atop the scarred pine table sat a blue enamel sugar bowl, its white dunes of sweetness pure and undisturbed. Everything was neatly in place—worn white dishtowel folded over the drawer handle, a deck of Bicycle playing cards stacked next to a pad with a long tally of penciled-in points. On his night table, which doubled as a plastic milk crate turned sideways, there was a battered Larry McMurtry paperback. Next to the book, a pair of wire-frame reading glasses comically magnified half the title. "I can't talk about all of it."

"I'm not asking you to. Tell me a little of what you *can* talk about."

She let out a long breath. There were a thousand miles between this simple room and the PICU floor of the Presbyterian hospital with the piped-in air flooding the ultraclean hallways, but sometimes she could swear it was all only a step away, through the next door into knee-shaking fear. "He got sick overnight. A fever of a hundred and three. The next morning I found him passed out on the bathroom floor. Deeter and I—a family friend—we took him to the hospital. At first they said it was nothing, just a virus. But it wasn't that simple. The fever went down, but Peter kept on sleeping. My sister. . . " Her voice grew thick.

Owen started to move toward her but stopped himself, keeping the distance between them clear and distinct.

"To make a long story short, I came up with this last-ditch idea that maybe his dog could wake him up. They had. . . ." She cleared her throat, staring down at the droplets of dishwater that had fallen from Owen's hands to the cement floor. Even if it meant telling the rest of this story through clenched teeth, she was not going to cry. "A special kind of friendship. He rescued her from that junkie outside the health food store, and then. . . ." she crossed her arms and looked out the window toward the truck parked outside, its pale green doors sanded down to primer in places. In her old California neighborhood her neighbors would write down the license plate, call the police, if that car so much as parked on the street. "It was kind of like she rescued him back."

"And it worked?"

"Yes. Not right away, but eventually. We got lucky."

Owen whistled.

Pride and pain trembled inside her. "It seemed like the first good idea I had in about seventeen years."

Owen rubbed his stubbled chin, waited a moment. "Had yourself a second one?"

"Well, I moved here."

His deep laughter drew her in. She hadn't laughed in months, and at first the sound came out harsh with the effort at letting go. Apparently it was this man's way to chuckle through difficult times and to leave the judgment making to others. With her thumbs she swiped at the tears that had gathered in her eyes.

Out by the barn, he showed her where he stacked the firewood. "I'll be cutting another couple of cords the next month or so. If you like, we can split the cost. It should just about cover us if we wear sweaters and don't overdo the cozy fires."

"I'm sure I have enough wood to get me through the winter. There's a huge pile near the house."

He laughed again. "Trust me, that's not enough to get you through Thanksgiving. I'll haul a load up in a week or two and stack it near the back porch. You finding the Starr place comfortable?"

"It's like stepping back in time forty years. I love the kitchen and the fireplace—those smooth river rocks. I'm only using two rooms upstairs—the bedroom on the west corner and the smaller room for a studio." *Where Mrs. Starr expected to raise her babies. All the babies God never saw fit to give her. . . .* Lulu Mantooth's words came back to her each time she opened the door.

"What kind of studio would that be?"

She blew out a breath. If he didn't think she was pretentious before, surely this would clinch it. "Someday soon I'm hoping to get up my nerve to start painting again. A long time ago I was. . . " Halfway decent, she wanted to say, but something stopped her. How could she explain to this cowboy that since then she'd forgotten which end of the brush to dip? That the plan was to dink around with watercolor, gouache, maybe try some acrylic, terms that wouldn't mean anything to him? "Right now, I'm just filling up sketch pads with scribbling that would shame a kindergartner. Listen, I'd better let you go on to work."

His hazel eyes held her fast. The left one, tucked into the scar tissue at the temple, seemed permanently amused. "That's the thing about work, isn't it? It'll be there in five or ten more minutes." She pulled a tough stalk from a hay bale and dragged it through the packed-earth barn floor, making a jagged line between them. "Draw me something," he said.

"I don't carry my drawing things with me."

"Here, in this dirt."

She laughed nervously. "In the dirt?"

"Sure. Just use the stick."

What could it hurt—one scuff of her tennis shoe toe and it would be earth again. She drew the outline of his dog. It was pretty terrible. Probably the dog could have done his own portrait with more finesse.

Owen looked up at her. "Well, that's. . . " His voice trailed off as he dropped his bait, trying unsuccessfully to get a compliment to bite. She made it easy on him. "The thing is, I usually use a fine-point stick."

He smiled. "I won't pretend I know anything about art."

"Animals are difficult! Everything is when you've been out of it as long as I have. I do better on paper, honest. Give me a few months and I'll try it again." She added some detail to the ears, a few strokes to indicate hair.

"That drawing might seem like nothing special to you, but to me the whole thing's a kind of magic. I can't hardly manage a stick figure."

She backed awkwardly into the barn siding, the rippled metal warm against her back. Behind her bridles and halters jangled, and she threw out her hands to get her balance.

"Careful now," Owen said, catching her by the upper arms and steadying her. "Don't want you to knock yourself out before the powwow."

He was still holding on to her, those capable hands holding her steady, his warm flesh against her own. She looked up from scrutinizing her shoes to catch Owen's friendly smile. He let go, straightened his hat, and looked away, politely giving her time to collect herself. As she regained her footing, she wondered what he was really about, this quiet man living in a bunkhouse off a barn, tending other people's animals, not having a beer alongside everyone else in the café, making do with ice water and the cheapest items on the menu. Her upper arms retained hot phantom impressions where his hands had been, and she was suddenly aware of him as a man, a sexual being, of their close proximity, their nearest neighbors nearly a mile away across a river. Despite well-intended resolutions, anything might happen. A man could kiss you in an instant.

Then Hopeful came flying into the barn, knocked over a toolbox, and fled to the top bale in a stack three bales high, leaving a scrabble of footprints in her dirt-drawing.

"Critics," she said, breaking the tension. "They're everywhere."

Owen sighed. "That dog'll choose his moments to go insane."

"It's only dirt. What do you suppose spooked him?"

"God knows. Sometimes he goes as crazy as a woman's watch. My friend Joe will tell you it's because animals aren't deaf to the rhythms of the earth, and nine out of ten times something'll happen to prove him right. Big rainstorm, thunderstorm, hail once, size of tennis balls. Hope takes weather personally."

Atop the hay bale the dog trembled, his stumpy tail tucked down as low as it could possibly go between his back legs, his pointed ears pinned to his head like wilted leaves of lettuce. "Speaking of dogs, I'd better get back and check on mine."

"Thursday night," Owen said, walking her out into the New Mexico sunshine. "Keep your fingers crossed for good weather. I might even wash the dog and clip all twelve of his toenails."

She spent the rest of the morning filling her newsprint pads with struggling sketches—Hopeful begging eggs from the bed of Owen's pickup, Echo asleep in a pile of clean towels just in from the dryer. Alone beneath the cottonwoods' soughing branches, she felt at home, but in town she bumped along like a fly caught between panes of glass. No way could she go to Blue Dog Days, whatever they were. When she next looked up, one entire sketch pad was filled, and she kept flipping back to two particular pages, which held drawings that looked suspiciously like their subjects. Afternoon light painted the pine floor the color of clover honey. Her stomach rumbled. It was three-thirty; she'd missed lunch, forgotten to go into town for the quart of milk and the paper towels she needed. She ate cold leftover macaroni and cheese from a Tupperware container while leaning over the kitchen sink. Still she was hungry—something in her just wouldn't fill up. "Come on," she called out to the dog, who was hidden in the nest of towels except for the tip of her nose and one ear. "We both need the exercise."

They took their time meandering down to the oversize mailbox at the end of the gravel road, exploring rustles in the rabbitbrush, Margaret doing her best to avoid the stickerweed, each intriguing clump suddenly so irresistible to Echo she had to stalk in and pounce on nothing, resulting in a time-out for both as Margaret patiently removed brambles. There was no need to fire up the car to hike a half mile. No reason to hurry. Her mail could have waited until the weekend, but maybe there would be something from Peter. All other personal mail she routed through the attorney in California. She was paying him enough; let him deal with Nori and Ray. When the last brown envelope had arrived, Deeter's letter and check among the bills, she'd had a bad moment when she felt her resolve to stay anonymous weaken. *Maggie, where the hell are you? When I said take off, I didn't expect you'd take me so literally. . . .* It wasn't fair to punish the man who once was her friend with silence and distance. But if she spoke to him, Nori would weasel her address out of him and come after her, armed with all her sensible reasons for taking Deeter to bed and accusations coupled with more questions than Margaret could or, at this point, cared to answer.

Strung like a Halloween decoration, a dusty, tattered spiderweb nearly three feet in across spanned the distance from her mailbox to the rail fence. A medium-size brown spider was in the tedious process of respinning what the wind had undone. Margaret watched the spider work each sticky filament toward the corresponding rib with desultory interest until she knew she was prolonging the inevitable and opened the mailbox. A bill from the electric company for the hookup deposit lay against the ribbed aluminum bottom, and her fifth Blue Dog Days flyer. Shoved alongside lay a brown-paper mailing tube tied with string. There was no writing on it, no address. Maybe there was a card inside. She undid the string and wound it around her hand. Twelve sheets of d'Arches watercolor paper—the expensive stuff—might go for twenty dollars back home. Who knew what it cost here, trucked in from the city? She shook the paper out, looking for a receipt or something to identify the giver. Nothing. As paper went, it was thick and ridged, art by itself without anything painted on it at all. She unwound the string from her hand and studied it—brown twine like the hardware store tied her box of supplies in. Owen Garrett thought she needed good paper on which to draw terrible dogs?

Life's little mysteries were everywhere—from the legend of

Blue Dog, which no one had explained to her, to a son who preferred a community of strangers to family. Throw in a sister who skulked behind your back, planting the idea in his head to go away to school, to live with foster parents in the first place, and top it off with a cowboy who made a life on the fringe, who could cook up eggs that would shame most restaurants, but thought so well of her dirt drawings he made her a gift of expensive paper.

She walked back to the farmhouse carrying the paper. Maybe it was a bribe; owing him, she'd have to go to the parade. At her side Echo sniffed the fading sunflowers, squatting by several to bless them. That was male dog behavior; probably it meant she had some kind of hormone imbalance. She should take her in to the veterinary, have that shot, have her spayed. But some other day. It was nearly ninety degrees. There was breeze enough to lift the hair from her hot neck and keep the insects from being bothersome.

Owen said that when winter came, you spent enough time indoors that you could teach an old dog new tricks. Struggling with the card table through the screen door, she moved her work downstairs and outdoors, took out new tubes of watercolor in sienna, umber, warm gray, white, and black, and set them on the table. The shakes hit her instantly. Why paint anything except your fingernails? The world was full of dilettante artists, women who changed their names from Susan to Siouxie and started wearing caftans and African trade beads in hopes that an exotic exterior would imbue their art with dimension and definition. Anyone could approximate the costume, throw paint at a canvas and sign it, pontificate on style and postmodernism. And there was a surfeit of successful painters dedicated to their craft who had logged in decades of work, work that had evolved and grown way beyond a few hopeful canvases a professor praised in graduate school. She could paint twenty-four hours a day and never catch up. She should get a job checking groceries and live like an ordinary human being; start a library like the childless Mrs. Starr; when the divorce settlement was final, give her money to the Indian Children's Health Services or, better yet, take a vow of celibacy and meditate for peace. Instead she picked up a sheet of the good paper, traced the sketch of Hopeful's profile on it lightly in pencil, and pinned it to the easel. Onto the saucer she was using as a palette she squirted a dab of umber paint she would feather over the pencil to define the dog's blunt forehead.

I am no damn good at this, she said to herself as she dipped the paintbrush for the first time, watered the paint down to a fluid consistency, and made exploratory strokes at the paper's edge. I am forty years old, and in fifteen years I haven't worked on anything more ambitious than Peter's elementary school Halloween costumes. This will end up in the trash, good paper, wasted. I'm killing time in a town I chose because twenty years ago I had this romantic notion that weavers and red rock could teach me about art. These summer wildflowers I keep arranging into bouquets—they're weeds, and they won't last out the month. Was I crazy to think I could live in snow again? My son can't even hear me tell him how sorry I am for his going deaf or for failing to keep his home life intact.

As if to break her trance of self-recrimination, overhead a magpie burst into song. Its teal-blue plumage was a blur in the cottonwood tree. In New Mexico the bird was as ordinary as a California blue jay, but to Margaret, every time she saw one, it was startling.

She managed a fair rendering of the slope of Hopeful's muzzle. One line in there somehow mysteriously worked. She traced over the paint with her pencil tip, trying to feel how she'd maneuvered it. Knew at once, instinctively, that she'd gotten the ruff hair wrong, and that what she needed was to add warm gray to correct the tone.

If you paint one good thing, make yourself attempt another at once. Professor Brownwyn again. She taped the sketch of Echo in the laundry to the easel and painted her, dark nose buried in a nest of purple towels. This one took the flowing drapery award— the towels were overdone to the point of cartoonery—but the curve of the dog's head—that wasn't bad. When the paint dried, she would send it off to Peter. No more letters begging him for responses, just a reminder that his dog was fine, here upstate, in case he wondered.

The light was gone now. Dusk hung in the cottonwood trees and the birds had gone silent. Echo lay curled up in Margaret's denim jacket. Margaret hugged herself against the drop in temperature and cataloged the sounds around her. The bawling of hungry cattle across the way, the wind rustling the leaves. No cars racing up and down the street, no loud music, no boats or smell of bay water—just clean dry air and the sound of her own breathing. She was on dry land, a stranger on the corner of a street in a foreign country. With the light falling all around her, it occurred to her she never wanted to leave.

She took her things inside, shivered, and turned on the teakettle. She'd lied to Owen Garrett—she'd brought one dress with her. It was peach-colored watered silk, a short-sleeved summer dress that hit her three inches below the knees. Maybe she would wear it, and then again, if she went at all, maybe she would just go in her jeans.

S TORM CLOUDS," MARGARET SAID AT THE FRONT DOOR WHEN
Owen came to pick her up for Blue Dog Days.

He craned his neck to check out the sky. "Maybe.
Then again, maybe not."

"Yes, they are. Cumulosomething. The kind that bring rain.
Shouldn't we call off this outing?"

"How about that—didn't know I had me a weatherwoman
for a neighbor."

"Weather weary is more like it. I remember the kinds of
clouds only because my son went though this cloud phase when
he was five, that's all. Had to know all the clouds, all their names.
Forget dinosaurs, it drove him berserk there wasn't some kind of
cloud museum we could visit. The weather's too predictably
balmy in Southern California for anything but a few wispy stra-
tus. Storm clouds were his favorite. You never saw a kid who
liked rain as much as Peter."

"A little rain can't stop a New Mexico powwow," Owen
assured her. "As Joe might say, that's just Father Sky's way of
blessing the event. Holy water from above, and the rainbow gift
that comes after."

Margaret sighed. "Well, it was worth a shot."

"I like the color of your dress. Did you go out shopping?"

"Excuse me?"

"You told me you gave all your dresses away."

She smiled flatly at him. "Well, it's the only one I didn't throw out and older than I care to admit. You can check my closet if you don't believe me."

"Oh no, ma'am. I believe you." Owen smiled back. He opened the pickup door for her. The truck interior was swept clean from the tattered upholstery down to the metal flooring, and he had splurged and bought one of those scented pine-tree mirror kebabs that made the interior smell like Pine-Sol perfumed alfalfa and evergreen sheep wool. He turned the ignition key, and the motor obediently kicked over. "Tell me what you have against social events."

"Let's just say I put in my time with social obligations."

"Tough marriage?"

"Put my time in one of those, too."

"Well, you're in a world of company. At least you got your boy out of it."

Which was only true in a manner of speaking. Technical custody, but Peter chose to live with the Hidalgos. "How about you? Do you have children?"

"A daughter. College girl. Knows it all, does my Sara Kay. I don't begrudge her an education. I miss her, though. Once upon a time I could do no wrong."

"Now?"

He pressed his lips together before answering. "Sooner or later they see how human you are, don't they? Then it takes them twenty or thirty years to forgive you for it."

"If ever." Margaret rested her elbow in the open window, leaned her chin on her fist. In twenty years she would be sixty, grandmother material. By then Peter might have sorted through his own childhood and want children of his own. How did a deaf father teach his child? Would the hearing child of a deaf parent be willing to sign or, just like a second-generation immigrant, would the pull of the spoken word keep him a world apart from his father?

"Your boy. He's okay now?"

"Do you know any fifteen-year-olds who seem okay?"

"Not really." Owen slowed the truck and pointed a finger to the roadside where a well-fed coyote trotted toward low hills. "Hello there, *Señor Chivito*. You're looking particularly hearty this year," he said to the retreating animal. "It's a good idea to keep your dog in at night, Margaret."

She had noticed ads on the bulletin board at the supermarket for coyote hunters, men who made a living hunting down and eradicating the animal. You couldn't pass a produce stand without seeing four or five skulls for sale, bleaching in the sun, recently scraped clean of skin and fur. It sickened her. "Tell me what you'd do if you were alone in this truck, Mr. Garrett. Would you take out your rifle and not even think twice about shooting him, or would you let him go?"

Owen turned to look at her and smiled. "Never shoot anything from the dog family during Blue Dog Days. It's like asking for a decade of terrible luck."

"And if it wasn't Blue Dog Days?"

"Well, the Navs like to say if you kill a brother coyote, you only end up trading places with him. Still, he'd make the start of a nice coat."

She shook her head. "Nobody wears fur anymore. In California animal activists throw buckets of pig blood at the movie stars in their minks. Of course, no one asks the pig whether he minds contributing."

He reached over and patted her hand. "Good thing you left that state. Sounds like it's full of a bunch of people weak north of the ears."

Main Street was cordoned off with sawhorses. In the cool summer evening, tiny white Christmas lights blinked incongruously around every storefront. Vendors had set up booths to sell food and crafts. Owen kept hold of her arm, guiding Margaret through

what she guessed was Blue Dog's idea of a sidewalk crowd—
twenty people here, thirty more across the street—to where
Indian women stood cooking up frybread and assembling Navajo
tacos. "Name your preference," he said.

"The bread looks good."

"You want powdered sugar or honey on it?"

"What do you recommend?"

"Oh, honey, by far, if you're after a traditional experience."

"Then I'll have honey."

"Smart woman." He paid for two rounds of the hot bread,
then handed one to Margaret.

The warmth of the bread seeped through the paper plate,
comforting against her hands. She pinched off small pieces of
dough drizzled with syrup. The butter melted immediately, pool-
ing with the honey. Margaret tried to eat carefully so she wouldn't
make a mess. Owen tore his bread into expert strips, folding
them to avoid spilling. Unabashedly he ran his tongue across his
thumb to clean the honey from his fingers.

The high school band played, the horn section louder than it
needed to be, most of the time on key. She watched the baton
twirlers, those smiling small-town girls with their whole lives
ahead of them, all that passion and heartbreak and disappointment and hard work. Their spangled white leotards fit like virgin
skin, announcing youth and fertility beneath hard-working muscles. These girls could do it all—smile, march, kick their legs skyward and perform remarkable saves as the baton spiraled through
the air. Riders on shining horses in silver show saddles and Spanish costumes waved to the small groups gathered on the sidewalk; a team of draft horses brushed to a glistening shine pulled
an old restored dairy wagon painted a bright yellow; a Scout
troop marched; and the mayor drove slowly by in a red Ford con-
vertible. Finally the town's impossibly shiny fire engine passed by,
the volunteer brigade marching behind. But because Blue Dog
was so small a town, the parade was over in little more than half
an hour. She wished they'd turn around and march everyone
back the other way, just so she could watch it all over again.

When she looked up, her last chunk of frybread in her mouth, her hands as sticky as a child's, Owen was staring at her soberly.

"What?" she said. "Do I have food on my face?"

"No. I wondered if it might embarrass you if I took hold of your hand. Your free one, that is."

"Why?"

"Parades and kids. Call me a fool, but they make me lonesome."

He looked old and tired, squinting in the last of the sun. Silver hair mixed with the sandy blond above his ears where the hat didn't cover it. She didn't quite know what to say. She looked back at him, trying not to be suspicious. Was there really one man left in the world who still asked, who didn't just grab at what he wanted as if that was his right? Or was this benignly poetic pass so especially clever that she was missing the point? "If you don't mind getting honey all over yourself, be my guest. Just return it at the end of the evening."

"Margaret, you sure don't make it easy on a man."

She'd already done that, for seventeen years, and it had gotten her nowhere. She felt his fingers close over hers and give a friendly squeeze. Down in front of the Chamber of Commerce, a circle of seated Indian men were beginning to beat in unison on a large drum. From everywhere, it seemed, dancers began to emerge. Indian women in beaded deerskin and moccasins fastened with silver conchos left the street sides and formed a wide circle. Men stripped down to loincloths and feathers, faces painted in primary oxides, wove past her into the street. Small children attempted the same staccato dance steps as the adults, their tiny brown faces masks of seriousness, and were led by the hand into the circle of dancers. She recognized Mr. Yazzi, Owen's friend from the restaurant, among them. Over his bare chest he wore a necklace of bear claws. His chest and abdomen were crisscrossed with scar tissue and so many stitch marks she couldn't count them. In spite of the manners her mother had force-fed her since she could toddle upright, she gasped, then, ashamed, touched her fingers to her mouth.

"Vietnam," Owen whispered in her ear. "When he got back to Blue Dog he spent about a year in the hospital, trying to remember who he was, while doctors come up from all over and took pictures of him. Half his organs are in the wrong places. Nobody knows why he keeps on breathing. Somehow he does. The government gave him a sackful of medals, and they send him a check every month, but none of it can ever hope to erase what happened."

"What happened?"

"Everything you can imagine, and a lot more that you wouldn't want to. He's a good man, Joe is, but part of him runs wilder than the old Blue Dog himself."

But Joe danced as if his skin were free of blemishes, and no one in the long line of performers excluded or shied away from him. In college she'd volunteered to train for draft counseling, where scared young men with high draft numbers tried to keep themselves from being turned into reluctant soldiers. Sometimes they found a way, or their parents could afford an influential lawyer. Other times they just went and tried to get it over with. She wondered what had happened to those boys, whose faces in her memory now seemed no older than her own son's. It had been too easy to ignore the Vietnam veterans, but that was what had happened. When Joe's back was to them, she turned to face Owen.

"Hey—you were going to tell me the legend of the Blue Dog. How about it?"

That winking eye winked for real. "Night's still young. Be patient."

They wandered the streets and studied the offerings the vendors displayed. Margaret admired a strand of silver tooled beads. "I make you good price," the woman urged, but Margaret shook her head no. She didn't need to buy anything to have a good time, and silver beads didn't exactly mesh with her current budget. But she picked up a leather wristband with inset buffalo nickels, and said yes to the woman's request for five dollars. "To send to my son," she explained to Owen. "He's still at the age where he likes bracelets."

"He back in the great prune state?"

"Riverwall, " she answered, then realized Owen Garrett was gathering clues here and there, adding them up. "Listen, I'm not telling you one more thing until you explain the blue dog, so you might as well quit asking me questions."

He feigned surprise. "How's the painting going?"

"How did you know I was painting?"

"This blue dog told me."

"The same one that told you to leave that paper in my mailbox, I'll bet."

"Will you look over there? It's the tribal president," Owen said, ignoring her. "He's going to make a speech. Must be important business for him to come down off the rez."

Like the abrupt absence of a heartbeat, the drumming ceased while the mayor gave a little talk about the town and its recent achievements, how the successful fund-raising for the fire engine now had them functioning at a state-of-the-art level with Albuquerque. Then he turned the microphone over to the Indian president, who welcomed the dancers in the Navajo language. His words were glottal clicks and foreign syllables to Margaret, but Owen knew enough to translate the gist of his speech.

"He's after changing their name from Navajo to *Diné*," he explained, pronouncing the word *din-AY*. "Navajo was the name given them by the Spaniards, and it means 'thief,' or 'clasped knife,' depending on whose translation you buy. *Diné* means 'the people,' and he feels it's a more accurate description, so he's asking the tribe to vote to make it a permanent change."

Angry words were exchanged between the chief and some of the high school kids. Owen laughed.

"What did he say?"

"The boys don't agree. He told them their minds were wrecked from satellite dish television and that they ought to spend time studying with the elders if they want to redeem themselves as members of the *Diné* nation."

The boys hung their heads and melted back into the crowd of their peers. Unlike Peter and his friends, these kids still seemed to hold respect for authority, or at the very least they bit their tongues in public.

After the speeches the dancing resumed. Joe Yazzi danced by Margaret again, his muscled body glazed with sweat. He was sober faced, there with her and Owen in body, but his spirit was caught in the dance of some other world. Turkey feathers, painted to resemble sacred eagle feathers, trembled as he matched his feet to the beat of the drum. He moved into the crowd and took a tiny baby from a woman's arms and hugged it to his scarred chest, then danced it along in the circle. Despite the noise and the jouncing, the baby didn't cry. The drummers were chanting now. If it had started out as a celebration of a small white town, that layer had peeled off and blown away in what seemed to be the last of the summer season. The street and the land beneath it belonged to the Indians now, the *Diné*, who had been here grow-ing food and praising the earth long before self-supporting libraries, mysterious cowboys, or itinerant mothers moved in.

The darkness gathered them together. Owen's hand released Margaret's and he casually placed his arm around her shoulder, tucking her into the warmth of his body. They were so near the same size that from the back, they might have been brothers. But their differences went beyond gender. He was a lonely man with enough integrity to ask outright for her hand, risking her saying no. She ached to hold on to that baby Joe Yazzi seemed to cele-brate with such ease, but she did so in a silence she could not bear to break. She longed to feel the music move through her the way Joe did, transporting her from a tall, displaced woman on a small-town sidewalk to wherever it was he went.

When the dancers took a break, the children brought out their entries for the Blue Dog competition. They ran the animals through a modified version of the companion dog course; Mar-garet recognized some of the commands from the Westminster show on cable television. Back home, recuperating, bored to death, Peter would flip channels, settle on the dog show, and make fun of the obese handlers in their sequined gowns, running around with sculptured poodles and beribboned Maltese. *Quick, which one's the dog?* he'd say too loudly, having not yet figured out how to modulate his voice. But behind his sarcasm there was genuine interest. He wouldn't have let on, but he would have enjoyed this competition. Margaret missed his snide remarks, the easy way a teenager who couldn't ever imagine himself old or obese spoke. She missed his rainbow hair colors, different from one week to the next, and the earrings glinting in his pierced lobes. There were times she felt close to missing picking up his damp towels from the bathroom floor.

"I'm putting my money on old Sadie over there," Owen said. "She does what she's asked, all right, but I think she's holding back. That old shepherd mutt's got a surprise or two left in her. You watch."

Owen was right. Though she'd tied in points with two other dogs, Sadie stole the show when it came to the talent segment. With nearly invisible hand gestures that made Margaret think of ASL, the chubby adolescent girl handling her was able to make the dog perform several extra maneuvers; walking low to the ground as if stalking prey; guarding her mistress with quick darts and feints, as if she were herding an errant sheep; mournfully howling out loud when the girl turned her back and pretended to walk away. When the girl asked her to come, she did so, circling back to pick up a fallen bell tie one of the dancers had dropped and returning to offer it to the girl. In unison, the street full of spectators let out a collective "Awww."

It was official. Sadie accepted her award—a collar of bells and blue beads—and walked entirely off leash next to her handler, Olivia Maryboy, who earlier that evening had also been crowned Best Girl.

"'Best Girl'—what's that mean?" Margaret asked Owen.

"The tribe's singled her out to the others as an example," he said. "She had some trouble last year, and now she's back on track, so she's wanting to pay back those who helped her."

Olivia handed out "gifts" to the crowd: bags of candy, lengths of fabric, skeins of wool, loaves of homemade bread. People cleared space in the street for the girl and her family to pass, and the crowd was silent except for the low drumming of the men.

"Some say the legend's as simple as this," Owen said into her ear as they watched. "Long time ago, a man traveling horseback through Four Corners neglected to take enough water along. He got delirious in the desert, fell off his horse. The rank old horse took off on him. Being just a man, he'd lost his animal instincts and was too weak to follow. To further this insult and prove luck just wasn't with him, he lived through three long days and nights craving water. On the third night, under a three-quarter moon, this blue dog appeared and said, 'Mister, I'm telling you true, plenty of clean water's right over that next ridge. Follow me, and I'll sure enough take you to it. But I want something in return.' The thirsty traveler was more than ready for any kind of bargain, so he followed the dog, crawling on his hands and knees like a baby. True to his word, the hound led him to the Animas River, clean enough for drinking, and the man kept his promise."

"Which was?"

"Some say to name this town after the dog. But I don't know. It's one of those things that changes depending on who you ask. Twenty years back, there was talk of changing the town's name to Fuller, after an oilman who settled here and built up a bunch of the Victorian houses. The Blue Dog diehards wouldn't hear of it, started up the parade, and now kids'll spend all year training a dog for the competition. Keeps them out of trouble, anyway."

Or from cutting school and swimming in polluted pools, Margaret thought, but said nothing about Peter, or the events leading up to his meningitis. On their way out, she stopped and bought five chances on a Navajo Storm Pattern rug to be auctioned off the closing night of the festival.

"Five dollars for paper chances. You must fancy weavings," Owen said.

"They've had a hold on me for twenty years. Sometimes, in the right light, they remind me of the stained-glass windows I used to stare at in church, rather than get scared by the priest's sermon, back when I was a child. They give me that same reverent feeling but none of the fire and brimstone. I could look at them all night."

He adjusted his hat. "Well, you came to the right town then. See that woman in the purple dress? That'd be Verbena Young-cloud, one of the best weavers in the state."

"You know her?"

He smiled, that same enigmatic cowboy grin, the one that said little out loud but much in its silence. "It's a small town. I can introduce you."

"She looks busy with her family."

"True enough, there's no shortage of children or grandkids when it comes to that household. We'll catch up to her another time."

Margaret realized they'd bought their bread at the weaver's booth. Twenty years ago, what she would have given up to meet this woman, ask her questions about art, about vision. But now those concerns seemed foolish, the shallow musings of an immature girl who had yet to learn what constituted art. The weaver was surrounded by children, many of them still in costume from dancing. A few hugged and kissed her as they showed off ribbons and helped to pack up the makeshift kitchen.

It was the end of the evening, and people were heading home. Loosening herself from Owen's grip, Margaret took back her hand.

"Wait here. I want to give you something," she said as he opened the front door of the Starr farmhouse for her. She ran up the stairs to the studio bedroom and picked up the watercolor of Hopeful. She hadn't stretched the paper ahead of time, so it didn't lie flat. It wasn't really finished, but it was more of a dog than the dirt drawing had been. Echo at her heels, she returned to Owen, who stood just inside the doorway, hat in hand. She pressed the paper into his hand.

"It's nothing great, just my way of saying thanks for giving me that push, buying me the paper. And for tonight."

He chuckled at the painting. "I'm going use my employee discount to invest in a frame for this one. Thank you, neighbor."

"You and your dog are both welcome. Good night."

▪ ▪ ▪

That night, after he'd gone, she lay awake upstairs in the dark, stroking the dog, her restless hands making their way through the manual alphabet just to keep in practice. The therapist had told her to practice by spelling out a word, visualizing what she spelled as she made the letters—*L, lamb*. She tried to imagine the sheep Owen tended and their forthcoming babies. *M, money*— had she enough to live on? Yes, if she was careful. *N, Navajo*— and in her mind's eye she pictured the Best Girl and her award-winning dog. *O, Owen Garrett*—neighbor and stranger. *P—paint-brush*. Her hands stopped. That hadn't been her initial impulse— Peter's name had. She saw his profile the day he finally began to consider what the doctors were trying gently to break to him, that he would never hear again.

As an adult you could unequivocally state that there was a limit to what the human heart could take. You could even imag- ine the cut-off point where painful truths no longer felt sharp. But as a parent, watching her son sit in the middle of his hospital bed while a team of doctors stood over him, their arms crossed, faces drawn into impassive, deliberate lines, she knew all that was a crock. When it came to children, their capacity to withstand pain was never ending. When Peter said, "I can *so* still hear," his fists clutching the white sheets into wrinkled flowers, she knew that at the same time, he was edging painfully toward that truth that said, Okay, you guys win. I'm deaf.

But what came to her now as she lay in her bed was another shock, strangely related. For years, after she had shunted aside brief, awkward glimpses, Peter's going deaf had provided her with an understanding of the reason she abandoned art when she mar- ried Raymond. It wasn't about Ray's insistence that she stay home and devote herself to having his babies, a decision she'd ulti- mately embraced as sensible and desirable. When Peter went away she could no longer couch her excuses under the heading of motherhood. Art took time away from other things, certainly, but creativity was a state of mind you fertilized and tended, not something you made room for. Even throughout those years when she wasn't doing it, she remembered how art worked. The way color and texture carefully built their layers to create a story, the way pure emotion could leap out from the canvas and lodge in your throat. Peter had shown her that early on. He'd ask to have one of her cartoon drawings, and she would tear it off the scratch pad and give it to him. He'd carry those drawings around with him all day, and later she would find them, slightly the worse for wear but there on the same shelves as his favorite toys.

She knew with enough instruction, over time, anyone with a shred of talent could learn to approximate craft. But the really frightening part was that so much of the time you spent facing down the colossal disappointment of your work remaining ordinary, derivative, bound to the canvas, unable to grow the necessary inches required to take the human spirit for a ride. Art thumbed its nose at you—Go on, peel off another layer of skin. Try harder. Simply put, she had turned away from art because *good* art exacted too heavy a price for her, one she was not willing to pay.

Even if you did everything right—stayed married, kept painting, watched your child make the honor roll—he still might go deaf. Bad luck was as random as her miscarriages had been. When Peter went deaf, she realized that nothing in her hands was going to make it better. Not art, no amount of perfect parenting— nothing would make her child hear again. Her understanding had begun in that hospital room, with coastal sunlight streaming in through the window backlighting her beautiful damaged son and ended here in a dark bedroom of a rented house. Sun and angle and eye had given Peter's profile a chiseled perfection the artist in *any* mother would cherish, and any practicing artist would sacrifice a finger to capture. But to harness the real thing, to make art, you had to peel your heart raw and constantly leave it open.

Profound adventitious deafness. The organ of Corti is missing in both basal turns. Striae vascularis *atrophy. . . tectorial membranes ensheathed in syncytium. . . .* Margaret hadn't wanted to believe the permanence of those words anymore than Peter. To believe meant there was no footing beneath either of them, that they were stepping off the same steep cliff. Was it arrogance to dip her paintbrushes in the summer sunshine while her son struggled to re-order his world, a world she could never fully enter? All she knew was, right at this moment, she had nowhere else to go.

Owen showed up two nights later. He couldn't possibly understand how many hours Margaret had spent at this kitchen table, the *Perigee Visual Dictionary* in front of her, trying to get the words right.

"Like a fool, I let Joe talk me into team-roping. Come on along and watch us. We'll be wearing our numbers upside-down, riding for the practice, not money, but who knows, I might fall off Red, dent my hat good, and give the crowd a laugh."

She'd kept him standing on the front steps, the door open only a few inches. Outside the door existed an ordinary world a divorced woman could step into by choice. Inside she had a new language to learn, if she ever wanted to speak to her son. From divorced parents to broken ears, his world was a jumble. She wouldn't be fit company for the walls in the house, let alone this good man who deserved more than her dark mood to spoil his evening. "I'm sorry," she said. "I can't. I hope you understand." And gently she closed the door in his face.

In late September she watched Owen Garrett, on his own initiative, spend the better part of his Friday afternoon well into evening splitting firewood outside the barn. When he was done, he drove a truck bed full over and dumped it outside her front door. Margaret helped to stack it, wiped her brow, paid him in cash, then took him a tall glass of iced tea, and mumbled, "Thank you," for his hard work. When she turned to go he called out.

"Margaret. All this sweat and sawdust deserves some kind of reward. Go for a swim with me."

"The downtown pool closed at five."

He pointed across the pasture. "The river's not too deep, and there's not much of a crowd after nine o'clock."

"It'll be too cold."

"Just a quick dip. We can wrap in blankets after and burn up a bunch of this new firewood."

"I haven't unpacked all the way. I don't know where my swimsuit is."

"Damn, Margaret, dunk your feet or swim in your underwear, I don't care. It's dark out, and I promise not to look."

Mild as it was, she took note. It was the first and only time she'd heard Owen Garrett use an expletive. It wasn't as if he was asking her to skinny-dip. Get wet, get out, cool down in the process. The shock of cold water felt good to her feet and legs. As her underpants and bra took on water, she was aware at how they shone in the moonlight, the white fabric bright enough to show off her slight tummy, the V of her pubic hair. She sat down in the shallows, folding her legs up so that the water hit her just above the breasts. Owen followed.

"Cold?"

"Terminally."

He laughed. "Keep moving and you'll warm up." He looked up at the night sky. "You know, this is probably the last night we can do this, weatherwise. It's fall, all right, shortest season of the year."

She rubbed her arms as they moved through the dark water, the moonlight occasionally illuminating their limbs when the cloud cover shifted. There weren't that many stars; other nights she'd seen them in greater numbers and been dazzled by the white points piercing the sky. The cold water felt warmer now, her body buoyant, as if the river were a hammock. Tree branches scraped at each other like spindly arms. Against the swift current, she fluttered her fingers and found Owen's hand, then interlaced her fingers with his. "My turn to take a hand," she said, and felt him move closer, until she could sense his warm body next to hers, every solid inch of it.

"Haven't seen you out and about lately. What have you been up to these last couple of weeks?"

She sighed. "There've been a lot of changes."

"Haven't got your legs yet. Don't worry, you'll grow them. How goes the drawing?"

"I'm getting pretty good at mediocre."

"That's a far step beyond terrible." He let go of her hand and swam out a few strokes to deeper water, where a tree limb hung low and thick enough for him to grab onto. He held on there. "You know, Margaret, one of these days I'm going to try to kiss you."

"Sooner or later I figured we'd come to that."

"Is it such a terrible prospect?"

She shook her head. "It makes me a little sad, Owen. Here we've been getting along so well as neighbors. Now we're going to screw everything up by throwing sex into it."

"Despite what movies would have you believe, one kiss don't automatically mean sex will follow."

"It's never just one kiss. Not with people our age."

"Our age what? I'm fifty-two, but I call myself a gentleman. How old are you?"

"I'm forty. You're still a man."

"Forty? That's a grand age. All the nonsense of your thirties is behind you. You got ten long years before fifty hits and scares you into spending every day you've got left like it's your last two bits."

He let go of the limb, moving closer through the dark water until she felt the warmth of his bare thigh graze hers.

"All this fretting over something we haven't even done yet." He placed his arm around her shoulders, drew her in, kissed her full on the mouth, his lips closed, as he promised, a gentleman's kiss. He held her to him, breathing naturally, his hands solid against her back, then kissed her cheeks, her ears, and tilted her chin back so that he could bend down and kiss the length of her long, white, wet neck.

That was the place—if she'd been a spy captured by the enemy in wartime, if she'd embezzled money from her employer, or if she was some kind of international art thief—all anyone would have to do was send in a handsome man to kiss her neck and she'd spill her secrets as easily as this river water flowing between her legs.

He held her there, her breasts grazing his chest, their ankles touching, hands staying like good children in the careful territory of arms. "You're making me wish I still drank. About now I'd down the better part of a fifth to give me courage."

"To do what, I'm afraid to ask?"

"Kiss you again."

She thought that over a moment. She knew what her sister would have done—kissed him back first. But she wasn't Nori, and for all she'd lost, she still retained the power of speech to say no when she felt like saying no. "I don't think we need liquor." Taking hold of his right hand, she moved it slowly up her body until it came to rest on her left breast, that mound of flesh made nearly weightless by the water. She felt him shiver the length of his body, felt the shock of his response through his lips as he kissed her again, the quick darting movement of his tongue inside her mouth.

That kiss said something she had needed to be reminded of—outside this river, on dry land, where contiguous states bumped each other at their borders and telephone systems chattered all night with orbiting satellites, nothing really mattered except two people in a river, making a night pass by holding on to one another.

When they came apart, breathing as shallowly as if they'd been swimming under rock toward a small pocket of air, Margaret said soberly, "Your dog the day we met. Is he some kind of mind reader?"

"Just a clever animal who makes the most of what little he's got."

"Maybe you ought to enter him in the Blue Dog competition next year."

Owen grinned, a flash of shining white teeth in moonlight. "He's already got too high of an opinion of himself."

She shivered. "I'm glad you talked me into swimming, but I'm really starting to get cold."

"Me, too. It's going to be a bone chiller of a race between this water and your farmhouse, but if we cut through the trees, my bunkhouse is closer."

She shook her head. "No way. You get me in there, start playing love songs on the radio, I'm doomed. A couple of kisses and swimming in my underwear is as far as I go tonight."

"Warm blankets and a hot cup of tea, nothing else. You have my word, Maggie."

Somehow, in two kisses, without alcohol, he'd executed the name change, baptism by river. Half teasing, she said, "How do I know your word's something I can trust?"

"It's the only thing about me that hasn't sold itself at one time or another. You take that to the bank. Folks there'll vouch for me."

Not believing him, beyond caring what that meant, she went.

6

IT TOOK MOST OF OWEN'S INNER STRENGTH AND ALL HIS REASON-
ING to wrap Maggie's bare shoulders in the faded rainbow-
colored Mexican serape when what his body told him to do
was strip away the blanket, the wet underwear, and what was
left of his resolve. She sat shivering in a rickety birch chair at
his kitchen table, dripping river water onto the cement floor,
three feet from his single bed with the overly soft mattress.
Depending on how you arranged your bodies, wouldn't be hard
to make room for two.

But even if you only got so far as stepping into natural water,
you still could learn plenty about a woman. Whether she could
swim, for example—she could—or if she was the type not to
want her hair getting wet—dunked it under, first thing—or best
of all, leaned her graceful neck back and let water wash over her
in some kind of elemental pleasure. That was the way he would
commit to memory the end of this year's summer—when he
christened Maggie Yearwood in the Animas River, the water
touching her everywhere, the way he wanted to but wouldn't,
because he'd given his word, and tattered as it was, he stood by it.

"You call this Indian summer?" she said, rubbing her hands over her arms in an attempt to get warm. "I could see my breath all the way up to the barn!"

"Coffee," he said firmly. "I'll make us a fresh pot."

She shook her head. "No thanks. I'll be up all night." The chill pebbled her flesh and blued her lips. Owen offered her a dry shirt and she turned her back, letting the blanket drop long enough to ease her arms inside. The sleeves were five inches too long. On Maggie, a flannel shirt took on all kinds of impractical significance.

He watched her wring her wet things out at the sink and dry her feet on a towel. Then she said, "We probably ought to talk about what happened down there in the water."

"Why?"

"Because kissing changes everything."

"Now, see, that's the trouble with you Californians, always wanting to talk everything into a corner, paying some lunatic a hundred dollars an hour to give you a theory on why or why not to kiss a man who takes you swimming on a hot night. We're human, Maggie. What we did felt good, that's all there is to it."

But that wasn't all there was to it. Kissing her, then, with her permission, touching her breast—the last time his heart had such a workout was when he'd met a Colorado state trooper in downtown Farmington. He'd smiled to the man, tipped his hat, and gone about his business, but he couldn't eat the entire day thinking about it, not even after Lulu Mantooth explained there was a convention of badges over at the Holiday Inn, and sure enough, they were a bunch of *agarrado* cheapskates who tried to argue her down on the price of turquoise keychains.

He got up and went to Maggie, taking her by the arms. "Let's get you home. I'll drive you. That way you won't catch a chill."

She looked at him uncertainly, as if she didn't believe he'd let her go without forcing the issue.

Up close, her skin smelled slightly sweet. She knew good and well what he wanted, and as much as he wanted it now, it could wait until they were of a similar mind. "Go on, get in the truck." He gave a whistle for the dog.

"Such a worthless day, might as well cut wood," Owen said outside Rabbott's Hardware, where there was a sale on insulation and
microwave dishes. The former was selling well; the latter they
couldn't give away, not even below cost. But Joe Yazzi was being
as silent as his white mule, Lightning. The mule had never been
much to look at, but since the Police Department had impounded
Joe's truck—a fish they were willing to throw back only if Joe
paid his outstanding fines—the mule took Joe where he wanted
to go and seemed to tolerate the city streets of Blue Dog. Owen
gave the well-fed animal a pat. Sometimes when Joe was low on
cash, the animal grew thin and poor in the coat, but if you looked
closely, Joe always looked worse. What Joe's sheep hadn't
trimmed down to nothing, the mule ate.

Thanks to the year's ample rainfall, there had been forage this
fall, but even that was meager as they headed into November.
Owen suspected Joe fed the mule instead of feeding himself. All
through the months of September and October, when the colors
were fading from the trees and grasses, and the tourists came in
fewer droves, farther between, you could find Joe just about anywhere, being Mr. Goodtime. If he wasn't making fun of the line
dancers in the Trough, or holding a female body close against his
own for a slow dance, he was driving a couple of pretty girls
around, in search of team-roping practices.

Lately, Owen thought, it seemed like Joe was retreating, inch
by significant inch. He didn't go out much, he missed a few
Thursday nights, the entire truck incident seemed off. At the core
of things, something felt so wrong it vibrated through the quiet
like an alarm. "You're not drinking, are you?" he asked, but Joe's
ready answer was to whip him at gin rummy, add the year's tally
of points, and remind Owen how many hundreds of dollars he
owed. When he did remember to meet Owen for Thursday sup-
pers, they chatted, but Joe's smile, like his storytelling and his
come-and-go pretty girlfriends, was like the sun, peeking through
now and again, but mostly dwindling down to nods in the grasp
of the oncoming winter.

Owen tried again. "It could also be a good day to accompany

a friend while he cuts wood. No work's necessary. Maybe the friend could use some company."

Joe squatted down face-to-face with Hopeful, who cocked his furry blue-roan head as if trying to understand Joe, too. Joe mumbled a few words in Navajo, then stood, pulled himself up on his mule, situating the worn chevron-patterned blanket underneath his scrawny butt, and gathered his reins in his left fist.

"How about if I stop by later and bring you some wood?" Owen asked, and watched the Indian silently ride his white mule down the length of Main Street, fall leaves and litter blowing up around the mule's pasterns as they ignored the single traffic light.

It had been too long a day, loaded with jigsaw puzzles. That morning Maggie had closed up the Starr farmhouse and—before getting into the gray-blue Toyota—asked him to watch after her skinny dog. Sure, he'd walk over twice a day and feed Echo— what was one more dog but company? "Santa Fe," she told Owen, tight lipped when he flagged her down at the mailbox and asked where she was headed. "I might stay a week."

"Off to see some of the local art? Or are you planning to hook up with your boy in Riverwall?" It about broke his heart when he saw her check the mailbox every day, hoping. After a few weeks he started leaving her things, a wildflower now and then, a clearance-table tube of purple paint, more paper when he saw she was running low, hoping to lessen her disappointment.

She'd looked at him, exasperated. "Can't I just drive to Santa Fe, or is that a crime?"

"Well, no, ma'am. New Mexico's a free territory since gaining statehood in 1912. We got freight, passenger, and steam railroads, natural wonders in the Caverns, *santuarios* if you feel like praying for miracles, and some wide-open spaces where you can worship dirt and stickerweed if that's what tickles your toes. You can pretty much do what you like."

"Thank you for the history lesson. And don't call me ma'am. I am not old enough to be a ma'am." There was that dry tone again, the one she put on when she was feeling sad.

He threw up his hands. She drove away, stubborn mouth set. *Santa Fe. A week.* He wanted to reach inside the car and turn off the ignition, throw her keys in the tall weeds, take her into the farmhouse, and kiss her breathless until they got to the bottom of this. Instead he agreed to look after the place, feed the dog, pick up her mail, check the pipes in case of a freeze—unlikely as that possibility was, since he'd wrapped them himself. In nearly three months he'd only touched her breast that one time in the river. Oh, she was generous with kisses, had a surplus of those, and there was no mistaking the electricity he knew wasn't sparking in his loins alone. Twice a week or so she had him to dinner—Maggie could make a mean beef stew with carrots and onions simmering in a juicy gravy—but she could also turn things off between them quicker than a stack of unpaid utility bills shut down your lights.

Sometimes she could be so bullheaded. Out there in the yard, planting bulbs six hours at a time, she wouldn't hear of him helping her. Stacking her firewood all by herself, as if she had to prove herself worthy of the heat they'd provide by earning a back full of sore muscles. Standing under his shower some mornings, turning the knob all the way to cold to settle his blood, Owen decided she flat-out reminded him of the Rio Grande. Opinionated when it came to direction, it came brawling out of Colorado, strong, clean, and deep, rushing down the soul of the state, so treacherous in places it could drown a man. There were the fine parts to Maggie, where the water ran clean and honest; a man could drink from there forever. But there were also deceptive shallows, where a trickle of dark water flowed stingily through sharp rocks and hidden cracks, like the days he'd catch a glimpse of her sitting at the kitchen table, that open book in front of her, her right hand in the air, practicing gestures that never seemed to satisfy her. He had no clue as to why trying to teach herself sign language seemed to upset her so. During those times, those dark-water passages, it was best to just walk around, not even dampen your boot tips.

He went to his truck and opened the door for Hopeful, who

gave his usual athletic three-legged leap inside. They'd travel northeast toward Dulce to cut wood, even though not so many miles north lay Durango, the town he had to avoid. The wood was cheap, plentiful, and if he got industrious, maybe he could sell a few spare cords to make some money. They were heading into winter, and the middle of the week was an unlikely time to meet up with anyone.

The whine of his Little Beaver chainsaw burned his ears. For as much time as one might save you over an ax, they exhausted your arms twice as much. He cut for three hours, then hauled out the wedge and started splitting the wood into stove-size lengths. Above him the sky darkened and a light rain began to fall. He studied the clouds, imagining Maggie's boy, the cloud fanatic. He'd sure enough know what to make of these—they were snow clouds. It was getting colder. Anytime now, that light rain might go to snow. He stopped to wipe his face and tie his bandanna higher on his face to keep the damp wood chips from his nose and mouth. Over his cowboy hat, he wore a plastic cover, a "hat rubber," Joe called it—when Joe was speaking. Hopeful lifted his head and sighed, then backed the majority of his body beneath the truck.

Between Owen's shoulders a warm heat began to spread. He set his mind to the task before him and tried to forget that the two people he cared most to spend time with were in some kind of twist where they wouldn't tell him anything. Just before dusk an Apache from the Jicarilla reservation rode by on his horse and dismounted, preparing to haul back some wood himself. Owen nodded hello to the man and continued loading wood into the pickup bed. The man nodded back and began cutting, creating his own small pile.

"I know your face," the man said, after ten minutes or so. "Didn't you used to live in Trinidad?" He snapped his fingers. "No, Durango, wasn't it?"

Owen shook his head no. "Guess that's the curse of having a common face. People say I look a little bit like everyone. Rapid City, that's where I come from. Transplant to the Land of Enchantment."

"You must have a twin, brother."

"They say most people do."

The Indian eyed him again, then took off with his load into the woods.

Owen sat down on the truck bumper and wiped his face. Maybe it was time to grow a beard again, just for the winter. He sure didn't want to leave Blue Dog. As much as he'd tried not to, he'd sunk roots here. Hopeful silently nosed his leg. No matter what, he wouldn't leave the dog. Joe. Maggie. How could he leave any of them? He reached down and petted his dog, scratching between the shoulder blades, where the vet had taken the muscle and wrapped it tight, leaving a smooth absence where there should have been leg. "You're wanting your supper, aren't you? Well, this work'd go a lot quicker if you'd help me out and load a few sticks into the truck."

At the sound *stick*, surely one of the finest words in the English language, the dog picked up a twig and dropped it at Owen's feet. He held on to the animal's muzzle, giving it a good-natured shake, then threw the stick into the truck bed.

All that night the rain hammered at the windows. Owen couldn't sleep. He set aside *Lonesome Dove*, which he'd read before but remained a book that had never once failed to settle his nerves. Until tonight. Like a silent movie, he played the memory over and tried to fit dialogue to the scenes. He could clearly see the brand of beer he wanted to be drinking, Coors. He could taste the whiskey he'd graduate to, any old brand, and recall in terrifying clarity the Apache's voice: *Durango, wasn't it?* After twisting the sheets into clammy rope, he got down on his knees beside his bed, shut his eyes, and put his head into his hands.

Dear God: This old ghost won't turn me loose and the only way I know of to shut him up is to drown him.

The windows rattled with wind. Rain shot like pellets against the glass. The cold was everywhere, in his bones, turning the blood that pumped through his heart cool. Pack essentials, leave behind nothing that might connect you to this place—he'd done it before, and surely he could do it again. He knew the routine. It helped to have a drink or two for courage. He dressed in his Wranglers and boots, then threw his Carhartt jacket over the thermal underwear he'd been preparing to sleep in. He could hear Hope's toenails on the floor, up and ready to go wherever they were going, but he told the dog to stay behind.

A slight problem presented itself. There were no liquor sales after 10:00 P.M. in Blue Dog. The law was engineered to keep the Indians from liquoring up late at night and driving to their deaths. Too many hand-lettered white crosses dotted the sides of the highways as it was. Owen wasn't the type to keep an unopened bottle in the house to test himself; he knew better than that. But Maggie had no truck with liquor. He'd seen wine in her kitchen, and a small bottle of sherry in the cupboard next to where she kept the ranch salad dressing and boxes of fancy crackers she was so fond of serving. Just one taste. One swallow. A slug would either settle him into sleep or give him the gumption to pack his duffel bag. Medicinal. It was supposed to be good for the heart, they said, in moderation. Prevent strokes, too. One drink, enough to put him out. Tomorrow there was plenty of time to regret. Tonight he wanted unconsciousness.

Rain stinging his face, he walked across the pastures ignoring RedBow's whinny and the bleating of his pastured ewes. Joe would come for the sheep. He'd be happy to tend the new babies once they were born, sell off the rams. In his pocket he fingered Maggie's spare key.

But when he got around to the front of the darkened farmhouse, her Toyota was parked at a slant across the front lawn. He felt the hood—still slightly warm under the water beading up on the paint. Three hours down and four back in terrible weather—depending on the muddy roads, she might have finally got the chance to use her four-wheel drive for something besides a status symbol. Plenty of hotels—he wondered why she hadn't stayed in Santa Fe. He knew she slept upstairs and her room was dark, as was the rest of the house. That long drive and the cooling-down hood probably meant she had turned in for the night. Sneaking in to borrow a bottle wouldn't wake her.

But she wasn't upstairs. She was in the darkened living room, surrounded as usual by sketch pads and half-finished paintings, mostly watercolor studies of animals and trees he recognized as subjects that lived just outside her front door. He'd startled her. Still wearing her jacket, she sat in the overstuffed chair, one hand covering her mouth, as if to speak would be a greater crime than Owen could imagine.

"Didn't mean to scare you. I just came by to check the dog before I went to bed. When did you get back?"

"I don't know."

"Something go wrong down there?"

She made a noise, a sound of disgust. He couldn't figure what that was supposed to mean. He went to her, knelt down by the chair, and tried to get her to turn to him. She pulled away. His eyes adjusted to the dark and he could see her face was wet, as was his own, only his was from rain. The skinny-legged dog was in her lap, one paw batting Maggie's chest for attention.

He knew better than to ask her to tell him what had happened. She looked intact. No dents in the car. He made her a cup of tea, lingering for a moment by the wine bottles, one of which would fit neatly into his jacket pocket on his way out the door. If the old Higher Power was ever to speak to him at all, Owen knew he would say wait on the wine, have a cup of Lemon Mist alongside your neighbor.

He set the cup down on the table near her and took her in his arms. Never had he met a woman so silent on whatever was bothering her. Maybe it was hard feelings from the divorce she wouldn't discuss, but this son of hers seemed to be at the heart of it, the mysterious teenager who was away at school but couldn't be bothered to write a letter now and then to the woman who'd given him life. Had she seen him in Riverwall?

He took a sip of his tea. It tasted a little like one of Joe's herbal concoctions but otherwise didn't do much for him. Maggie ignored hers. The steam from it rose like a tendril of woodsmoke around her face. "Come on," he said, and pulled her by the hand to a standing position.

"Where?"

"We're going upstairs."

"Owen, no."

"Look," he said. "You're all bottled up. I've been patient, I've asked questions and waited for some answers. Nothing. Let's get you into your long johns and tuck you in for the night."

She pulled away and reclaimed her seat in the chair, sighing. "Contrary to male opinion, the solution to every problem in the world does not lie in between bedsheets."

He chuckled softly. "Rein it in there, Mrs. Yearwood. All I was planning on was rubbing your back for you until you fell asleep. Get your mind out of the gutter."

He could just make out her face in the light from the window. The furrow between her eyebrows deepened as she searched for a reply that would silence him. Her jaw trembled and she swallowed hard, that racehorse neck of hers flexing its lovely muscles.

"It's Ms., not Mrs. anything, and don't you forget it."

"Yes, ma'am."

"Dammit, Owen!"

He knew he was pushing limits hauling out the "ma'am," but at least she wasn't crying anymore. She let him walk her upstairs, and she didn't need to be tripped to stretch out on the double bed with the painted iron frame. He took off her jacket and hung it over the chair near the window. Rubbing his wide hands over her muscled shoulders, he located twin knots of tension in the arc of her shoulder blades.

"I learned this from Verbena's brother, Abel. You press hard on the muscle until it gives up, straightens out, and behaves."

She stiffened. "That hurts."

"I know. Kind of like breaking colts. You'll get a little sore in the process, but the end result's worth it."

Soon he felt the muscle begin to loosen. She sighed with relief, but on the edge of that letting go, he heard tears gathering, like the foul-weather clouds near Dulce.

"Cold out tonight," he said, rising from the bed and fetching the chair with her jacket over it. "Old Man Winter has set his suitcases outside the Blue Dog Hotel and rung the bell for room service. You can curl up and go to sleep. I'll just sit here and keep the bogeyman away. "

"You can't," she said into the pillows.

He turned the chair around and straddled it, resting his arms across the back rail. Echo nudged her head up against Owen's knee, and he gave her a friendly scratch. Maggie sighed and rolled over, facing him. He reached down and traced her cheek with his index finger. "I can surely try," he said, softly.

She didn't answer.

Glass rattled in the windows as the rain beat against them. "I guess those old frames need puttying after all. I'll have to get out there tomorrow and work. Will you hold the ladder for me, Maggie? Bake me some Toll House cookies if I do a good job and don't break anything? I like them crisp-to-burnt on the edges. I'm particular when it comes to cookies. That's one of my major failings."

"Stop it right now."

"Stop what?"

"You know what I mean. Trying to distract me talking about windows and cookies."

He scooted the chair closer, until it touched the bed frame with a small click. "Here's a little secret about me. Don't tell Joe. I'm scared of heights. Looking down from a horse's back is about as high-up comfortable as I get. Second-story windows on an old slate roof take more courage than I humanly own. So I put those cookies in mind while I'm up there shaking in the wind. In my mind I mix up the pure white flour with the soft butter, crack in two fresh eggs, measure out the brown sugar. I make fixing those cookies last all the way to smelling them baking as the putty knife seals up the last cranny. Otherwise I might do something foolish, like let the windows go through winter, or worse yet, think about taking a drink to lessen the distance between me and the ground."

He could see her blink her eyes, trying to keep the tears at bay as she listened to his words. The furrow between her brows looked about to become permanent. He took off his hat and held it in his hands. "Let me kick off these boots and lie down beside you, Maggie. Tell me that'd be okay."

She had no clock in the room. In place of ticking there was a different kind of time passing, marked by the sound of her dog scratching a nest in the laundry basket, the persistent rain outside, and his unanswered question growing like a cobweb in the corner.

"Okay."

The chair threatened to topple when he rose from it. He steadied it, toed off his boots, and lay down beside her, feeling the softness of the old mattress as it accepted the weight of another body. When he kissed her mouth, keeping his lips chastely pressed together, she locked arms with him. Where their bodies met, his chest against her breasts, the mutual pocket between them felt warm, like springtime dirt, fertile, eager to be worked. He held her against him, wanting not to stop the kiss but stopping it all the same, tucking her under him so his chin rested on the top of her head. Immediately the crying he'd caught scent of earlier kicked in. One choking sob escaped, then another, softer this time, and then she was in the hardest current of it, treading her way to finally being honest. He held her while she emptied herself, feeling dampness spread onto his neck, wetting the neckline of his thermal shirt. He expected when she was empty, she'd fall asleep, her head tucked into the crook of his arm, sleep more deeply than she had in months.

But from the tears she turned to him, her mouth hungrily on his neck, shaking from what he believed to be equal portions of exhaustion and risk. Her hands tried to move everywhere at once, as if to be in the middle of things would be easier than this awkward starting out. That wild hair of hers fell across his face, and he spoke to her through the strands against his mouth. "Go slow," he told her. "There's no hurry." Taking her hands in his, he intended to let her direct them. Straining, she kissed her way up his face, chin, cheeks, forehead, and he realized he was holding his breath, beginning to feel lightheaded, and blew it out in one single whoosh.

"Here?" he questioned, his hand beneath her sweatshirt, where he felt the slight curve of her left breast in his grateful hand, the nipple nudging his thumb. She sighed, bringing his free hand to the right breast.

In the river she'd been shy about giving up her clothes, but in the privacy of the bedroom they fell away, barbed-wire fencing easily cut. She surrendered the shirt, unsnapped and flung off the flimsy softness of bra, facing him naked for the first time. He looked at her skin, ran his fingers over her ribs, tasted her bare skin. When he reached down, unzipping her jeans to stroke her belly, she stopped his hand.

"Don't."

"Why not?"

"I have scars."

Against her protest, he slid down to take a closer look. Across the arc of her belly there were two scars, upturned at the edges like smiles, the skin there less taut than the rest of her body. Maybe she'd birthed two children through surgery, or just the one, then had one of those female operations, not that it was his business to ask. He traced the ridges of the scar tissue with his index finger and heard her intake of breath. "There's history here. Same as on my ugly old face, but yours delivered you children, and all I got was beat up." He waited a moment, then continued. "Maggie? We can stop this right now if you want."

She shook her head no. "Give me a minute."

He felt her reach down in the dark to touch his face, seeking, her fingertips finding his damaged eye. The fat lump of scar tissue was nerve-dead, had been for years. He felt the pressure of her hand but little else. Prying her fingers away, he pressed them to her own scars, every inch of them, edge to edge, then followed where her fingers had been with his lips and tongue.

Her tension began to loosen under his mouth. He edged the jeans down, stroked her inner thighs, like chamois to his calloused hands. He touched his thumb to her pubic hair and wasn't satisfied with only touching. In the dark, Owen eased his body over hers, heard her groan in welcome. The moment was pure grace. Just the touch of her hand had been enough to cause him to harden enough to enter her. Swiftly, before either one of them could voice all the reasons to stop, he did. Inside she was slick and tense, a soft narrow tunnel that held him in. Oh, he tried to take things nice and slow, but with Maggie crying out his name over and over, her strong arms up over his shoulders, pulling him deeper inside her, there was no such speed as slow. She pressed his fingers against her, and then boom!—like a crack of lightning, the upward and downward strokes meeting just right, shock waves carried her away. She grabbed hold of his shoulders hard enough to make him commit to memory the pent-up need and passion she'd been carrying inside. In the window light he tried to watch her fall away into that dark, soft no place where the body could take you, but once she arched her long neck and the moonlight spilled on it, he was on his way there himself, too, blindly arching above her, hollering her name into the dark. Then, too soon, they were back inside themselves, together, heads bent, faces touching, laughing breathlessly at the simple thing they'd discovered they could do to save each other, the one option humans always forget they have, which must be rediscovered over and over again but to work its magic, need be no more complicated than breathing.

"All I did was ask him to come spend Thanksgiving with me," she said as they sat in bed in the dark eating crackers with slices of sharp Cheddar. "Just drive up for the day and let me cook him turkey. Well, actually, with Peter it would have to be vegetarian turkey, textured vegetable protein, tofu or seaweed, some damn thing I'd slave over all day that would come out wrong. He doesn't eat meat."

"What happened? Dad get to him first? Kids'll play you like checkers around the holidays. Don't I know it."

"No. He said he'd rather stay at school, have dinner with his host family."

"Host family?"

She set the plate of crackers aside, and her face was fierce. "It's hard to explain."

"I can tell without you saying you're a good mother, Maggie. You love that boy and I'm sure you do right by him."

"Thanks. Wish I could make myself believe it." She pushed on one of the crackers until it broke under her finger, spilling sesame seeds and wheat particles onto the sheets.

"His father have anything to do with his deciding not to come home?"

"Ray didn't force it. Unusual, because when we were still together he tried so hard to force everything. Me to be the perfect wife, his work to succeed, mold Peter into the son he thought he should be—there never was any dividing line between any of that for Ray. It was something different." She scraped the crumbs into her palm. "Kind of like an exchange student, I guess you could say. Peter decided he wanted to live with another family after his. . . illness."

"Well, for God's sake, Maggie. Excuse me, but maybe what the boy needs is a good whipping. What did he catch that turned him so mean? The thirty-year measles?"

For an instant a smile crept over her sad face. "That's very funny, but no."

"Then what?"

"He cut school with some of his buddies. They'd been drinking, and then they thought it would be hilarious to go swimming in a pool down in TJ."

"TJ?"

"Tijuana, Mexico. Of course the pool was polluted, and he got sick, so sick he damn near died. The whole thing was some kind of dare. He'd lose status if he stayed in class and studied. The doctors said he was lucky to only lose one thing." She swiped at her face, angrily scrubbing the tears.

"What'd he lose?"

Her eyes glittered in the moonlight, and she cocked her head, looking for all the world like a teenager herself, cornered into telling some truth that would convict her of a terrible sin. "His hearing. He's deaf. And yes, it's permanent, and no, I don't want to talk about it, so if you want to do something constructive, you can keep your mouth shut and hold on to me."

He did. He saw her face turn toward the window and watched the dampness in her eyes spill onto her pale skin. The rain, which had been pounding at the old glass so hard that a couple of times it came close to drowning out their conversation, was suddenly still, and he knew without looking that it had begun to snow.

7

DUSTED OVER WITH SNOW IN THE DISTANCE, SHIPROCK MONU-ment had transformed from the red rock pirate's ship run aground in the desert to something out of a fairy tale. Now it was a castle, fashioned by a wizard's child, its fine white crystal blanket blowing up into the morning wind. Maggie leaned on her elbow and looked out the window of the Land-cruiser. If Owen wanted to drive, it was fine with her.

"I'm taking you out to breakfast," he'd said when she turned him loose earlier this morning. "So don't start in about not being hungry, Ms. Yearwood. The way I see it, all that exercise, it's bound to make you as starved as me. I'm not even sure these legs will hold me until then. You took more out of me than chopping six cords of wood."

Then he had headed for her shower, leaving her in bed, feel-ing as full as he claimed he was empty. Now, wherever breakfast was, they were about to leave Blue Dog, head onto reservation land, two dogs in the backseat, each pretending the other didn't exist. Echo had claimed the car blanket; Hopeful sat up with his face to the window, alert, always watching Owen to see what he might do next.

Next to her Owen unbuttoned his jacket halfway, his faded flannel shirt and thermal underwear covering the skin she'd claimed for her pleasure last night. His body had surprised her. The skin was weathered where it had worked in the sun, loosening with age, but everywhere she put her hand or tensed her thigh, she encountered absolute firmness in this workingman's frame. His chest was covered with blond-to-graying hair that appeared coarse, but as she pressed her breasts against him, she discovered its softness and warmth. His hands were knowledgeable as he cupped her here, stroked her there, but it wasn't the precise, flawless lovemaking Ray had practiced. There was a thoughtful, let's-just-give-this-a-try attitude in his hands. When whatever he'd done elicited a happy response, she could feel the charge drive though him as strongly as into her own flesh. It was silly to have held out so long, but she realized she hadn't done it out of any latent moralistic notions. She simply hadn't wanted to be hurt again when he notched his belt and went on to his next partner. She had probably scared him half to death, jumping on him this morning before she'd even made him a cup of coffee. Her body felt hungrier than her stomach. Why was it when there was nowhere else to go, yourself was the last place you considered for comfort?

"You mind?" Owen said, his hand on the radio.

She shook her head no. She'd owned the car four months, lived in Blue Dog for three, and during all that time, hadn't gotten around to setting the stations.

He tuned the radio to KNAV, where after a long interlude of musical chant, the announcer broke briefly into English.

"Ladies and gentlemen, that was 'Last Year's Dancing Partner,' coming to you from the Four Corners Singers, and this here is KNAV radio, all Navajo, all the time. We got some R. Carlos Nakai on the Native American flute coming up with his fine group, Jackalope, so stay with us." Then he repeated the same information in what Maggie guessed had to be Navajo.

"Every hour or so they set aside time for open mike," Owen explained. "Good or bad weather. People needing to get messages to family and neighbors can go to the station and talk on the air."

"Why don't they just phone each other?"

"Well, some of them are a little bit like you when it comes to the telephone. You need power lines to install phones. Money to pay for both, something the rez sadly lacks. You know, I can just about fold the Shiprock phone book up three times and fit it in my back pocket. Radio's a lifeline on days like today."

Maggie couldn't make out a single word coming from the dashboard. Every once in awhile Owen laughed out loud at what was being said.

"Maybe I ought to go on down there myself, leave Joe a message."

"Does he listen to the radio?"

Owen looked back at her doubtfully. "If he forgot to turn it off three days ago, he might. Joe's mind isn't all that. . . straightforward, sometimes."

"What direction does it take?"

"Well, sometimes he's fighting old Charlie in Thanh Hoa, and the next minute he'll be a kid selling corn to the tourists, dreaming about getting rich. You never can tell when what'll hit. Something'll trigger it, and he'll go so deep inside himself I couldn't exactly tell you where."

"Because of Vietnam?"

"Oh, partly. Some of it, sure. But Joe never was one to let things fester. He speaks up. He might not've been born early enough to get involved with the AIM uprisers or bury his heart at Wounded Knee, but you'll sure enough see him out waving complaints against Columbus Day. He's got himself good and arrested a few times."

"Every time I've seen him he's been a sweetheart."

Owen tuned the radio volume down. "That's mostly how he is. But Joe's been stubborn from the get-go. The way he tells it, they tried, but nobody could make him to go off to Indian boarding school. Later he had to know *why* it was Indians couldn't drink alongside white cowboys in the bars. Shoot! Wanted to be able to drink like them and have the same good times. But it turned out he couldn't handle it any better than his own momma, who died of alcohol poisoning out at the clinic when he was a teenager. He never got much from his daddy except a smack in the head now and then. Verbena's Minnie said he used to run with a different blond girl every week, just to rile the old man. Trouble was, pretty girls only wanted him until the dance was over or he stopped making them laugh. Then they were back with the white fellows, and Joe was just one more pretty-faced Navajo."

"That's rotten."

"Yeah, it is. His engine runs a little better when he takes his pills."

"If they're so much help, why does he stop taking them?"

"The *Diné* aren't keyed into this medicine thing the way you and I are. And Joe fancies himself an herb doctor, thinks everything he needs is growing right there in his backyard. He remains, as they say, to be convinced."

Beyond the casual talk, she could sense how worried Owen was. There was a good friend inside this sheeprancher/stock clerk at Rabbott's Hardware, this man driving her car. The hardware store had begun to carry a small line of Winsor & Newton gouache, Maggie's favorite paints—Owen's doing. She'd said nothing about her preferences; one day she walked in to pick up vacuum cleaner bags and there were the white tubes on the art supply shelf, all the way from England to Blue Dog, New Mexico. All night he'd held her close in his arms, good strong arms that wanted her—tears, bad mother, and all—making love, he'd told her so with every movement of his body. He hadn't refused to see her as her son had, after she'd driven through narrow roads and freezing rain to Riverwall with nothing more than a Thanksgiving truce in mind. Owen had shown up on her doorstep at the lowest point of her evening, had made her go upstairs, lie down in bed where she belonged. Perhaps all along his intention had been to get into bed alongside her, use her to relieve his own tension, but if that was so, his patience was on a grander scale than Job's.

▪ ▪ ▪

As if it were a Catholic notion, her mother had always set the topic of sex on a level with wifely duty. Whenever Maggie had asked her questions about sex, Colleen met them with steadfast impatience—"There are areas of marriage that are more important to a man." The subject, like the Lenten obligation of giving up your favorite vice until Easter, was no more open for discussion than that. Nori insisted sex was mutual friction that worked on the body like a good massage, and seemed to be in the process of making her life's work one endless backrub. Women's magazines claimed the need for touching and joining deepened and grew with age, but Dear Abby insisted if all you were dealt was comfortable companionship, that could be enough.

Comfortable companionship was no substitute for passion. Making love with Owen had made Maggie feel as if her feet were once again meeting solid earth, the horizon before her level enough to trust. Yesterday the highway had been skewed, untrustworthy, like a landscape in a Dalí painting. It took more than a marriage to make sex good between two people; it took willingness to open yourself, because who else besides a man could cut your confidence to ribbons by turning to another woman, dispensing with you when a younger and more fertile model came on the market? Even her own son was a man in training. She rubbed away the fog her breathing had created on the car window.

Late summer, when she'd driven this way to see the monument, as per guidebook suggestions, she'd carried in her own food and water. But Owen knew the area in ways she didn't. What looked to her like a dirt road to nowhere was a shortcut as far as he was concerned. She pressed her forehead against the icy window. Snow everywhere. For all her years in New England, shoveling frozen gray slush from the sagging porch steps, suffering the feel of soggy wool against her chapped hands, California had erased all but the wonder of winter from her memory. It lay pure white and chaste against the rocky earth, lending grace to ramshackle houses and weatherbeaten trailers they passed, cloaking everything in silence as if to say, Wait a moment, look here, God has put his hand to this landscape, see how he loves his own creation.

Then Owen hung a U-turn at the crossroads and turned back toward town, slowing as he neared the trading post. Outside, a nearly new blue dual-axle Ford truck was parked beside a battered Dodge. Snow dusted the bumpers of the blue truck; the Dodge didn't sport bumpers at all. Owen led her inside, and she wondered if there was some kind of coffee shop around back she'd missed on her previous visit. Pawn turquoise hung on the walls, dozens of necklaces in fat sky blue and sea green nuggets, the yellowed claim tickets fluttering in the forced-air heat. Past the exterior room with its predictable tourist fare of boxed Taos moccasins and mass-produced pottery, they entered a smaller back room where blankets hung or lay everywhere, beginning with turn-of-the-century Germantown in faded brown and beige wools, museum-quality, interspersed with the occasional Chief's Blanket North Phase, the odd pictorial, or a circular rug woven on an old wagon wheel rim. Here, beyond the larger blankets, chained off from the tourist crowd, was a tiny nook filled with newer weavings, more patterns than she knew existed from her books. A Burntwater design, woven in pale pinks and greens, undoubtedly the end product of vegetable dyeing, which she'd read some of the weavers were turning back toward in an effort to reclaim their craft. On the wood-paneled wall at the rear of the store, a massive Two Gray Hills was displayed over pine dowels, its brown, black, gray, and white colors so finely woven into the geometric stairstep design that Maggie thought she might trade everything she owned to possess that rug just for one moment in time. The pattern dated from the early 1900s, when women from the Crystal area, north of Gallup, went to visit their fellow weavers in the Chuksa Mountains. It somehow reminded her of that game she'd played as a child, where you folded paper to create a four-sided fortune-teller, and beneath numbered choices your fortune was revealed in the unfolding. Maggie could see how stretching the design out, lengthening it, perhaps talking as the women wove experimentally side by side at their looms, had led the weavers to create the Two Gray Hills pattern. Easily twenty feet across, and incorporating a complex geometric design into the border, depending on the weaver's name, the rug could be worth as much as the sailboat she'd sold to her friend Deeter.

Though the transaction had taken place on the same day she'd discovered the woman Ray was leaving her for was pregnant with his child, the memory of that bad day now made her smile. At Deeter's suggestion, they'd each drunk two glasses of Ray's oldest and most expensive cabernet, toasting first each other, then wishing Ray twin daughters who would reach puberty early and give him ulcers. Then, for what had surely been the umpteenth time, Deeter looked longingly out at the Catalina sailboat tethered at the dock and said, "Thirty-six feet of fiberglass hull, Loran-C computerized navigational systems sitting there idle. She's Bristol, and Ray ought to go to jail, not just for what he did to you and Pete, but also for criminal neglect of that boat."

Maggie'd asked how much money he had in his pocket, and Deeter'd answered, typically, that he didn't know for sure, forty or fifty dollars, but she was welcome to it. She'd asked for the wallet, extracted a one-dollar bill from the twenties and fives, held up the dollar, thinking that of all the foolish acts her soon-to-be-ex husband had done, putting the boat in her name had to be near the top of the list. "A down payment," she'd said. "Deeter, go kiss your new boat." And he had, but not before shaking his head and giving her a long hug that, midway, turned into an embrace. He might eventually have become more to her than a friend, maybe even have gone so far as to fill the position of what Nori referred to as "transitional man," the one you slept with as an experiment while you were healing, then shrugged off in search of a more permanent fix—something that sounded easier in theory than practice. The boat was a dream come true for Deeter, a small act of rebellion for Margaret. That was all a lifetime ago, when she lived in a bay-front house she'd scraped and scrimped to revive from the foreclosure bargain they could afford. You couldn't sail a boat like that by yourself. The only material item she really cared about was the thrift-shop rug she'd found at Secondhand Clothes—forty dollars, one corner looking like a puppy had teethed on it. When things got loud between Ray and Peter, she'd walk down to the guest room and fix her gaze on the weaving, imagining how the maker had taken time to thread the loom carefully, choose her yarns, develop the pattern in her mind. Once Ray had walked in, screamed at her that it was her fault their son had turned out belligerent, and then punctuated his outburst by throwing his drink at her rug. Gin and tonic. The stain was as much a part of its history as the single ragged edge. Maybe all along it had been a case of cost versus quality—if your husband wanted a younger woman, a new family—fine, let him go. You could turn to your child. Concentrate on raising him, find a way to numb the other pain into something tolerable. But if your son opted to dwell with strangers rather than his mother, well, then. You could make your life in the shadow of a rock in a small town on the edge of nowhere. If you chose to bed down with strangers, no one would bother to accuse you of poor judgment, ridicule your choices, or christen them with drink.

Now, standing there in the trading post chatting beside Lulu, it seemed to her that Owen's kind smile might take her years to grow tired of watching. It was genuine, solid, even if it happened so infrequently you wondered if something inside kept him permanently sad. Was she throwing her last few shreds of respectability out the window, taking him into her bed? Lulu Mantooth unabashedly adored him. Joe Yazzi, sound of mind or not, ate dinner with this white man every week, called him brother. People warmed to Owen, no questions asked. Maggie Yearwood? All she knew for certain was that she didn't want this day to end without feeling him move inside her once again.

All three of them were pretending not to watch the Navajo weaver argue with the shopkeeper, each holding a corner of the beautiful rug.

Owen motioned her over. "This here is the real thing. Once

Benny gets to dealing, the price starts dropping quicker than last night's barometer."

"Hah," Lulu said. "What you call dealing, I call foreplay. Them two both end up satisfied as two fat nursing puppies. Don't let any of this fool you, Maggie. I'm going to make some fresh coffee. You could waterproof fence posts with this other—we'll save it for tourists. Now don't you two leave without saying good-bye, promise?"

Owen put his hands in the pockets of his jacket. The sheep-skin was lightly covered with melting snow at the collar, and Maggie ran her finger across it to chase the wet away from his skin.

He whispered, "Thanks," and she blushed at the intimacy in his lowered voice. This cold, snowy day seemed to call for that kind of speaking, extra blankets, a nap.

"This Storm Pattern *extremely* fine work," the weaver said. "You take a look, Mr. Benny. Tell me rug won't sell."

"I don't know." He pretended to examine it for flaws.

The weaver was dressed in sweat pants, a crinkly maroon velvet blouse trimmed with white rickrack and buttoned with sil-ver *conchas*, a large blue-and-yellow L.A. Rams jacket draped over her shoulders. Her heavy hair was wound into a bun, which was secured with a silver-and-turquoise barrette styled in the needle-point design. Though she was only a little over five feet, her weight more than ample, she held herself with elegance.

"Fine work deserve good price. I think thousand dollars about fair."

"A thousand dollars? Jesus Christ, Verbena honey, you been watching too much 'Price Is Right.' Who told you old Benny would pay out that much?" The man shook his head and laughed. "How about a cup of coffee so we can get normal? Lulu, what are you doing back there? Helping Juan Valdez pick the beans?"

The weaver smiled, showing even white upper teeth and wide expanses of pink gum on the lower half of her jaw. She tried again. "Nine-hundred-fifty dollar keep my horse in hay, my grandchildren in Pampers, buy me a few skein of halfway decent wool to make you another, maybe, if I find energy."

Benny, his Lucchese cowboy boots with the pointy lizard toes and high heels trying in vain to make up for his bald head and beer gut, skinny imported cigars sticking out of his suede vest pocket, looked up from the desk, where dozens of color photographs, rugs, and papers threatened to topple to an equally crowded floor space. He wriggled a finger in his ear. "Excuse me? Must be time to flush the wax again. It's a nice weaving, Mrs. Youngcloud, but she's no nine-hundred-dollar rug. Let's get serious here. . . " He took out a tape measure and began to calculate.

Owen's shoulders were shaking with mirth. He fiddled with a box of cassette tapes offering lessons on speaking the Navajo language, and Maggie wondered just what it was he found so funny. She'd seen the poverty on the reservation. Yes, the rug was small, but it was beautifully crafted, nearly dizzying with its diamond points and sawtooth border. The Navajo people lived on land so barren nobody else wanted it. They received little in the way of compensation for having been moved from their homes, and as far as Maggie could see, they complained about the whole deal even less. In Southern California a rug like Verbena Youngcloud's would have gone for two or three thousand dollars easily.

But Benny the rug dealer held firm. Maggie and Owen drank coffee with Lulu, heard who was cheating on whom in town and out, listened to the latest gossip from the Chamber of Commerce—It seemed Lynda Yellowhair was angry with Mary Begay, who wouldn't acknowledge her son now that he was marrying that Las Vegas showgirl he'd run off with. What good could come of leaving your family behind for a man-made city of devil liquor and neon lights? One of them sin hotels had a gas-fired volcano now, trying to copy nature just so tourists would stay there and spend all their dollars. . . . By the way, had anyone thought to check on Joe Yazzi, now that it was snowing good and hard? She'd heard he'd wrecked his truck the day the cops returned it, and maybe you could go a lot of places muleback, but the clinic was far away, and that was one Navajo white man's medicine had done some good, providing Joe had pills within reach, not sitting around gathering dust in some bottle in the pharmacy. . . .

Maggie listened to Lulu's news report with curiosity, though some of the names meant nothing to her. Owen promised her he'd look in on Joe. Then the telephone rang and Lulu was momentarily distracted. While she talked Owen gave the pawn watches some consideration, and Maggie turned back to study the dealer and the weaver.

A hundred years ago dealers like Benny had given the Navajo weavers commerce, influencing them to switch from weaving strictly garments to rugs, which the tourists were keen to own. Bastard or shrewd businessman, Mr. Benny chewed the price all the way down to three hundred dollars, which the woman accepted. Then he asked Owen if he would mind taking two Polaroids of himself and the weaver with the rug.

"Why not?" Owen answered. "Just show me which button to press."

The weaver took off her glasses for the picture and smiled at the camera as each of them held on to a corner of the now-sold rug.

"What's the point?" Maggie asked. "After all that bickering, it seems like the last thing either of them would want is a picture of the other."

"Like signing a contract," Owen explained. "Mrs. Youngcloud gets a copy, so does Benny. That way it's proof they made a deal, in case one of them suddenly gets amnesia."

Lulu cackled. "I wish I could get me some amnesia, particularly where my daughters are concerned."

Owen laughed politely, and Maggie wondered about his daughter, Sara Kay, who seemed to have done just that—forgotten she had a father entirely. Maggie watched them proceed from the dealer's office to the area of the store that stocked yarn and load up on "top of the lamb" skeins. These the dealer didn't charge her for, though at the cash register they came close to a hundred dollars. It was Verbena Youngcloud, the weaver he'd pointed out to her months back, at Blue Dog Days.

"Never thought he'd go past two-fifty," the weaver said to Owen under her breath before wrapping him in a hug. "Hey, sheepman, king of Rabbott's Hardware, how come you never come out see Verbena anymore? I have to depend on daughter for news. That Minnie, she's a dreamer, would just as soon tell me something made up about Tommy Cruise in Hollyweird as let on what you up to."

"Been busy, that's all. I'm working on raising rams these days, trying to turn a few dimes."

"You still saving me wool off that old ewe?"

"Absolutely. Ruby's got your name on every inch of her fleece. I'd like you to meet my neighbor, Verbena. Maggie Year-wood. She's rented the Starr place. Out there painting some awful darn pretty pictures."

The Navajo woman looked Maggie up and down hard. "Well. No wonder you never call this old woman." She turned her head back toward the dealer's office. "Benny, don't think you can give me coffee and forget about check."

"Allow a minute for the ink to dry, woman!"

Owen stepped closer. "Come on over here and hug me again. I need some warmth today. It's getting cold out there. Can't say for certain, but I think summer might be just about over."

Before he handed Verbena the check, the dealer stopped at the register. In black marker, he penned a price tag for his newly acquired merchandise: eight hundred dollars.

Maggie watched Lulu Mantooth turn away and begin to dust already spotless pottery. Verbena said, "Seem like winter year-round in some folks' hearts."

"Come with us to breakfast," Maggie said impulsively, and the woman gave her a blank look.

"Where you going?"

"Why, your place, of course," Owen answered, and Lulu and Verbena both began to laugh.

Inside Verbena Youngcloud's government-issue two-bedroom house, there were few pieces of furniture: a fat woodstove, a nineteen-inch Sony color television, and a shiny new black Kenmore washer-and-dryer set, displayed almost as proudly as the Two Gray Hills rug at the trading post. No couches, no chairs except for a cedar rocker with a broken arm. The once-beige walls were smudged from cooking and the hands of many children. Verbena went to the kitchen and started reheating a pan of grease among the pots on the stove.

Turned loose, the dogs wove themselves in and out of her legs, accepting pats from assorted grandchildren drifting in from the huddle near the television. Now and then she stopped stirring and measuring to stroke a small head and exclaim over childish scrapes, then turned back to knead her dough on a wooden board.

Frybread—she was making triangles of dough to drop into the crackling fat. Any minute now Maggie expected to hear herself start whining like one of the dogs for the first piece, cool enough to eat or not. She watched as Verbena ladled honey onto the first round of dough, still so hot the honey smoked and sizzled. The children waved their hands over it, trying to hurry the cooling process.

Outside a window with a frayed gray-white curtain, Maggie saw Verbena's late-model pickup, gathering snow on its shiny blue paint job.

Owen caught her looking. "The Two Gray Hills on the wall at Benny's? With her check from that one, Verbena bought the truck you're looking at. Don't worry about her, Maggie. She's an old hand when it comes to trading. If anybody tried to screw her on a deal, she'd only have to let word out she was looking for another dealer. They'd be on her like horseflies on the thoroughbreds at San Juan Downs."

Owen settled down on the floor with the children and watched cartoons, tearing off chunks of his frybread to soothe whoever was feeling left out, hugging assorted dark, wide-eyed faces to his, finding pennies in his pockets for every hand.

Maggie stood, taking in the easy family scene before her. Verbena's house reminded her of those friends' homes all the kids gathered at after school—a kindly mom, good snacks, nobody worried about crumbs getting in the couches. Where were their parents? Working, or out grocery shopping for the upcoming holiday? It would be Thanksgiving soon. She'd always tried to make the holidays a special time, cooking a goose ordered special from Pavilions, trying different recipes out of *Gourmet*, or making reservations at some trendy new restaurant where Ray wanted to go. Ray reveled in the idea of rituals, but Peter made it known he despised every enforced minute of such holidays, refusing to eat anything but potatoes and salad or going on some fruit juice fast, mocking the paper cuffs the chef placed on the turkey's legs: *That's right, dress a dead bird in stockings so we can forget the terror it went through before it made it to our table. Want me to tell you about factory farming? Did you know they cut off the beaks and the feet so the birds can't clean themselves, or even fight when they get cornered?* So often what started out as celebration ended with harsh words, a gesture that went a little too far, resulting in something accidentally getting broken. Then Ray would leave the table, his son brooding sullenly, his wife sweeping crystal shards into a good linen napkin. His implication was clear—break *things*—you can always afford to replace things. But what you really wanted to break was the mouth of the child *she* brought up to turn out this way. Maggie set down her bread and hugged her arms to herself, her mind focused on a series of such scenes that added up to their holiday traditions. Verbena squeezed her shoulder.

"Come outside a minute. Help me grain this mare. Go on, get jacket."

The Youngcloud barn was elderly corrugated aluminum, a tissue-thin skin against the winds northern New Mexico winters engendered. In an arena constructed of fallen tree limbs and old baling wire, a sorrel mare stood alone, snow gathering on the plain of her furry back. Verbena Youngcloud made a low noise in her throat and the horse lifted her head, moving toward the sound. Maggie noticed her eyes then, milky blue orbs, out of place in the otherwise hale animal.

"Is your horse blind?"

Verbena nodded, shaking the oats in the Folger's can so the horse could locate her. "Everyone tell me,'Verbena, shoot that old blind nag. She no good to you.' But old Lady Rainy Mountain throw such pretty babies. If you pony her along, you can use her for light work. Her and me, two old ladies nobody else want. So I keep her." She cupped her hand and shook grain into it. The horse moved her lips over the hand, whiskers sensing each crimped oat, taking it all, nickering in delight at this body-warming treat on such a snowy day.

"Just because she's blind doesn't make her worthless," Maggie said. "My son is deaf."

Verbena waited until the mare was finished, crinkling her forehead thoughtfully. Then she wiped her hand on her pants. "My sister Geanita's boy William in prison for stealing Chevrolets. Such a thing for those cars! Just that one brand, no other. With boys, you struggle all the time. If not tribal police on your doorstep, it hearing them out there shooting prairie dogs. Bang, bang. Don't use skins or meat, just leave bodies to rot on prairie. Coyote, too. Always have to make sure gun still works, don't they? Such big problems men have. I notice this. They aim anger on car, gun, always a big motor making loud noise. But with daughters, it silence you need to listen for. Now they're hard ones to raise. Right?"

"I suppose you're right."

"You got no daughters?"

"Only the one who never opened her eyes." Maggie remembered her only pregnancy to go full term, the short, too-easy labor, and the stillness in the delivery room when everyone could see this was not going to end up a day for birth announcements and celebration cigars. "She was stillborn."

"I lose two that way. Probably easier. Spirit at rest before got chance to get hurt." Verbena nudged her glasses up her nose and stared at Maggie. "My Minnie wears the hearing aid. She get along, work with Owen over to Rabbott's, the cash register, good job, regular money."

"That's great."

"Wants to move to California. Imagine! What kind of life for her there? Better to stay home, learn weaving."

Maggie smiled, agreeing. "Your rugs are lovely."

Verbena stroked the mare's fuzzy winter coat. "We both buried daughters and been deviled by men, huh? I like you, Maggie Yearwood. Just what kind pictures you paint? Stuff I know? You one of them what-you-call painters who do the crazy mess stuff?"

"Abstract? No, I'm not like that."

"A good word for it, abstract. Big word meaning confused in the head." Verbena laughed hard at her own joke.

"I noticed you weave both Storm Patterns and Two Gray Hills. I thought weavers in the Shiprock area concentrated on Yeis and Sand Paintings."

"You read in some *sevaho* book! I work design the way it come to me. Storm Pattern clear way for whatever coming next. Yeis and Sand Paintings, they take long time up here." She pointed to her head. "You can't rush what dream send you. You wait, listen. Then, hardest work in here." She placed Maggie's hand over her heart, where through the jacket she could feel the woman's full breast. "But you already know that, painter."

"I don't know *what* I know anymore. I just lift the brush and say a prayer."

"Good!" Verbena whistled, and Hopeful came loping over to her. Echo stood just outside the back door, sniffing at a pile of refuse she apparently found fascinating. Maggie watched her extricate a C-shaped paring of horse hoof and trot beneath the truck with it. A country dog.

For the first time since she'd told anyone about Peter's hearing, she felt the weight of the burden rise from her heart and dissipate into the steamy breath her words had made. Deaf for life or stealing Chevrolets—Verbena Youngcloud placed no value on either crime. She didn't feel so much as one single thread sorry for Maggie Yearwood—she had a good mare to feed, grandchildren to spoil, daughters she'd buried, her rugs.

On an icy patch, Maggie took hold of her arm. "Sometime, it

doesn't have to be today, could I watch you work on your rugs?"

The wrinkly Navajo face frowned and looked up toward the horizon where snow swirled across flat land. "Some of my people might get mad at question like that. Then there others who say okay, fine, you pay me, you can watch a little."

"Which category do you fit into?"

"I'm not resister like Joe Yazzi, Maggie. I took government house. I got grandchildren to raise, and unless I want to watch them die of pneumonia one by one, might as well do work I got to do inside walls as inside hogan. But hear this. No way I want to join white man's world. Aside from Owen Garrett and Benny over to the trading post, I don't got good friends out there. So I guess neither one."

Maggie faltered. Whatever she chose to say, she was throwing her words as blindly as that mare negotiated the arena. "I'm sorry if my asking put you on the spot."

Verbena hooked her arm through Maggie's, and they started back to the house. "How about you let me see your paintings? Then we talk weaving."

She would have to go home and burn them all, start over, or leave town. "Okay," she said, feeling small and cold beside the strength this woman emanated. "Sounds fair."

Verbena grinned, stepped gracefully over a rotting frozen tire, and opened the back door to the house.

Inside, she took Maggie down the hallway to a room with shelves along one entire wall. From every nook, hanks of colored yarn spilled forth, ranging in shade and hue from a muslin white all the way through the color spectrum to black. On a twin bed made up with a faded orange bedspread, lay an art book on the Impressionists. Verbena opened it, and Maggie could see that several years ago it had belonged to the Blue Dog library. She pointed to a quotation beneath one of Gauguin's well-known Polynesian women. It read, "Oh, you painters who ask for a technique of color. Study carpets; there you will find everything that is knowledge."

Verbena had no way of knowing that that phrase had been the original epigraph to her master's thesis, the one she never finished. Maggie's eyes widened in surprise. "Paul Gauguin?"

"He couldn't have thought of it unless Spider Woman sent him dream weavings. That Minnie, always trying get me read books for better English. This one interesting. I keep it."

Maggie set the book down on the bed. On one of the shelves, she saw a pillow-size weaving, rolled into a cylinder. Verbena took it and pressed it into Maggie's hands. "False start. You like, you keep."

"Verbena," Owen said as they walked to the Landcruiser. "Once again, you fed me and warmed my insides. How can I thank you?"

She smiled in delight. "*Nizho'ko ani-hiye, tro-tlanastshini-ye be jinichltan laki*, Owen Garrett."

"Yes, ma'am." He kissed her cheek.

Maggie hadn't dared unfold her weaving until they were on the highway, past all the bumpy roads with their slick ice patches. It was a pictorial, maybe a trial weaving on a smaller scale for something Verbena might try later, perhaps something that had come to her in pieces of dreams and hadn't panned out for a larger rug. On a background of sandy yarn that was just the color of the reservation earth in summer, a small male figure stood against a turquoise blue sky filled with falling arrows. They were of the traditional design, the type the Yei dancers usually clutched in their lineup. A crooked pine grew to the figure's right, and in the background an auburn-red horse had one foreleg lifted as if he had been frozen in mid-trot. Two fat sheep grazed at green wool tufts of forage.

"That horse is about the color of your hair," Owen said.

"My hair when I was about fifteen years old," Maggie answered. "There's more than a little gray here, in case you haven't looked closely."

"Maybe I didn't mean the hair on your head." He smiled and kept his eyes on the bumpy road.

She looked at him for a moment, stunned. "Well. You don't miss much, do you?"

"Not when it's that fine, and offered up to me."

She could come up with no adequate response that wouldn't lead into more uncomfortable territory, so she quickly changed the subject. "What was it Mrs. Youngcloud said to you just before we drove off?"

"Just a little Nav to make sure I'm keeping current with my languages."

"Tell me, Owen."

Now it was his turn to be embarrassed. "Well, she blessed us, and basically let me know I was lucky to be feeding in a field of such delicate flowers."

"Delicate flowers?"

"That's the gist of it."

Maggie covered her mouth to hold in her laughter. "I've been called any number of things from the fifty-foot woman to a worthless bitch, but never a flower."

All at once Owen pulled the Toyota to the side of the highway, shoved the gears into neutral, put his foot on the brake, and took off his hat. "Don't you know how decent you are? Hell with your ex-husband, your son blaming you for his hard luck! I'm about down on my knees, today, thankful. Last night I was ready to try old Jim Beam for comfort. Instead I got you. Come over here."

He took her in his arms and kissed her, his mouth opening hers roughly. She felt his tongue slide against her teeth seeking passage until she opened herself to him. When she did, he moved inside her mouth in a deliberate echo of the previous evening, that well-oiled rocking rhythm, hauling her to him so needily that she grasped the seat, afraid she was falling. When he let go she gasped, trying to get her breath.

He adjusted his hat, threw the gears back into drive, silent, the smile gone, and started driving. She had no answer to his question beyond the throbbing in her lips.

She held the weaving tight in her fists. To her left Shiprock loomed beyond the highway, immovable, beyond grandeur, a holy presence. Inside her skin, Maggie felt her blood running hot and strong through her veins, as thick with need as it was with loss. *Peter, you can push me away; I can't stop you. You can live with other people, celebrate your holidays without me, too. You can even hate me, and sometimes I deserve it, but there's no way on earth I will ever stop loving you.*

8

"HOLD OFF STARTING THAT FIRE," OWEN SAID A FEW DAYS LATER in the doorway to the Starr farmhouse, where Margaret was fussing with the woodstove. "We're on a run of good luck here. Why stop? How about you grab your clothes, I throw an extra flake to RedBow, check the ewes, then go after Joe Yazzi to come housesit and feed?"

"Where are we going?"

He smiled. "South. Santa Fe'll be a zoo of rich Texans come the Christmas season, so we'll beat the rush, take us a little vacation midweek, while things are still quiet."

"I don't know. I'm not in much of a museum-going mood."

He could sense her uncertainty and knew it had more to do with Santa Fe's proximity to Riverwall than museums. "Nobody said nothing about museums. I happen to know this flamenco dancer who always goes home for the holidays, and sometimes she shows up in this little bar off Canyon Road to try out her new routines." Remembering, he felt his face go as wistful and dreamy as the first time he'd seen her perform. "Wait till you see her dance, Maggie. It's like nothing else on earth."

"If she's that good, how can I say no?"

"She won't disappoint you. Now grab your red panties and sketchbooks, and if you wouldn't mind feeding the dogs, I know Señor Hopeful'd be as grateful as me. Be back in half an hour."

He took his truck and set off toward Joe, wanting to find him huddled up in a blanket keeping warm, not gone from the hogan he called home. He hadn't the courage to tell Maggie what happened the other times Joe quit taking his pills. She didn't need to know how he'd been thrown in a jail cell in Albuquerque for "public drunkenness," left to sit for three days in his own vomit and excrement until Lulu collected enough donations to make his bail. She didn't need to know the truth about Joe's dog, either— how in a state of confusion he'd tied the poor thing to a traffic median in a wealthy suburb of Rio Rancho, where it was shot by a concerned citizen who thought *prairie niggers* should stay out of his neighborhood and get back on the rez where they belonged. At best he hoped he'd find Joe drunk, passed out, a temporary setback. That he could deal with.

Outwardly nothing had changed. Chicken-wire mesh still covered the small, murky windows. Sand-filled tires weighed down the snowy roof. The basketball hoop fashioned from a hub-cap was still nailed to the dead-tree backstop Owen had helped Joe put together the summer before, when they played one-on-one in the cool evenings until it was too dark to see the ball.

He found Joe around back, kneeling in the snow, his face to the ground. He made himself walk over slowly, crouch down, and give his friend time to notice his presence.

"More than a little cold out here, brother. Want my jacket?"

Joe turned his panicked face and looked past him. "I dug a hole past the white stuff. Still can't get to them. They're trapped. Earth's humming with murder of the Old Ones, Owen. Holy People down there in the cold. They don't like winter, Owen. Got no blankets to keep warm." His eyes were filled with true concern.

"Well, let me have a listen." Owen put his ear where Joe's had been. He heard the crunch of snow and felt the stinging wetness

on his ear, nothing else, and was a little sorry to have to tell that
to Joe. "Nobody much cares for winter, Joe. Let's go inside and get
you something hot to drink. When's the last time you ate a meal?"

"Can't eat when so many go hungry. Got to find a way to feed
everyone."

"Where's Lightning? You turn him loose in this snowstorm?"

"Possessions weigh a man down. Rode him to town, gave
him to Verbena's Minnie at Rabbott's, walked back. She always
liked that mule."

"Well, Minnie knows as well as anyone Lightning's yours,
Joe. We'll go and fetch him back in a few days."

"Nah, she can keep him."

They could argue about that later. "Got your truck running
yet?"

Joe shrugged.

"What will you ride into town? How you planning to move
your sheep this spring?"

Joe thought it over for a minute. "Man shot my dog, Owen.
He was only sitting where I tied him. Not doing nothing wrong.
A big old bullet took out his shoulder, blew it away just like
Jimmy Tso's over to Bai Thuong."

Owen helped his friend to his feet. "That was a terrible thing.
The man will have to answer to his own Higher Power someday.
Take some comfort in that. You know what? You ought to get
yourself another dog, but maybe one that isn't mostly wolf. Maggie's found herself a nice companion in her boy's Echo. Hopeful
finds her attractive. Maybe we can arrange to get you a pup out of
her this spring."

"No. Never can tell when a white man might shoot his gun."

Owen gripped his friend's shoulder. "I'm telling you, that
kind of thing is rare. Think about it and let me know. You feel
like spending a day or two at my place, tending ewes? I got a
cupboard full of Campbell's soup. That cocoa mix with the little
marshmallows you like. Hot shower."

Joe looked toward his snow hole, not wanting to give it up.
"My people been hungry a long time."

"They're inside Grandmother Earth, aren't they? Have a little faith. She'll direct them to the corn eventually. They can melt snow for water."

Joe looked at him uncertainly.

"We've done it, haven't we, that time we got stuck up in the mountains?"

"Yeah, but—"

Owen took off his jacket and wrapped it around his snow-dusted friend. "We'll stop by the clinic, stock you up on your medicine. You got to keep taking them pills, Joe, then these memories won't grab hold of you so hard. You listening to me?"

Joe wiped his face, where tears washed the full, dark cheekbones women found so irresistible. "What I'm talking about, my people, happened a long time before, didn't it?"

"That's right."

"And my dog?"

"Years back."

Joe looked surprised. "It don't feel like years. I can still hear him barking at me to get up. When do I have to go back to the army?"

"You're in Shiprock, New Mexico, Joe. Vietnam is miles away from here. You don't ever have to go back. That nonsense is over and done with. We got us a pile of presidents come and gone since then. None of them much good, either."

Joe said, "They need a woman to run this country."

"That's right. Think Verbena Youngcloud might be interested?"

Joe shrugged.

"Come on. Can't you just picture her, moving her sheep down Pennsylvania Avenue, turning them loose to graze on the White House lawn? Cooking up frybread for the Secret Service suits?"

The men laughed as snow continued to fall on their shoulders. Joe began walking toward the hogan. "Owen, I take them pills. But when I feel good, I think, What's the point?"

"That's understandable. We all put a leg down off the wagon

now and again, just to test the ground underneath our wheels. You got to remember to climb back on again when the ground starts getting shaky. Will you try that?"

"Yeah."

Inside the cabin, Owen helped his friend pick up the accumulated mess, return the strewn bedding to the blue-ticking mattress and crumpled clothes to the cardboard box that served as his dresser. They rehung the tattered American flag that time and previous episodes of confusion had sullied, and with chilled fingers tacked it into the rough beams. The only things untouched were the shoeboxes of herbs, each cellophane packet carefully organized according to potency and desired effect. Owen thought about the tea Joe had concocted the day he saw Maggie for the first time. Some kinds of medicine were unquestionably good, he thought, wondering with what exactly his friend had spiked his tea. He'd never pass judgment on Joe, remembering that he'd nearly fallen off the wagon himself a few nights ago, fear and despair embracing each other in his psyche, coming up with a dozen good reasons why alcohol was the only salve left to soothe his fear. The nearest bottle was next door, so that's where he'd headed. Instead he ended up between the precious thighs of Maggie Yearwood. Therein, he knew, lay the difference between himself and Joe. Eventually, even if it was dangerous, Owen would seek out the company of others when he found himself stuck in the dark places. Not Joe. Joe bellied up to shadows and phantoms. Bought them drinks. Listened to their answers, no matter what nonsense they fed him. He'd give a try to whatever they suggested, and every time, they'd abandon him, leave him facedown in the nearest puddle, his dog bleeding to death in the middle of traffic.

Maggie was quiet until they'd cleared the gravel road. As soon as they hit asphalt, she started in on Owen. "All right. I've waited long enough for you to tell me. What's in the little packet Joe handed you? You told me you didn't mess with alcohol, I assumed that meant you left drugs alone, too."

Owen patted his shirt pocket. "You know better than that.
Joe fancies himself the great herb doctor. He made us a holiday
tea, *raíz del macho*."

"What's it supposed to do?"

Owen took the packet from the pocket of his Carhartt jacket
and set it on the dashboard of the Landcruiser. "Nothing. It's just
a drink."

"With a name like *macho*?"

"I didn't say I planned on sneaking it into your food."

She smiled and met his eyes, then looked out the window.
"Good. Because you know you don't have to."

How women had changed in the last few years. No doubt
about it, straight talk was a timesaver. It made a man shy, though,
wondering if he should just be sitting there grateful and happy, or
if there was some modern kind of etiquette expected for dishing
it back. Owen drove carefully through the winding roads and
hoped they wouldn't encounter any closed passages. They might
make Santa Fe before suppertime. He wanted Maggie Yearwood
hungry when they hit town; there was nothing better than feeding a hungry woman, one who wasn't too shy to eat. If a lady
relaxed enough around you to satisfy herself with meat and potatoes, when you hit the bedroom, look out.

"Whatever are you thinking about?" she asked. "I haven't
seen you smile that wide since the day your dog deflowered
Echo."

He pulled a blank expression. "Eating. You like regular
American cooking? Meat, potatoes, salad that looks like a salad?"

"Owen, you seem to know what I like very well. If it's not
raw and there's hot bread alongside it, I'll probably have a long-
term relationship with it."

He grinned. "The way you put things, Maggie. Sometimes I
wake myself up laughing."

Even off-season, they had to stand in line at the Red Cloud Café,
but the blue potatoes mashed with cream cheese and nutmeg,
and Mom's "regular" meatloaf, were worth snow, damp socks, and
a forty-mile hike any day. Here they served up the food family

style, a mixing bowl of steaming potatoes, a milk pitcher of gravy, brick-size slices of meatloaf studded with diced onion. A king-size bottle of ketchup sat on the tabletop, the kind you had to stick a knife in to get it to pour out. The dessert tray held equally large portions of cherry and apple pie, and a hefty bowl of Indian pudding swimming in maple syrup. Those Maggie declined.

"I've been here before, once, but I was smart and didn't eat. It's going to take me two days to sleep off this meal."

"No, it won't. You'll brighten up where we're going next." He took her hand beneath the table. "Trust me."

"I do."

Whether he was worthy or not, he knew she meant it.

It was a small bar-restaurant off the Canyon Road, lit by *luminarias* and a battered wooden sign. Centuries ago the road had been used as a footpath by Indians. Now it was the main drag of an art colony, and the small adobes and shacks had been converted into trendy storefronts and high-priced galleries. Come summer, you'd be lucky to move a car down the road for all the people crowding through.

They parked and hiked in from Paseo de Peralta, taking small steps in the snow.

Inside the bar each of the patrons cherished the same wonderful secret: Before last call a celebrated flamenco dancer would take the stage in her white lace, rose-covered shawl and give them the souvenir of her dance. If you were in Los Angeles, Chicago, or New York City, you would pay upwards of fifty dollars a ticket for the privilege of watching the woman move. Here, in her home-town, off-season, she came by to try out new routines on old friends, who bought drinks and left a few dollars in the musicians' tip jar. The lucky few who heard the whispers and rumors knew enough to keep the information to themselves, but as soon as she took the stage each of them turned selfish, staring at her as if for the brief time she was on stage, they owned her, from the dark, chiseled Indian face tucked inward to the flowing embroidered cape covering her perfect muscular shoulders.

Owen ordered two coffees spiked with cinnamon and settled

Maggie and himself at a table in the back of the bar, where shadows kept them anonymous.

This past week was the best he could remember living through in a very long time. Waking up next to Maggie, breakfast with Verbena, and hugs from her grandchildren. Two days' honest work, then some time off. The challenge of driving in snow in a car built for it, a bellyful of good American cooking, and now this tall woman next to him, her thigh grazing his. He said, "Cold weather brings up your color. You look so darn pretty, I'd kiss you if we were alone."

"Kiss me anyway." Then she took hold of his shoulder, pulled him close, and kissed him—a serious kiss, one he felt all the way down to his socks. Before he could respond, the bar band struck up a Paul Zarzyski/John Hollis tune, homage to the *flamenca duende* who would follow their act. The kiss had him all knotted up. Much as he wanted to, he didn't take her hand and hurry her out of there just yet—certain things needed savoring as much as good food took time to digest. The motels would still be there in two hours, all those clean sheets and Gideon Bibles with the stiff spines in the drawers nobody opened. He watched Maggie's face soften in the atmosphere of the rough music, its sentimental lyrics take hold of her heart and give it a tender caress, making her forget everything from that viper-tongued son of hers to the bad mood she'd worn a few nights back like army boots.

Before she came to Blue Dog, he figured her life had to be like something out of one of those slick decorating magazines Minnie Youngcloud loved to pore over on her lunch break. He imagined sofas covered in pastel fabrics, thick white carpet, fragile china vases full of fresh flowers, everything in such good taste a man like himself wouldn't feel comfortable taking a seat anywhere. The most he knew of taste was a meal at the Red Cloud. Sure, he admired the craftsmanship of Molesworth furniture, and could spot a decent weaving and name its region, thanks to Verbena, but he knew he would never possess the means to own either in his lifetime. Sometimes the detours you took decided the larger issues—and there wasn't any turning back. They were two completely different people, their common ground a few acres in Blue Dog, New Mexico. Both had pasts they'd tried to leave behind; both enjoyed themselves in bed; and no two ways about it, both had children who were troubled.

Sara Kay *was* deaf, in her own way, and he'd been the one to foster that silence. He saw her in his mind that coltish year she turned thirteen, her chest starting to bud out. One minute she was loving up to her horse, the next she was applying warpaint to her eyelids, strutting across the living room in a way that made him leave the too-small house and go muck stalls for relief. Her attention-getting was more like asking for directions, but when she voiced the questions he wanted to run. *What do I say when a boy asks me to the movies, Daddy? Am I old enough for dating? Help me find the way*—some of the answers were within him; he just was too sidetracked with cattle and malt liquor to handle her growing up so quick. There were opportunities galore for talking. When they were in the barn, grooming horses, trimming hooves, or he was standing at the arena fence, telling her she better start leaning into her horse earlier around that second barrel or she'd never shave a second from her time. He'd been a poor excuse for a husband, drinking and gone so much. He wasn't much of a daddy either. When Sara was little, her diapers needing changing, that day-to-day stuff seemed like such a nuisance. Now he saw all of it was precious.

Maggie took mothering as serious as world peace. They hadn't talked about what she'd told him a few nights back—her deaf son—what was there to say besides how sorry you felt, and what a crying shame it was? That the boy had lived after the illness was more of a miracle alone than you dared hope for. It'd be natural enough for him not to handle the change well. No one could wake up to silence and not have trouble. Teenagers were the most listening breed of creatures ever created. Music, gossip, schoolwork, their ears were lower to the ground than Joe Yazzi's, wanting messages that might help them grow up different from their sorry folks. Riverwall School—the buff-colored adobe walls behind the chain-link fence—he'd driven by there dozens of times on his way home from Santa Fe, never giving it more than a moment's thought. He knew Maggie wanted more than anything to see her son, but only if he wanted to see her. Well, it was coming up Christmas season, the time for *milagros* if there ever was one.

An expectant silence came over the room as soon as *she* stepped from the shadows onto the stage. He recognized the musical arrangement, *tres alegrías*. Three Hispanic gentlemen plucked guitars to accompany the dancer. She slid onto the wooden stage and dropped her embroidered cape. Beneath it, her bare shoulders and brown back underscored the animal nature of each person sitting in the room. It was impossible to watch her suddenly expose a taut thigh from beneath the rough cloth and not feel the echo resonate in your own sexual being. Owen rested his hand on Maggie's knee. After a minute, he felt her hand press his, urge his fingers higher on her leg. When she touched him like that, he understood what she was saying. That place he wanted to go would once again be his comfort before this night was over.

He wasn't about to let Maggie pay for any of this trip, so they were staying at the Ocotillo Motor Court, one of those early fifties motels designed to outwardly resemble forts, complete with free steam heat and complimentary fresh-brewed coffee in the office. The off-season bargain rate was twenty-nine dollars a night, affordable if he cut back a little on his next month's food budget. Other than a trucker already tucked into his bed for the night and two Winnebagos who'd apparently had it with RV camping, the place was empty. Owen laid his money down on the Formica desktop and took the key to room twelve, which was located around back, off the busy street. He drove the Landcruiser around to their parking space in front of the door, painted that peachy pink trimmed with aqua.

"Home for tonight," he said as he opened the door. The shoebox of a room smelled musty and chill. It sported a double bed with a graying chenille bedspread, one terrible painting of a mother brushing her daughter's hair, and a partially cracked full-length mirror on the wall opposite the bed. Maggie immediately turned on the wall heater and sat down on the creaky bed, rubbing her hands together.

"I can go get us some of that fine complimentary coffee," Owen joked nervously. "Or maybe if you hop in the shower it might warm you up. Let me go turn it on, get it hot for you." He started for the bathroom, but she caught his hand.

"Sit here with me a minute."

He looked down at the worn carpet. "Sorry it's not the La Fonda, Maggie. I don't have the *dinero* to keep you like you ought to be kept."

She stroked his face. "Will you hush?"

"Well, I know that's what you're used to."

Her auburn hair was kinky from snow dampness, and she pushed it away from her face. "Fancy hotels, chocolates on your pillows, the little pleat they make the maid fold into the toilet paper—you think I need that? When it comes right down to what you get out of a hotel or a motel, there's not much difference. We've got the bed, haven't we, the only thing we need for sleeping."

When snow was busy blanketing the highways, providing a good nights' work for the plowers, and time was the only commodity you had an abundance of, there was no need to hurry. This woman knew it as well as she knew her own name. She made him lie back against the pillows while she unbuttoned his jacket and shirt, slid him out of his pants, ran her hands over him as if she was searching him down for hidden weapons. If he put up a hand to touch her back, she *tsk*ed him and stroked it across her own breast before placing the hand back down on the bed. The sight of her stiff nipple beneath the flannel shirt—he thought his heart would gallop right out of his chest.

Then she undressed herself, letting him watch. He sat up for this. She was no flamenco dancer. Her body wasn't hewn of muscle and bone and long hours at the ballet barre, but she did make fine use of the mirror.

She stood up and stepped out of her jeans, kicking them away. His favorite red panties hugged her bottom. She flicked them away with her thumbs until they were nothing more than a bright handkerchief against muddy green carpet. In front of the mirror she ran her hands over her hips, down in between her thighs, back up to her breasts, cupping and lifting them in her hands, looking all the while at the two halves of herself reflected in the cracked glass. Owen watched her take inventory, his blood rushing into his ears. Didn't she know she had more than everything he needed, more than he deserved? No, she wasn't hearing anything he had to say on the subject, she was deep inside herself. She pressed her hands to her belly now, against the overlapping scars, as if by covering them with her palms she could will them invisible. He saw her face nearly break then, and orders be damned, he'd had enough of this waiting game. He stood up and went three steps to her, turning her to face him, pressing her back against the mirror, pinning her there with his hands over her upraised forearms. She gasped with cold when the glass met her back. He bent his knees slightly, cupped her behind and lifted her up onto her tiptoes, then onto his erection, moving carefully until they were joined, his penis so deeply planted inside her it he felt it touch the end of her passage.

He began to rock toward her, carefully holding back, scared he might hurt her, trying not to upset the delicate balance it took to hold her this way. Each nerve between them quivered. It wouldn't take long. Already Maggie breathed harshly in his ear, and he had found her rhythm, started moving against her relentlessly, until her cries grew hoarse and ragged.

He jockeyed forward, holding her to him, forcing her to fall into orgasm, feeling her body arch up tautly, then slacken until she lay against him dead weight, breathing unevenly, the spirit of her far away, walking by itself on some rocky landscape. Walking back toward him, finished, she started to cry. He held on to her, feeling the warm fluid their friction created sluice down her leg, well up between them where he held one of her legs up tight against his flank. Her breathing settled, but the tears kept on spilling. He kissed her forehead. "What's wrong, sugar? Did I go too deep?"

She shook her head no. "I just feel sad."

"Why?"

She sniffled and scrubbed her eyes. "This was incredible, but you've got to let me down."

They disengaged, and she shocked him, pulling him down to the bed, moving down his chest until her face was at his belly. He held on to the back of her head, lifting her hair until her neck was exposed. The sight of her pink skin, the thought of where her mouth was—he was harder than he'd been before. "You don't have to," he whispered.

She stopped for a moment and looked up at him, wet-faced from crying and sweat. "But I want to."

She reached up and put his hand back on her neck and continued exploring him with her mouth. He didn't last very many minutes before he was over that same ridge she'd gone to, and somewhere in the back of his conscious mind, he was thankful they had no neighbors on either side of them to hush this human music.

For a long while he lay there, spent, her face against his chest, quiet. It seemed like hard work just trying to reorder his breathing, running his fingers through her hair. Finally he said, "Whew. I feel like I been slingshot to the moon and back. Is it polite to say thank you?"

"Oh, I think so."

He tucked her hair behind her ear, traced its outline with his fingers. "Maggie, tell me what got you crying earlier. Something I did?"

"No. I just miss my son. Thanksgiving is tomorrow. I keep wondering who's going to fix him his vegetarian turkey. Make him bow his head and act thankful, even if he isn't."

He heard the sadness choke off her words and knew that whatever he might try to say, none of it could make up for what was hurting her. "Well, my goodness," he said. "What have we here?"

"What are you talking about?"

"This business right here. My necessary equipment seems to still be in working order. I thought the days of twice-in-one-night were long past me, but if you're interested, I'm willing to risk a try."

Later, wrapped in blankets, Maggie's head tucked into his shoulder, he had one comment. "That business about the toilet paper. I believe you. Rich folks don't mind spending to frip up the basics. Were you that rich, Maggie?"

"Never." She snuggled up, and whether she was lying or telling the truth didn't at that moment seem important.

She slept like an overtired child, occasionally fussing her way through dreams. Owen lay there beside her, wakeful despite the marathon they'd run, thinking hard. Maybe it was motels, giving permission to let everything tip over to physical sensation. The sight of her down there on the shabby bed, asking permission to let her please him—he would never forget her eyes wide open to him, risking him saying no.

He thought of Sheila, her wild requests to copy positions she'd read about in those marriage books, her purple bra where the nipple area was nothing more than a lacy cutout. For her, solutions to their problems came in the form of naughty lingerie, sex toys ordered through the mail he was always afraid Sara Kay would discover, an aggressiveness that made him want to run away. She worked herself into a sweat going after passion, as if she might rope it once and forever hobble its feet. All those times he'd failed to conjure what she needed—what a sorry husband he'd been. In a motel room or on a patch of soft ground, desire lay somewhere between two people, didn't it, a tiny invisible vapor that probably entered the body someplace unlikely, like the ears or the feet, charged its way into your heart and blood, and made you brave, making love standing up in front of mirrors, leaving a steamy imprint of shoulders and buttocks on the cheap glass, you two locked together, falling in a heap to the bed.

The *flamenca duende* tapped a stiletto-heeled rhythm over his

worries, forcing them back into the dark earth. When she suc-
ceeded in tamping one down completely, she arched her long
neck and shouted, *"Olé!"* and went onto the next. Drifting into
sleep, Owen smiled, thanked her, and slept hard, not moving
once the remainder of the night.

9

RED CHILE *RISTRAS* HUNG IN DROOPING, SNOW-DUSTED ARCS from the eaves of the café where Owen suggested they have breakfast. The special was a spinach omelette stuffed with mushrooms and *queso blanco*, only $4.99, including potatoes and toast. Owen ordered that, so Maggie asked for coffee and raisin toast. He'd spent enough money on her, and she could do with a spartan meal after last night's feast. This morning in the motel she'd woken before him, turned from the thin, doubled-over pillow to observe his sleeping face. Sleep changed everyone. Bone-tired or catnapping, sleeping adults once again became baby-innocent. She'd never seen him so relaxed. Now Owen's cheeks were stubbled with a fine sheen of whiskers, blond against his tanned face. His tough skin made him look older than he was, but that wasn't just the result of years of working outdoors, or even the sexual gymnastics of last evening—she sensed it was worry. He was generous, funny, thoughtful, an able and consider-ate lover, but his past was curtained off in an opaque, seductive drape, and behind it she guessed were events that troubled him. She'd pieced together her own ideas: He'd left behind more than his drinking self, some other terrible person he'd been back then now lay in that smoldering wreckage. Whenever a sheriff's car drove by, he became decidedly calm—maybe he'd been involved in something left of the law. Or it might be something else entirely, some self-inflicted punishment for his own failures—his wife's infidelity, his daughter's bad choices—when lovers came to each other at this stage in life, they were tired of telling life stories and offered only the highlights.

She would probably never know the man well enough to say for certain what he'd run from. Whoever he was back then, this was Owen now, drinking his coffee and chatting with the wait- ress. Give him five minutes, he'd know her favorite color, shoe size, all her pets' names. If he'd chosen to be a salesman, that charm would have made him wealthy by now, his past forgotten in all that success. But he wasn't; he was a clerk in a hardware store, and about as open as the Blue Dog library. You could check out only five books at a time, and in two weeks you had to return them. Now, as unlikely as the possibility seemed a few months ago, her neighbor was also her lover.

When her world had begun to fall apart in her California house, she thought she'd spend the rest of her life there, alone, raising Peter. Instead, she'd come to New Mexico so others could raise him. Sometimes she made herself recall the house she'd left behind, standing with perfect posture next to the lapping water, remembering how, on the surface, everything couldn't help but look cleaner near the ocean—perhaps that was California's best trick—the white sailboat clusters, the tart scent of ocean, the unflagging sunshine. You couldn't see the PCBs fouling the water, the widening hole in the ozone. You couldn't even see her unhap- piness. She'd broken free from a husk more beautiful than the one she wore now, honest but plain. Mrs. Raymond Sweetwater. Dear Margaret. Giver of parties. The wife of a man who was going places. A smart dresser. Someone you could depend on to help sponsor a charity event. Now, having reclaimed her maiden name, she was Maggie Yearwood, someone who rented a house, slept with her neighbor, tried to paint, and heard nothing but silence from her son, who was home with his foster family in this very town.

Owen said, "You're about as quiet as a tree full of owls this morning."

Maggie smiled at the image, wishing she possessed the bird's legendary wisdom. She bumped his knee beneath the table with her own. "Happy Thanksgiving, neighbor."

"Back at you."

She took his hand and ran her fingertips in between his knuckles where the skin was a shade lighter, and softer. "Probably too late to buy a turkey, let alone cook one."

"How does cheese and crackers in front of the woodstove strike you? Some cider? That break too much with your traditions?"

She wanted to laugh, burst out with the stories of different Thanksgiving menus she'd attempted over the years, wild-rice stuffing, searching for saffron to make paella, tofu fajitas—how all of them had not so much failed but ended in domestic wrecks of one sort or another. Owen would understand. He'd laugh along with her, even at the sad parts, because in retrospect all that stuff seemed like so much bad acting. But she didn't need to say anything, he knew what she felt just by looking at her. "Cheese and crackers in front of the woodstove sounds perfect."

He kindly avoided the road that ran past Riverwall school, pointing out little shops off the avenue and museums she might have missed hearing about before they headed north. Peter wouldn't be at school, of course. She couldn't help it—it still hurt. Maggie knew she could have forced the issue, could have made herself an unwelcome guest at the Hidalgo dinner table, but all that would have netted Peter was yet another uncomfortable holiday meal to add to those he'd previously celebrated. Did they fix a southwestern supper on Thanksgiving, steaming tamales, roasting corn, or were they traditionalists? Would they make him peanut-butter sandwiches, considering Peter's stance on meat? Maybe they ate out, at a place like the Red Cloud, regular food, nothing remarkable. Her boy—fifteen years old, heading into his first Christmas season in New Mexico. She hoped he was in a warm place, lying comfortably on the floor, playing a soundless version of Sonic the Hedgehog, that video game where if you traversed enough hurdles, stomped enough of the plants that snapped at you and stole your golden rings, you ascended from impossible chase sequences to an odd-looking maze that kept turning as you maneuvered your way around, trying to capture glittering "chaos gems" for extra points and longer "lives." Weren't they all, holiday or not, trapped in just such a sequence, white-knuckling the controls, hoping?

"Owen," she said. "Pull over. If I'm going to live in this state, I have to learn to drive in snow."

He stayed awake just long enough to make certain she was pointed on the right highway, then tipped his hat forward and went to sleep. White crystals whirled against the windshield. Every so often the intermittent wipers came on, scraping a clean arc through the accumulated snow. It made her think of her sister, one minute there for her and Peter, helping out; the next, attending to her own selfish whims. Nori's logic—you needed a manual to decipher it. It's all in the way you view things, Maggie thought. One minute you're positive there are patterns in what piles up, and that it all means something significant. The next minute something scrapes it away and you have to start all over. She lifted her right hand from the steering wheel and touched Owen's leg. He turned toward her slightly but didn't rouse. He trusted her enough to sleep. No matter what failures lay behind her, his trust counted for something.

Just before the big left turn toward Blue Dog, Owen sat up. "You shouldn't have let me sleep like that."

"Why not? You were tired."

"I could have helped with the driving."

"I grew up in Massachusetts, where snow is serious. I asked to drive, and besides, you drove all the way down."

"Call me old-fashioned, I just think a man ought to do the lion's share of the driving, especially in bad weather."

Maggie gestured to the snowy fields outside. "All this is adventure to me. It's Thanksgiving, I'm wearing my blue jeans, didn't even buy canned olives, and I'm driving in a snowstorm. It feels refreshing."

"You trying to tell me skipping turkey is about the worst thing you ever did in your life?"

She signaled for the left turn. "No, I've done worse. I used to lie every week at confession, back when I was a good Catholic girl. So good that I never once told the priest about my impure thoughts regarding Bradley Madison, or how much I resented my beautiful younger sister. The sins of omission, Owen, they're just as bad as the real thing."

"That's a fine way to bring up a little girl—have her sit in a dark box once a week and tell some celibate old fart she's thinking about boys. You and this Bradley fellow—anything come of it?"

"He taught me the fine art of French kissing behind the candlepin alley, but that's all. I was a virgin until I met Raymond. All around me everyone was practicing free love because that's how it was in those days. I probably would have done the same, had anyone asked, but no one did. What about you? What's the worst thing you've ever done?"

"Do we start from the cradle? If so, we could ride bad road till Easter."

"Owen, you're the most upright person I've ever met. If you found a dime on the sidewalk, you'd spend ten dollars locating its owner. Were you always such a saint, or did you develop this trait late in life?"

He bristled. "You want me to drive now?"

"No, I want you to answer me."

He stared out the window, shifted position in the seat.

"Owen."

"Don't."

His voice was low and solemn, and she instantly regretted she'd teased him. "I'm sorry. I can be a first-class idiot sometimes, in case you haven't noticed."

"I guess you have good reason to ask me questions, and a right." He rubbed her arm with his knuckles. "I've done some things I'm ashamed of—you know any man who hasn't? I stopped drinking and I follow my twelve steps, though they don't lead down the same path others might take. But there was a whole period of years where I was what you might call reckless. Once I jumped off the tip of a twenty-foot-high roof, this silly bar with a huge steer head constructed out of plaster on top. Seemed like an awful good idea at the time."

"Twenty feet? Didn't you get hurt?"

"Oh, lady, alcohol is the cheapest form of insulation you'll find. I cracked my leg some, but it didn't cripple me."

She looked at him, waiting for more from this polite man who wouldn't share his checkered past. "What else?"

He offered nothing. The fierce look on his face almost frightened her. In a few miles they would bump down the gravel road and park the car in front of the Starr farmhouse. Joe Yazzi's presence would smooth over the awkwardness she felt now between them in the car. They could share Thanksgiving crackers, play three-handed hearts.

Embarrassed at how far she'd pushed him, she concentrated on taking the road slowly. Owen had told her over and over again that the faster she drove on rock, the sooner she'd be having body work and a paint job done. The old Starr farmhouse wasn't hers, but it looked like home, all two stories, the red roof laden with snow. She could see RedBow racing across the pasture; he knew his master was home, and any minute, she expected both dogs to bolt from Joe's company and chase the car until they parked. Everything would be okay. They had nothing but long winter days and nights ahead of them.

But as she cornered the loop in the road, she saw dual sets of tire tracks. They led to two cars parked where she usually left the Landcruiser—a burgundy Range Rover replete with rhino bars and the bumper sticker: LUXURY RENTALS, BERNALILLO. Next to the Rover there was a Colorado state trooper's car.

Her first thoughts were of Joe. Then, "Oh, God." She looked

at Owen. "Something with my son, maybe? But why Colorado?"

He bit his lip. "Maybe not. Maybe it's something about me."

A cold shiver ran through her, past the silk long underwear and the down parka, settling in her skeleton. "Owen?"

He looked up from staring at the cars to meet her eyes. "I don't know what to do, Maggie. Part of me wants to cut rope and run. The other part wants to stay with you, no matter what happens."

She took his hand. "Whatever it is, we'll see it through together."

His hand in hers was gloved, distant, but she kept her grip strong. He let go to open her door, and she could feel coolness replace the warmth where his fingers had been interlaced with her own. She started to pocket her keys, then dropped them. There sitting at the round pine table in the kitchen was Nori, drinking red wine from a long-stemmed glass. Sitting next to her was the handsomest policeman Maggie had ever seen. He was having coffee, her coffee, and from the look on his face, Margaret could tell, he was hoping later he'd be having Nori, too.

"Owen, this is my sister, Noreen Yearwood."

He shook her hand politely and nodded to the cop. "Sir."

"She got a little lost, folks. Just helping her find the way and getting a warm-up cup of coffee for my time. Hope you don't mind."

"No problem."

"Be on my way, then."

Nori didn't get up. She set her glass down and stared hard at her sister. "You should have known I would track you down one way or the other, Mag. It was stupid to run away. Did you think you could just cut me off along with everyone else? I'm your sister. Doesn't that mean anything to you? Where will you run to this time? Antarctica?"

Owen tipped his hat and mumbled about sheep and horses needing tending. He was out the door and gone before Maggie could process her sister's words. The cop's radio crackled, but it said nothing understandable. Why, Maggie wondered, for all the technology of the nineties, did those things still spit whirling static?

"Go home," she told Nori. "Whoever's bed that is these days. Steer somebody else's children away from them. It's Thanksgiving, this is my house, and I want you the hell out. Now."

She shoved the cork back into the wine bottle and put it away where it belonged, in the cupboard where she kept the cleaning things, right next to the lye for clearing stubborn drains.

Riverwall

I came in and found the moonlight lying in the room.
Outside, it covers the trees like pure sound,
the sound of tower bells, or water moving under the ice,
the sound of the deaf hearing through the bones of their heads.

ROBERT BLY, "AFTER WORKING"

10

AFTER THREE MONTHS AT RIVERWALL, PETER DIDN'T NEED ONE of Dr. Kennedy's twice-weekly, professionally understanding, this-is-part-of-the-agreement counseling sessions to tell them what he already knew: They hated him here.

He hadn't lost his sight. His roommate, Berto, barely made an effort to sign with him, and after their first week together he had put in for a transfer as soon as was possible, following Christmas vacation. Most of them didn't even bother to wait until his back was turned. They made fun of him at every opportunity, signing "green" or "asshole" whenever he tried to use his hands to communicate. The only thing worse than his trying to sign was if he forgot the rules and committed the unpardonable sin of *speaking* to help get his point across. It was reflex. Sometimes he couldn't help using his voice. Was that a crime? Sure, the teachers, who all had some level of hearing, appreciated it when he spoke, and nobody dared rag in front of *them* when Peter signed and spoke simultaneously. But when the teachers weren't looking, the students turned away from him and acted as if he wasn't there at all.

Sometimes he thought maybe they were right, and he *wasn't* anywhere, he was floating somewhere between worlds. But his eyes told him he was in Riverwall, New Mexico, in English class, Mr. Linder's third period, the one class where he, the out-sider, the-not-*really*-deaf kid, kicked serious ass, while fifteen of the legitimate deaf struggled to put words into a logical sequence. They were way behind everything he'd read in junior high. They hated having to reorder the perplexing grammar of English. Linder had such a hard time getting anyone to crack a book that he gave Peter free rein—let him jerk off by reading Dean Koontz, Stephen King, Christopher Pike, even those cheap choose-your-own-adventure books. Talk about bullshit. But anything was better than looking at the smirking faces around him. He'd made it past the whooshing silence that sometimes drove him so crazy he'd scratch his ears raw. Sometimes, if the story was good enough, and he lost himself inside it, he could sort of "hear" the words in his skull, this tingling, fleeting echo of old voices. It was weird, like the first time he'd smoked mari-juana, everything so slow and drifting, a little scary. The harder he tried to make it happen, the less often it did. But when it did happen, it was so *trick*. He dreamed sound. Heard everyone dis-tinctly, all the way from whispers to screams. Just before waking up he could almost pretend things were like before. That is, until the flashing light of the alarm clock rudely erased all that, or Berto startled him out of a dream by smacking him, signing, *Wake up, fag*, or he smelled the diesel stink of a truck and had to get up to see it rumbling soundlessly by the school, have his vision confirm that he would never again hear traffic. Bonnie Tsosie, the girl who sat in the front row, liked reading books, too. Sometimes he saw her walking across the campus, her brown face buried in the pages of one of the lame library's better selections. Today her thick black braid hung like a single rope between her shoulder blades against her black turtleneck sweater. If he circled the width of her hair with one hand—

something he imagined doing way too often—he knew in his fingers that heavy hair would feel warm and silky. In one of their first counseling sessions, Kennedy pointed Bonnie out to Peter, held her up like some shining example of what Peter could become, if he put his heart into mastering ASL. Forget the fact that Bonnie had been slowly losing her hearing since she could walk upright, or that she had years of practice under her belt to his five months. She also kept a small amount of hearing, which, when amped by her aid, gave her the best of both worlds—a clear voice to communicate with the hearing, and fluent sign, passage into the world of the deaf.

She's like you, Peter, Dr. Kennedy insisted. *What little hearing she has left she uses, even if it takes technology to get the most from it. Now, can we discuss the cochlear implant again. . . ?*

No, we can't. Maybe that justified Bonnie wearing a hearing aid in her right ear, but it wasn't any reason for Peter to submit to surgery to put some Terminator crap inside his skull. He'd told the audiologist to fuck off when he saw the array of instruments set out in her office. Ugly flesh-colored plugs, harnesses that "fit unobtrusively" on the earpieces of glasses he didn't need. And what did all that hardware get you? A series of buzzing noises you could learn to memorize—*that's* the doorbell, that other buzzing is your *name.* Buzzing wasn't hearing. He was deaf. He had to get used to it. It was just taking more time than he thought it would.

Bonnie's signing was awesome. It didn't stop with her hands, knowing all the correct movements. Like dancing, she used her body to give each sign her personal signature. If she was telling about a hike she'd taken over the weekend, she put you right there: the smell of piñon, cold wind stinging your face, hawks circling overhead in a clean blue sky. You watched her hands sign "dusty trail" and smelled the dirt under her boots, felt each loose stone she stopped to turn over, and saw those she chose to pocket. Her face was dark amber, her skin smooth and clear. Her flint-gray eyes reminded him of Echo's, if that wasn't a stupid comparison to make—they were always wide open and looked slightly wet. Her cheekbones were high and pronounced, and except for how skinny she was, she looked like a full-blooded Navajo. Kennedy said she wasn't, she was more like Peter, a mixture of different tribes and races, and that she sometimes felt like she didn't belong anywhere because of her background. She was signing with her seatmate, Ruth Castro, now. *Water. . . whales. . . color. . . fishes. . .* She signed so fast Peter only caught half of what she was saying. Unashamedly her face contributed to the signing in a sensuous way. Her eyes opened wide as she described the whales. *Big fish!* Mammal, Peter wanted to tell her, warm-blooded like us. Mostly her facial expressions worked because she wasn't afraid to use them. Peter was. In the mirror it looked completely bogus. He couldn't even come close to mimicking her expressions without looking like a total idiot. As if to punish him for his thoughts, she turned in her chair, looked right at him.

"Peter," she signed, "come here." He had to acknowledge her. He had to go.

She was reading a library book about some ancient hokey sea adventure. Jacques Cousteau—another candidate for Dad of the Year. Jacques always stayed aboard while his sons swam with the barracudas. She opened the book to a photograph of a huge wave combing toward the shore of some unspoiled island. "Waves," she signed. "You swim waves in California?"

He nodded.

"You. . . " she frowned, then finger-spelled, "s-u-r-f?"

He nodded his fist for yes. He'd surfed maybe a dozen times; surfboards weren't his thing. They got in the way of riding the wave.

"Tell me how."

He thought a minute. With his hands he tried to show her the curl of waves unfolding, spreading his fingers out, then raking them back in. "They rock," he signed, striking his fists.

She looked at his hands and frowned. "Hard?"

"No," he said, squeezing his hands, "soft."

"Oh, you mean rock, like *sway*," she finger-spelled, then

signed "rock" correctly, smiling gently at his confusion.

He felt his face darken with embarrassment. "Yes. Wet. Salt. Cool. Beautiful," he signed frantically. "You find currents and ride. Words can't explain waves. Wish I could show you."

She nodded, her smile probably just good manners, but around her, he could see the others snickering. Ruth tugged Bonnie's arm, and together they leaned back into the pages. Bonnie's braid fell across her arm, and she was lost again in the underwater world she could only imagine, the one he had taken for granted. Back in his seat Peter couldn't find his place in his book. Stephen King was a geek, determined to freak people out, taking a thousand pages to populate every dark corner with a monster. Major time waste. For really scary, all he had to do was take away a guy's hearing and then try and have him talk to a girl.

Fifteen minutes until lunch. Linder was busy tutoring two slowpokes. Why couldn't he have spared everyone and just died in the fucking coma?

At lunch the shitheads mimicked his clumsy sign while he ate, until he couldn't finish the broccoli and pasta in front of him, so he left to take a walk around the grounds. Even though outside it was cold enough to snow at any moment, it felt peaceful. Tall, thick-trunked trees, soft yellow-colored buildings, and it wasn't likely anybody from the old cemetery next door would come out to torture him. Someday, when he got the chance, he meant to explore that place, read all the names on the gravestones. Maybe Bonnie might go too. She didn't seem like the kind of girl who'd get spooked in a graveyard. She'd asked *him* a question. But for all her retained speech, maybe in defiance of her upbringing as part of the hearing world, she never talked in class. The other kids accepted Bonnie as deaf, but she was a girl, and they were always nicer to girls. Maybe it took longer for them to do that if you were a new guy. Or didn't look quite as Indian. He knew how white he looked compared to all of them. Was it his fault his color didn't show? Or did the people at Riverwall think because his dad made movies he'd come from some Hollywood–Disneyland–Tar Pits kind of town, and was scaling down, slumming his shameful deafness here in New Mexico?

Occasionally, when Bonnie gave him a good-morning smile, took the time to correct his lame attempts at signing without managing to go totally aggro over it, he thought she might like him just a little bit. He wondered for the millionth time just what it would be like to touch her, to accidentally brush against her brown hand once.

But here in Riverwall beautiful Indian girls were not interested in flabby seven-eighths-white boys, hearing or otherwise. It had been so long since he'd swum his stomach muscles were gone—nothing there but loose flesh. His hair was growing out a weird shade that looked about the color of burnt-umber shoe polish. He wasn't even special enough to be ordinary; nothing he was, nothing he did, was so outstanding it would grab her attention. Sometimes she looked at him like it pissed her off if he smiled back at her, or turned to her girlfriends when he signed "hello," signing away from him when he walked by in the cafeteria or outside the classrooms. He would never fit in here. Might as well give it up.

In California he'd worked being alone to an art, because being a loner elevated you in status. *Peter Sweetwater? Oh, he never eats lunch, he stands over by the fence and reads. He's like, this total philosopher or something.* He only did it because it was easier than having to talk to people for an hour. It was an act then, and like some parental threat, his scheme had come back to haunt him. He wanted friends, people who heard the same rushing gray nothing that he did and knew how to walk away from the world of concerts and MTV and find an equivalent in this one. That was why, when Nori told him about Riverwall, he'd wanted to come. It was more about trudging off to where he belonged than slicing himself up between his parents after the divorce, though he didn't really relish having to pick between them. Okay, so Riverwall hadn't turned out like he planned, and nobody here wanted anything to do with him. Bottom line—it was easier to be lonely here than choked to death in the land of waves and movie stars, packing your life into a suitcase every other weekend.

At night Bonnie visited without hesitation—in his dreams she was a regular. Oh, she had plenty of company. His dog, Echo, leaping around the perimeter of the pool at Harbor, anxious for his cue that the coach was off in his office and she could join him in the water. Why couldn't people be easy with each other, the way dogs loved everyone? Did everything get weird once you started having sex? He spent a lot of time thinking about it, though he'd never done it—yet. Sometimes he wasn't even sure if he wanted to—look what that had done to adults. His father, especially, whose new wife looked like she'd gotten her braces taken off last month. Some people refused to buy into that marriage crap, like Deeter. Deeter was cool. He kept life simple. Sure, he had girlfriends, but he stayed single. He quit working before he turned senile, and lived off his savings account. He hadn't changed either, just because Peter had gone deaf. He still made jokes and challenged him to swimming races. Deeter and Nori were about the only ones who still acted normal.

Crazy Aunt Nori—she sent him faxes once or twice a week, just notes about what she was up to, nothing vital, but he could tell it made an impression on the other kids. Probably they thought it was more Hollywood tactics, but they didn't know Nori, who didn't think it was worth her time to wait for anything, including the time it took the TDD operator to translate her intimate thoughts. She modemed her news instead, and once or twice a week, Peter got called into the office to pick up the faxes from Mrs. Woodward, whose frown as she handed them over had "spoiled brat" written all over it.

But his mother, his father, his father's wife. . . those bottomless worries occupied his thinking twenty-four hours a day. He'd learned how to replace them the moment they came into his head by imagining Bonnie Tsosie, looking him in the face, *speaking* clearly so he could speech-read her dark mouth, acknowledging that they two were more alike than the others, smiling, him smiling back, and then somehow, though this part wasn't very clear, the fantasy always ended with the two of them kissing.

He was alone in his dorm room, now that Berto had gone home sick. For months Berto had made a career of blaming Peter for how tired he was, having to constantly show around the lame new kid, but it turned out Berto had mono, not some terminal roommate disorder. He might be gone as long as a month, which meant Peter would have the room to himself, and privacy, however lonely, sounded good. Down the hall he could feel the throbbing floors, which meant someone had his stereo turned up full bore. You could do that here. No one went off on you until late, when the dorm staffers came back to their quarters. Sometimes he could recognize the beat of certain songs: Tone Loc's "Funky Cold Medina," Herbie Hancock's "Rockit." Not exactly MTV's top ten, but stuff with heavy bass was the music of choice because you could feel the vibrations, enter into the rhythm through the baseline. More than anything, he missed music, but not those rank old songs. He'd give anything to hear some Bob Marley, just one cut off the *Legend* CD. "Is This Love" would be killer. "We'll share each other on my single bed. . . ." But the song wasn't much more than a looping rhythm without Marley's voice, and what came through the dorm walls today was nothing more than pounding, sort of like a bad headache minus the pain.

He got up and took down his *Basic* text. He needed to spend more time practicing his signs so he wouldn't screw up again, like he had with Bonnie. But alone in his room he didn't feel like pushing his aching fingers through the drills again, when there was nobody there to sign "whoops," when you got it wrong, or "way to go," when you got it right. He glanced over at Berto's side of the room. On his bulletin board he'd tacked pictures of his family standing next to a fading red barn with one shabby mule occupant. Berto had two brothers and a sister. He also had a World Wrestling Federation poster, his prized possession, the Hulkster glistening like some oiled blond sausage. Maybe Peter would customize it while Berto was home—give the Hulk a few ballpoint tattoos, an eyepatch.

Peter's side was empty blue cinder-block wall. He kept Nori's faxes rolled into a cylinder on his bookshelf, next to his textbooks. On his small, battered desk, he unlocked the Apple system and turned on his Mac, scrolling to his journal files. There were two. One contained stuff he'd written in California, the other was junk he was writing here at Riverwall. His hand hesitated on the mouse as he studied the file icons. Someday he would get the courage to go back and read about his old life. It was like looking into some giant garbage disposal, seeing it all mixed up in there: his friends who were no longer his friends, his mother and father framed in a permanent argument, the waves Bonnie Tsosie dreamed about, the old house with the bay right next to the deck; outside, the sunny weather like a painted backdrop. The new journal entry he'd titled, "Try to Remember Mexico."

It was one of the goals he shared with no one, not even Dr. I'm-Your-Pal Kennedy. He had to piece it back together alone. But trying to remember what happened right before he got sick felt like trying to make sense of a bad dream. Certain memories were still whole, and those he could pull out and look over to figure out what the differences were between deaf Peter and the old Peter, who was a fuckup, but a *hearing* fuckup—someone who used to go to the movies with friends and trade Seattle grunge CDs, someone who hung out at the Alta coffeehouse just for something to do, got jittery drinking espresso, and made fun of the overly serious poets. But Mexico only came to him in jagged pieces that wouldn't fit together.

He remembered cutting school—try and tell me that my fucking *dad* didn't engage in such heinous activity once in awhile—and that it seemed like a brilliant idea when he heard Travis lay out the plan. School was glorified day care for adolescents. Mrs. Dornan, his English teacher, was always on the verge of a nervous breakdown. She'd sit at the desk with her head in her hands and tell them to just read a chapter out of *Lord of the Flies*, quietly at their desks, please, *Talk among yourselves if you must, but quietly. Quietly* being the operative word. That's what happened to you if you tried to make a career out of teaching teenagers literature, even if you approached the task ultra*quietly*. But Peter had a soft spot for the old lady. She was an ardent reader of mysteries—twice he'd seen her on the bench at lunch with a James Lee Burke paperback. Too bad they couldn't have read that in class—*Lord of the Flies* you could finish in two hours, and they were supposed to drag it out over a month. Consecutive attendance was hard to pull off unless you broke it up with rewards—cutting classes, taking days off, going places—like Mexico.

Travis, who had been held back twice, was permanently up for adventure. And Brian. Brian had broken his arm body-surfing at the Wedge once, stood up holding the weirdly bent thing out to show them the radical new way his elbow worked, and gotten back in the water for three more waves before they made him quit, laughing his ass off even as they drove him to the emergency room. Brian would smoke notebook paper if he thought it might get him high. Peter didn't know why he had been nervous at first about the idea of TJ—something about it just sat wrong in his stomach. It would mean they'd have to drive up and back in one day—a long way to go, especially in a heap like Travis's Cabriolet, which he'd already rolled once. Peter was going to call and tell him no, catch you next time. Then he'd picked up the extension and heard his father on the telephone in the guest room, murmuring, *Sure, baby, you know I want you, too*, while some starlet gave him verbal head via AT&T. How weird that when you went deaf there were some things you could never *stop* hearing.

He couldn't remember them drinking either, but it wasn't like he hadn't done that before. He didn't really like mescal. Travis claimed the worms in the bottom of the bottle were hard-on material, big johnson medicine, and he'd eat them up, smacking his lips. Peter didn't want to eat anything that moved ever again after seeing the "60 Minutes" thing on slaughterhouses. Panic-eyed cows screaming while some no-brainer *humanely* clubbed them to death. Two guys holding a pig down while another one cut its throat until it bled itself silent. How could they do that, then go home, eat a bloody steak, screw their wives, tell their kids right from wrong, get up and do it again the next day? He'd heard the animal screams on that show. He made himself stop eating meat that very night of the TV program, not so much as one slice of bologna or even beef-fucking-jerky crossed his lips.

Which he guessed was why he'd been stuck pulling off bits of tortilla while the rest of them chowed down on fish tacos. So of course the mescal *would* hit him twice as hard on an empty stomach. But the rest of it—sneaking into the closed hotel's pool and swimming in the murky water—he had to depend on Travis's recollection for that part.

Dude, Trav'd written on a pad of paper when he came to visit him in the hospital, *you don't remember the awesome cannonball contest? The algae in there thicker than kelp? Peter Sweetwater, alias moss man, wearing that shit on your head all the way home?*

No, Peter didn't.

Not even the lovely señoritas who climbed over the fence with us?

There were girls?

Dude, you must of like erased your memory or something while you were copping the major Z's. Brian got lucky. But you and me, we got stuck with this one fat chick and her ten-year-old sister.

Travis also told him he hadn't looked all that great even before the swimming. *But hey, Pete, it wasn't like you ever were in the same league with Johnny Depp. So when are you getting out of here? When will you be, like, you know, regular again?*

Peter read the words on the notepad and took a moment before answering back. "Regular" meant, "When will you be able to hear?" If Travis had to ask, that meant anything but regular was never going to be okay.

Soon, he told Travis. Everything'll be regular, we'll shave some waves, blow the speakers out in your car, cut History for sure.

The look of relief that came over Travis's face said it all—he'd never be back when he realized Peter was deaf. None of them would. Funny, neither Trav nor Brian had gotten so much as a cold. The brilliant doctors wouldn't say for sure what had led to the meningitis. Peter had looked it up in one of Nori's medical books. It could be as simple as a flulike thing, someone sneezing in your face, but he figured somehow it had to be the dirty water, punishment for what they'd done. Hey, go swimming. People do it every day. Having a good time? Great. Now give up your hearing, because every goddamn thing in life requires a trade.

He quit typing into the computer and took down one of Nori's faxes. *Joke time, Pete. How many doctors does it take to create the universe? Stumped? Only one, but it has to be a surgeon, because everyone knows they're gods!* The school for the deaf back home would have taken him, and though it was an out-of-county drive for his mother, he knew she would have picked him up every weekend without complaint. That was 90 percent of her problem—she couldn't say no. Not to shoe salesmen or husbands who slept around. He could have stayed where he was, going back to Harbor in the fall with a state-provided interpreter. He knew how that would go—his mother fretting and driving him to school every day, everyone so damn *sorry* about his hearing, one or two skanky girls anxious to be his girlfriend just because the whole situation was bizarre enough for them to want to get next to it— but he wouldn't be playing water polo—you needed sound for that. Actually, he bet if anything would ever get his ugly butt laid it would turn out to be his going deaf. *You can't hear? Oh, Peter, how totally sad. Take your pants off and let me make it feel better. . . .*

Because Nori was in the medical field, selling implants to surgeons, she knew doctors all over the Southwest. She kept after the doctors in the hospital, checking up on them, and she had made the series of calls that led him here. He told her he couldn't live with his parents and asked if maybe he could live with her in Phoenix for awhile, just until he got used to this whole thing. She was never home, really, not with all her traveling. Then she found out that Riverwall had a foster family program for those "audiologically challenged individuals" who wanted to immerse themselves in the deaf culture. He figured, Why not? At least here he would be in the same boat as everyone else, and no one knew how he was before. There was one catch, the school's resident policy. But, as Nori insisted, every catch has a built-in loophole, and it turned out she was right. You could enter under another umbrella: You were automatically eligible if you possessed Native American blood. His father did, and therefore so did he. His parting gift at the pathetic birthday party they threw him was spilling the news that he didn't want to live with either of them. His mom hadn't even tried to hide her crying. She and Nori had a big fight about it, but of course he hadn't heard the details.

Echo was the only one he let himself miss. Deeter—well, maybe he missed Deeter a little. The only cool friend his mother ever had, Deeter hadn't backed out on the promised birthday sail to Catalina just because his passenger was no longer of the hearing variety. They'd packed up the cooler and taken off for the island the day after he turned fifteen. Watching Deeter's hands on the sailboat rigging, just sitting in the sun alongside a guy who wasn't telling you what to do—their trip to Catalina was not about talking, it was snorkeling through the kelp, checking out fish, catching rays. They'd seen one nurse shark—Bonnie would have been impressed. Deeter let him have a couple of beers if he wanted, didn't make a big production over handing him a washcloth when he got sick over the side of the boat. And because he knew it would have wigged out Margaret to spring it the night of the party, Deeter had ordered a special birthday cake to take along on the sailing trip. He brought it out the last night, just before they had to sail back. A black cake. A mariachi band of skeletons played atop black icing. The letters on the cake read, WELCOME BACK TO THE LIVING, PETE. That cake *raged*.

On the weekends the Hidalgos, Leocadio and Amparo, both deaf, made him sign everything. *We're out of toilet paper. May I have a bowl of Cheerios, please? Good morning. I slept well, thanks for asking.* He thought he might come off a little scary to them, with his pierced earring and black wardrobe. But they seemed unimpressed. Their own kids were living in D.C., one doing grad work, the other interpreting at the Smithsonian. Every week when he arrived on the bus, Leocadio signed him the same question: "So, Mr. Serious. What you want to do with your life?"

In sign all that was abbreviated, of course. And he could tell Mr. Hidalgo found the question amusing by the way he delivered his signs. Off to the side of the body, it was almost like whispering, especially if he didn't want Amparo to see. Oversize, exaggerated signs meant he was as tired of asking the question as Peter was of "hearing" it. The cut-the-crap grammar of ASL made English seem absurdly wordy and self-centered. Peter didn't know what he wanted—maybe he'd apprentice himself and learn woodworking from Leocadio. Wood waited under your hands and tools to become what you made of it. Dovetail joints, arms for a chair, even those sucky howling-coyote statues Leo made from time to time, when he needed a quick couple of tourist bucks to tide him over to the next custom job. He was willing to try. Maybe he would end up sitting in the Plaza like the hopeless-faced Indians who barely tried to interest tourists in their silver jewelry. One thing for sure, he knew he was never going to get married, and he'd die before he turned into the Hollywood hustler his father had become. Look at his mother—the only thing she was good at was pretending her husband was faithful and rotating the flowers in her goddamn garden so that something was always "colorfully in bloom." Like some hopeless shadow, she'd followed him to New Mexico, even when he specifically asked her not to, settling herself in some pinchy little hooterville 150 miles north. Why? Were they low on floral arrangements? Like he'd really *want* to spend time with her in another unknown town, with more complete and total strangers feeling sorry for her, stuck with this burden for a son. The woman was clueless. Blue Dog—what the hell kind of town could it be—country-and-western bars, drive-through taxidermists?

She'd had the nerve to come down here, show up for lunch, sit there with her *Perigee Visual Dictionary*, determined to sign her way through this conversation, a backup pencil and a yellow pad just in case, trying to keep her smile from wobbling right off her face. She'd asked him to come home with her for Thanksgiving. He didn't need to read her painfully slow signs—he was a natural at lipreading when it came to his mother. He could still "hear" her voice, clearest of everyone. But he'd made a pact with himself not to speak to her until she learned to sign to him. Thanksgiving. Let's see, what shall we be thankful for this year and in what order should we put it? Your divorce first; second, my going deaf? With great difficulty she managed to sign, "Peter, Blue Dog's nice. I rented a farmhouse. Your own room. Horses and sheep next door."

It had taken her about twenty years to get the signs out. She kept having to look stuff up in the goddamn book. He had no intention of seriously considering her invitation, but he let her finish anyway, just to watch her try. "If I get tired of riding the horses, I can always have sex with the sheep," he signed back, but his mother was lost halfway through his sentence, and she just smiled at him hopefully.

She took it hard, his signing no, but she didn't break down, he had to give her that much. "Maybe another time," she spoke, forgetting to sign completely, looking away. Didn't even mention Christmas—just stood up and left, not even trying to kiss him goodbye.

Whether he answered or not, she wrote him once a week. Today he'd received an envelope with a sketch enclosed, no letter at all. It was a watercolor of his dog, asleep in what he guessed was a pile of just-dried purple towels. Purple—not one of her neutral colors. That fuzzy patch of white on Echo's cheek where the hair grew in different—she'd managed to paint that so accurately he could remember how it felt under his fingers. Apparently his mother was using pencils and paints to kill time these days. Art therapy. He smoothed the creases from the heavy paper and tacked it up above his computer, next to the bookshelf. Warm towels out of the dryer—Echo's favorite. He remembered that funny creaky sigh she'd give when she made herself a nest. His dog's eyes were closed, her lips relaxed and slack as she slept on in canine bliss. He remembered how it felt to have her greet him at the door, her back end in motion, the welcome-home leaps and squeals. He also remembered how when his father went ballistic over something really minor, like the time he brought home that D in Spanish, Echo could squeeze herself flat underneath his bed. The only thing animals offered freely was no-strings-attached love. His dog cuddled with him when he'd mouthed off to his mom, and followed him to the kitchen like he was a god, so grateful when he threw her potato chips he almost felt he was one. Even if his face broke out like Mount Pinatubo, Echo wanted to give him a kiss. She was eternally up for a game of ball. Too bad Amparo Hidalgo was allergic to dogs. Or that Riverwall didn't allow them. Maybe he'd skip dinner again tonight. Tomorrow he was going to the Hidalgos for Thanksgiving, the universal family day of gluttony. At least this year there'd be no fighting.

He lay on his twin bed, across from Berto's lying empty, stripped down to the bare mattress. He shut his eyes, trying to will sleep to come to him, working hard to keep the tears from spilling over.

School was officially out for the holiday following the primary kids' Thanksgiving program. Dressed in Indian buckskins with a few token Pilgrims thrown in, the grades one-to-three children, who ate their lunches an hour earlier, began signing the Thanksgiving prayer of thanks. Peter had seen them preparing for weeks, painting murals, constructing paper headresses. Now their small hands moved in unison, looking like overturned baby starfish, the pink exposed. They went slowly, had a good time, and only needed a few cues from the teachers.

"I am making the sacred smoke that all the people may behold it," they began.

Peter looked away, across the room to Bonnie. Two tables away, she was standing at her place, signing back to the children, smiling, her soup forgotten, cooling.

Dr. Kennedy came over to join him. "Vegetable soup," he signed to Peter. "Your favorite."

"It tastes okay," he signed back.

"Mind if I sit with you?"

Peter shrugged. He tried to concentrate on the elementary kids, to immerse himself in their short skit of the first Thanksgiving, delivered Indian-style. He saw the janitor turn on a cassette player and the kindergarten teacher cue the children to begin signing to the music, but the only one he wanted to watch was Bonnie.

"What song?" he asked Dr. Kennedy.

"Read the signs."

"Just fucking tell me the music, will you?"

"'Amazing Grace'," he signed back. "You know it?"

Peter set his spoon down and nodded. Of course he did. They weren't completely without culture in California. "I don't have amnesia," he finger-spelled to Kennedy.

Dr. Kennedy signed, "She's very attractive."

What was he supposed to say—No shit, Sherlock, what was your first clue? If he stayed out of trouble, kept his grades up, Peter didn't have to attend more than one counseling session per week, and he wasn't getting suckered into another one over a bowl of kindergarten soup. He knew what Kennedy was really after—why Peter wasn't going to be with any of his family for the holiday—he didn't buy the story about how since the divorce, they didn't make holidays into a big deal. He'd probably had a little chat with Mom when she came down.

Finished with their song, the children signed in unison, "Thanks." They joined hands and bowed. The audience's hands rose in unison, swaying from side to side in deaf applause. Peter's throat constricted.

"Aren't you hungry?" Kennedy signed.

He couldn't have swallowed soup to save his life. He left the table on the excuse that he had to pack.

While he waited outside for Leocadio, it began snowing lightly, small spatters hitting his face. Though it was only early afternoon, it felt much later—the high New Mexico sky foreshortened by snow clouds moving in. Nimbostratus—he'd only seen that kind of cloud in books until now. The Sangre de Cristos were shrouded in heavy-duty weather, and Peter wondered what it might be like right now on the ridge of those mountains. Bonnie'd said she climbed them all the time. Actual snow outside of a ski resort—the reality exhilarated him, and he felt the urge to run charge through him. They weren't much for sports here at Riverwall, but maybe a snowball fight, when there was enough on the ground. It was holiday weather, and it called for something spirited. Lacking any reasonable options, he stood off to the side of the group of kids waiting for their buses or parents to take them home for the holidays, the desire in his blood beating itself faint.

Bonnie Tsosie came down from the girls' dorm carrying an old army duffel bag. She was dressed in a hot-pink down jacket that made her skin glow. Her black hair, set free from the braid, had some kind of kinky waves he'd love to touch his fingers to. She was laughing, shaking her head, her snowy hair wild and free. Her girlfriends boarded the school bus, waving to one another, blowing kisses, signing, "Miss you! Love you! Don't forget me!" Then she was standing alone, none of the older kids left except the two of them. Peter walked over. "How come you're not on the bus?" he signed.

"I always go home to reservation for Thanksgiving," she signed back. "My Uncle Eddie come get me. We drive together."

"Where?"

"Shiprock," she finger-spelled. "North, about three hours from here."

"Is that anywhere near a town called Blue Dog?" Peter signed, proud that he'd remembered the sign for *blue*—the shaking *b*, and *dog*, a snap of the fingers.

"Yes," Bonnie nodded her fist excitedly. "Near. Why?"

Now he had to sign slower, remembering how to say things. "My mom lives there."

"Your mom? I thought she lived in California?" Bonnie smiled and made a sign similar to his "waves," but more accurate this time.

"Not anymore." He made the "waves" back, copying her movements. "She moved. My parents are. . . " He forgot the sign for *divorce,* and snapped two fists apart, for *broken.* As soon as he'd done it he remembered—it was easy—two shoved-together *d's*, then separating. *Why* couldn't he remember the right signs when he needed them?

She circled her heart with the letter *s,* the sign for *sorry.* "Come see me over the holiday. Let me write down map."

He reached out a hand to stop her. "I'm not going home for Thanksgiving."

She looked surprised. "Why not, Peter?"

"Because, like a stupid asshole, I decided to stay here," he blurted out loud.

For a moment she was quiet, taken aback by his outburst. Then she started to laugh. Right then he *swore* he could hear her, the sound of her laughter deep and clean, smelling of the wind in high places, clean, perfect, accepting, surrounding him like smoke from a campfire.

"You're not an asshole, Peter," she said.

He didn't argue. The snow was making the tips of his ears ache.

Then, impossible as it seemed, she leaned over and kissed his cheek. His eyes were starting to water from the cold. Everything was blurry. An old red pickup was at the curb, Bonnie was waving goodbye, scrambling to get her bags into the truck bed. He had to shield his eyes to see the truck disappear into the traffic.

Leo picked him up ten minutes later. At a red light on the way home, he kidded him, signing, "Where you got that goofy look—what you thinking about, boy? You figure out what you want to be yet?"

"Smart," Peter signed back to him, the first time he had an answer for the question. He knocked his forehead, making the sign for stupid, ignorant, dumb, then pointed to himself. "If I can't hear, I want to learn not to make an ass of myself."

Leo kept his hands on the wheel and spoke so Peter could

practice reading his lips. "Does this have anything to do with women?"

Peter made a face. "You read minds, too, or just signs?"

Leo laughed soundlessly, ruffled Peter's hair, then took him to a little shop off the Plaza, where they had to buy two pounds of blue *masa* for Amparo, holiday orders.

No!" AMPARO HIDALGO SLAPPED PETER'S RIGHT HAND AWAY from the steaming platter of vegetarian tamales. Then she shot him one of her darkest frowns, the kind that sent her husband scurrying to tend to whatever chore he'd forgotten, and Peter to his room. Only a moment later she was smiling, but Peter kept his distance. When it came to Amparo's tamales, he had no willpower whatsoever. She made them by hand, stuffed the corn husks with blue cornmeal paste, filled them with roasted sweet peppers, dozens of spices, finely chopped onion, and cheese until they were fat and straining, mouthwateringly irresistible. Where some people might keep a bottle of ketchup on the table at all times, Amparo had a special covered blue ceramic dish of green chile.

"Please," he signed, circling his heart, feeling brave enough to venture one more try. "Just one. They're so good." Before him, the tray was filled with at least three dozen. "Nobody makes them like you."

Amparo smiled at the compliment, then shook her red apron

at him, shooing him from the tiny kitchen as if he were a spoiled dog, begging at the table for people food.

"Food's for the *santuario*, for the poor. Even a stick of a boy like you can skip a meal. It will help you to understand the nature of hunger." Her broad hand made the letter *c,* then dragged it down her spare chest, the fingers coming together at just about the place where Peter's stomach was tree-trunk hollow and howling, juiced up from smelling the impending feast in Amparo's kitchen.

"Go help Leo with the carvings," she signed and turned back to her stove, where a tall aluminum pot simmered with soup stock.

He tapped her shoulder. "No dinner?"

Patiently she explained. "On Thanksgiving we fast until after services, share our food with others, and eat only a little when offered. That's our way. Now out, hungry boy."

More food than he'd ever seen, and 90 percent of it had no meat in it, so he could have sneaked an afternoon snack and there would have been plenty left over. Amparo's initial reaction to his vegetarianism hadn't even rated a nod. *The poor have been eating that way for generations.* Now he was supposed to learn about hunger on Thanksgiving Day. That was never the situation at home, though there were plenty of times he fasted on holidays, just to annoy his parents. They'd make reservations somewhere expensive, his father would order for everyone without asking you what you wanted, then act like a know-it-all sending the wine back, running the waiters ragged, leaving a miserly tip— that was your typical Sweetwater Thanksgiving.

Weary of smelling the things he wasn't allowed to eat, he ducked out back to do his laundry. The house rules here at the Hidalgos' were: If you dirtied it—dish, sock, bathroom sink—you cleaned it up. After one load of boxer shorts turned mottled gray from washing everything with his black sweatshirt in hot water, he started reading detergent labels and following directions. The washer and dryer were outside on the patio under a sloping roof. It was strange to stand at the washer measuring in Tide while a few feet away snow piled up in white mounds along the small courtyard. He looked out at the patch of visible sky, gray and dense with weather. It was the same northern New Mexico sky Bonnie Tsosie was under 150 miles north. It might be a little grayer up there, because it was colder in Shiprock, at least according to Leocadio's guidebook, which Peter'd borrowed from the living room shelf last night and read in bed, trying to force the small print and black-and-white photos to reveal more of this suddenly important landscape. Arranged by regions, the book gave a description about each town's founding year, population, industry, any history quirky enough to draw a tourist. Even dinky Blue Dog rated space—one whole half page!

Blue Dog (pop. 2,500 and "one or two good dogs," see below) is not really typical of northern New Mexico. Here among the cotton woods growing alongside the Animas River, folks'll stop you on the street, just for the opportunity to change a stranger into a friend. Blue Dog, est. 1867, is home of such American staples as Rabbott's Hardware, "hub of the community," run under the same family ownership for over one hundred years; some noteworthy examples of Victorian architecture; and one of the few self-supporting libraries in America (patrons pay ten dollars yearly, which supports staff, new acquisitions, and cookies for story hour Saturday mornings). In late fall, the whole town turns out for "Blue Dog Days," a week-long festival featuring an old-fashioned parade, the coveted Shiprock blanket auction, fine edibles prepared by the Reservation Association and local church groups, culminating in the yearly Blue Dog "best of show" companion dog competition ("turn out one or two good dogs a year and make a friend for life") and a locally sponsored rodeo, wherein some of the local working folk have been known to polish up their spurs and mount a wild horse or bull, "lookin' for eight" all-important seconds of ride time to place in the money. The nearby Navajo reservations, one of the state's finest examples of trading posts, hiking, good New Mexican cuisine at affordable prices, and the majesty of Shiprock National Monument within drive-by distance. We recommend the Enchanted Cactus Motel; Holiday Inn; bed & breakfast at Aunt Sally's Hideaway on Main. Good fly fishing on nearby Navajo Lake, catch-and-release not a law, but standard practice. Permit required.

His mother, armed with paintbrush, in the middle of that postcard? Right—she'd rent the nicest house in town, one some poor old farmer had scraped to build with his life savings, then lost to the bank when his wife came down with terminal brain fade. She'd tastefully accent all her rooms with floral arrangements that blended with those throat-clearing shades of beige she always went for, then buy seventy-dollar throw pillows, arrange them, and wait for her life to happen.

But by the time he got to the rinse cycle—Amparo had shown him how he had to stop the old machine, pour in the capful of softener, give the agitator a quick spin to get it rotating again—he couldn't quit picturing the map of Blue Dog's nearness to the Shiprock reservation. Shit, you could probably hoof it from Blue Dog to wherever Bonnie lived.

Leocadio came out of the garage carrying a load of carved wooden animals in one arm. "Help me," he signed as he jostled to keep them from falling. Peter set aside his washing and took a few.

"Thanks," Leo signed, his free hand touching his lips. "Got to get these in the truck and help Amparo with the food. Good clothes tonight—hope you didn't wash everything you own."

Inside Leo's workroom Peter began wrapping the more fragile carvings in newsprint. Leo favored birds and dogs, and somehow he could make his knives and rasps unearth paws and beaked faces from scrap wood. Peter ran his thumb over the flank of a dog—just a generic pooch, no particular breed. He started as Leo dropped a box on the floor, nudging his foot.

"You like that one?"

Peter set the dog into its newsprint nest. "I like everything you make."

Leo shrugged.

"No, really. They're so real. How do you do it?"

Leo began arranging the wrapped animals in the cardboard box, the heavier pieces on the bottom. "Focus on what's in your heart and the wood before you. God grants me the—" he stopped signing to finger-spell *ability,* then resumed speaking with his hands. "I try to honor my—" he stopped again, spelling out *burden.*

"B-u-r-d-e-n?" Peter questioned.

Leo nodded his fist yes, yes, yes. He pointed to a sign that hung above his worktable, next to well-tended tools and lengths of unused wood. In red marking pen, someone had lettered, ¡NACES PENDEJO, MUERES PENDEJO!

Peter's two years of junior high Spanish had prepared him for *albondigas* soup, trips to the *biblioteca* to check out *libros*, but not for translating aphorisms. He looked to Leo in bewilderment.

Leo spoke. "It means, if you're born a dickhead, you will die a dickhead."

"Then why bother?"

Leo's gentle brown face broke into a wide grin. He pursed his lips and blew on his fingertips, like a small breeze. "Words on a sign aren't permanent, Peter. Nothing is. You can change just about anything, if you want to and you work hard."

Amparo draped her best white wool shawl over her purple down coat; Leocadio's threadbare brown suit had monstrous lapels and an exaggerated pinstripe. It was so dated it had come back in style. He looked like a *pachuco*, and Peter complimented him.

"Cool threads."

Leo sucked in his belly and held his arms out to his wife. "Come here, woman," he signed. "This handsome man wants you."

"Stop this foolishness and drive the truck," Amparo signed back, heading determinedly toward the pickup.

"In my youth I could charm her," Leo signed to Peter. "Now I do what she tells me."

They drove to the *santuario* from Española on 64, passing the small farming community with its glut of weavers and artists who helped stock Santa Fe with the art they sold to tourists, but who couldn't afford to live there. The way to Chimayo was down a winding two-lane road, made narrower by banked snowfall lining its edge. Peter watched three mules look out toward the road from their wintry pasture as the truck passed by. They flicked their tall ears to dislodge snow. He thought of the horses he and his mother visited one time, out in the Southern California canyons when things weren't going so well at home and a drive seemed like a better idea than listening to his dad yell. He didn't miss California, not really. It was sunny all the time there. Here he liked how the weather matched his mood. Cold and wet, going nowhere for a few months. He could relate.

But holding Leo's carving had reminded him how much he missed other things. Echo—how she came along to water polo. About now the team would be going into the Division III finals. Then came playoffs, quarterfinals, semifinals, and the final game, swum on complete adrenaline rush. If your team won the championship, there was a banner, trophies for the school, the patch for your jacket, your name over the loudspeaker at the athletes' banquet. No way he would have worn that stupid jacket, but still—just to have it. If you were part of a winning team, colleges would come looking for you, might even offer you a free ride, and then you could go where you wanted to, not where your parents said you had to. They'd have a month of preswim before the coach started everyone in on weights and laps in the morning, laps and weights in the afternoon. You swam three thousand yards each time, and the minute you got out of the water, your thighs and biceps took on what felt like a ton of weight. Stadium runs up and down the bleachers—how he hated them. But it was a kind of brotherhood-of-pain thing when you all had to do it. One time, after his second tardy, Carpenter made Travis swim five thousand yards in his street clothes, including his Doc Martens. *Sons of bitches are supposed to be waterproof, aren't they? Get in the pool!* Trav wasn't late again. At Riverwall they didn't have a pool. It would have frozen in the winter. Besides, if you couldn't hear your teammates or the referee's whistle, you couldn't exactly play polo. There were times, despite what he said to Kennedy, he wondered about having that cochlear implant thing. But the thought of something like that in his head, changing music and people's voices from the echoes he remembered into a manufactured noise—it made him want to puke.

He knew he was right to shut the door on his past. Travis and Brian, school, everything—just forget it. Nori hadn't pushed him into Riverwall, like his mom accused her of doing. She'd just pointed out that there were other avenues open to him besides staying home. And for once, maybe the only time he'd do it in his lifetime, he'd thought his dad might have agreed—taken a hard look at an insurmountable problem and said, Fuck it, cut your losses here and move on.

So why did the place in his chest that ached with hunger suddenly feel so much emptier? *Pendejo*, he thought. That's what I am. Fucking imbecile. I could have gone to my mom's and put up with her, played with my dog for a few days, eaten a filling dinner, and maybe even seen Bonnie. Remembering his Spanish grammar drills, he conjugated: *Pendejismo*—that's what it was he was feeling, a by-product of its more familiar cousin *machismo*.

The church at Chimayo was as tiny as the Hidalgos' house. Mounded adobe walls with ragged wooden doors opened into a small courtyard filled with old, barely readable gravestones. Then you entered the church proper. It was narrow in width but tall ceilinged, decorated with gilt candelabra and twelve of those horrifyingly ornate paintings of the stations of the cross. Some of them would have made amazing T-shirt designs. At least the Hispanics painted the agony like it was—this Jesus stumbled and bled; when he drank the vinegar, his face showed it. Peter was surprised that even without being able to "hear" the mass in Spanish, he remembered when to genuflect and when to kneel. At home, church got hauled out only when his mother was feeling guilty. Easter Sunday services or a midnight mass on Christmas, she'd drag him along. *Come on. It won't kill you to put on decent shoes and sit with me for one hour.* Sure, he'd been baptized, probably more to appease the sainted Yearwood grandparents than for the good of his soul, but that was about as Catholic as Mom got. *I won't have you growing up under that load of guilt. Maybe all it did was repress me, but your Aunt Nori is a perfect case in point why religion backfires.* Okay, so Nori went a little too far occasionally, like when she got that tattoo on her ankle, but she did have it removed. And he knew she slept with way too many guys than made sense, but so what, it was her life. Sometimes, like now, with the smells of beeswax and incense in his nose, sitting next to believers in the straight-backed pews, and that old guy up front in the satin and brocade robes messing with the candles and the chalices, he wished they had kept on going to church. It wasn't so much that he believed if there was a God that he or she gave a crap if you ate meat on a Friday, or swore sixty times a minute, or even if you got raging drunk on mescal once in a while. It was more about the guardian angel thing—that fairy story—believing you were never alone.

On the altar the priest was lifting the sacred host skyward, changing the simple gift of bread to symbolic flesh through his blessing. *This is my body and this is my blood.* Outside, in the bed of the truck, Amparo's tamales and tortillas were kind of like communion too. The cave in his chest sent out a bellowing echo he couldn't hear, but felt. When Leo and Amparo got up to take communion, he went with them, knelt at the altar, and took the small host in his hand, then placed it on his tongue, letting its flat taste dissolve into his mouth.

Following mass, while Amparo visited with friends, Leo shouldered Peter into the chapel of the *Santo Niño*. "Church and shrine have healing power," Leo signed, gesturing to the paintings, statuary, and hundreds of crutches and braces left behind by generations of miracle seekers. "People scrape dirt from the floor when no one's looking."

"Why?" Peter said.

Leo frowned. "Sign, Peter. Don't be lazy."

Chagrined, Peter made the gesture for *why*.

"To eat. Some say it's holy and can cure the incurable."

Holy dirt? Nickel-colored *milagros*, tiny, crudely fashioned amulets portraying different parts of the body were pinned to the skirts of one robed doll dressed to represent the Virgin Mary. Various shrines bore handwritten notes on yellowing paper, some in Spanish, others in English, asking for cures to physical problems. Leo signed, "Farmer might leave one in the shape of a horse, if his animal was ailing." He took Peter to a glass-encased carving of the *Santo Niño,* whose palm was upraised in eternal blessing. The Holy Child's face was starting to lose its layers of paint, poor bare-plaster-nosed *niño* in his crumbling robes. Beneath the glass box there was a large ledger with handwritten entries. Using the wooden page-turner provided, Leo flipped back a hundred pages, then pointed out one particular entry to Peter. It was written in Spanish, way back in 1954. Fly spots decorated the paper.

"See those words? I wrote them. When my son was born deaf, I prayed hard, certain God would restore his hearing. When my daughter was born deaf, too, I thought maybe booze. *Pendejo* that I was, I did not see the gift they already were to me, hearing or deaf. It's in my genes they cannot hear. Mine and 'Paro's. Some people will tell you that being deaf is to be part of a special culture, and that is so, for when you have no choice, you work to find your specialness within. But your hearing was lost. If there is anything medical that can be done, you must seek it out. If that doesn't work, okay, in time, you will learn that silence, too, is a gift. Now let's go eat many tamales and be thankful men."

While everyone was having flan, Peter went back inside to look at the statue again. He'd eaten two tamales, felt satisfied, and thought long and hard before reaching for a third. During his hunger he could think of nothing but filling his face with all that food. Watching the others at the table eat, taking small portions so everyone had enough, he'd changed his mind. He didn't see how gorging himself made this any more of a holiday. Inside the small room the thick walls felt warm and close, so comfortable it might be spring outside. He looked closer at the statues now that he was alone. One of the wax Madonnas wore black lace skirts, like some kind of Spanish dancer, and somebody'd painted her mouth with peach-colored lipstick. He smiled. It looked like some well-meaning visitor had wanted old Mary to keep up with the times and lent her a little Cover Girl. His mom didn't wear much makeup, but Nori piled it on with a trowel. On Nori it worked. In fact, without eye shadow and lip liner, Nori looked older than his mother, and so pale and tired out she was kind of scary. However, to put any kind of makeup on Bonnie Tsosie would be serious overkill.

Peter knelt and pinched some dirt between his fingers. It looked ordinary, but lots of great things looked ordinary at the start. Carefully, checking to make sure no one was watching, he folded it into a scrap of paper he had in his wallet, some receipt, the ink so faded it was no longer readable. Leo had a point. For Peter to eat magic dirt and wish for hearing was like saying God's designs made no sense. But in between that thought and acceptance, there was a large gap to step over. Peter had almost fifteen years of sound for reference: human voices, birds calling, the ocean slapping onto the sand. And some of it he'd sneered at: his father's yelling, the alarm clock, static on KROQ because where he lived the station didn't tune in clearly. Had he ever once said thanks for any of it? Still on his knees, he faced the *Santo Niño* and bent his head. He had never learned any prayers except for a simple grace and the Our Father. He remembered the kindergartners at Riverwall signing their blessing: "Make the Earth Bright and Thanks." Most of the words were gone, blown away in the wind, like Leo's gesture to him back in the workroom. His hearing was never coming back, even if he let the doctors put transistors and telephone cable in his head. He would have to learn to listen in his own way, more closely, to everything. And to see Bonnie anywhere besides in class at school, he would have to smooth things over with his mother, and that meant going to Blue Dog for Christmas.

Dear Mom,

I hope you had a nice Thanksgiving. Try not to faint, okay? I went to church with the Hidalgos. It was tolerable. Listen, thanks for that painting of Echo. I wouldn't mind if you sent me some others, you know, stuff you just have laying around.

Okay. The big question. If it's okay with you, could I come there for Christmas? It's not a problem to get a ride from some kids who live up that way, so you won't have to drive down or anything.

Peter

While the letter was printing, he unfolded the paper in his wallet. He studied the contents, trying to see if here, by desk light, the magic was any more perceptible to the human eye. It was just dirt from the floor of an old church where people went when they lost all hope, in search of miracles that would never happen. He opened his mouth and tossed it down his throat anyway, swallowing the dusty sweetness with a sip of Classic Coke.

12

INSTEAD OF A PHONE CALL IN RESPONSE TO HIS LETTER—HIS MOM trying not to cry through the TDD, asking him what he wanted for dinner, offering up some little holiday fable about mother and son trimming the tree—to which he'd already rehearsed his replies—she didn't call at all. He was starting to panic. All the kids were making holiday plans, some of them getting permission to go home with each other, arranging ski trips to Angel Fire, all kinds of plans that didn't sound too rank, actually. If he didn't ask Bonnie for that ride soon, there might not be room for him in her uncle's truck. She might have made other plans, or have offered some other guy a ride.

His father was awaiting the impending miracle of birth. The last note he'd gotten from him said he'd "catch you after the first of the year, if filming goes according to schedule." He'd probably almost forgotten what his son looked like. He'd forget he had a son completely when the new baby was born. Maybe his mother didn't want him home for Christmas. He supposed the Hidalgos would let him share their family reunion, but he didn't want to.

The Friday before Christmas break, a brown envelope arrived. He checked the postmark—Blue Dog—and tore it open in front of the mailboxes, screw what the other kids standing there thought. As he slid the paper from the envelope, he saw it was another not-a-letter. On an 8½-by-11 sheet of nice paper, his mother had drawn a cartoon strip, four frames' worth. For a second he remembered when he was little, sick in bed with a strep throat so sore Chloraseptic didn't even come close to numbing it, how she'd taken out a pad of paper and gotten in bed next to him, ballpoints, pencils, and crayons between them on the blanket. *You tell me what you want,* she'd said. *Just name the adventure, and we'll send Peter the Well there. Does he need a horse? I know you like horses. How about a Percheron? That's a good, sturdy breed for rough terrain. . . .* It seemed like the most natural thing in the world, her fingers making the pencils move, drawing her way into a whole other world. Her pictures had done more than pass the time. They made him forget his fever. Changed the scratchy sheets to a slightly more bearable softness. Made him somehow be able to swallow juice and drift off into a deep, restful sleep.

In the first frame of this cartoon, she'd drawn a tiny Echo, curled up napping, little commas to indicate her paws were twitching with dog dreams. In the large thought balloon above her head, his dog envisioned a skimpy pine tree bearing a single ragged, half-burnt-out string of lights. Beneath the tree a plate of dog biscuits and bowl of milk were set out for Santa. In the next frame, Santa, who looked like an elderly golden retriever with a beard, came down a chimney, sampled one biscuit, then sat down to read Echo's note. *Dear Santa: I've been a good dog this year, except for that one time I dug a rather sizable hole in Mom's garden. But I'm not chasing the sheep anymore! For Christmas, I can do without that fancy rhinestone collar, and I guess I don't really need a new squeaky toy. This one's ratty, but it still works. What I'd like more than anything is to see my boy Peter again. But if you can't make that happen, I'll still try to be a good girl. Say hello to Dasher and Dancer. Hope you liked the biscuits—made them myself! Love, Echo.*

The following frame was the one that made him bite his lip

and run down the hall for the privacy of his room. In it Echo was just beginning to stretch awake as the sun came in her window. The dead tree, previously sketched in light pencil, now transformed through more serious lines and shading into part of a larger, living forest. The half-broken string of lights had become snowflakes and fat winter birds. Next to the tree there was a Christmas-wrapped package in the shape of a person, with twin airholes cut into the nose area. On the package's tag, his mother had drawn each hand shape for the signs, so that it read "For Echo" in the manual alphabet. The last frame of the cartoon was blank. He knew what that meant. She wanted him to fill it in, to make the next move. He took that for a yes.

"Maybe sometime you should try wearing different colors," Bonnie signed to Peter from the front seat of her uncle Eddie's pickup. She gave Peter's collar a tug, then signed, "Black's nice, but so are other colors."

Peter nodded stupidly at her easy grin. She was wearing her faded blue jeans, that pink jacket, a dark green turtleneck peeking through the collar. The warm colors made her skin glow, and he thought he'd never seen her looking prettier than right now, even with her hair tied back in a plain rubber band. He'd stood in front of the mirror in the bathroom at the Hidalgos' for half an hour, just trying to decide what shirt to wear under his jacket. In the end he picked a solid black flannel. It was one of those shirts his mom had bought that he'd never worn, what she called "a nice shirt," which probably meant it cost megadollars and had an impressive label. He thought maybe Bonnie might like it. But Bonnie was basically letting him know that his wardrobe was funeral material. California and New Mexico were only two states apart. How could what was cool in one place be so stupid in another?

He looked out the window at the freeway overpass they were approaching. He'd passed it before, when he drove with Amparo to buy chiles and wondered what the spray-painted letters on the gray concrete arch, KEEP WIPP OUT OF NEW MEXICO, meant. It had struck him funny, that kind of message versus some tagger's *placa*, or gang-affiliation marking boundaries, like on the freeways at home. He signed to Bonnie. "What's WIPP?"

"Waste Isolation Pilot Project."

"What's that?"

"Government wants to use Carlsbad for a dump."

"To dump what?"

"Radioactive waste."

He'd never thought of stuff like that as *belonging* to anyone before. Back in California, when the alarm went off for San Onofre's nuclear power plant, it was usually a mistake, or some test they were doing to make sure the alarm still worked. Below the twin domes on Trestles beach, he just kept on bodysurfing. Trav made jokes as they drove by—*Dude, cover your nuts, or your children'll be mutants.* It sucked—all that bogus crap you inherited from your parents, one day their shit, then suddenly *your* problem to fix. There was so much wrong that couldn't be fixed. When the doctors stood around his bed, trying to explain to him that what he was "hearing" was really nothing more than leftovers of all the sounds he'd known before he got sick, he refused to buy into it. Okay, on some level he knew they were right. But he couldn't let them know. He figured out he was deaf—it didn't take ten years of medical school not to hear doors slam or not understand the nurses' voices. He thought the hardest thing in his life had been that one moment he realized they were telling him the truth. But, no, what was really fucked was every hard moment seemed destined to be replaced by another, even worse. The nuclear waste might not end up in New Mexico, but it sure wasn't going away. The thought of government trucks filled with barrels of it, driving around, trying to find a place to put it, God! He knew some night soon he'd sit up with the light on, worrying about those barrels, and that somewhere in the back of his mind, now that he knew they existed, he wouldn't ever be able to forget them. But what was worse was knowing there was something else out there, too, something even darker, just waiting its turn. He'd thought the hardest thing he'd ever done in his life had been asking Bonnie for this ride. He'd been so nervous his palms were sweating, and he was sure she noticed when he took her aside as they were leaving the cafeteria to sign his request.

"Any chance you have room in the truck for me to catch a ride as far as Blue Dog?" He'd rehearsed and rehearsed, memorizing the signs.

Bonnie had looked up at him, her arms full of textbooks stacked atop her notebook. Her lips parted slightly, and he thought she might be about to speak, but she didn't. "No problem," she signed back, left for class, and then all that was left was the waiting.

Bonnie's uncle, Eddie, a quiet, short guy in a Levi's jacket with worn sheepskin lining, hadn't seemed to notice Peter was there. He threw his stuff in the truck bed, and Bonnie scooted over on the seat to make room. Eddie kept his hands on the steering wheel and drove just under the speed limit. They were slowly climbing in altitude. Probably the old Chevy couldn't do any better on the grade, even if he nailed the pedal. But there wasn't any real hurry. This ride could last all day and Peter wouldn't mind staring at Bonnie, just inches away, even if he had no clue what to say to her. He wanted to *talk*. To use his voice, and even if he couldn't hear her, have her use hers back. She spoke to Eddie. He saw her turn her face to her uncle and saw Eddie's lips move as he answered. But those unwritten rules at Riverwall applied here too. She wouldn't talk to him.

They stopped once to buy lunch—burgers Eddie and Bonnie relished and Peter turned down. Amparo had packed him lunch. Well, you could call it a lunch, or a little more accurately, a Peace Corps relief package. It weighed about ten pounds. It would have looked stupid to start unwrapping all that food in front of Bonnie, like he was tapeworm boy or something. Pretending it was Christmas presents, he'd stowed it in the truck bed along with his duffel bag of clothes—black clothes, he reminded himself. Maybe Blue Dog had a store like JC Penney's, or New Mexico's equivalent of Miller's Outpost. Wouldn't Mom have a joy attack if he asked her to take him shopping?

It was kind of like all of them were spending Christmas in foreign countries. His mother in Blue Dog, his father in London. White Christmases, with piles of snow. You could always count on Dad to send another big fat holiday check for Christmas, though, merry and glad tidings, just so long as I don't have to see you, son. It might already be there waiting at his mom's. Oh, well. Might as well spread his money around Blue Dog as anywhere else.

Eddie drove slowly over the icy road indicated on the map as leading to the house. Peter craned his neck against the window to look. A brown horse ran across the pasture, parallel to the truck, as if he got off on trying to race it. Behind him snow sprayed up like the wake off a speedboat. Near a small barn, he could see an old green pickup and, for just a few seconds, some cowboy dude standing there, looking back at him as he fed some dirty-looking sheep. The farmhouse was like something out of one of his father's old TV series. He couldn't picture his mother being comfortable with shoulder-high weeds, dirty snow, and livestock crapping nearby. He remembered her jeans and sweater when she came down to ask him home for Thanksgiving, how she looked different, but he couldn't say what it was about her that had changed. Now it struck him. What had been missing were the little ironed-in pleats and the tasteful designer labels. At first, he almost hadn't recognized her. He guessed her life had changed, too, and that he was a geek to think she could move to a place like this and stay the same. She'd moved by herself, rented this house on her own. Like that cartoon she'd sent him that almost made him cry, his mother was not the same person. She was getting along, and he wasn't, unless you counted Dr. Kennedy's sessions as having a friend.

Bonnie insisted they walk Peter to the door of the farmhouse. He was secretly glad that she wanted to, but if she'd dropped him off at the top of the gravel road, he could have scoped out the place and endured his mother's hugs and the welcome-home tears in private.

"What are you thinking?" Bonnie signed.

A girl's favorite question. He made O's with his hands, and drew them over his chest, opening them as he did so.

"Nothing? Liar. Why you look scared?"

He drew his thumb under his chin. "I'm not."

She smiled, then made the sign for "Good." "Eddie has friends in Blue Dog. Some night, we come over. Play–?" She made a sign he didn't know, and his face burned with embarrassment.

"P-o-k-e-r," she finger-spelled, then repeated the sign.

He nodded, color flooding his face. They were in the driveway now, so close to the house he could see the woodpile behind it, as tall as his shoulders. Frost rimmed the lower windows, and a set of icicles hung along the north side of the roof.

As Eddie cut the engine, Bonnie signed, "Save your Christmas money, Peter." She made the poker sign again. "I always win."

On top of being pretty, she had to be a card shark. He opened the car door. Cold air hit his face in a bracing slap. He stretched out his legs and began to gather his bags from the truck bed, wishing there were ten more miles between this truck and his mother, wondering how it was going to be spending these weeks with her.

Bonnie walked briskly alongside him to the red front door of the farmhouse. Eddie lit a cigarette, and the smoke smell was sharp in the cold air. What if Mom hated Bonnie on sight, had his weeks sewn up with endless planned outings to make up for lost time? He couldn't wait for Bonnie to meet Echo. Bonnie'd like the dog. He eased the scowl from his face. Unsure whether or not it was okay to just walk in, he lifted his hand to knock at the door. His mother opened it at once, as if she had spent the day standing behind it, waiting. She smiled at him in a way that made everything seem okay, then said hello to his companions. It was funny, when she moved her mouth, he could still hear her voice in his head, clear as ever. She had a funny voice, one of those deep sopranos that sometimes grew creaky with laryngitis—her weak spot. In his dreams Bonnie sounded the same way. To his surprise, Bonnie was talking now. She signed simultaneously, so he could tell exactly what she was saying. "Hi, I'm Bonnie, Peter's friend. This is my Uncle Eddie. We live in Shiprock, on the reservation. Merry Christmas. . . ."

His mother gestured for everyone to come in, get warm. Then all at once, Echo came flying at him, a mutt bullet traveling at warp speed. He knelt to let her properly welcome him home. Dodging licks and paws, he looked at the room around him. Woodstove radiating warmth, pale yellow walls, an overstuffed couch and rocking chair. Maybe in a little while it could feel like home. But right now the only thing he recognized was the old dresser from the guest room, and the threadbare rug his dad used to make fun of, which now hung above the mantel. The rest of the place was crowded with easel, sketches, crinkled tubes of paint and half-finished canvases. Several of them, he noticed with embarrassment, were portraits of himself.

Eddie said they had to go, that people were waiting on them, and as he and Bonnie walked back out the door, Peter wished he knew how to combine the goodbye he wanted to say—putting his arms around Bonnie, burying his face in her hair, smelling enough of her clean girl smell to hold him over until the next time he saw her—with the polite goodbye wave of his hand. He watched her get back in the truck and drive away, the outside rush of cold air infiltrating the warm house until the lights on the truck disappeared around the curve in the road. Then he was alone, his dog scratching at his leg for attention, his mother standing behind him, waiting for him to say or sign something.

If she was nervous having him there, she was doing a damn good job of hiding it. She made pasta for supper, stir-fried carrots and broccoli, then dusted everything with Parmesan cheese. The vegetables were a little burned, classic Mom, but she didn't apologize and even went back for seconds, the first time Peter could remember her doing that. She was the kind of mother who ladled out her own tiny portions of whatever she fed him. Lots of nights she just had salad and crackers. She bought herself fat-free everything, from cheese to yogurt, stuff Echo wouldn't even bother begging for. They sat across from each other at the kitchen table, silently cleaning their plates. She refilled his water glass without his asking, and if he shut his eyes, he could almost pretend they were back home, on one of a million nights his father was "working late."

"School's going okay?" she signed when she laid her fork down on her plate.

He shrugged.

His mother looked down at the table, as if concentrating hard on getting her signs right. "Your friend Bonnie—nice."

Rapidly he shot back the letter F, ASL shorthand for *fine*. He could see she didn't know what that meant. Too bad.

"I missed you," she signed.

She was using the letter *I* to indicate herself—which was practically forbidden—that was like holding out your pinky to drink your tea, like sticking your nose in the air as if you were some snobby Englishman. He smirked at her blunder.

She looked embarrassed and excused herself. He buttered a third slice of French bread. She took her plate to the sink, rinsed it, and disappeared upstairs. After five minutes of waiting for her to come back down, Peter went looking for her.

"Some mother," he said aloud in her doorway, as she looked into a dresser mirror, dressed now in a purple silk shirt, brushing her hair. "My first night here and no dessert?"

She looked over at him, startled, and signed back as she answered aloud, the signs lagging so far behind her mouth they were pointless. "My God, Peter. It's been so long since I heard you speak. Of course there's dessert."

She ran the brush through her hair once more, then she said, "Whether I brush it for three hours or not at all, it ends up looking the same. Wild." Then, as if she had just remembered he was deaf, she signed "wild" and pointed to her hair.

She smelled nice, like soap and lotion, clean and natural, not marinated in perfume, like the old biddy who worked in the library at Riverwall. "Your hair looks okay. Your signing's improving. You can talk to me. When it comes to speech-reading you, I kick ass."

"Thanks, but I need the practice. I was hoping you'd help me. For dessert, there's cherry—"

Peter watched her hands make the sign for pie, that unmistakable wedge shape. "Since when did you learn to make pie?"

She abandoned her signing and simply spoke. "About two months after I watched your father flush my life down the toilet." His heart sped up. He didn't want to talk with her about that. Ever. It was over. If he didn't think about it, there was no other family, no half-brother or -sister on the way, nothing.

"Pete, relax. I'm not going to try to convince you to hate your dad because he decided he loved some other woman."

He made an *O* with his right hand and circled it with his left index finger.

"I don't know what that means."

"It means asshole."

"Lovely things you're learning at school." She shook her head no. "Well, he does have moments where he definitely qualifies. For a long while, I hated him."

"Now?"

She turned the brush over in her hands and touched the bristles. "I don't know, Pete. Part of me's still hurt. He's just trying to make sense of his life, the same as you or me."

"By fucking actresses?"

She smiled. "Another one of my favorite words! I was wondering where that one had gone to."

"Sorry."

"Try to understand, Pete. Sometimes sex is how people initially go about finding their happiness. It's not like marriage, but sometimes it leads there." She gave his shoulder a shake. "Don't *you* get any ideas in that department, you hear? Oh, there's the door. Come on downstairs and meet—" She stopped and fingerspelled the name: "O-w-e-n."

O-w-e-n?

"It's fixing to blizzard," the man said, shaking snow from his shoulders, and Peter watched as his mother signed the translation, though this guy spoke so slowly he didn't need her to translate what he'd said. He'd pictured this neighbor she'd invited for dessert to be some old maid his mother'd befriended, like the Welcome Wagon lady. Not six feet of cowboy on snowshoes, carrying a carton of vanilla ice cream to go with the goddamn pie. *Fixing*. Jesus Christ, was this guy the same one out there feeding the sheep? The handyman? What?

Owen held out a hand for Peter to shake. He was all smiles and good manners. Peter left his hand resting at his side. Margaret, halfway to the kitchen, *fixing* to serve her pie, missed the whole exchange, but the cowboy didn't. Not missing a beat, he reached over with his left hand, shook his own right one and gave Peter a look that said, "Okay, for now we'll play it your way." He went back to the door, opened it, and let in a small spotted dog with three legs.

Then Owen left him standing in the living room and went to the kitchen. Both he and his dog had been here before. They seemed to know the house—both floors, as the dogs took off up the stairs in a game of chase. Peter pulled the living room curtains aside and looked out the window at the heavy snow falling, making peaks on the hood of his mother's car, the only car around. If the man came on snowshoes, he had to live close by, like say that shack off the barn where he'd glimpsed the sheep feeder. Maybe it *was* the same guy. Driving in, the nearest house they'd seen from the road was way across the river, and cherry pie wasn't that humongous a draw in two feet of snow. He peered into the kitchen, and saw the man place his hand on the small of his mother's back as she leaned over to take the warming pie out of the oven. He saw his mother lean ever so slightly back into that hand, like she'd done it before.

"I'm not really hungry," he announced.

His mother gave him the palm-down sign, which meant he needed to lower his speaking voice. "That's okay," she signed. "There's plenty if you change your mind."

She'd cut the cowboy a huge wedge, then topped it off with a generous scoop of artery-hardening ice cream. No one in this state had ever heard of nonfat frozen yogurt, and his mother, standing there licking the spoon, seemed to have forgotten about fat-free anything. It looked to Peter like she was doing him.

"My dad makes movies," Peter said when Margaret and Owen were well into their pie. "What do you do?"

The cowboy patted his mouth with a napkin before he answered. "Clerk in a hardware store, raise a few sorry sheep."

"What for?"

His mother set aside her plate to sign as Owen spoke. "Money. To sell. For meat."

Peter said, "Let me get this straight. You raise them, feed them, and then kill them?"

"Not exactly. You skipped over a few steps."

His mother interrupted. "I can make cocoa—anybody want cocoa?"

Peter ignored her, intent on watching the cowboy. "So you don't kill them?"

"No, son, I don't."

"But you pay someone else to, right?"

The cowboy was trying hard to follow his logic. "*Slaughter's* the term. After I sell them, what people do is their business."

"You're right. *Slaughter* is a better term. But you don't even need to think about what to call it, really, if you sell them."

"It's a fact animals give up their lives for people to eat."

His mom had quit trying to keep up the pace, but he didn't really need to know what the guy was saying at this point. "You know what? I'm not your son. And not everyone eats meat. Breeding sheep—what's that mean, essentially? Fucking?"

The cowboy didn't respond, but his mother stood up, tensing, giving him the look that said he'd gone over the edge.

Peter said, "Hey, we're all adults here. It's just an expression for sex. Kind of like 'fucking your lights out' is also an expression for sex."

"Peter! That's enough."

The cowboy set his pie down on the table and placed his

hand on his mother's arm and patted it twice. Crudely pointing, "You-me, go-to-snow," in elementary sign, he said aloud, "Pete, let's go bring in some firewood. Blizzards can last days. You need to know where the wood is, and how to stoke the stove. That is, unless you feel comfortable with your momma doing all the work around here."

He was trying to get to him with that old reverse psychology bullshit. "A slight problem. I don't have boots. You wouldn't want me to catch pneumonia, would you?"

"Use mine."

"Owen," his mother said. "I can get the wood. I do it every day."

"Maggie, sit tight. You went to the trouble of making this delicious pie, the least two men can do is fetch firewood."

Maggie. He was calling her Maggie.

Owen was already snapping the laces over Peter's Doc Martens, the dogs sniffing and prancing nearby at the brilliant idea of going out in the snow. His mother was staring at her pie, the ice cream starting to melt in a slushy, blood-colored puddle studded with cherries. Her shoulders were hunched forward, and the silk shirt had lost some of its luster.

If Riverwall had been cold, by comparison Blue Dog at dusk was Antarctica. Snow knives in your face—and he was talking *cojones*-freezing cold. Peter trudged behind Owen the ten feet from the house to the woodpile. Owen took a pocket flashlight from his jacket and turned it on for Peter to follow, though it was still light enough to see clearly. The snowshoes kept him from sinking, but he could only move like he was dream-running, pointlessly strug-gling to move out of some gluey muck, getting nowhere fast, until the man came and guided his arm, lifting him up and pulling him along.

"Thanks."

The cowboy nodded. He shone the light on his own face. "Fell flat on my ass the first time I tried them. You got to remem-ber to lift your feet."

At the woodpile Owen stopped and took out a notepad, removed the fat glove he was wearing, and gestured to the pad.

"Your momma says you read lips. How well?"

"I'm what they call a goddamn natural at it. My teachers all think I'm 'gifted.' But sometimes I miss stuff if you speak too fast."

"Then I'll talk nice and slow and write you a note when I don't want you to miss anything." He leaned against the woodpile and scribbled onto the paper. Peter stood there, awkward in the oversize shoes, waiting while the cold pierced him. Finally the cowboy handed the note over along with the flashlight.

It read: "You treat your momma meaner than an abscessed tooth. She may not win no mother-of-the-year contest, but she's trying."

Peter gave him a frank appraisal. "Tell me why should I give a shit what you think? Because you're screwing her?"

The cowboy rubbed his thumb across one of the split logs, then turned back to Peter's face, smiling. "You're a long-headed little mule."

Peter shrugged. "And you're an asshole."

He penned more words onto the pad. "If you think you can get away with a nasty mouth because God saw fit to take your hearing, think again."

Peter handed him back the pad.

Owen pocketed it, chipped loose a stick of wood from the icy pile, then spoke. "I'm not your dad. To tell you the truth, I wouldn't exactly be eager to adopt you. Your momma brightens my days, not that it's your business. You seem downright anxious to get into it with me. I'm no fighter. I left that nonsense behind me some time ago. But you keep talking trash about your mother, I swear I will be happy to haul in your neck and hobble both of them useless ears permanently."

Peter said, "Oh, write that down, would you? In the King's English for those of use who didn't grow up playing cowboys and Indians."

Owen the cowpoke laughed hard at that. "I think you got the

gist of it. Now hold out your arms. Let's see how much wood a little whiner like you can manage."

As if screwing the "Bonanza" extra in private wasn't enough for her, his mother had to go out with him as well. Day after day, snow or not, they went out to dinner, said they were going shopping, but he knew what that really meant. Oh, they always asked him to come along, but no way was he going to say yes and watch them make cow eyes at each other. They were probably regulars now, renting a room at the Easy-Eight, not even bothering to use fake names. While his mother painted trees and birds onto canvases, three endless days passed, slower than a gas leak. The paintings had all started to look the same to him. Perfectly accurate representations of the outside world, a place too cold to go to. Echo was about as tired of fetching the ball as he was of throwing it to her. He looked forward to going outside to get firewood, because even having to scrape away snow, get splinters in his glove, and snort away freezing snot as his nose ran, at least the woodpile was a change of scenery.

He wondered what Travis and Brian were up to. They had planned a ski trip a million years ago, when they were still friends. No biggie, just a couple of days someplace close—like Bear Mountain. Probably they'd gone without him. He wondered about Aunt Nori, too, why she hadn't come by—she practically lived in airports—it was unbelievable that his mom had no telephone, that her mailbox was enough of a hike you had to stop and rest on the way back. What if something happened to them out here in hooterville? He'd read all her back issues of *Redbook* and thought about trying the macadamia-nut cookie recipe he'd read about in the July "Let's Have a Backyard Luau" article, but the Blue Dog market probably never stocked anything more exotic than beer nuts. He was beyond sick of sitting around—he felt like he might explode before Christmas got here. When he had half-completed the old waterwheel jigsaw puzzle that had undoubtedly been left behind by God's grandchildren, he thought maybe he might get out the map and borrow the cowpoke's snowshoes and go off in search of Bonnie. Even rejection would be more interesting than finding the green edge pieces and the blue water shapes. He shoved the puzzle off the kitchen table back into its taped-up box. Maybe, in between her dates, his mother could find the time to drive him to Shiprock.

Around five she cleaned up her paintbrushes at the kitchen sink, then went upstairs. He knocked at the half-open door of her bedroom and saw she'd changed into a whole new outfit.

"Where are you going?"

"Dinner with Owen. We'd sure like it if you came along."

"Right."

She sighed. "Okay. There's frozen cheese pizza in the freezer. How does that sound?"

"How would I know? I can't *hear*."

She sighed again, rolled her eyes at him, and tried two different earrings against her lobes, a silver disc with a house and tree carved into it, and a long beaded green one that lay against her neck, drawing attention to its length and curve. "Which do you think goes better?"

"If you're trying to get Roy Rogers to slip you the tongue, why don't you just rub chewing tobacco behind your ears?"

She laughed. "That's pretty funny. But Owen doesn't indulge."

"Why not? I thought that was a cowboy requirement—Skoal can in the back pocket, lip full of chaw. Is he some kind of saint?"

She didn't answer.

Maybe, Peter thought, he had no time for it, since he was so busy indulging in something else—like his mother. She unhooked both earrings, set them on the dresser, and he looked at her, her hair tucked behind her ears. Next thing she'd probably start wearing miniskirts. Go with them to dinner—like they were going downtown to chew barbecued cow bones, this happy little "family," pretend they weren't groping each other under the table. She reached for the beaded green earrings, and just the thought of it, his mother's neck, that cowboy's mouth—he left the room and went downstairs.

When she joined him in the living room, he said, "The least you could have done was gotten a goddamn television set with closed captioning. What the fuck am I supposed to do here for three weeks? Learn macramé?"

She stopped at the closet door and turned to him. "That's up to you. I don't really need a TV, do I? Up until a week ago, you made it pretty clear you didn't want to see me or come here. If you're bored, you might try getting hold of that girl you have the crush on."

He walked across the room until they were standing elbow to elbow, the heat of the woodstove surrounding them. "How am I supposed to do that?" He was yelling now, just like his dad. Echo was trying to fit herself under the couch, her skinny back legs scrambling against the floor. "You don't even have a goddamn telephone! Am I supposed to send her a fucking smoke signal?"

She slapped his face. "Lower your voice. In case you've forgotten, I'm not the one who's deaf. And you might want to rethink that last little racist remark, considering your father's background, not to mention your friend Bonnie. Now, if you will excuse me, I have a date."

And after applying burgundy lipstick to her mouth, rolling the gold tube shut, and dropping it in her purse, she went out the front door, started up the Landcruiser, and was gone, leaving him absolutely alone, five hundred miles from anything remotely resembling civilization.

He hated himself for not being able to will the tears back inside. They slobbered over his cheeks, had him wiping snot on his pants, and breathing in hot, fist-size gasps. Nothing made sense. There were trucks filled with radioactive chemicals driving around looking for places to dump poison. Some woman, not even ten years older than he was, was about to make his dad a father. His mother wasn't even trying to hide what she was up to with the cowboy. Echo slunk across the floor until she was next to him and tentatively placed a paw on his leg. The old familiar gesture only made him cry harder. At once, she came into his lap, moving lightly, arching her neck until she could butt her head into his face, lick away the tears that just wouldn't stop. He put his arms around her. Not so long ago he could go to his room, turn on music to soothe away bad feelings, even something wanky like Morrissey would do it. Or go over to Harbor, swim a hundred laps to bleed out the panic, make himself so tired he could fall asleep. He couldn't hear. He didn't have a vocabulary for how much that hurt. Sometimes his hands throbbed from trying to explain.

His throat ached, and he realized that he had been crying so long and so loud that he'd torn it up good. Echo sighed against him, settling down in his lap. Against his cheek, her ears felt like warm velvet. Outside Blue Dog was white and forbidding, and in three days, like it or not, it would be Christmas.

13

To Maggie's eyes, downtown Blue Dog sparkled like the glitter on those Hallmark cards she'd loved as a kid. Tiny yellow-white twinkle lights and silver garlands festively transformed ordinary snowy street corners into a small-town magic that caused her to slow down her ingrained California Christmas-shopping pace so as not to miss a thing. Even the life-size statue of the red-and-white steer outside the Trough restaurant sported his own personal wreath, wound with red chili pepper lights, a crust of ice ridging his backbone. It was a bone-numbingly cold evening, but at least the snow had stopped blowing momentarily. People traversed the sidewalks in small groups, hurrying in their heavy coats, taking advantage of late shopping hours the stores offered in hopes of squeezing a few more holiday dollars from everyone's pockets. To keep the blood flowing, Maggie stamped her feet inside her Gore-Tex lined boots as she waited outside Rabbott's Hardware for Owen to finish with his customer. As soon as his break time arrived, they'd eat dinner. Looking forward to dinner was what was getting her through the days, made even longer by Peter's sulking. Through the plate-glass window, she could see Owen helping an old lady buy a wok. What Owen knew of the attributes of Chinese cookery was a mystery to Maggie, but he had the old lady squinting at its slop-ing black steel bowl with informed consumer awareness. After a few minutes Maggie watched him take the larger of the boxes to the register, where Minnie Youngcloud stood waiting to ring up the sale. Then he laid his work apron on the counter, held up his hand, the fingers spread wide—he'd be hers in five minutes. Using the few gestures he'd mastered, he signed, "Please wait," and that touched her. Here he was, working two jobs, being insulted by Peter on just about a daily basis, and still managing to find time to learn the basics of her son's language.

So much between them these days was left unsaid. By tacit agreement neither had brought up Thanksgiving, that horrible close to a wonderful time away. In the space of twenty-four hours Maggie had managed to remove her sister, and Nori drove off toward Albuquerque in her rented Rover. Maggie held firm, telling her, *Look, I moved for a reason. Don't call, don't write, and don't tell my son what to do.* Emotionless until the end, Nori'd hung in, yelling before she pulled out of the drive: *Did you ever stop to think maybe Peter loves me, too? We're related, Mag, and we're all the family we have left.* Just like her father—overwhelmed by one of Nori's many shenanigans—used to say: *You'll find no tears in that one.*

The morning after Nori left, Maggie had gone to Owen's. In the too-neat quiet of his room she discovered a note, indicating he'd taken a sudden trip out to the reservation. In town Big Lulu confirmed it. Yes, he said he was going off to help Verbena with her sheep, but when Maggie drove out to the reservation, Verbena hadn't seen him. It was winter—what could you do with sheep in the snow besides throw a little supplemental feed their way, and make sure nobody got caught on the fence? Then Joe Yazzi appeared at her door, shuffling uneasily, asking for a ride back to his place. In silence she drove him where he wanted to go. Mag-gie went to the barn every morning and evening, measuring out

four-inch-thick flakes of hay for Red, who came running as soon
as she approached, whinnying questions for which she had no
answer. She fed the sheep; she had watched Owen mark the
charts, slowly upping their grass-hay as more and more snow
covered the ground. While trying to court sleep, she listened for
the sound of his truck, his three-legged dog—anything—nervously straining her ears for a sound that didn't come.

Then one night, long after midnight, she woke to see him
standing next to her bed, a good start on a beard covering his
cheeks and chin. He'd put a finger to his lips, shushing her questions, undressed in the dark, and climbed in beside her. After the
shivering subsided, and he was thoroughly warmed in her arms,
he began to tell her with his body that nothing mattered more
than what they were doing right that moment. Maggie didn't
want to speak; sound would mar the physical sensations. Tears
filled her eyes. Relief rippled through her muscles. He seemed
never wiser than just then, taking her underneath him, opening
her legs with one sure hand. It made her ache with longing just to
remember, but behind the rush of pleasure, what he'd said about
the state trooper still haunted her. *It might be about me, Maggie.*
They would have to discuss what he meant. But not now. Not
while their bodies offered this quiet corner in which to forget. It
could wait. After Christmas, they'd have a big talk, clear up the
mysteries and start the new year fresh.

He shut the glass snow door and gave her a quick smile outside Rabbott's. "I'll testify to a warming trend. It must be at least
half a degree hotter than yesterday, although that could be due to
my present company." He appraised her from her Isotoner gloves
to her black overcoat, then whistled. "Hello there, pretty lady."

"Hi yourself." She clutched her shopping bag and smiled.
They were a pair of fools, weren't they, standing on Main Street
pretending they had no past, perfectly aware that same past
dogged their ankles like newly hatched fleas. "Are you hungry?"

"Always. I could put away a plate of your stew or forget eating altogether, kiss you till morning. It's your call."

"Given Peter's current emotional state, we're probably safer eating take-out burgers and thinking about renting an armor-plated hotel room."

"You know, the other night I almost felt sorry for the little pea-pecker."

"Sorry? How can you feel sympathy for him when he's practically choreographing his misery?"

"That kid doesn't know what to do with himself, and he sure won't take any advice from me, now that he's figured out what I'm doing with his momma."

"He's working hard to be the perfect little shit. When I think of how many tears I cried, wishing he'd come back home." She blew out the sigh that had been caught in her chest all day, huddled up next to the guilty memory of slapping her son.

"What is it they say? 'Be careful what you wish for?' "

She finished the sentence for him. ". . . For you may surely get it. And I did."

Owen took her free hand in his, and they set off walking toward the restaurant. "He's just yanking your chain, Maggie. He'll quit once it snaps back and smacks him upside his smart mouth."

She bristled at his word choice—why had she gone and hit Peter, something she'd never had to resort to before? "Never mind. I don't want to spoil your appetite talking about it. Let's just go pretend food will fix everything."

Inside the steakhouse Maggie told Owen she wanted the herb-and-rice chicken special, then let him order while she stared out the windows, which someone had needlessly sprayed with decorative flocking, creating swirls and banks of pretend snow. Shop owners did that in Southern California, romanticizing the element they never had to endure. Outside on the Blue Dog sidewalks, the real thing had been painstakingly shoveled away so people could pass. The storm had begun down in the Florida Panhandle, dumping snow in three- and four-foot amounts everywhere it went, leaving destruction in its wake. Already people had died from exposure, and she couldn't help being glad Joe had once again been talked into staying warm at Owen's, that in this weather he wasn't trying to heat that worn-out hogan. As soon as the blizzard started blowing in another direction, she'd made Owen take the Landcruiser and go check on Verbena. Verbena was doing just fine, thank you, no little snowfall was going to get the better of her, he said, describing the hot pink long underwear peeking out from beneath her Rams jacket. But the storm was serious; the governor was talking about calling in the National Guard if it didn't let up soon. In the Blue Dog library, she'd stopped looking through art books long enough to flip open a copy of the *Los Angeles Times*, its familiar front page there before her like an old friend. Some reporter had taken it upon himself to christen the storm "the Mother of All Blizzards," as if an act of nature was just one more thing to blame a mother for. But that kind of thinking didn't stop with newspapers. Yank your phone wires, and your sister would find a way to fax you nasty letters, like Nori had, straight to the only copy shop in town. They'd called Lulu Mantooth at the trading post, she'd told Minnie at Rabbott's, and eventually Owen had delivered her the news, so the whole town had probably read the fax before she had. *Just because you gave birth to him doesn't mean you can make me stop seeing Peter if he wants me to. . . . Morally, I have as much right to see him as his father. Damn it all, Mag, why are you being like this? Because of that one night I slept with Deeter? Give me a break! He wasn't even that memorable, if you want the ugly truth. . . .* Maggie'd crumpled it up, told the clerks to throw whatever she sent next away, just send her the bill and she'd pay it.

But silence, too, had its own punishment. Maybe she *should* buy Peter that television set for Christmas—closed captioning might even him out for a few hours, ease up the pressure he was foisting on her to be a type of mother that matched his ideal. If she had learned any truths since her husband had left her, one was that she didn't miss television and had managed to fill the space where racket used to blare into her life, insisting she respond, with a rich peacefulness, and from that serenity, somehow, she was painting again. But what kind of mother slapped her kid and tried to justify it? Here he'd gone through eight months of hell, watched his parents split up, lost his hearing, and she couldn't bring herself to locate a shred of sympathy.

"Maybe I should get us some counseling," she said aloud.

Owen dropped his fork, and it clattered against the ironstone plate. "What did I do?"

She smiled at his confusion. "Not us. Peter and me. A therapist. Somebody who understands teenagers. A professional."

He chuckled with relief. "Well, if there was such a thing, some old fool with a rule book, sooner or later I expect the teenagers would catch on and change everything, just to keep the deal tipped in their favor. You don't need a headshrinker, Maggie, but you do need to grit your teeth and hang on for the ride, because I'm telling you, it's only going to get rougher."

She twirled the greasy salt shaker under her fingers, sprinkling grains in an arc across the red tablecloth. "Well, that's happy news."

He took the salt shaker from her and set it back next to the pepper. "From where Sara Kay stood at thirteen, it must have looked like my leaving was directed at her. Until they're about fifty, kids think the universe rotates around them. You can't take that kind of logic personal."

"Why not?"

"Because it'll drive you to the nuthouse. Now go on and eat your dinner. I guarantee you, everything looks more manageable on a full belly."

She pushed the chicken around her plate with her fork tines.

He set aside his apple-stuffed pork chops and reached across the tablecloth for her hand. "You know, when you pout, you look so much like him I start looking for the extra pierced earrings. Of course, you've got nicer hair, and you're a little friendlier."

Under the table he nudged her knee with his own, that familiar warmth bringing her worrying to a halt. He was willing to wait, yes, but what was it that would keep, and how long would it even be there? With Joe camped out at Owen's and Peter's resentment crowding every room of the farmhouse, the only inevitabilities they could count on this Christmas were a set of equally frustrating unrelieved tensions: Peter's—God only knew when that would end—and their own, at having to sleep apart.

If his mother could justify dinner out every night with O-w-e-n, Peter thought, fine, screw the rules, and went through her desk. No love letters, no loose wads of bills, not even so much as a journal in which she recorded her whining. She was up to date with the gas and electric, boring, but Jim at Minuteman Copies in town sent her monthly statements for faxes, so maybe Nori was sending her messages, too, though he couldn't find any hard evidence to prove it. Behind the bills there was a brown envelope from the lawyers, and inside, legal papers. He took it over to the armchair and sat down. Echo jumped up in his lap, turned a circle, tamping down some distant primal memory of prairie grass, and made a nest out of his jeans, resting her head on a throw pillow.

So okay, here they were, the final papers. His dad didn't want to be married to his mother, he wanted to be married to the woman he'd knocked up. Those were the facts. He got her pregnant, and unlike a lot of people these days, they wanted to have the baby. He imagined seeing a picture of her. The baby would have to be a girl, wrapped in a pink blanket, looking like a humanoid burrito, as all newborn babies did. But this one would be his half-sister. Her eyes dark and wet, like the glass eyes on a stuffed animal. Her ears in perfect working order.

Dr. Kennedy, in their never-ending counseling sessions, was always on him to discuss the divorce, saying that his parents' splitting had "impacted" on him even before the deafness. Peter always answered this ridiculous inquiry the same way, "Just because two people can't hang on to their marriage doesn't mean I feel erased." Kennedy rolled in that like a dog in stink, as if his word choice revealed something swimming under the surface of this psychological swampwater. What did he expect from the son of a screenwriter? His father used to give him a hard time when he didn't try to amp up his vocabulary, as if words were right up there with breathing. Like a simple-minded cat, Kennedy chased

Peter's words all around the office, batting at them, trying to get them to roll over and show their bellies. Around them there were volumes of books on the child's mind, the trouble with adolescents, so many books on the subject of sex that Peter began to wonder if the people who wrote them weren't more obsessed than those who admitted to having a few problems and stupidly went looking for help.

There was a crappy handmade ceramic vase on the shelf between the two chairs Kennedy liked to sit in. It was glazed sloppily, so that big gray drips marred the design, which was a hand signing the letters *I, L,* and *Y* simultaneously, shorthand for "I love you." Peter wondered who on earth, deaf or hearing, could find something in Kennedy to love. His thinning black hair, which he grew long on one side and then gelled into an Elvis comb-over to fake nobody out? His hey-bob-a-rebob minibeard growing in the center of his feeble and otherwise hairless chin? He could just see Kennedy snapping his fingers to some Dizzy Gillespie riff while girls in sequined gowns waited for him to notice their cigarettes needed lighting. He often made references to the sixties, warbling about peace and community, Spaceship Earth. Such bullshit. That whole generation had their consciences wiped Windex-clean. His dad, starring in *Family Man*—the sequel; Kennedy, the ultimate brain-fuck; Owen the cowpoke poking his mother—your basic male role models, Pete, my boy.

He read the divorce papers for awhile, then got bored with the legalese and put it back in the desk. It was six-thirty, the time his mom usually had dinner on the table. His stomach in a knot, that frozen cheese pizza was the last thing he wanted.

The cowboy had left his snowshoes by the front door. Probably he was planning to sneak home after midnight and didn't want to fall down in the snow. Peter told Echo to stay, strapped them on, and went for an exploratory hike across the now-white pasture toward the barn and bunkhouse in the growing dark. He didn't really have a plan—he just needed to breathe air, no matter how cold. Lifting his feet carefully, he made his way across the pasture, leaving waffle-iron footprints. The red horse he'd seen the day he drove up was standing in one of the stalls, looking out hopefully at Peter's presence. Now Peter understood that the horse belonged to the cowboy. He unlatched the snowshoes and went over to say hello. It was a decent horse, friendly, with halfway intelligent eyes. Peter leaned across the stall door to scratch the horse's neck, burying his gloved fingers in the thick fur, pulled them back and sniffed his hand deeply—if only people smelled that good, nobody would ever need cologne.

He found a light switch and flipped it on. It looked like the cowboy was a neat freak. Except for his own footprints, the dirt was hardpacked and bare, even in the corners. Every tool and piece of equipment hung from a nail, and what was too heavy to hang was covered with burlap. Pulling one cloth away, he found a plain Western saddle straddling a sawhorse, cleaned and oiled, well kept, but none of the silver tooling he expected. Against the back wall there were bales of hay stacked like stairsteps ranging from one bale high to as tall as three. He climbed up and sat on the second tier, folding his arms across his chest, watching the horse worry the wooden stall door, thinking about the last time he'd sat on a hay bale. When people had the worst news to deliver, they liked to take you someplace natural—outside, down to the beach, to a park.

His father had that weatherbeaten kind of face that made him seem like a man who spent a lot of time outside, hiking, fly fishing, as if he would be as comfortable in this barn as he was in Hollywood. But Peter could count on one hand the times they'd done stuff like that, father and son. Sure, they made plans, and once or twice they'd actually gone on vacation, but when your dad carried a cellular phone in his jacket and had to pick up faxes at the front desk of the lodge before you bought bait, it kind of civilized the wilderness out of a camping trip.

The real reason he looked craggy was because he was one-fourth Cherokee Indian, the rest of him a blend of races—what he called mutt. He'd grown up in a small town outside McAlester, Oklahoma, and he still had relatives there, but when he talked about those people, it was like they were trash or something, embarrassing, and he only mentioned them when he wanted to make a negative point that illustrated his own point as correct. *Look at me. I brought myself up, Peter. I never had the nice things you have. You want to know what it was like living where I did? Fine, I'll tell you. Imagine wearing secondhand underwear, somebody else's piss stains in them. Or not to have a working toilet, or better yet to go to school every day, trying like hell to make something out of myself, only to have white kids throw me in with the Indians, or as they called them, goat ropers. There was no sailboat out in front of where I grew up. No new cars. . . .*

That kind of yap was the preamble to one of his "B" arguments; when "A," simple logic, failed, he brought out the heritage lecture. *What the hell is this D in algebra about? You need a tutor? You stupid, or what? People who shit on their education live second-class lives, Peter. Someday that D could be the one point that makes a difference between you getting into a name school or having to go to State. Look around you. Tell me you could be happy with less.* Which was pretty funny when Peter thought about it, because his father's leaving had made all of them live with less—all of them except his father.

They'd gone for the horseback ride the weekend he told him—like he didn't already know. They drove out to Coto de Caza, where his dad knew some people who owned horses, and they were going to take a ride, or so he said. But before they got on the horses, he took Peter over to the stacks of hay bales and said, *Sit down, let's talk for just a minute.* He knew what was coming next, long before the words "irreconcilable differences" and "someone else" had even formed on his lips. Travis's parents had split up when he was ten. Brian's mom was on marriage number four, to some guy who thought punching Brian in the stomach made a fun hobby. He really didn't know anyone whose parents had stayed together, so why should his own life be any different? He remembered the bright sunshine beating down on his shoulders, burning through his T-shirt, and that there was no shade anywhere. The horses switched their tails and shifted their feet like they couldn't hack it either. The smell of the hay, the scratchy feel of it against his jeans, his father's voice, trying so hard to be unemotional and sensible that it came out clipped, like when he tried to lie, and that his one "I'm sorry" sounded so fake it should have been laminated in plastic. Then, as they got on their horses—like taking the ride would somehow ease the bad news of divorce—how his father on the horse ahead of him, turned, and he noticed a stalk of hay stuck in his hair, his perfect haircut that was never too long or too short. That one piece of hay was all it took to undo the Italian suits, the power deals, the credits for every show he'd ever written. Of all his lectures and lessons, this unintentional one was the one Peter would always remember. The hay stalk stamped him with the single word he hated most, "Oklahoma," and nothing would ever erase that.

Joe Yazzi rapped on the metal door of the barn, and Peter felt the vibration twang against his back. He sat up quickly as the sliding door he'd slid through swung all the way open. "Who's there?" Joe held a teapot out, pointed to it, mimed drinking a cup of tea, and motioned for him to come inside the bunkhouse. Following the Indian into the rooms where the cowpoke lived was not first on his list of fun things to do, but neither was freezing to death in the barn. He cleared his throat and tried to make his voice come out normal, regular. "That's okay."

The Indian came back and gestured with the teapot. "Get your ass inside or I'm telling Owen you were out here messing with his horse," he said.

He couldn't speech-read everything the man said, but he could follow the few signs he'd used: *Go-to, Inside, Not-say-Owen*, and intrigued that he knew any of them, Peter followed.

Inside Joe signed and pointed to a deck of cards. "Sit down. You play?"

"A little." He watched him deal out cards, counting. Eleven for Peter, ten for the Indian, that meant gin rummy, one of his aunt Nori's favorite games. He picked up his hand and began sorting, found a run of three and discarded a jack of spades, keeping his points low in case Joe ginned early.

The Indian picked up the jack, smiled at it, and tucked it into his hand. He said something, but his face was half hidden by the cards and Peter missed it. Instead of asking him to repeat it, he pretended to be engrossed in his hand.

Four discards later, guessing that Joe hadn't done any more than partner the jack next to one dealt him, Peter went out for four.

The Indian threw his cards down, then signed, "Good."

Peter said, "Okay. Where did you learn that?"

"Signs? Owen showed me. We been practicing on each other from this book your mom gave us. I'm good. Owen tries, but he's an old white man. Can't hardly teach him nothing."

Peter shuffled the cards, feeling the wind they created as he snapped them together. "Owen didn't tell me that."

"Maybe he tried, and you didn't listen." Joe refilled his teacup. "You should come help us with the sheep in the mornings. Could use some help."

"Right. What do I know about sheep?"

Joe smiled and tipped his black hat back on his head. "You can learn."

"Maybe I don't want to learn."

Joe leaned forward and began tucking the discarded cards back into the deck. "Pretty Voice Tsosie and me go way back, all the way to Nam."

"Who?"

He wrote the name down on the tally pad, and Peter picked it up and read it. "Pretty Voice. Am I supposed to be impressed?"

Joe took the pad back and added to the name. "Pretty Voice's niece listens to everything he says. He tells her watch out for a certain boy, Bonnie minds."

Peter let the pad drop to the table. "Bonnie Tsosie? You know her?"

Joe smiled, and Peter watched as Joe finished his tea, cleaned out his thumbnail with a toothpick, then yawned. He was waiting for him to say more. When he did, it wasn't what Peter wanted to hear. "Just asking for some help with the animals. Lot of hard work, animals. Better get home now and sleep. Morning's coming up. Sheep eat early."

"How early?"

On the pad, Joe wrote a big block numeral 5.

Peter smacked the table with his hand. "Man, this is black-mail," he said, too loudly. "That sucks."

Joe smiled, the silver eyetooth glinting like tinsel, then put a finger to his lips and shushed him.

"Awful nice of you to get up early two days in a row and help me feed sheep," Owen said.

"My dog wakes up about five to take a leak. Figured as long as I'm up. . . ."

"Peter, I do believe the Christmas spirit has infected you."

"Spare me, okay?" He was wrecking his gloves picking up the withered moldering lettuce Owen told him to rip into chunks and toss in the trough, an old hot-water tank cut lengthwise, its sharp edges hammered over to a safe smoothness. The lettuce was slimy stuff, and it smelled no better than the rotting apples had. While he did the dirty work, the cowboy went over the sheep one by one, checking their hooves, grasping individual muzzles and taking a brief look at their teeth. Where in hell was Joe Yazzi, Navajo blackmailer? Probably still in bed. Probably had no intention of telling Bonnie's uncle anything. Merry flippin' Christmas.

Owen had made him core the apples and measure out grain and hay into a hanging scale in the barn. What was the point, if you were going to throw it into the trough? Owen said, with exaggerated slowness to each word, "These sheep look tough, but they're delicate creatures. Too many apple seeds is toxic. Too much grain, you go upsetting the rumen, nine times out of ten you get bloat. Don't pay to feed cheap hay, 'cause you just end up having to feed more. Good hay costs good money, and it's got to last, so we measure it."

Whatever the hell rumen was. When they were finished with the sheep, Owen let his horse out of the stall and showed Peter how to brush him. "He likes the feel of that old shedding blade. Teeth are pretty worn down. Have at it."

When Peter tried to prove his horse knowledge—two weeks of summer camp lessons on nags, his father's occasional rides— by attempting to pick the horse's feet clean, Owen yanked him away by the shoulder so hard he could hear his vertebra crackle.

"Fuck you!" Peter cried out.

"Nice mouth you got on the Lord's birthday," Owen said, catching him by the wrist. "Here I was trying to save your miserable little life. Red's sensitive about his feet. He'll pretty much kick anyone in the head, given the opportunity."

He took down hobbles from the barn wall and tied one of the horse's rear legs up. "Don't want to spoil your momma's Christmas with a trip to the hospital, getting a horseshoe removed from your forehead. Now you can pick his dainty hooves to your heart's content."

When his red face had quit burning, and the shame of trying to impress Owen had somewhat dissipated, Peter looked out at the sheep and said, "It's disgusting."

"Them sorry sheep of mine?"

"No. That people eat them."

"Son, you can't look at everything so hard. They're here for a for a purpose."

"Right, going into people's guts, coming out shit. Nobody needs meat to survive."

"Maybe so, but some choose to, and that's one way I make my living."

"It's wrong."

"You can't expect the world to change its mind since you got mad." Owen pointed to the old Merino. "Ruby's my charity case. Her I'll be sad to see go. She and I have covered some trail."

"What about your horse? Would you sell him, too, if someone offered you a bunch of money? Let them turn him into dog food?"

He shook his head and breathed out a sigh that showed steam-white in the cold air. "No way. Likely I'd take a bullet for

Red. He's too good a horse to ever let go. We'll be together until one of us forgets to take a breath, won't we, boy?" He reached up and scratched the horse's neck. "If something ever happened and I couldn't take him along, I'd find a way to come back for him, no matter how long it might take. I love that horse."

Peter said, "Really?"

Owen nodded.

"Then maybe you should think about your sheep the same way. They don't deserve to be anybody's dinner either."

"Must get that stubborn streak from your momma. Let me bridle Red and you can ride him around the barn a few times."

"No. Thanks anyway." One of the reasons he didn't want to was because Red reminded him of the horse he'd ridden with his father.

"Go on. It's Christmas. Give Red a thrill."

The other reason was that he didn't want to fall. Since he'd lost his hearing, heights scared him, even just that few feet up on horseback seemed unmanageable.

"You scared?"

"Do I *look* scared?"

"If you're scared, I won't make you."

"Jesus! I said I wasn't scared."

"Then give me your foot, and we'll get you aboard."

Whatever happens, please don't let me fall and have to be rescued by the cowboy, Peter prayed. But beneath him the horse was gentle and solid. From his back everything about the property looked different. The white two-story house where his mother lay sleeping seemed to rise up out of the ground warm and sturdy, something the wind could howl at but never penetrate. The thick-trunked bare trees down by the Animas made a kind of black lace framing the farm way across the river. The dingy sheep were full of energy after their feeding, spazzing around, snow and icicles strung from their heavy wool. Between his thighs Peter could feel the warmth of the horse, the collected muscle waiting there, just aching for permission to run but well-mannered enough to wait to be asked. Before Mexico he might have tried it. Just smacked his heels against the horse and hung on, gone for it, whatever happened, whether he fell, cracked his head open, or somehow managed to stay aboard. That was before he believed in consequences. Now he was too scared to do anything but walk.

Owen let him get down off Red by himself, take off the saddle and bridle and hang them up. When Peter had groomed the horse, wiped his gloves on his jeans, and fed him two carrots, Owen said, "You handled him kindly. If you want to ride him again, you have my okay."

Peter didn't know what to say. Just the fact that he hadn't said anything about how scared he was or held the hoof-picking attempt against him seemed surprising. He tugged Owen's jacket sleeve and signed, "Thanks."

Owen signed back, "You're welcome. Pete, go clang a pot lid inside my bunkhouse. Get Joe up out of that bedroll. That lazy 'skin can at least help us cook breakfast."

Peter used an old baling hook and the lid to a twenty-five-pound tin of equine Stride. Maybe he couldn't hear, but from the cranky look on Joe's face, *he* sure could.

⌐14⌐

TOO EARLY ON CHRISTMAS DAY, MAGGIE WOKE TO THE SOUND of Echo's yipping. She had slept fitfully, pestered by the kind of dreaming that kept her so busy she woke expecting to receive a paycheck for the last eight hours. Still drowsy, she splashed her face with cold water under the faucet. Downstairs she could hear voices—Joe Yazzi's deep baritone and Peter's odd tone shifts, which meant he was trying to carry on his end of the conversation by reading lips and answering without using sign. It was a dangerous practice that "led to the newly deaf being ostracized," or so said the school's brochure on immersion. They would not approve. She heard chairs scrape across the pine floor. The smell of frying bacon tickled her nose and made her stomach growl with hunger. She pulled on her wrap, a heavy white terrycloth men's robe from the JC Penney's in Farmington, toed blindly into her slippers, and made her way downstairs.

"The sun isn't even all the way up. What time is it?" She looked at the men in her kitchen: Joe with his boots propped on the woodbox; Peter, dressed in black sweats, peeling an orange by the sink. Echo was mad for oranges—just stood there yipping and drooling until Owen, who was at the stove, finally turned, threw a dish towel at Peter, and said, "Son, have mercy. Give the hound a slice."

Peter, smiling at his dog's antics, nodded his fist yes and let a segment fall. The dog growled over her orange as if it were her first kill. Hopeful, unimpressed, lay with closed eyes near Owen, all three legs stretched toward the stove as he soaked up the heat. Joe was buttering a stack of toast and had three kinds of jelly lined up beside him. It was a montage of homey comfortability she might have expected in an English novel, everyone cordial owing to the holiday before them. When had they formed this brotherhood? When women's bridges formed, they were structures spanning childbirth, marriage, and shared agony. With men, who could tell? Sometimes they had to batter each other into a bloody mess or tear up all their muscles moving an object that didn't want to be moved. Their bonds were sweat, endurance, and heft. For that matter women's weren't so different, possibly a little more complex and—thinking of her sister, she was certain—more painfully broken. With a sharp pang in her throat, she wondered where Nori was spending her Christmas. In what five-star hotel she was staying the night at the corporate rate, and which first-run movie she was paying to watch on cable to waste enough time so that the holiday would pass and she could go back to where she was most comfortable—work. Here, in Maggie's rented kitchen, her private domain, things had changed. Somehow, overnight, in a way that left her standing outside the circle, these men before her had become friends.

"Are we going to do the present thing?" she said, and the men looked at her, surprised to see her still there.

"Later," Owen said as he handed her a mug of coffee. "Drink up," he said. "And you might as well turn loose of this day. From bacon to bird, we're handling it."

"Nice robe," Peter signed. "Big improvement."

She knew he was referring to her last year's Mother's Day gift—a silk robe covered with bowling-ball-size tulips—something Ray had undoubtedly had one of his secretaries pick up on Melrose during her lunch hour. Last thing she'd used it for before throwing it in the trash was waxing the car. "At least I don't have to fight Liberace for this one."

Owen looked at her, puzzled. "Excuse me?"

How could you explain private jokes from a life that happened an ice age ago? "Nothing. Well, if I can't do anything here, I guess I'll go take a long soak in the tub."

Owen was busy lifting bacon with his spatula from the pan to the waiting plate. When she left the room, no one seemed to notice.

Breakfast finished, Joe and Owen ducked out, leaving mother and son alone to the business of exchanging gifts. Maggie watched as Peter began to work the tape free from the corners of his first Christmas present. His father had sent it FedEx, in care of the trading post, and Big Lulu had set it aside for Maggie with a loaf of homemade banana bread. "Take this, too, for your skinny son," Lulu said as she handed Maggie the bread. "Don't worry. Keep feeding them and eventually they grow up."

It was not the Ralph Lauren shirt she figured his new love would send—a nice, neutral, stepmotherish gift. It was too heavy for that. Sadly she saw it was as she expected, the script to the film he was shooting. Peter's face said it all as he turned over the cardstock cover.

Maggie leaned over and looked at the note Ray'd written on the first page: "Pete, this is what kept me preoccupied the last three years—hope you like it. Hang on to it—might be a collector's item someday."

She had decided at the last minute to give him the first painting she'd done, the one of Shiprock. No, it wasn't her best work, in fact, the dimensions were slightly goofy from the tension of her early efforts. But standing in the room surveying her choices, somehow this initial, risky painting, with all its flaws, seemed the right choice. Now, with Raymond's script in his hands, she felt her self-absorbed idea of what a fifteen-year-old might treasure was equally as large a blunder as her ex-husband's. Maybe Peter wasn't interested in what it had taken for her to pick up the brush and didn't give a damn what trying had done for her. Why should he be? He would never hear the whistling of wind against his ears the way she had, feel the sleepy hum as it curved around Shiprock, luring her into staying until it was dark, and she was painting on blind instinct, unable to stop her hand. Given her many disappointing features as a mother, he might turn both his parents' presents to the wall or give them away.

He said one word about his father's manuscript, "Cool."

She didn't think his heart was entirely in it. The script set aside, he now tore away the tissue paper covering the painting and she watched his face grow fierce, deliberately unemotional. He studied every corner, looked away, then signed, "This is good. Thanks," with a rough wave of his right hand.

She signed back, "You're welcome," and heard a car door slam shut outside. Had Owen and Joe driven the truck around, rather than walk? It was cold out there. She didn't blame them if they had, but was surprised to hear them this early. She waited for the knock at the door; Owen always knocked. But the door opened with no announcement, and she followed the barking Echo toward it.

Nori wore a duster-length olive green silk coat. Her red boots were mottled with snow and grime. She balanced several packages in her arms. Her smile wobbled back and forth from the usual sizing up of the situation to what-in-holy-hell-am-I-doing-here? "Don't worry," she said. "I'm not going to stay and wreck your Christmas. I just came to drop these off."

But Maggie could see she was hoping to be asked, hoping for forgiveness on this day hard to live through alone. "Merry Christmas, Nori," she said evenly.

"Same to you."

"Did you have a long drive?"

"Not really. Flew into Albuquerque. I've been staying at the Holiday Inn a couple of days, over in Farmington. Trying to gather my courage."

Maggie smiled. She looked beyond her sister to see a white Taurus parked in the drive. "That's a different car for you. Scaling down?"

"I was afraid if I rented the usual, you'd see me coming, move again or something."

With a casual elegance, Nori possessed all the trappings of a successful life—the wardrobe, the undoubtedly costly gifts lurking inside the spangled paper. Yet standing there in the doorway, she looked as starved as a deer forced to peel bark from winter trees. *Maggie's farm*, she had once kidded her sister, what seemed like a lifetime ago, when they had sat on the bayside patio confessing their dreams, what they would do if they could start their lives over. *I'd go back to school and get my goddamn Ph.D.,* Nori had said. *I'd do research, juggle numbers and chemistry, never put on another goddamn business suit or pair of high heels as long as I drew breath.* Maggie said, *I'd go live in that town where the weavers are. Rent some big old house, keep horses, try to remember how to paint.*

"Maggie's farm" indeed. The only horse lived next door and wasn't for sale. The painting was admittedly weak. Nori was only out of the business suit temporarily, and it had been a time long ago when both set aside their differences to log in interminable hours at Peter's hospital bed. Between the two of them, it seemed like their collective faith would be enough to bring Peter back whole. But the way it turned out, large pieces had been sacrificed: Peter's hearing, only the most obvious loss. On the night of his birthday party, when Ray was being such an unreasonable shit about who owned the sailboat, and Peter made his announcement about wanting to go to Riverwall, Maggie had been too shocked to blame anyone except herself. Sleeping with Deeter was an idea she'd come to on her own, some kind of temporary salve to rub over the raw skin. To discover her sister had thought of it first, and gone ahead and acted on her idea with no more thought to it than to which color socks she'd chosen, started a crack between them that widened and had led to this chasm between them now in the foyer. Inside it there was a lifetime's worth of sisterly resentment, and right now all of it seemed about as petty as arguing over borrowed clothes and hair curlers.

The dog was leaping in joy. Peter was coming to see what was happening, and this was the present he would like best of all. "Nori," Maggie said in a hoarse voice. "Come in. Let me take your coat and get you something hot to drink."

15

H EY, PRETTY LADY," JOE YAZZI CALLED TO MAGGIE AS HE CAME in the back door of the farmhouse, lugging an armload of wood for the stove. Joe set the wood down. "What Christ-man presents you get?"

Hands deep into the flour bag, she turned and said, "Hey yourself."

"Any perfume? Women sure like that good-smelling water. New teapot, maybe? You could use a new one of those. Your old one's got cracks in it. Do okay for heating water, but try and make good teas in, I tell you, the medicine finds them cracks and hides."

"Really?"

"It's true. Maybe if you ask nice, Owen will bring you one from the hardware. Rabbott's got 'em to spare. Blue, yellow, red, black, they got plenty of the teapot, just not enough customers. Everytime I go in, people standing around, talking, talking, never can say enough, just keep on talking."

Owen, two steps behind Joe, shook off the snow and

unloaded his armload of wood. "The idea is to *sell* teapots and make a profit, Joe, not give them away."

"What's Dave Rabbott need profit for? He got a nice house and two big smelly cars. He should learn to share if he don't want to piss off the powers. Get himself thrown from his horse in Blue Dog rodeo. Worse, maybe."

Maggie, who was now rolling out dough at the counter, said, "I'll see what I can do about that new teapot, Joe. How about you? Santa find his way to your tree?"

The Indian pinched off a piece of biscuit dough and rolled it between his fingers before popping it into his mouth. "The People don't hold with killing a tree in the name of poor dead Jesus, no matter how great whites say he was. We need all the trees we can get in Blue Dog. Come March the wind here'll show you what I mean." He held out his left wrist to Maggie. On it was strapped a massive gold watch with a silver-and-gold band. He wiggled it. "What you think?"

"That's some timepiece."

"Ah, really just an old Foolex I traded some hay for, but come summer, it'll impress tourist women. My best part of this Christmas thing is supper." He patted his stomach, muscled and flat. "I been saving up room awhile now."

"Well, good. I like watching you eat."

"I could come over and enjoy it again tomorrow."

She laughed. "Any time, Joe."

Owen saw Peter sign for his mother's attention. "After dinner, Joe's taking me to Shiprock."

She signed back, "It's Christmas. I want you here."

"But. . . the reservation. . . kids don't get Christmas. . . ."

Owen was getting better at figuring out signs, but that finger-spelling business had him counting his alphabet in his head. Maggie usually spoke and signed simultaneously, which was both a lesson and an ease. Peter, however, was more selective. If he wanted an audience, he would let rip with that funny fluting voice of his, which grew higher in pitch the angrier he became; anger seemed to be about nine-tenths of this young fellow's marrow. He knew why the boy wanted out, and it sure wasn't to take canned goods to any Christmas-poor Indians. He wanted to see that Bonnie Tsosie, with as many miles between himself and his mother as possible, and at age fifteen, why not, more power to him.

But before Maggie could rebut Peter's last good reason for bailing out on Christmas, here came sister Nori into the kitchen, trailing store-bought fragrance. She was one surprise Owen hadn't counted on. He thought he'd seen the last of her Thanksgiving Day, when Maggie all but chased her out with a broom, but apparently she was no more of a quitter than her sister. Thank the Lord, this time she wasn't toting a state trooper. She wore skintight pants the color of sun-turned hay. If you looked at them quick, it almost seemed like she wasn't wearing pants at all, just soft gold summer skin up and down those endless legs. Owen hadn't imagined there could be any more leg to a woman than Maggie Yearwood. But here before him was another one with a thirty-six-inch inseam. Three feet of legs and sister to Maggie, the woman he slept with. Lord God, help me stop thinking with my equipment and use the good brain you gave me for something besides skull insulation.

When Joe saw Nori, he took off his hat. "Sha! Must be of one them Christmas angels. I shouldn't of made that remark about your Jesus."

"Joe, Nori's my little sister," Maggie said.

"Little?" Joe echoed. "She's taller by a good six inches."

"It only seems that way. *Younger* sister," Maggie clarified. "By eight years."

Nori smiled, hugging her arm around Peter, who beamed with attention.

And close up, taking a good long look at her, Owen thought, What sane man wouldn't beam with serious candlepower? While Joe shook her hand and smiled, Owen forced his deliberations to stay pleasant and polite and tried to banish from his mind the notion of how widely spaced breasts like hers could fill up empty hands. It wasn't working too good. He blindly chugged after his train of thought, which at any moment seemed likely to derail off the side of the nearest mountain, just like the narrow-gauge Cumbres and Toltec out of Chama always felt like it might. Where Maggie was long-term good to be with, her sense of humor the kind of comfort he looked forward to after a good day or a hard day, either one, this sister of hers offered an entirely different experience. She might have been eight years younger, but he sure couldn't find proof of that anywhere in the hazel, cat-quick eyes. Maggie's were blue, quicker to take in the softer side of life. Sister Nori's had charted harsh sights and recorded every one of them right in her tough little heart.

Joe smiled broadly, showing off his silver tooth. "Say, Younger Sister, you like my fine new watch?"

Nori stared back at him, unimpressed by both his words and his dental work. "I think I can tell what time it is."

Joe took another tack. "You got one of them inner clocks, do you? Lucky duck. Never have to set an alarm."

"Well, I don't know about that, but I can usually tell when someone's giving me the time of day."

Joe laughed, and Maggie turned away, greasing up her baking pans, putting her elbow muscle into the chore.

Owen watched her, curious. She was moving about the kitchen in her "efficiency mode," stacking little rounds of dough for what his own momma used to call Parker House rolls. All this food! She had two pies ready to go into the oven, in addition to the already-baked peach cobbler she knew he favored. When Maggie started in cooking like that, as if she were expecting the governor for supper, it meant she was trying hard to work out in kitchen pots and pans whatever was troubling her in the world outside. This sister of hers looked like she had never owned a fry-pan of her own long enough to figure out you were supposed to take it down off the wall now and again to burn dinner. Maybe that was the sore point with her sister, some twenty-year feud over who did the dishes.

Peter was watching the whole scenario closely, maybe hoping his mother might cave in and let him go with Joe just to simplify the equation. But Owen could see that another part of Peter, the cautious side, was worried, like he'd been on Red, afraid that at any moment this quiet holiday might spontaneously combust, like hay could if it got baled up while it was too damp in the middle. And by the look on his face, Owen figured if it wouldn't come as that big of a surprise to Peter if and when it did.

But Maggie was all smiles, a fierce grin that had all the men a little cowed and both dogs seeking a quiet corner. "Dinner," she said, wielding an oversize fork and lengthy knife intended for the turkey, "in case anyone's interested."

No one hesitated; they found places at the table, pulled out chairs, sat ready to eat. Everyone bent their heads while Owen said the blessing, the same one he silently said to himself every time he sat down with people he cared about to share a meal. "Thank you for the opportunity to fill my undeserving belly in the company of these good friends." And though he and Joe had done the hard work of roasting the turkey, peeling the potatoes, heating up the gravy; at the thought of Maggie's desserts and the flaky rolls, he felt all raw nerves and the usual dollop of male guilt endured whenever a woman went all out in the holiday *cocina*. He hoped it was enough of a blessing to cover them all.

His mind wasn't on holidays, prayers, or even Nori's legs any longer, it was on Maggie's reaction to the present he hadn't yet gathered his nerve to give her. Verbena had helped him find it, had taken him over to the trading post and forced the backroom keys from Benny's fist. Together they sneezed through the dust, tried to decipher the yellowed pawn tickets that had faded to scribbles as they bypassed pots and turquoise trade necklaces in search of rugs. Something about the weavings moved Maggie in a way that made them more to her than simply rugs. The first night they went out to Blue Dog Days, he'd seen the way she looked at them, how she knew the patterns and the wool types right off, and concluded that she had studied the books hard because the real thing wasn't an option. He couldn't afford much, and wished he'd gotten lucky at the Blue Dog auction, but he had saved seventy dollars out of the money he'd gotten selling lambs. With Benny's prices, it didn't look like it would go far. "I want something she won't get tired of looking at," he said as they flipped through rugs too worn for Benny to sell up front, yet not old enough to qualify as "museum pieces" and therefore fetch ungodly sums for their charming disrepair.

"Then you ought to give her something more than rug," Verbena said. "Like jewelry."

He sighed. "This ain't about romance, Verbena. It's just about one rug. Can't afford nothing else, not this Christmas."

"Not all presents have to cost arm and leg," Verbena countered.

"Is that so?"

"Yes. Some say best things in life are free."

"You read that off some cereal box, or is this the wisdom of talk-show radio?"

"Don't smart-mouth me, Owen Garrett."

"That's not my aim. It just raises my hackles when people hand you little sayings, like you're not right in the head."

"Don't take a wise man to know what I know. You should be able to come up with more clever present than shabby rug."

"Verbena, honey, she likes rugs. Can't we just settle on one and be done with it?"

"For smart white man, sometimes you awful stupid. Your life is work in the hardware store, sell a few head of sheep, rest of the time maybe sit and read book? Hah. You're as knotted up as any of them others got that nonsense dangling between legs. They lead you in circles, built-in stupid compass."

"I give up. You win. Where's your inkblots, Doc? Let me take a look, try and find my poor old momma in one."

She smiled. "Suddenly you roll over like a dog and show me your belly. I wonder why?"

"Maybe it means I want your help picking a rug before summer."

"Well, don't get nervous." Verbena's careworn hand flipped corners back, checking to see which rugs' patterns were mirrored on the backside. Those that didn't go to the trouble she *tsk*ed at and gave no further inspection. She sat back on her heels in the storeroom and sighed. "Owen Garrett, you already in deep, up to your heart's bones."

For the first time in a long while, he wished he had a cigarette, a drink, something to do with his mouth besides fumble an answer.

"Trouble is, we're looking in wrong pile. What we want is something not so much regular pattern," she went on. "I think only thing your Maggie never grow tired of looking at be your ugly white face. But you say a rug for her, so I say best look for pictorial. Benny Mota!" she called out, and the stocky Texan stuck his head around the corner.

"I am not giving you the keys to the goddamn museum rugs, Mrs. Youngcloud."

"I don't want smelly old rugs you found on some old rancher's porch and now you're trying to sell as valuable antique. You might get rich on money now, but big punishment in your future. Mark my words. Where you keep them old pictorials, Benny?"

"What on God's earth you want with those old rags? They're fire damaged from hogan smoke. I can't give them orphans away."

"Maybe I'm looking for some cleaning cloths."

He set his face slyly. "Maybe you know something I don't yet. Like suddenly this kind of rug is getting hot with collectors."

Verbena put her fists on her hips. "Come on, Owen. Let's drive to Farmington. Blue Dog ain't only place to find a rug."

Benny stepped between them and the doorway. "Verbena, sweetie, don't be giving me the evil eye. And for God's sake, don't you go showing your face in Farmington. You're my best weaver, darlin'. Pictorials're over there in the chest under the Airwick Solid. Take your pick."

Owen lifted the lid and Verbena happily dug in. She spent awhile studying a Tree of Life design with different-colored birds sitting on each branch. The background was a harsh limeade green, but the weaving was handsome, detailed down to pinfeathers. "How about that one?" he said. "She likes birds well enough. I've seen her paint pictures of them."

Verbena shook her head. "Puke green wool? Plus sloppy knots here, no spirit trail. Bad luck. You always got to leave exit. No wonder this rug ended up in white man's cedar chest. Probably cause of Benny's piles, may their tribes increase."

Her hands went next to some gray pillow-size weavings, portraits you could just about base a timeline on. A fifties era Indian chief's face in profile, the stereotypical headdress sporting a trail of carefully stitched feathers, each outlined in black. Beneath him there were some Mickey Mouses, with their fat white button gloves and perpetually cheery smiles. "Sometimes," Verbena said, her voice low and slightly weary, "we just do it for money."

He got up from his crouch and went to stand by the wall of pawn saddles. Their three-month tickets sported so many renewals they looked like kite tails. It would be hard to give up a saddle you loved. Nothing worse than riding an ill-fitting one, or having to go long distance bareback, like he had, leaving Durango. His knees creaked and he felt older than Old Man Time himself. Somewhere between the years of fifty-one and fifty-two, it seemed like the aging process had sped up in a deliberate race. The box, where every man eventually came to rest, toes up, in a cheap suit and clean underwear, had looked as misty as oasis water for years, maybe even decades. Now every sharp corner and handhold for the pallbearers to grip was clearly in view. So I grow old in this bunkhouse, he had told himself when he first settled in at Blue Dog. Say I die in this bed one night, or get myself kicked good by some bad-tempered livestock and I lie in the snow until I lose enough blood to slip away. No one'll waste much hanky over Owen Garrett's passing. He had believed that. But when Maggie Yearwood moved in, with her funny dog and the itch to paint everything from apple trees to prairie weeds, suddenly every ticking second of every minute seemed as precious to Owen as hard rain after a season of drought—you hustled your fanny setting out barrels, old coffee cans; moved seedlings into the stream. Finally, you stood there open-mouthed, trying to catch every drop.

"Now we're talking," Verbena whispered, holding up a three-by-five pictorial on a beige-and-gray background. "This here's promising. But don't you go offering Mr. Benny more than twenty-five dollar. He'll try and find way to change your mind, he will, and he's no better than horse's backside for missing what in this here box so long."

And then the wide Navajo woman who was a better friend to him than his own daughter turned to show him what she had discovered in Benny's trash/treasure chest. As rugs went he knew this one was special, not because of who'd done the work, but because of the care with which she'd done it—the sawtooth border, executed in three colors, not two. Owen's breath seemed to forsake him, yanked up out of his hardworking lungs, leaving him scratching his head in wonder.

Verbena's face peered over the top of the rug, grinning. "Told you I find right one," she said smugly. "Red horse and man planting seeds for future. I think things Maggie likes to look at. What you think?"

Viewing the weaving, he thought that women had to be God's most mysterious creation, their ways of knowing seemed so close to infinite. Furthermore, if they were after electing a queen to foster them along in these somewhat disquieting ways, Verbena Youngcloud would wear her crown and reign with a wicked good humor. "That's a good one," he said. "Think Benny'll want more than seventy for it?"

Verbena laughed, thrilled to be getting ready to deal with the dealer.

What could have cost Owen a hundred dollars or more ended up taking his wallet down only twenty, plus she got Benny to gift wrap the rug and throw in some sage smudge sticks tied in a bright red string to decorate the package for absolutely nothing.

"Going to reservation for cocoa and some visiting," Joe Yazzi explained when the table was cleared and everyone's belly was full. "Got our own kind of Christmas party deal. Peter's friend from school asked after him. Thought we maybe stay over at Verbena's if the roads are bad. That would be okay by you, right,

Maggie? Wouldn't want us screeching tires over dangerous ice. You could take a hot bath in them herbs I made. Visit with the tall sister. Then take a good long Christmas nap."

Nori, who had stood quietly by while the negotiations were ongoing, spoke up. "Actually, Joe, I'd like to tag along. I've been to Europe and Australia, but never to a reservation Christmas party. I can keep an eye on Peter if Maggie's worried. Nobody better than an overprotective aunt for a chaperon."

"Well, better ask." Joe looked to Maggie.

Nori finished stacking the plates. "I don't want to be in anybody's way."

Owen saw Maggie frown at those words and wondered, Now what? Let her go, he wanted to say, let them all go and give us two minutes alone, but it wasn't his place to say anything, so he held his tongue.

Joe said, "I got Owen's big old pickup. Plenty of room. One more always makes a party better. But it's cold out there, and they don't got much wood for heating. You might want to get different shoes or something."

Nori stuck out one well-tooled toe. "What's wrong with these boots?"

"Fine boots like them, you'll spoil 'em in snow."

"I don't care."

Nori continued to look at her sister, and to Owen it seemed like everyone in this kitchen, including the two dogs, anxious for scraps, was waiting for a kind of permission only Maggie could deliver.

Clearly she yet hadn't made up her mind. Peter was the reason. Owen signed to him behind his back, "Get firewood." Peter rushed out, then returned, carrying out an armful to add to the Youngcloud Christmas package. "I though Mrs. Youngcloud might appreciate some wood," he said aloud to no one in particular. Then he left the room to join Nori and Joe.

Maggie stood at the sink scrubbing hard at her roasting pan. If it had been Owen's choice, he would've let the dogs work on it awhile, soaked it overnight in hot water, cleaned it in the morning when the scrubbing would go easier. No task on earth was built to defeat this single-minded Yearwood woman. Her pretty hair was kinky from the steamy dishwater, her face flushed with effort.

She wrung out her sponge and set it on the counter. "Owen, why do I get the feeling I'm being set up?"

"Don't know what you mean."

"Oh, I think you do. Everybody's clearing out at just the right moment—like they spent all afternoon rehearsing."

"I can't speak for your boy or your sister, but I spent my afternoon playing gin and losing ten bucks to Mr. Foolex."

"Then maybe Joe orchestrated it."

"Well, maybe that's his present to you. Is it really going to tie a knot in your Christmas if your boy goes off to see that girl he likes so much he can't even say her name to you?"

"No, it's just—"

"Just what? That you're scared to let him go and find out he doesn't need you—or don't you want to be alone with me?"

He went to her, stood behind her at the sink, and pressed himself into her back, closing his arms around her. The front of her pretty green holiday blouse was damp with dishwater. He palmed the hair away from her neck and kissed her there, whispering, "It's been awhile. I want to be with you."

She sighed and nodded her head. He shot a thumbs-up sign to where Peter stood, just outside the doorway, and heard his small ebullient whoop in celebration.

When Nori was off finding her coat and Peter was loading the truck with the last of the wood, Joe returned to the kitchen. "Ain't so bad," he said, "you two being alone on Christmas. You could think about that poor dead Jesus, pray for his spirit. Fix him plate of turkey, throw him some tobacco."

Maggie gave him a look. "All right, Joe! Go. Take Peter, take Nori, take the tree and the lights. But I'd better see all of you tomorrow before lunch, right?"

He nodded. "Oh yeah, sure. No problem."

"Take Mrs. Youngcloud this package of leftovers, too. Otherwise we'll be eating turkey until March. And wish her happy holidays for me."

"Anything else?"

She wiped her hands on a towel and flicked her thumbnail at a stubborn spot on the roasting pan. "Look after my boy, Joe. For all his tough looks and the earrings. . . he's still pretty raw."

"Maggie, anybody mess with Pete, they answer to Joe."

"Thanks."

Joe took her hand and one of Owen's, squeezed them gently. "Dead white man's birthday or not, it was some great feast."

When he was gone, Maggie untied the dish towel from her waist and folded it, tucking it over the handle of the oven door. She let out a big sigh and stretched her arms, then hugged herself, fingering away the curtain from the kitchen window. Owen watched her looking hard out that window, as if instead of steamy glass reflecting her uncertain face, and his behind hers, she would see clear over to Shiprock, follow her boy, that sister who drove her so crazy, and Joe at the wheel, traveling the icy road safely.

"I got you a present," Owen said, trying to take her mind off Peter. "It's nothing much, and I don't want you to feel like you got to give me anything in return. This dinner and sharing your family has been present enough."

She turned to him. "You shouldn't have."

He pulled the package from his jacket. The plain brown wrap and smudge sticks made it look like ordinary mail. Not festive, like a proper Christmas present. Ghosts of past Christmases came rearing up in his consciousness like rank horses: all the bright, patterned paper and shiny bows, store-bought toys for Sara Kay, things that broke before she got tired of them, wore out costly batteries. Everything you wanted in life generally disappointed. Had that many of those days ended in tears? He remembered the year he got Sara her first saddle, cheap suede, but she didn't know the difference. The smell of new leather permeating everything. Bayberry candles. Candy canes and Sheila's unfortunate yearly attempt at rum cake he pretended to eat but later fed to the dog.

Maggie was holding on to the package, smoothing the red twine in her fingers. Tears ran down her cheeks as quiet as the beginning of spring snowmelt. Was Nori really the taller of these two? "What's the problem? Joe thinks the world of you. If he gave his promise, you can bet he won't let the boy out of his sight."

She sat down at the kitchen table. "Oh, Owen, there's no problem. No problem at all. Peter'll do whatever he's going to do." She cleared her throat. "When I was a girl, I read too many books. I kept waiting for some boy to come along and treat me with concern, as if I was worth that. What I got was this great-looking man who just couldn't seem to keep his zipper zipped up whenever a pretty woman walked by. Will you tell me why it takes until you're over forty to find your way past the bedsheets? To see what it's really about? How come you have to be old and scarred up before you get wise?"

"You're a long way from old, and I'm friendly with your scars." He shifted his weight from his left boot to the right. "I don't know. I guess for human beings we're pretty slow on the uptake."

"But we don't learn anything from generation to generation! Here I am treating Peter the same way my mother did Nori and me, all hard rules and suspicion when he isn't like he was before—he hasn't even done anything wrong except swear a couple of times. I can't let go. It's a little late for rules, wouldn't you say?"

"So, loosen up a little, but not too much. Kids all ages like to know where the fences are."

"Why? So they can rip the seat out of their jeans jumping over them?"

He chuckled. "Yeah, that's about right."

Despite her tears, she found a smile. "If I still had the working parts, which we both know for a fact I don't, I'd swear I was pregnant. This has to be hormones. I hear a MasterCard commercial on the radio, it chokes me up." She gestured to her face, where the tears still ran. "I'm wrecking your Christmas."

"Last year I played solitaire on my bed and put an extra

spoonful of sugar in my coffee." He went to her, urged her up from the chair into his arms, held her to him, and pressed one hand to her belly. "Wish I'd been the one years ago, filling you up with children."

She looked away. "I couldn't keep a baby. I lost every single one of them but Peter."

"How many?"

"Four."

"Oh, honey." He tightened his grip. "You would've kept mine. I would've carried you from the john to the bed all nine months, scaring those kids into staying parked until their rightful birthdays. We wouldn't have had your easy life in California, but I'd have tried my hardest to make you happy."

"I know."

They were quiet a moment, and Owen felt himself tugged from this imaginary past back into the present as rudely as some schoolteacher yanking him out of a daydream. "Open your present." His voice was husky. "Now."

Her strong hands peeled away the paper. A few petals dropped from the sage bundle. For a second a brief, dusty summer perfume scented the kitchen. She unrolled the rug on the tabletop. It was a turn-of-the-century pictorial, late eighteen-hundreds; Verbena insisted you could date it by the use of early commercial wools. One edge was frayed, the wool crisp where it had gotten too close to the fire. And worthless or not to Benny Mota, the weaver must have poured her all into the piece, taking that risky step from known patterns to shuttling real life across her loom. *Look here at this false pathway*, Verbena had said, running a hardened thumbnail across the border. *See the wiggle? She did her sawtooth regular, like I do, then left these two S-shaped exits. Whoever she was, she was scared of this wool, scared of how true it become in her hands.* But it wasn't the border that made the rug a perfect gift for Maggie, it was what happened inside the border. Under a blue sky with rounded cartoonish clouds, the weaver had invoked a small farm on the long expanses of Blue Dog prairie. There was enough green to conjure up late spring, the time when winter was reduced to nothing more than the occasional chill you shivered through before you made yourself go inside for a jacket, and some afternoons you swore you could smell summer coming, hiking up the state, yellow flowers clutched tight in its fists. A red horse galloped in the distance, none of his four hooves touching the ground. In the foreground, just the back of a bent figure caught in the act of planting was visible, but you could tell it wasn't a woman, it was a man, tucking something into the earth that would blossom and bear the fruit of a single season's worth of hope.

Maggie ran her hand over the weaving. Owen circled her waist with his hands. He could feel her trembling.

"You don't like it," he found enough nerve to whisper.

"You're going leave me one day," she said flatly. "Then all I'll have left of you will be this rug."

He waited a moment before answering. "We all got to go someday. Sooner or later you get called, you go on back. This whole deal here is temporary."

"Don't talk that way."

He held her close and spoke into her neck. "I'm here now."

"Don't hate me for saying this, Owen."

"Saying what?"

"That I love you."

Her words echoed in the kitchen, over every inch of the town of Blue Dog, its chilly Christmas silence, the rented house, everywhere, and deeper still, lodging in all four chambers of Owen Garrett's heart.

16

D AMMIT, JOE," NORI SAID, RUBBING HER ARMS AND LEGS. "DON'T you have any heat in this truck?"

"Well, sure. Why didn't you ask before we gone so many miles?" He switched on the heater, slammed the dashboard to convince it he meant business, and a feeble tepid wheezing began at Nori's legging-clad knees. "If you're cold, maybe you should of worn underwear."

"You have to be looking awful darn close to be that certain I'm not."

In the glow of the few dashboard lights that worked, she could see Joe's face crinkle in amusement. "The thing is, see, I'm kind of like an underwear detective. By looking at a girl, I can tell what's under her clothes. Lots of men can. It's a gift, passed down from my grandpa Joe I got my name after."

"Scientists all over the world would kill for a peek at your DNA, Joe."

"Yeah, I know. But them damn doctors over at the clinic got too much Yazzi blood already."

Peter sagged against her arm, and Nori nudged him awake. "Move over, Mr. Lively. Some Romeo you're going to make if you can't stay awake past seven o'clock. Who's this babe you came all the way to your mom's to see?"

Peter smiled sleepily, tucking his jacket up under his head for a pillow. Not in the least interested in abandoning his nap to follow her conversation or her crude signing, he was going to be little company on the drive to Shiprock. She turned her attention back to Joe. "So, any little underwear detectives running around Blue Dog, scouting the elementary-school-crowd females?"

"Ain't heard of any so far. Every day, though, I'm looking hard for the right woman to bear me a mess of daughters."

"I thought all men wanted sons."

"Few sons would be okay. Teach 'em to team-rope. But daughters, now, they take care of you, cook up pots of good-smelling eats, listen to your advice. You take care your own daddy?"

"I used to. He's dead."

"That's too bad. Old people can tell you stuff, help you live your life in real smart ways. You like horses?"

She uncrossed her long legs and rubbed her calves, which beneath the Lycra-and-cotton fabric, felt about the temperature of the hamburger section in the market. "Set me on a halfway decent quarter horse, I can whip the sissy boys at polo or leave them all behind, jumping fences."

"Hmm." Joe looked impressed. "You prejudice against the mule?"

"The mule?" Nori studied this good-looking Navajo driving the borrowed truck. He wasn't like the Indians she came across in the bars she frequented in Cave Creek, north of Phoenix. They sat in dark corners nursing the same beer all night or betting on each others' games for quarters and pitchers, shooting pool with serious intensity, silver bracelets glinting off their dark arms sexily, in a way white men could never pull off. She tried to imagine Joe in Little Winston's, her favorite haunt. He'd be asking all the pretty girls to slow dance, not taking no for an answer, trying to talk them into taking him home, and getting the crap beat out of him by rednecks who didn't like Navs moving in on their territory. She could see Joe in the alley behind Winston's, cactus studding the butt of his jeans, that silver tooth poking through his lip courtesy of their fists, still grinning, certain whatever few lumps he garnered were worth time with a pretty girl. "Mules. Come on, what's the punch line, Joe?"

"There ain't one. Mules're no good for roping, but you can't beat 'em for going places. I got one. You can meet him tonight. He's living over with Verbena's Minnie until it gets warm again."

Nori sighed. "Maybe I should have stayed back with the two lovebirds by the woodstove. I'm starting to find it hard to believe it will ever get warm again."

"Oh, you ditch the poor-sister routine, it might get tropical warm tonight."

"Poor sister?" She pointed a magenta porcelain nail at him. "Don't make the mistake of thinking you can read a very complicated situation by sharing Christmas dinner with me."

"Before this night's over, we'll share more than dinner, something tells me."

"Well, don't go betting your mule on it. How long till we arrive at this mythical party?"

"Relax. You're on Indian time now. Sing your favorite song. Dream some good summer dreams to warm you up. We got plenty of time for talking. By time we get to Youngcloud's, you and me'll be friends for life."

Lacking even the energy to say she doubted him, Nori opted out of the conversation entirely and looked out her window. Dirtied by tire tracks and irregularly shaped stains of dog pee, the snowfall along the highway possessed little of the prettiness common to Blue Dog's snow-dusted Victorian houses off Main Street. She'd walked by them after having breakfast downtown two days in a row before gathering the nerve to come to her sister's. They reminded her of their old family home in Deerfield, the three-story house nowhere near as charming, but with wonderful nooks and attic rooms for creating your own personal hideouts.

Mag filled hers with painting stuff, stuck those plastic hippie daisy decals on the painted wood floor, put up posters of Janis Joplin and spun 45s on her record player. Nori's rooms were more about caging up squirrels she'd managed to coerce into trading their freedom for peanuts. Or her tropical fish tank, which ended in disaster when the power went out and their water turned frigid. Mag told her that would happen, and that she'd neglect the squirrels, too. Mag always knew the grim future. She took the responsible, long view of things, making Nori, no matter how many A's she got on her report card, emerge looking like a flake. But for all their years together, the squabbles, the silences, Mag had never once turned her away as coldly as she had on Thanksgiving. She knew her sister was pissed off—that one night she slept with Deeter had really punched her buttons. But she had that cowpoke now, so why wouldn't she forgive her? The lobby of the Farmington Holiday Inn—two stars were better than none—with its rattling Coke machine and ever-present stench of Carpet Fresh, made Nori feel more at home than eating Christmas dinner in the farmhouse. Damn, she hated it when her mind started going off like this. Would this road leading to Shiprock *ever* end?

The few houses they passed on the highway were just a notch above hovels, deteriorating right through their patched roofs and dented siding. Those strung with lights blinked feebly where the bulbs weren't burned out altogether. When you began to feel sorry for yourself, all you needed to do was look around— someone else always had it worse than you did. Or you could open the Lew Magram catalog, order a silk blazer, anticipate its arrival. That worked until the bill arrived.

Nori braced herself as Joe drove them slowly down the rutted road leading onto reservation land. But for the snow, any one of these paint-peeling prefab boxes could be a hard part of Phoenix, somewhere she avoided driving through even with her doors and windows locked. She'd traveled all over the world with her job—in Munich, watched Germans celebrate with flowing beer and mass craziness. In Portugal lavish religious holiday custom disguised the poverty until everything looked so quaint she wanted it on a postcard, a picturesque self-contained memory, hers to keep forever. Deep down, though, she believed all towns were the same, halfheartedly making a stab at holidays they couldn't afford, fooling only the foolish, and running the Master-Card up to alarming heights in the process.

Meanwhile, back at the ranch—farmhouse—whatever-the-hell you wanted to call it, her sister Mag was no doubt in the process of giving Owen the shepherd his hour of Christmas cheer—and wasn't that a little crèche scene in itself? She laughed aloud, imagining the two of them—Owen, his cowboy witticisms and dinner prayers, and her sister, all that caged-up desire cut loose.

"You got a nice laugh there." Joe took off his hat and cocked it over Peter's head, who was sleeping between them. "Glad you decided to ride along."

"What was I supposed to do, stay at the house and listen to them pant and moan upstairs?"

"Sounds like you might be wishing you was back there instead of your sister."

She made a disgusted sound in her throat. "Trust me. The last thing I need is a cowboy draining my bank account. I can do that fast enough by myself."

"Maggie says you got a big fancy job in the whiteman medical world. I myself have an interest in medicine. You one of them paramedicals?"

"No, I'm in sales. I sell saline and silicone implants to physicians."

"Saline and silly what?"

"Silicone implants. Don't pretend you haven't heard of them."

"Well, maybe I heard of them. Explain 'em to me, I'll stop you if it sounds familiar."

She sighed, automatically going into her simplest sales pitch. "Beneath a thin pocket of plastic, a medical-grade silicone or saline gets deposited, and then shaped like human tissue to form a prosthesis. What's nifty is the material approximates the same weight as normal body tissue, and it feels similar inside the body.

They were calling it a major breakthrough until the FDA started blaming it for everything from nosebleeds to cancer."

"What do people need them for?"

"To augment areas of the body where they believe tissue deficiencies exist. Body builders after larger muscle mass, men who've lost their precious testicles for one reason or another, but most commonly women seeking larger breasts."

"Don't sound like medicine to me. Sounds more like too much looking in the mirror."

"Plastic surgery's not always about looking beautiful. Women who lose a breast to the big C have a right to look normal again. Or if they didn't get that much to begin with, and it's making them obsess, why not have implants put in? La-la, instant D cups, the doctor gets rich, woman gets her underwire bra, husband has two new toys to play with, and I get a fat commission."

Joe grinned, and she realized he'd been playing her for a fool. Just another nutwood making her yammer on about tits for a cheap thrill.

"Now tell me why a woman want something fake like that inside her body?"

She'd had enough of this game. "Joe, cut the shit. It's Christmas, my sister is back there getting laid, I'm sure as hell not, and unless you or Pete have fevers, all three of our asses are freezing to death on this less-than-comfortable seat."

Between them Peter began to snore. Nori shook her head. "Will you listen to him!"

"All tired out from feeding sheep. That boy gets up too early."

The cowboy hat began to tip, and Nori removed it, set it in her lap, smoothed Peter's ragged hair back away from his face. At her touch Peter sighed and the snoring ceased. Though she knew he had no way of ever hearing her again, she couldn't make herself stop speaking to her nephew as if he always would. His face, not yet bristled with whiskers, was innocent, untempered by testosterone and male posturing. She wished she could freeze time, believe in her heart he would always respect her, keep Pete fifteen forever. "You're going to get your mom's hopes up, Pete. She'll want you here for the whole summer."

Joe said, "All summer be so bad? He could get job working in town. Lots of kids do."

"He's deaf, Joe. What's he going to do? *Intuit* what people want on their burgers?"

"You must feel worse about his broke ears than he does, if you're worrying on it that hard. Lots of jobs it's better if you don't hear nothing. Don't need twenty-twenty ears to saw boards or feed animals. Or throw newspapers at a mailbox."

"You don't know what you're talking about." Nori rested one of her pricey boots on the dashboard.

"Them boots of yours look wicked soft, but I sure bet you can't do much work in them."

"I had them handmade down at Paul Bond's in Nogales, by this old rodeo cowboy. He makes separate molds of your feet. You sit in this chair and he measures each foot, lets you choose the skins and how you want the designs to go. Made me feel like a princess when he did it. And they fit like a goddamn glove. They're pretty, but I think I hate them."

"Nothing in life worth hating. Boots are boots. I always got to stick cardboard in bottom of mine. Got bad feet after the war."

"Which war?"

"One everyone tries to forget. Nam."

"Imagine. I was about ten when you were off killing the enemy."

He kept his eyes on the road, and his mouth tightened into a thin line. "You was lucky to get born when you did, and a woman."

"Because I couldn't get drafted?"

He nodded. "Plus you possess powers to make babies, that's real medicine."

"I don't know about that. I think my sister's generation was the last one that could ever hope to relax a little, take time off to have a real life, reproduce. This time I'm taking off now I had to steal."

"Busy job like that must make you lot of money."

"Hell, I'll be out there waitressing if this bullshit with the FDA and the implants doesn't die down."

"Man! All you working girls got trash mouths. How come you swear so much?"

She unscrewed a tube of lipstick that matched her nails and redid her mouth. "Because we can get away with it."

"It scares men."

"Another good reason to do it."

"I'd sure love to see you in a waitress uniform."

"I'll bet you would. But I intend to go down fighting with the FDA. I've got thirty claims to discount every one of theirs. It's totally ridiculous. As if silicone is some new invention. Christ! Every time you get a needle inserted for an IV, a shot, blood drawn, the damn thing's coated with silicone. Goes right into your bloodstream. Nobody's died of that yet that I've heard of."

"Sounds like you're trying hard to convince yourself. If you hate that job, why you don't quit and find another one?"

"When did I say I hated it?"

Joe slowed to make a left turn onto a slick driveway where pickup trucks were parked three and four deep in front of a well-lit house, twin to every one of its neighbors. "Honey, you didn't have to."

Peter, fully awake now and smoothing down his corners, was itchy, anxious to get going. "Hurry up!" he signed.

"Keep your pants on, sport," Nori said. "And I mean that literally."

Unfolding his handkerchief outside the truck, Joe revealed a dozen worse-for-wear sugar cubes. "Been carrying these three days now. They give 'em away free at coffee shop in town. For my mule. Brought Lightning this sugar on account of he's a Christian mule, this here being one of his most holy days."

Standing there ankle deep in the grimy snow, the snow and cold no more bothersome to him than a buzzing housefly, Joe could have been one of the wise men who never made it into the catechism stories. Nori hugged herself against the cold. "Joe Yazzi, you're like one massive concentrate of every greasy pickup line I've ever heard."

"I know," he said back, smiling, the silver tooth revealing

itself for one brief flash. "But pretty harmless. Just one more thing. Case no one's ever told you, you don't need those implants."

"Will you guys come on?" Peter yelled, stamping his foot, his squeaky voice all adolescent urgency and nervous expectation.

Inside the Youngcloud house, adults and rambunctious children crowded the kitchen and living room, each of them balancing wobbly paper plates of food. His mother's leftovers were duly distributed and disappeared in ten minutes. He watched Nori accept a serving of corncake from Joe, even though she kept telling him she wasn't hungry, and Peter knew for a fact that she only ate one meal a day in order to stay so skinny. Joe, on the other hand, bottomless-stomach man, methodically made his way through the crowd and another full meal, gleaning something tasty from every plate he passed. Peter's stomach was as tense as his jaw muscles.

The reason for his tension sat across the room. Bonnie. Her pink headband was a candy-colored stripe against her long dark hair, hanging loose, the way he liked it best. Seeing her, he couldn't have gotten both his jaws to cooperate in the act of chewing without biting his cheeks or choking to death. At once every sign he knew seemed to fly out of his head. He watched as she tucked her loose hair behind one ear, her hands in perpetual motion as she signed with the girl who was refilling cups with a pungent-smelling cider. Even her hearing aid, that yellowing clear plastic arc at her hairline, looked somehow attractive. His knee joints would loosen and collapse if he had to get up and walk over there. If he didn't find the nerve to try, later he'd beat himself up for hairing out. The massive, muscled guys fooling with guitars alongside her must have been her brothers; she'd told him her whole family were musicians, and there was enough family resemblance in the broad faces to back his impression.

They had purple Vox Flying V guitars, cheap copies of the late-fifties originals, chrome whammy bars Peter thought were an insult to the original Bigsby. Back in California Travis'd had one. It spewed too much treble, he remembered, and was prone to serious string buzz. After six months it developed a warped neck, and Trav traded it to some eighth grader for a Baggie of sin-semilla. The brothers were tuning up now. He wondered how much of their music Bonnie could make out, and what it sounded like to her. If it was faint, like somebody's radio tuned low, or if maybe it faded in and out, muffled, like the way he recalled it could if you weren't listening closely, like if you didn't think the song was important.

He tried to think of the perfect music to go with this night. On Christmas in California, his mother played unbelievably stupid Christmas CDs: that hallelujah choir bullshit, Fred Waring and the Pennsylvanians, and this one tolerable disc, *Blue Yule*, which had some funky R&B stuff. Sometimes he spent whole days reciting songs in his head. Though the melodies were fading into unreliability, and that sometimes panicked him, nobody could take away the lyrics. Peter'd always meant to learn guitar. He was planning on settling down before he'd gotten sick. Get better grades so he could go to college and become some-thing, learn guitar, saxophone, too, because it was a killer horn; maybe he'd even learn to sail Deeter's sailboat, work his way up to them navigating a trip to Hawaii together. He wanted to see the North Shore, Maui, the Big Island. Instead, he was in a ratty government-issue house on an Indian reservation way out in the middle of nowhere, New Mexico, sitting in a crowded room while all around him strangers who'd endured centuries of poverty hap-pily carried on in voices he would never hear and no amount of money could buy back. It was like being trapped inside some for-eign flick, crappily dubbed, where the subtitles never match the actors' movements.

He thought of his dad's movie, that pet project he cared about more than his ex-wife or his deaf kid. Back at his mother's, next to that weird painting she'd given him, the script waited for him to read it. Merry Christmas, son. That was as much of his dad as he was getting this year. As soon as the new squeeze spawned their perfect lovechild, the cards and presents from Dad would dwindle down to once a year—he'd seen that happen to his friends.

Suddenly everyone was finding jackets, making their way to the door—all this way and he hadn't even spoken to her—now she would go. Joe palmed his shoulder and Nori finger-spelled, "Church," then threw up her hands, as if she couldn't quite believe she'd come all this way to get out of having to put on good clothes and feel guilty in the house of God, and Joe, of all people, wouldn't let them escape.

He guessed it was church, but there was no bloody Jesus stapled to a life-size cross. Instead a multicolored weaving hung in its place, high above a plywood altar with only blazing votive candles to assure Peter this was a somewhat Catholic assembly. None of the attendees felt committed to staying in the few ramshackle pews. People were here to dance, if you could call that foot-shuffling they were doing in the aisle dancing. The younger men were braver. They employed trickier moves and some were waving their arms in arcs, their brightly colored cowboy shirts as flashy as peacocks' feathers. Up on the altar, where the sacraments were pushed to the side, Bonnie's brothers played their guitars. After the first song Peter could feel the music in his feet against the floor, and sometimes in the tiny hairs that lifted on the back of his neck. Then Bonnie left her parents in the pew and joined her brothers onstage. One of her brothers came to her side and lowered the mike to her face. She looked a little nervous. At her side he sang with her, like a guide.

Peter would have cut off an arm to hear her voice. Everyone else here could. That he never would didn't seem fair. He yanked Nori's sleeve, demanding translation.

Nori's expression was soft, the closest he'd ever seen her to tears since that time in his hospital room, when she thought he wasn't looking. She finger-spelled "Bonnie," then made the signs for *write song*. Aloud she said, "I'm glad you can't hear it. This would break your heart," and she made the "breaking" motion, her fists snapping apart.

"Tell me the words."

She shook her head no, pulled a tissue from her purse. "It's about saying goodbye. Excuse me. I need to get out of here."

Catching most of what she'd said, he watched her retreat to the rear of the church, clutching her wad of Kleenex.

When the singing was over, Bonnie waved to him. She signed low on her right side, as if she didn't want to call attention to what she was saying. "You-me, talk Youngcloud's, yes?"

All right. She hadn't forgotten him.

In the rear of the church, Joe joined Nori. He sat down next to her, saying nothing for a long while, just watching the dancers.

Nori said, "God, I hate church. It always makes me feel so guilty. One of the little perks of growing up Catholic."

"Half our people worship Catholic religion," he said. "But they keep the Navajo custom, too. Double-strength prayers or whole lot of hokey, who can say? Myself, I like to watch, but I'd rather be scared into being good by Monster Slayer kachina than burn in hell with your nasty old Satan."

Nori said, "He's not my Satan. I left that shit in the dust decades ago."

Joe nodded. "Good trick. Tell me how to leave behind your creed."

She snuffled into her tissue, then balled it up and hid it in her purse among loose change, stray pieces of gum, credit card receipts she needed to list on her December expense report. "One day it all sticks in your throat. So you just say adios. You walk out of church and you don't go back."

Joe nodded. "Sure, that's a good way. So how come you're crying about it?"

"Damn, you're nosey!"

He smiled and handed her his handkerchief. "Maybe nosey. Maybe interested."

She looked down at his bandanna in her hands, a faded gray with the barely discernible words "Red Power" stenciled on it, a few grains of sugar still stuck to the fabric. Its smoothness between her winter-rough fingers felt as comforting as her own bedsheets, not that she ever spent enough time in them to remember. Up on the altar/stage, Bonnie's family was singing something foreign, Navajo, she guessed. Not understanding didn't matter one nit—she could tell this was holy music. Touching Joe's bandanna to her ruined mascara, she said, "Now I suppose I have to wash this."

"That's okay. Let me keep some of your tears. I don't mind."

"Well, maybe I do." This was certainly turning out to be among the weirder Christmases she'd experienced.

To Peter the night at Verbena Youngcloud's was measurable by neither time nor clock. If anybody left they came back later with a friend or two, more food, or contributed to the music by taking a turn at the drum or singing. The snow mounded up in small white cones on the horses' backs outside, but the horses were way too interested in the commotion behind the windows a few feet away to go into the warm barn. Joe went outside to feed his mule, and when he returned, he was dusted with snow, looking like a gingerbread cookie man, powdered with confectioner's sugar. Peter remembered how his mother used to make those, with honey and wheat flour, back in the days when she thought keeping him away from refined sugar would stave off all of life's most dire circumstances. He didn't like sugar that much, so he guessed her efforts had some positive effect. But she couldn't keep him from having to go through the divorce, could she? Or losing his hearing. Well, why wreck Christmas opening that can of worms? He stretched out near the woodstove, where, one by one, the kerosene lamps were extinguished so tired children could flop, piled together like puppies, share a blanket, and go to sleep while the adults partied on. This was the first adult party he'd been to where the kids weren't sequestered in another room and shushed. Here they seemed to be the heart of the celebration, and every adult stopped and took time to see what one needed, to cheer a sad face with a hug or a bite of food.

When most of the kids had found sleeping places, Bonnie sneaked over and curled up only a few feet away from where he lay. Joe and Nori looked as if they might stay up the entire night, Nori talking, Joe eating. Eventually Bonnie's body inched its way closer, until she was curled in front of him like a warm spoon under the blanket. He couldn't believe it. All his dreams and fantasies were nothing compared to this. He felt his erection pressing into her side, and wished he could will it back into softness before she noticed. How soft, warm, and curved every part of her was! He was afraid if he touched her, she would pull back. Gathering all his nerve, he signed into her hand, *Nice Christmas?*

Nice. You're here.

Didn't know you wrote songs. Sang.

Family thing.

That song tonight. Tell me name.

She nestled against him, spelling out her name with exaggerated slowness, *B-o-n-n-i-e.*

He teased her back. *Ha ha. Song in church.*

Later.

Please. Tell me name.

"Blue Rodeo." Quiet.

You wrote? What about?

Go to sleep. They'll move us apart.

Song about saying goodbye?

In answer she leaned back to kiss him, a hello kiss, definitely nothing in her mouth saying goodbye. He hadn't known it could be like that—so easy—a girl just up and pressing her mouth to yours. Trying hard not to think how to do it properly, he kissed her back. Touching her hands, feeling her fingers move, was awesome. She was right, they had to be very still. This took more strength than any idiotic sport he'd been challenged to in school, and it was definitely harder than algebra, or anything he'd ever experienced, including all those years of hearing his parents argue. She finished the kiss with a soft giggle he felt against his neck, her breath hot and sweet. Hidden behind the bodies of sleeping children, they kissed some more, until Peter's mouth felt worn raw and his heart stretched as thin as drumskin from all that pounding. He was sure people could hear them breathing this hard into each other, trying not to move beyond kissing, and he figured in the morning, there would be some kind of unpleasant consequences, but right now it was worth it.

. . .

Nori, feeling about as crabby as her morning face looked in the Youngcloud's bathroom mirror, gave up on repairing it and shut her compact. Other people were waiting to use the bathroom, so she had to go back out there eventually. All night they'd stayed up talking, Joe telling her stories, defining his dreams so clearly she could see every acre of the ranch he wanted, the sturdy barn, the decent stock, the houseful of laughing children. All the men she dated wanted basically the same thing—an indecent amount of money, the latest model of Porsche, Mercedes, or Lexus, and her panties off before the end of the evening. She'd run her own life similarly, working three times as hard as she needed to, knowing she'd retire at forty, thinking how great it was that when she settled down she'd never crave travel, since she'd amassed more frequent flyer miles than she could ever use. Listening to Joe had made her look back, inventory her plan. She discovered she was in roughly the same place as five years ago, when the plan seemed brilliant. Someone knocked at the door and she called out, "Sorry," opened it, and planted herself in the corner next to Verbena's loom, woven one-quarter of the way up with a streak of mocha lightning against a black background.

Joe brought her black coffee in a chipped cup.

"Uh-oh. You're wearing that pissed-off look again, wrecking your pretty face."

"I'm just trying to figure out how to tell Peter to knock that shit off."

"What shit? Him and Bonnie Tsosie helping clean up the mess?"

"That's not what I mean. You saw him last night, kissing her."

Joe blew on the surface of his coffee. "So?"

The hot coffee tasted surprisingly bitter to her seasoned lips. "He's too damn young to be doing this."

"How old are you supposed to be? Thirty-two?"

She made a face at Joe's mention of her age. "Look, he's fifteen. If he starts screwing now, he'll wreck his life getting into trouble with a girl he hardly knows."

"Last time I checked, screwing was a long ways off from

kissing. Besides, you said his life's already wrecked on account of going deaf."

Joe's dart hit its target, momentarily leveling her fierce logic. "Look, maybe I went overboard last night in the truck, but this is not a deaf thing, it's a sex thing."

Joe laughed. "Bull. Get off his back. You ain't his mother. Maggie is. You want some kids to boss around, make your own."

Nori felt her stomach start to crumple. Asshole—how dare he tell her a thing like that? She considered throwing the bitter coffee in his pretty face, decided she hated all Indians, and finished off her careening train of thought with a wish she often dredged up late at night, in hotels, when she had trouble sleeping. If only there was some rental service where you could pay fifty bucks and, in return, get some anonymous, sexually tireless man to screw away your panic, ask no questions, and keep his well-meaning advice to himself. She set down her coffee and stared at the weaving, waiting for her emotions to collect themselves, the same way she handled belligerent clients and all-male board meetings.

Softly, Joe said, "Hey, medicine girl. Look here." He pulled up his shirt, revealing his scars, the long lines of surgical tracks where the doctors had jerry-rigged bones and organs, then set to with staples and catgut to hold him together. "See this? Everything happens for a reason. It was my time to serve my country, my time to check out death, then my time to come back and do some more work here. Can your doctors fix this? No. I got to learn to live with it. It ain't easy, but remember, we all grow into each other like these here yarns in Verbena's loom."

She started to put her fingers to the longest scar, the one that snaked across his chest like the ammunition straps he'd worn in Vietnam. It was the stitchery of a child, a blind surgeon, *shoddy* was too nice a word for Joe's chest.

He grabbed her fingers in his and kissed them.

Sharply she pulled them back, afraid at what his touch had called forth in her, angry that her coping skills were flopping around like dying fish. "Don't," she whispered.

"Sorry." Joe took his coffee cup and drank it slowly, looking away from her. He was pulling back, thank God. She needed to be alone, that's what, to cry herself to sleep in her hotel room, the DO NOT DISTURB sign on her doorknob, the television on in the background for white noise.

17

USUALLY OWEN LIKED NOTHING BETTER AFTER MAKING LOVE than Maggie's predatory light massage, as she ran her hands over his face in silence. Her movements were gentle and knowing and had the power to settle him into sleep even better than the sore muscles that accompanied hard work. But tonight, when her fingers stopped abruptly at the scar over his eye and didn't move on, he got a bad feeling.

"Okay," she said. "Time's up. I want you to tell me how this happened."

In the dark he brought her fingers to his mouth and kissed her winter-roughened skin. Lately, her businesslike nails were stained with oil paint. Her palms sometimes smelled of the garlic she used in cooking. He doubted that, even in her former life, she'd taken the idea of a manicure seriously. Hands were instruments, tools—hers were capable of work as well as this other touching. He drew her to him and with two deep kisses, tried to interest her in a different activity, but he might as well have been barking at a knothole for all the good it did. She pulled away from him and sat up in her bed, waiting. "Maggie," he said. "Trust me. Better off you don't know."

"Granted, I was slow in starting, but over the past two months you've listened to me pour out my troubles, Owen. You've heard me confess more about screwing up Peter's life than I ever intended to let you know. Now it's your turn."

"Wasn't that sister of yours showing up a surprise?"

"Nori's like fog. Hell to drive through and gone by afternoon."

He chuckled. "Careful, you're starting to sound like you live here."

"Please don't change the subject. I do live here. And as hard as I tried to resist, I fell in love with you."

He turned on his side and tucked a pillow under his chin, whispering. "Thought my loving satisfied you, but you still sound hungry."

"This isn't about sex, Owen. You make my body sing."

"Lord God, will you tell me why is it women always end up pestering you for secrets in bed?"

"Probably for the same reason men won't tell the truth until someone puts a gun to their heads."

"Honey, that's just small-town attitude."

"Right. And it has nothing to do with Thanksgiving, or why you flinch whenever we run into anything remotely connected with the law."

He took hold of her hand and traced the long, sturdy bones. A pretty fair painter, more-than-able cook, determined gardener or post-hole digger, he had no doubt his Maggie would be this feisty into her eighties. He tried to picture her in this house forty years down the road, her blouses gone as faded and soft as these old bedsheets. Stubbornly wearing her Levi's until the seat wore out. Avoiding church, making the ladies in town gabble about her like turkeys. Everything around her would be categorized into a kind of comfortable rubble, canvases stacked against the wall, the dog she never could find the time to spay long gone, but probably some of her great-great-grandpups sleeping in the shade of the porch. She'd keep after her son until they'd squared their differences, like he should have done with Sara Kay. The only puzzle piece missing from the blissful scene was himself. He couldn't stay in any one place forever. Maggie would eventually replace him. Some other man would see how good a woman she was, court her in ways he couldn't afford. She pitched no fits when he was gone working. She wasn't afraid to stay in this big house alone. She liked thunder and shoveled snow alongside him; she made a hand worth hiring. She put him in mind of that O'Keeffe woman New Mexico revered more than its mineral resources. Maggie's paintings, however, while hardly museum quality, were more realistic. She wouldn't move for a prairie fire if she wanted something, including the truth about his past. And she was still waiting. He cleared his throat. "All right. Remember, I didn't offer this, you asked. And if I ever disappear, know it'll have little to do with you. I'd like nothing better than to stay tucked inside you for the rest of my life. Until I stop breathing, maybe."

"What did you do, Owen?"

"What you expect. Killed a man."

He heard her immediate sigh. "How?"

"With bourbon and half a pool cue."

He listened to her silence as she took it all in. She was a woman who had heard it all, from her I-don't-love-you-anymore Hollywood husband, to the team of he'll-never-hear-again doctors who couldn't wake her kid up when a dog could, to her nine-dollar sister saying I just spent the night playing slap-and-tickle with your best friend. He felt a momentary lightness, confiding in someone else after all this time, but the heavy bird hovering over them in the dark landed again, square on his chest, and he felt the familiar taloned feet close back over his ribs.

"Was it somebody you knew?"

"No. Just a stupid fight that got liquored up and fatal."

She turned in bed, moving away from him. "So what did you do?"

"Hit Colorado breeze for a healthier climate and didn't stop for kissing. Until I met you."

She touched his scar again. "But if it was self defense—"

He cut her off. "That's a mighty gray area, Ms. Yearwood."

"Why didn't you go to the sheriff and at least try to explain?"

She had a right to every question. He only wished he had some different answers to give her. "I was drunk. I hit him with the weighted end of the pool cue. That's what happened and that's all they would have heard. If not murder, then voluntary manslaughter at least. We're talking hard time."

"It's been years. You're living a decent life. Maybe they'd take that into consideration."

"A man looking over his shoulder at every piece of straight road hasn't exactly lived what others call a straight life."

"But you never did anything like that again."

"Of course not. But until I got sober, I did jobs that ran a little left of the law. Stupid stuff, like moving unregistered livestock. Selling transport papers. Other stuff I was so drunk I can't even clearly recall, but it wasn't legal. Let's just say it was enough to make Sara Kay want to change her last name, which she did."

Maggie rubbed his arm. "But you left rather than hurt her. That counts for something."

And it was also why he'd stayed so close—if there ever was a time he could go back, when he couldn't stand not seeing her, within a day's drive, he'd be close enough to get to her. "Say we called it an accident, Maggie. Truth is, the more years that pass, the more of an accident it seems."

"Sara's twenty. She'd understand."

"Maybe. Maybe not. But not everyone's going to see it that way. Think about that man's kin. Somebody was his mother. Maybe he had a wife, a baby on the way, brothers, sisters, cousins. In seven years you think they'd be any more likely to excuse what I did by calling it an accident?"

She lay back down next to him. He could feel the coolness of her flesh from having been out from under the covers so long. He started in stroking her, running his rough hands over her shoulders, down to the slippery skin between her thighs, traveling up to her solid firm breasts, and hugged her to him, this stubborn woman whose Christmas present was saying she loved his sorry carcass. He concentrated on how good it would feel to connect their bodies, but in the wake of their sobering conversation, neither one of the bodies in this bed had enough heart for making love.

"It's been a long day. Maybe we should just try and sleep."

Maggie turned her head away and he could feel the stiffness in her shoulders. He tucked the blanket up around her neck and lay on his back, staring up at the ceiling, where to his wide-awake eyes one lone crack in the plaster took on the curve and angle of the Rio Grande.

When Mag called and invited her to spend the rest of her holiday at the house, Nori checked out of the Holiday Inn as soon as she could stuff her clothes into the Samsonite. Now she followed her sister around the Smith's Food King in Farmington, picking up whatever hit her fancy: jars of Scottish marmalade, pricey tins of mushroom-and-garlic pâté, fifteen-dollar bottles of wine that sold so infrequently they were caked with dust. At a trot she hurried them into the cart because Mag was shopping at Mach twelve, launching her cart like a missile halfway down one aisle, grabbing boxes of cereal, then piling into the metal cart food she hardly even gave a second glance, including Pop-Tarts for Peter—junk food her sister normally denounced as contributing to society's breakdown.

Outside, the snowy parking lot looked grim under the light fixtures. The wind was blowing, too, and the red-and-yellow striped plastic banners that were supposed to make things look festive had tattered themselves to shreds. "You miss California?" Nori asked.

Mag stood there balancing two cartons of ice cream in her hands: Chocolate Cookies and Cream and Tin Roof Sundae. Nori knew her sister well enough to bet that the addition of chocolate to normally vanilla-based Cookies and Cream would be enough to send her plummeting into depression. Cookies and Cream was Pete's favorite—one of those sacred mixtures that satisfied a

teenager on a primal level. Tin Roof Sundae had chopped nuts—
not that many, but ever since he could handle solid food, Pete
had pushed aside the nuts. Mag put the Cookies and Cream into
the basket, shoved the Tin Roof back into the cold recesses of the
freezer compartment with its unsold brothers, and immediately
took it back out again to read the label.

Nori stifled a laugh. "I asked you if you missed California."

Mag frowned as if it was the first time she'd heard the question. "Right now I miss their ice cream selection."

"Come on. You know what I mean."

Nori watched her sister eye the few pints of low-fat frozen
yogurt caked with icicles and decide against them, too. Again, she
set the ice cream back into the freezer compartment. "Let's see.
Police helicopters, taggers' graffiti on the storefronts, beachfront
gridlock? Get in the car and let's go back right now."

"Come on, Mag. Snow? You don't have moments when you'd
like to put on your shorts, go sit on the deck, drink coffee with
Deeter, and discuss the thorny issue of middle-aged angst?"

Her sister shot her a look that revealed the depth of that sore
spot. "Sure I miss that. I miss pretending I had a stable marriage,
having a kid with two working ears and a somewhat manageable
future ahead of him. And I miss the shit out of having a friend
like Deeter."

Nori smiled sheepishly. "But I took care of that."

"Yes, you did."

"So when are you going to forgive me? All I did was spend
one night with a lonely middle-aged guy who knew he was never
going to get the chance he wanted with you."

Mag stopped the cart. "What are you talking about? Deeter
and I were friends."

"That's what you think. He wanted in your bed. Bad."

"Contrary to what your estrogen level tells you, not every
relationship has to end up there. If that was the case, which I
doubt, it was something we could have worked through by our-
selves. In any case I didn't need you to be my surrogate. Your
one-night diversion trashed a friendship."

"Oh, horseshit."

But Nori could see that Mag was gathering steam. "You grew up in Massachusetts, too, right? Snow's snow. Pretty in November, a pain is the ass in March, but it goes away eventually."

"Unlike sisters?"

Mag turned her face away, but Nori had already seen her expression. "I never said that."

Her older sister rolled the cart on, then stopped in front of the juice concentrates. In Mag's kitchen there was always a pitcher of pulpy Florida squeeze in the fridge. Multivitamins for Pete. Enough canned goods that they could survive a month without going to the store. A bottle of drinkable red and excellent white wine. Nori was home so infrequently she didn't bother shopping. She hit the four food groups occasionally varying her take-out.

"Why not? If it's how you feel, own up."

"Nori, for now my life is here. I'm making the best of things so Peter can go to school. Did you know they weren't going to let him in otherwise?"

"No."

"Well, it's true. You got him all fired up to go, then left. I had to go in and bargain or watch my son get let down a third time."

"Sorry."

Her sister sighed. "I know what you think of me. That I don't have much of a life. Probably you're right. I should have finished my degree, had a career I could go back to, but I didn't. It's still my life, Nori. Peter and I are speaking, my divorce is ambulatory, and I have somebody in my life I respect."

Nori laughed. "The way you put it, it sounds like you two spend all your time discussing great books instead of having sex."

"Maybe you have a problem with that in particular."

"No, you do. Who you screw should be your own business. Like Deeter was mine."

Mag sighed. "Owen Garrett isn't your trusted friend. I didn't drop in, hop in his bed, and drive away the next day."

"That's right. Who is he, Mag? What do you really know about him?"

"That he's honest and dependable. There for me. That he's *my* friend. Mine." She took a box of microwave popcorn from the highest shelf and put it into the silver cart.

"You don't even *have* a microwave oven anymore!"

Her sister stared at the box, at Orville Redenbacher's wholesome assurances of low fat and the minimum of salt—tenets Nori was certain she based her life on. Who could tell what she was thinking? No matter what Mag believed, Owen Garrett wasn't going to be able to patch over every howling hole in her life. From fathers to smart-ass Indians to the ones who seemed so like Mr. Right you heard bells chime during your orgasm, all men moved on. Mag could go back to California, live on her settlement, slip back into the fold, do all right anywhere. She was like that. When she died, Pete would still be *her* son, proof she'd done something worthwhile besides pay taxes. Nori reached up and put the popcorn back on the shelf, looked at her sister, then burst into tears.

"At least we don't have to worry about the groceries defrosting in the car," Mag said as they sat drinking cappuccino topped with foamy drips of hot milk. "We're probably the only two women in Blue Dog, New Mexico, stupid enough to be sitting in a frozen-yogurt shop drinking coffee when we could be home sitting by the woodstove."

Nori agreed. "It's colder than a witch's ass out there."

"Where did you pick up that little bon mot?"

Nori stirred sugar into her coffee. "Mr. Joseph Yazzi, Christmas powwow escort service and underwear detective first class."

"What?"

Nori waved her hand in front of her face. "Nothing. A joke."

"Joe's a decent man."

"Oh, I know. His only drawback is that he thinks he knows everything. Wonder what he kisses like."

"Please don't try to find out."

"God, Mag, you're so serious you can't even tell when I'm kidding. Lighten up. I'm swearing off men forever. Since I have such incredible luck with them."

As she said the words, she believed them, but the pull to fall into bed, give herself ten minutes' forgetfulness in the lock of bodies joining, was still there, just as strong. Behind the counter the Indian girl who'd made their coffee was leaning against the counter, focused deep into the pages of a paperback horror novel. Family—what was it? Relatives like herself coming and going, people who tried hard to get their work done, or just a sloppy genus term?

"I'm still angry with you, Nori. I'm trying to get over it."

"Because of Deeter?"

"Deeter's history. Much as I hate it, I suppose I can afford to lose a friend. But not my son. You steered him away from me when I needed most to be his mother."

This shocked her. "Are you serious? How can you be mad at me when Riverwall's turned out great?"

"I'm not denying that. Peter's different now. He even studies. I'm almost afraid to say anything, to jinx it."

"So be mad at me? That doesn't make sense."

Mag took a measured breath. "Nori, when he got meningitis, Peter could have died. He went to sleep and almost didn't wake up. When he did, he was deaf. And his parents were still getting a divorce. There was a lot of repair work we needed to do, and we needed to work on it together. I'm not saying he was my only anchor, but I am his mother. Going to Riverwall should have been a group decision. Peter looks at you and sees this free spirit, this intrepid, shrewd world traveler, incapable of failure. You used that. Took how much he adored you, trounced blithely over what was left of my family, and made all the choices for everyone."

Nori stirred the frothy milk into her cooling coffee and shoved the cup into the saucer. It wasn't fair. First Indian Joe, now Mag. She *wasn't* being selfish, she was just offering a sensible perspective on a difficult problem. Why couldn't Mag see that she had everyone's best interests at heart? "Well, what do you want? Me to say I'm sorry so you can feel superior?"

Mag's expression was pained. All over her face, that why-do-

I-bother? mouth pursed in judgment. Hadn't it been that way their whole lives? Nori creating shitstorms, Mag soldiering her way through, Nori labeled the bitch.

New Year's Eve, Rabbott's Hardware was making a profit selling plastic champagne glasses, corkscrews, and a few plastic chip-and-dip sets to town ladies planning parties. The shoppers were passing on the cocktail napkins, which Owen attributed to a basic flaw of design. Who wanted to pay ninety-nine cents for a hundred napkins featuring a wizened Father Time on one side, his weathered body ready for the bone pile, and that obese, too-cheerful diapered baby on the other? It wasn't a holiday he minded working. Too much time to think if he stayed home. Dave Rabbott, gone to Albuquerque for the duration, had left him the keys and a pad full of instructions: *Here's the order of lock-up, the combination to the safe—not that I expect any great haul after the holidays, but put the take in the green zippered bag and we'll worry about depositing it come Tuesday when the banks are back in business. Open the store for me and I'll see you around lunchtime, unless Enid gets into a shopping frenzy over to Dillard's. . . .*

Owen cut some plywood for a fellow who'd had bad luck with guests at his motel and needed to patch a window until the glass people could come replace it. He sold the complete inner workings to a toilet to a young man who said, "Christmas. You can tell anyone who might possibly be interested that contrary to popular belief, Legos do *not* flush." And he kidded a sour old woman who wanted to know what was "on sale."

"Everything but me," he answered, but she wasn't having any of Owen Garrett's holiday cheer while she was seeking bargains. Minnie Youngcloud stared rapt into her Sony Watchman at the register, one of her Christmas presents to herself. Owen wandered over and stood by her. It'd been a year or so since he'd seen anything more than a night of motel TV, and he wondered if during that period it had changed any for the better. "What's on?" he asked.

"'Unsolved Mysteries.' It's a show where people try and solve crimes the cops give up on. They call in and give tips. You get a big reward if they arrest somebody. Sounds like easy money."

"Sounds like making a buck off misery, if you ask me."

"Well, no one asked you. Shh. I'm trying to see if I recognize anybody. Then I can quit this job, move to sunny California."

He stepped back from the counter and started sweeping the floor. He didn't want to know—if they made a television show out of that sort of thing, there truly was no place a man could hide—and that was a terrible thought. He abandoned the broom and went to the back room to begin the process of shutting up the store. Hope was asleep under Dave Rabbott's chair and lifted his head when Owen walked into the office.

"Hello there, son." The dog stood up, ever ready to accompany his master down whatever path he might choose. He was a good dog, smarter than most, and comfort on cold nights when what you needed most was to hear the sound of your own voice, no response necessary, just the kinds of foolish utterings that convinced you you were still tethered to the planet. With his three legs, Hopeful was distinctive, but not all that unusual. In farming and ranching country, what with tractors and baling accidents, more than one three-legged dog could be found, and blue heelers abounded. Summer or winter, a medium-size dog was easily transportable. Not so with Red. Selling a horse legally left a paper trail. If you gave that good a horse away, you had to make certain it was to folks who would look after him proper. He could give him to Joe. But pills or not, Joe had that crazy streak—he might up and one day sell the horse for a meal at Embers on enchilada night, or turn him loose in the badlands when he got off on one of those Indian guilt-and-history jags he sometimes fell into.

"Owen?" Minnie said from the office door, holding her Watchman like a spaceman's pocketbook. "It's six o'clock. I'm heading home, unless you need help."

He shook his head no, wished her Happy New Year, shut down the store lights, counted the bills, separated paper and coin, and put the checks into the plastic envelope. He noticed there was more cash in the wall safe and set his envelopes on top of it. The quiet store felt like a cave. Its dark corners could easily have been filled with bats as merchandise. Running away from Colorado, sharing a cave with some enterprising bats, he'd discovered he didn't care for the animal. Half bird, half bug, despite their reputed intelligence and necessary link to the food chain, he'd just as soon never see a cloud of them moving around his head again. But for his panic at their numbers and the resulting sleeplessness, that cave had kept him warm.

He and Hope stopped at the Texaco on the way home. Joe Yazzi was there, outside the convenience store cash register area with two of his Navajo buddies, silent men who were bundled not too effectively against the cold, drinking what looked like Cokes. Owen wondered how his friend had gotten from the farmhouse downtown, and furthermore, what the heck he was doing—it wasn't a Coke in his hand, it was a Coors bottle. "Hey, Joe," Owen said as he laid his ten-dollar bill on the counter for the clerk. Half a tank of gas beat none. "What happened to Step One? 'Admitted we were powerless over the booze'?"

Joe gave him a distracted look and started in on eagles and bears, the way things used to be in the animal world before the white man killed everything off. True as the basic issue was, it was crazy talk. In Owen's marrow, alarm bells started ringing.

He tried kidding him. "Now don't go blaming me," Owen said. "I never ate bear in my life."

But Joe was acting as if he didn't even know who he was. Owen mentally tallied off who he might call to help as he went back out to his truck, opened the hood, and checked the oil, which was only down a quart. Dave was out of town, it was getting late, and the ugly way things were proceeding, he didn't want Maggie involved.

Alongside him a shiny red Ford dual-axle pulled up, its bed full up with cages containing silver-and-black-tipped huskies, show dogs by the look of them. "Nice-looking animals you got there," Owen said.

The driver slammed his door and lit a cigarette. "Yeah, well, if I get them to California by the end of the week, I pocket five hundred bucks and have time to watch a dirty hotel movie before I got to head back. Good thing they come with fur coats. Looks like it might snow again."

Both men looked up, automatically checking the sky for clues.

"You're probably right."

The man went inside to take care of his bill as Joe Yazzi threw his empty beer bottle into the Dumpster, where Owen heard it shatter. He watched him stop at the Ford and eye the dogs. Owen said, "Why don't you hop in my truck, Joe? I'd be glad to give you a ride home, or you can come along and drink coffee at my place. We could even grab a bag of enchiladas and take them on over to Maggie's, play some cards. Don't throw away your hard-earned sobriety. You worked to rack up those years."

Joe reached in the bars of the cage nearest him, letting the dog sniff his fingers. His face grew wistful, as if he were communing with the memory of his own lost dog, and Owen felt for him. He added the quart of oil he was down and fumbled with the latch on the hood, trying to urge the slightly askew hinges to shut properly. When he next looked up, Joe had set three of the four caged dogs free and they were running around the station— elated, confused, and headed for the only place they could go, the highway.

Joe stared at Owen with a face as dejected as it was angry. His voice was thick with sarcasm as he expelled whatever venom had made him drink in the first place. "The wolf is my *brother*. Don't you know his *spirit* must run free?" He shooed the dogs. "Get going, brothers. Track deep into the woods. If you're smart, you'll steer clear of bitches altogether."

"Jesus, Joe! Them are show dogs, not wolves." Owen ran, trying to corral the scared dogs. He whistled for Hopeful. Inside the cab of his own truck, Hope saw a job that needed doing, heard permission, dived through the open window, and set to heeling. The driver of the Ford emerged from the station, a Twinkie sticking out of his mouth and in his hand, a Styrofoam cup of coffee he immediately dropped.

"What the fuck you think you're doing, you stinking Indian?" He started into the traffic after the dogs, then apparently thought better of things, because Owen heard him yell to the clerk inside to call the police.

The Camaro that hit the unlucky dog stopped immediately. The driver was a young blond woman who reminded Owen so much of Sara Kay that he had to stop himself from calling out her name. She got out of her car, ran to the laboring dog, and bent over his body, crying, stroking its neck fur, and begging it to keep breathing, trying to will life back into the beautiful coat and glistening eyes.

"I didn't see him until it was too late," she kept repeating, as Owen patted her shoulders, urging her away from the dog.

"It's all right, honey," he said.

"No, it's not." She wept into the dog's fur, and hearing her grief, staring at her pretty blouse getting streaked with blood, Owen thought his heart would break.

The delivery man had a rifle set on Joe, and the store clerk was trying to talk him out of the gun. "Joe won't take off on you. Put the gun down before somebody gets hurt."

Owen put his arm around the crying girl, and in his head he heard a montage of voices, noises he'd tried hard to deafen himself to. *Daddy! Watch me jump this horse. Daddy? When are you coming home? Daddy?* The sound of a pool cue breaking. Maggie's singing in the summer sunshine. The impact of car meeting dog bone. The long sigh that made up the dog's last mortal breath. *Hello, my name is Owen, and I'm an alcoholic. The wolf is my brother.* . . . The keening cry of the young woman beside him.

Hope was bursting with pride; he'd seen a job that needed doing and gotten two out of three of the escapees. Number four was still barking safe inside his cage. Owen stood at the foot of the truck while Joe sat, shameful tears streaming down his face.

"White man come up and shot my dog," he explained in a shaky voice. "Gut-shot old White Dog, just bad enough so there weren't time to get him to no vet. I ask him please shoot him in the fucking head and get it over with, but he took his rifle and

went on back to his car." He paused to wipe his face, then continued rambling. "We shouldn't have burned them villages because
there was children hiding in huts no one could see. I can still
hear 'em calling out, like my own people calling out for water,
and she's the best-looking girl I ever saw, white or red, but I'm
just a stupid Indian and nothing going to change that. . . ."

Owen said to the driver, "He's got some troubles."

The Ford man took his finger off the trigger. "I don't give a
shit if he's Jay fucking Silverheels, he owes me one purebred
husky show dog, and I mean to get my money even if I have to
sell his tipi out from under him."

The sheriff's department was there in minutes. They dis-
armed the driver, set Joe into the rear seat of their car, and covered the dead dog. They took the girl's statistics before sending
her on her way. Her old year was going out with a bang, all right.
Owen wondered how Sara Kay was spending this night—if she
had a date, a steady young man, if they were drinking just one
glass of champagne or driving crazy with open containers, the
radio blasting encouragement. Owen did his best to explain to
the cops about Joe's condition. The cops asked him his name.

"Owen Garrett. I don't see why you need that."

"You're a witness, Mr. Garrett. We take witnesses' names in
case we need to follow up."

"Told you what I saw."

Impatiently they opened their pads and waited. "You want to
just let us take a look at your license so we can get on to our next
call?"

Owen started to protest, then realized his predicament of not
having a license went much deeper. If he didn't show it, they'd
run his truck plate, discover it wasn't registered. Either way they
were asking too many questions. "I'm ashamed to say I left it
home. Sorry. You guys probably have a long night ahead, what
with this holiday. Too bad it had to begin this way. Can I come by
and bring it to you tomorrow? Guy who runs the station will
vouch for me."

The younger officer went to the car to talk into his police

radio. Maybe he was calling home, asking his young wife to check if they had enough beer in the fridge for watching the game tomorrow, but then again, he might be one of those kind who went above and beyond the call of duty and did it all by the book.

When he returned he said, "Be sure you come by tomorrow, Mr. Garrett. In the meantime, a phone number where we can reach you?"

He had no phone at the bunkhouse. Maggie had none at the farmhouse. To say so would sound falser than calling the night sky pink. He gave them Rabbott's number and drove off, rolling his window down to signal his merge into traffic, sweat pouring down his armpits, Hopeful next to him tense as coiled wire, sensing his fear.

His mind ran in a loop, replaying the accident from the initial screech of brakes to seeing Joe's mouth close around that beer and clear back to Minnie's television show. He made a wrong turn, stopped the truck in the middle of a dark stretch of road, and stared at the houses in front of him, trimmed with Christmas cheer, lights in the windows, mailboxes with the names painted on in block letters. He could never do that. He'd been using the name Owen Garrett so long he almost believed it was his. He'd chosen it carefully, during the long trip from Durango to El Paso. The Owen part he'd lifted from the guy who wrote *The Virginian*, one of the first books he'd ever read, given to him by his momma, who appreciated a little romance to soften her hard life. The Garrett sounded enough like the guy who shot Billy the Kid that everytime he said it, he'd remember how the boy died and what he'd died for, but it was a modern name, too, you could find it in any phone book.

Time was up. It had been up a while now, and here he was, going through the motions of a regular life, pretending he had a right to one. The way you left a place was simple. You packed the essentials: three changes of clothing, no more. Razor, toothbrush, the few tools you needed to prove you could do a job. There was no room for getting sentimental. You destroyed anything that would connect you, swept away your tracks like dusting off your boots, and you went. It was best to lie low for a few days, circle around, then make your trail long and wide, boring to anyone who might come looking, to make a path through cities where people came and went in droves, just like it used to be working cattle on the big ranches. Find work as soon as possible, nothing special that might call attention to you, and act like you been there doing that job ten years. Volunteer to stay late, keep watch, work graveyard shift if they had it. Avoid bars, not just because the temptation to drink was greater than usual but because that's where the truly desperate soaked their sorrows, and they would sell your face to anyone who asked, if it meant a bankroll for the next night's drinking. Find a meeting, and let those one hour segments be as much medicine to your scared self as Joe's pills were to his mixed-up thinking.

Home in the bunkhouse, Owen rolled his bedding up into a sleepingbag size–coil, two sets of clean clothes flat inside. Dishes were anonymous and could be left behind. His paperback books, traded back and forth with Joe Yazzi, their names and comments to each other on the inside cover, he burned in the woodstove. The painting Maggie did of Hope stopped him. If he folded it, it would spoil. If he left it behind, she would think all the time this had meant nothing to him, and nothing could be more hurtful to her, or further than the truth. He could burn it, but then what she'd painted would never be anywhere else again. Though it wasn't a satisfying decision, he tucked it behind the cowboy painting on the wall, the one she fancied, hoping she'd take both, discover his hidden, somehow come to understand.

When he considered the sheep and Red going hungry and untended, he felt like his head might blow. Owen Garrett was not one to mistreat his animals. What could he do? That almost broke him, and he sat down on the bare mattress, ready to give up. He knew he had to go to stay clear of the law, but suddenly it seemed neither possible nor right to pack up his truck and head off in no particular direction and leave these people behind. He needed them. He was no longer able to handle all this solitary. He needed somewhere—or someone to go toward.

Sara Kay. Make up these last seven years.

He looked up, verifying that he was alone in the cabin. Surely he'd heard the voice, not imagined it. He listened hard, but it didn't come again. He put his face in his hands and reached out to his Higher Power, the same way he did when he wanted to drink so bad he could taste the icy-hot whiskey burning down his throat. He wanted to see his daughter. He'd never stopped wanting to make things right between them. But to go directly to her would be to put her in danger, and further, to once again postpone the step that came between him and his Program, what he really needed to do, which was deal with what had happened that night in the bar. But *I'm not ready.* Fluttering between his eyebrows, concentrating hard, he heard the same voice whisper, *Go.*

All those hours logged on his knees, never once hearing any answer that wasn't his own echo—well, if all this sober time he'd been asking for direction, he guessed at long last, he'd gotten his wish.

Peter was no trouble to track down. After stopping off at Rabbott's to leave his last uncashed paycheck in exchange for traveling money, Owen drove to the Youngcloud place. It seemed like everyone gathered there—from the smallest kid to the creakiest Indian. If Minnie's television couldn't cheer you up, chances were, Verbena Youngcloud's coffee and conversation could make you momentarily forget your troubles. He shook the snow off his hat and cleaned his feet at Verbena's door.

"Owen Garrett," Verbena said. "You come ask me for date?"

He smiled, kissed her, shook his head no. Three couples sat in the blue cathode glow of the screen, watching the surging crowd in Times Square—it always struck Owen odd that they got their holiday earlier, that you could tune it in on the ten o'clock news and all the kissing would be done with, the party hats and confetti so much trash. Bonnie Tsosie sat on Peter's lap. If they were watching anything, it was their own show. He signed to Peter, "You-me, outside."

By the truck Owen said, "Need a favor."

Peter frowned as if he didn't understand. "What?"

Owen took out a voided lumber receipt from Rabbott's, found a pencil stub in one of his pockets. On it he wrote, "Look after Red. The sheep, too. I got to take off for a while."

Peter read, then looked up with that sneer he'd worn the first day they met. "How long is awhile?"

Owen looked down at his boot toes in the dirty snow. He didn't know how to tell the boy that awhile could mean a length of time so unmeasurable and uncertain that whatever he'd answer would be perceived as a lie. "Awhile."

Peter pressed his lips together. Owen tried hard to think how to say what he wanted to say next. "It's not what I want."

When the fury erupted, as he knew it would, the force of the boy's response shocked him. That funny screeching voice of his made a piercing wail in the wind, and Owen looked toward the house, where any second he expected the door to open. "You dick!" Peter yelled. "Why'd you get her hopes up if you knew you weren't going to stick around?"

"Try to understand."

"I understand! You think because I'm deaf I can't understand when people leave?" He began to stomp away from the truck in no particular direction, and Owen caught his shoulder and hauled him back. He was young yet. His own father had deserted him. He wanted to say, Listen here, son, one of life's hardest lessons is learning that a man is nothing but flesh, bones, and bad decisions, but it would take too long to write, and the boy was too mad to lip-read.

Peter jerked away, and Owen again hauled him back, shoving him up against the truck. "I'm writing this note, and you're going to sit there until I'm done, okay?"

Peter, breathing heavily, folded his arms across his chest.

Owen wrote, "Take care of the horse. I can't leave him behind to starve. Ride him all you want. Keep him for me. Sell the sheep for firewood money for your momma. Please give Ruby to Verbena."

Peter read the note, crumpled it and tried to throw it away with force, but being paper, the note only fell a foot away from where they were standing. "At least find the balls to tell her goodbye."

He shook his head no. "Can't."

When Peter swung, Owen found the grace not to duck. The first angry adolescent fist barely glanced off his cheek, and he felt his neck creak in protest. The second punch was more surely aimed and caught him square in the nose, dazing him. He'd locked his knees and taken it fully, knowing that by doing so it would injure Peter's knuckles, give him something sore to nurse besides what was flaring up in his heart. If the kid needed to punch him a couple times to better take what was going down, so be it, and better he learn that there was damage in swinging as well as being on the wrong end of the punch.

Blood trickled down his nostrils, the smell metallic, familiar, bringing to the surface memories of the bar, the rattlesnake head-band, all of it. He wiped it away with his hands, his bandanna already packed for the road. Behind him he could hear Hope in the truck, toenails scrabbling against the window, trying instinctively to free himself to go to his undeserving master's aid. Maggie's boy stood in front of him, slightly hunched over, gasping, shaking his aching hand distractedly. Owen reached for it, hoping that Peter would shake his now, see that a gentleman's agreement didn't have to be based on total agreement, or on anything more than this sorry compromise, but bullheaded Peter would have no part. He gave Owen one last look, and in that look Owen saw the good in this boy rise up, shake itself off, then turn and walk through the blood-spattered snow toward the house, toward Bonnie and, eventually, his mother.

Owen smiled, though it made his nose ache. He was right to do this—Peter'd take care of those animals. He'd been that kind all along, but this new responsibility would find its way into any weak places and shore them up firmly.

He got into his truck and started the engine. It was going to be a long, hard drive in too many ways. He'd have to get used to looking over in the shotgun seat, seeing a three-legged dog sitting where a tall woman, one who was way too good for him, ought to be.

18

NEVER MIND WHAT THE POETS SAID ABOUT APRIL BEING THE cruelest month—obviously none of them had taken into account a Blue Dog February. Plenty of ice patches to slip on as she walked to the mailbox. Inside, there was a color postcard of the Eiffel Tower with Nori's scribbling on the reverse, another chunk of sisterly wisdom meant to be kind, but sounding too much like an accusation to be of any comfort—*Mag, I told you the cowboy would bail out on you. Forget him. That's men for you. . . .* She never thought of herself as Maggie anymore. Margaret tucked the card into the bottom of the mail stack. Next she uncovered an envelope postmarked Riverwall—Peter's letters were now a weekly occurrence, full of questions he made certain she had to answer in a letter of her own. *How's my dog? Are you making sure to feed Red that special grain I bought? What do you think about Bonnie and me going to Monument Valley for spring vacation?* Fine, as long as I come along to chaperon and you sleep in separate states, was what she thought, but she wouldn't phrase her reply in exactly those words. If it was the first of the month, there would be a check from Deeter, but she no longer looked for a note to accompany it.

With her mail spread out before her on the kitchen table, Margaret studied the cup of instant cappuccino she'd just made. It smelled like its label promised it would—"a magnificent blend of cinnamon and the finest blend of European coffees." Sure, it did—somewhere in there her nose registered a slight coffee aroma. Zero cholesterol, 99.5 percent caffeine free, so low in fat it wasn't worth mentioning, what really was the point of drinking such a concoction? She knew if she could locate the energy to lift the mug and take a sip, it would be a warming experience, which was what this cold day called for. Instead she reread Peter's letter. Monument Valley indeed.

Before he returned to Riverwall, he had become so attentive Margaret thought she'd go insane. She hoped his behavior wasn't an indication of how life would be when she was eighty—her son fawning over her doddering-old-lady helplessness. He'd left firewood stacked so high outside her kitchen door that when she did remove a length of wood, the gesture had to be accompanied by a strategic leap out of the way, lest the wobbly pile topple. It was true, firewood could go a long way in heating the body in winter, but there were limits as to its effect on the soul. Bless his teenage heart all the same—her son so worried that Owen Garrett's leaving had devastated his mother that overnight he'd turned good.

She stirred the coffee, watching the mocha clouds swirl into themselves. Just because he'd gone away, as he'd warned he might, everyone—including Nori—expected she would take to her bed in a vaporous collapse, spend the rest of her life crying. But this dry sorrow, with its accompanying absence of tears, hadn't surprised her a bit. The older you got, it seemed like juicing those lachrymal glands took serious effort. The last year and a half had depleted her reserves. Besides, what was one man's departure compared to divorce, a son's deafness, a sister always leaving wreckage in her wake? Ironically this was proving to be the one time Nori wasn't completely off base—men left. Short ones, tall ones, good ones, bad ones, even mediocre ones. They looked out for their own needs first, and when it was time to move on to wherever they were going, apparently they didn't bother saying goodbye.

At her feet Echo nudged her head against Margaret's ankle for the third time in as many minutes. Lately the dog was behaving strangely, demanding affection, turning her nose up at food, making beds for herself all over the house. Margaret thought about reaching down to lift her up into her lap, then petted her instead. It wasn't Echo's fault—things had turned lonely when everyone went back to their lives. The dog missed not only Peter but her three-legged pal as well. After reaching down, Margaret's hands felt impossibly heavy, and she knew that eventually she was going to be faced with the prospect of hauling them back up to the table—it all seemed like so much trouble.

In the living room her painting things stood gathering dust. She'd made herself finish the landscape she'd begun just before Christmas. Three cottonwoods growing along the banks of the Animas River, their winter-bare branches precisely rendered in shades of gray and black. But when the painting was done, those trees and rocks had somehow developed sharp, accusatory angles, and all the energy she had for painting anything else seemed to crawl into a dull hibernation.

Above the mantel her two weavings hung side by side, a pairing of presently passing life and the ancient past. On the left the secondhand remnant of an anonymous weaver whose work had come to rest in a trendy beach-town junk shop a thousand miles from home, the forty-dollar price tag hardly an indication of its worth. To the right hung the smoke-damaged pictorial. When she'd first unwrapped it in her kitchen Christmas night, it had seemed priceless. Now, whenever her eyes accidentally came to rest on it for longer than a second, that promise of a man planting his crop seemed like a cruel joke, both he and his horse destined to stay trapped in the yarn until it rotted. She wondered again what it was the weaver envisioned the man putting into the earth—corn, beans, or some tired relationship? There the weaving had failed to inform. Nothing bloomed in February, anyway—the short month seemed like it didn't even need to be here at all—some twenty-eight-day write-off invented to balance the calendar.

The wall on which the weavings hung was otherwise bare. There was certainly room for a third weaving. Margaret had considered hanging Verbena's "false start" there, but all arrows and business, the small rug seemed too warlike an omen, so she left it upstairs in a drawer.

Outside she heard the perpetually loud muffler of Joe Yazzi's approaching clunker truck, which ran about as infrequently as Margaret's desire to eat whatever she'd fixed herself for dinner. How about that—a rotten day like this, some decent mail, and now a visitor—things were looking up. Abandoning the full cup before her, she went to her front door and opened it, not bothering to wrap a jacket around herself against the cold, and waved to him to come on in. Echo flew out, barking.

The well-bundled Indian got out of his truck and went to the passenger side, wrenching the dented door open. Verbena Young-cloud emerged, hands stuffed in her coat pockets, a scarf wrapped around the lower half of her face. Two visitors.

Joe retrieved a large cardboard box. "Idaho potatoes," he said when he was within speaking distance. "Government commodities. Big suckers, tasty and free. Got so many I'm thinking, might as well share 'em. Great for cooking. Keep all winter long if you don't let 'em freeze. Everybody likes potatoes, right, Verbena?"

"She could use five or six on skinny body," Verbena answered. "Lose any more weight, her breasts disappear."

Joe laughed. "Never have to worry about Verbena beating around the bush."

Verbena unwrapped the scarf and pointed to Echo, who was digging furiously in the snow. "Something don't look right with that dog."

The truth was, nothing had looked right with anything since New Year's Eve. "She's off her food this week. Here, girl," Margaret called, but the dog took off running at her words, straight to the fence line to bark at Ruby, the only ewe Margaret wouldn't let Joe take when he parceled out the remaining sheep he didn't want for himself. Once they got into it, RedBow would get stirred up as well, and between the galloping, barking, and worrying, Margaret was plain worn out dealing with animals. "Joe, help me catch her and I'll keep her inside. Probably like everybody else, she's just anxious for some warm weather. You two want some coffee?"

"Coffee," Verbena repeated, walking past her into the house. "Good idea."

Inside the house Joe set the dog on the floor and got down the cups. "This blue cup's my favorite."

"It's got a chip in the rim. I keep meaning to throw it out."

"Nah, that just makes drinking from it a challenge. Now, blue is a spiritual color. You can take comfort in blue, the same way turquoise is a healing stone." He reached into his flannel shirt pocket for a cellophane bag. "Anybody for tea?"

Verbena held firm—she wanted coffee. But maybe Joe's tea and out-of-state potatoes were what was necessary to turn this gray day sunny. Margaret dumped her cappuccino down the drain. "Why not?"

"Where your sister at?" Verbena asked.

"Back to work. Nori delivers a paper at some medical conference every year about this time. She's in Paris, France, 'the City of Light'."

"You been there?"

Margaret nodded her head. "When I was twenty-two, on a student visa. I can't remember it too well."

Verbena smiled and sipped her coffee. "Big fancy place, Light City?"

Joe squeezed the cheesecloth packet of herbs into the teapot in front of him. "Probably they got more streetlights than downtown Blue Dog or something."

Margaret smiled. "I do remember that the light seemed to shine differently—onto people, buildings, trees. And that it cost around twenty bucks for one not-very-well-cooked pizza."

"Man, that's a lot of money."

"I thought so too, Joe."

Verbena frowned thoughtfully. "Maggie. You go Paris, then twenty year later, forget all about. Kind of like love."

Margaret pushed her cup forward toward Joe for a refill. Verbena Youngcloud, master weaver and legendary lover, at least according to her own stories, had a train of thought unlike anyone else on earth. "Honestly, Verbena, I can't see how Paris and heartbreak connect."

"Well, quit thinking like white woman, maybe you figure out." She shoved her chair back from the table and got up. "I make Joe bring me along because today I wake up and something say, Time for me see Maggie's paintings. Well, where's them paintings hiding at?"

"Right there, in the living room, hiding behind themselves."

As Verbena walked over, Margaret shot Joe a hard look tempered with affection. "Thanks, old buddy. Remind me to return the favor someday."

He threw up his hands. "Hey, Verbena decides on doing something, no skin can refuse. She's my elder, and I got to respect my elders or else—"

"I know, I know, you'll piss off the powers."

Joe smiled. "Well, when I say it, most white people believe it."

In the living room Verbena began turning canvases over and laying them out for inspection. Margaret stood behind her, chagrined at the pitiful inventory emerging: From her initial sketchbooks filled with Conté crayon scribblings of rocks and flowers she had leapt onto gessoed canvas attempting portraits—whatever was she thinking? Here was Peter, his features slightly skewed—one eye too large, the pierced-earring holes studding his ear looking torturous. Then, without provocation, she'd gone on to attack nature, sanitizing Owen's sheep in a pasture *never* that green, feathered out what she didn't know of Red's musculature with her brushes into a vague prettiness, the end result being some kind of astral cloud-horse who, on seeing this saccharine portrait, would have sought out his own shotgun. Finally Verbena came to the painting of the cottonwoods. "Hmm."

"What does 'hmm' mean? Good? Terrible?"

Verbena ran a fingertip over the spidery painted branches. "Not terrible."

Margaret felt a small inward sag of relief. "When I finished that one, I thought it was time to quit."

Verbena picked at a glob of acrylic paint, dried to hardness. "Why you think about quitting?"

"Because I tried to make something beautiful out of what I saw in those trees, and it didn't turn out anything like that."

Verbena let the edge of the canvas go, where it fell against its less successful brothers. "That what you trying do, paint everything beautiful?"

"Well, in a way, I guess. Art certainly should uplift, or question the known. . . ." She stopped, realizing that for all her schooling, despite these past months, she had no idea what art should or should not do, except the niggling awareness that her own wasn't performing at all successfully.

"You want Verbena opinion on painting?"

Margaret nodded. "Absolutely. I respect your work so much."

Verbena turned the cottonwoods painting over so the trees showed again. "Safe."

"Excuse me?"

"You paint good, safe tree here. No scary bark catch your skin on. No dead branch, smelling bad. No one strong branch to save yourself from drowning on, either."

Safe? At first, she thought she hadn't heard her correctly. Then, glancing at Joe, who was finding his chipped blue cup more fascinating than ever, she realized she had indeed heard the weaver, in her own way, tell her what she needed to do was to quit painting. Inside she felt herself falling into a dark place she thought she had been building handrails and stairs out of all these months. After a minute she found her voice. "Am I that bad?"

Verbena's dark eyes held her steady. "Go to Santa Fe. Painters selling there don't paint this good."

"Then what is my problem?"

The Indian woman pointed a finger, chest-high. "Heart made

up of dark and light. Them paintings got no dark heart in them. No light either. False start, always better put away. Sometimes it better not to do a thing than do and not care about it."

But she did care—more than anything, she had hoped to find in those brushes and paints something of her own to nurture when everyone and everything was gone. "You're saying I should quit."

Verbena waited a minute before answering. "Listen. Now, my Minnie, she could be weaver. Why not? In her blood to weave. Mother, grandmothers, way back, all weavers. But she got no heart for the wool, no wanting in her fingers. Better she run cash register down to Rabbott's than pretend."

That stung. "I didn't think I was pretending."

Verbena's face softened. "Ah, Maggie, put aside feelings! You trying so hard, got it all mess up. Just stop painting until you hear it call you back. Then start again." She patted her hand. "Now let's go drink more of that fine coffee you make."

Margaret tamped the aching down into the sore spot where it found immediate company. "I have half a loaf of cinnamon bread from the bakery. It'll mold if someone doesn't help me eat it."

"Some bread would be good," Joe said, too cheerfully.

She watched her friends finish their drinks and listened as they shared several recipes for which Idaho potatoes seemed essential. She heard their words and hers echo hollowly in the kitchen.

"Sure do miss that old white man," Verbena said. "He make me laugh, just like first man I marry."

Joe shushed her. "Maggie don't want to hear about that right now."

"Well, that is stupid way of thinking. Pain of losing don't go away when you tell it to. Remembering is best way to grieve."

"Sorry, Maggie. Verbena, ain't we better get going? Remember, you got business in town with Benny Mota."

"Don't boss me, we can go in minute." The old woman pinched off a piece of her bread and held it out to Echo, who skulked around the table, then pressed herself against the woman's legs. "Better feed this dog, Maggie, or when her time come she have too much pain."

"What time? What are you talking about?"

Verbena bent down, felt the dog's belly, and ran one of the dog's teats between her thumb and forefinger. "Pups," she said. "While yet before she deliver."

"Puppies?" Margaret sputtered.

"Feed her some government potato, potato good for mother dog."

"It's been nearly two months since Owen left—and he took the dog with him. How on earth could Echo be pregnant?"

Verbena smiled. "Sometimes they come into heat out of season. Minnie had terrier one time, he got so obsess with his grandmother that dog in permanent state of ready. Mostly though, the bitches go into heat weird time of year. Who can say? Too much light, not enough, spending all time with one dog. Sometime it almost seem like they fall in love."

"What am I going to do with puppies in February?"

"Well, for starters, keep 'em warm. She's frail-boned little dog, but probably only got one or two in there at most. Put notice in library. Folks'll ask for one. Pups won't be looking for homes till spring. Everybody get baby fever in spring. All but three of my babies born in February on account of spring feeling so good." She fed Echo another piece of bread. "Cute in the face. You'll find homes."

At the door Joe transfered his hat from hand to hand, looking down at the floor before speaking. "Say, listen. I been thinking. Maybe I'm ready now. Maybe I can take one of them puppies off your hands."

Puppies. Margaret, still in shock, could only manage a nod.

Daily Margaret followed Echo from room to room, trying to hunt down her potential choices for labor spots. She left bureau drawers open, not caring about the mess a dog could make of her good sweaters, created towel nests in the laundry area, which was the warmest spot in the house, hoping the dog would sensibly opt for comfort and cleanliness. Equitably Echo ignored them all. Nights, Margaret swore it seemed like she hardly closed her eyes, listening for the scrabble of toenails against hardwood floors. There wasn't any time to feel bad about Verbena's words when Peter's dog could go into labor at any moment. She sleepwalked around the property feeding the animals in the daytime, keeping Echo in sight. As she opened the front door at two in the morning and stood there watching the dog survey several spots that deserved her urine, Margaret told her, "Don't start getting used to this treatment."

But she fed Echo carefully. One night she cooked up a rice-and-lamb casserole, the meat chopped finely, and when it was cool enough, set down a small bowlful on the kitchen floor. Echo dug in, as if she found this dining a distinct improvement over canned dog food. Watching her son's dog eat, for the first time in a long while, certainly since Verbena's visit, Margaret Yearwood felt useful again—needed in a way that had begun to seem obsolete.

"Come down to Embers," Joe Yazzi insisted the following week, a slightly warmer Thursday. "It's enchilada night. I'm sure getting tired of talking to myself."

"You're a ladykiller, Joe. Go find some pretty girl and buy her supper. Then take her dancing."

"Ah, them town girls are looking pretty gray this time of year. I need me a tall, good-looking dinner companion. One who can listen to my troubles, and one who don't throw up after she eats."

"You have troubles?" Margaret hesitated, looking over to where Echo lay sleeping in her newly purchased dog bed, lined with imitation, machine-washable fleece. "I'm happy to listen, Joe, but I'm nervous about leaving the dog. What if she has the puppies while we're gone?"

"She ain't looking too ambitious sleeping there. We'll be gone an hour. Nothing going to happen in one hour."

But sometimes all it took was a brief passage of time to change an entire life. In the few short hours she'd left Peter at home with his fever, he had slid into a coma. In less time than that, Owen had disappeared. Margaret said, "I don't know."

Joe put one boot up on her kitchen chair. "Look, I wasn't going to say nothing. But when I hear from Lulu Mantooth she ain't seen you since Christmas, I figure it's time to come pry you loose of this house. It's a nice house, Maggie, but you need to get out of here sometimes, breathe some car smoke, talk to strangers."

"Great—now everyone downtown is talking about me?"

"Just Lulu and that guy Jim who runs the copy shop and Minnie who's sure you got to be out of coffee filters by now. Come eat. I want to ask you about your sister, anyhow."

Warning bells started ringing like windchimes in a full gale—now she had to go to dinner. She said a silent prayer, hoping that Joe wasn't becoming interested in Nori, the only woman she knew who could out-story Verbena Youngcloud when it came to the subject of men and love. She bent down and gave Echo a scratch under the chin. "You stay tucked into bed and don't start anything until we get back, you hear?"

Echo rolled over, showing her now-plumper belly, wanting and receiving a few gentle strokes from both people.

At Embers Joe tore into his enchiladas hungrily while Margaret toyed with her bowl of tortilla soup. The grated cheese on top sat there in a lump she knew her stomach would perceive as solid rock, so she spooned it out of the bowl and set it on the saucer, alongside two slightly wizened decorative olives.

Between mouthfuls Joe said, "Been wanting to talk to you about something a while now."

She put up a hand. "Not about him, Joe. Trust me that I'm dealing with it in my own way, okay?"

"Oh, hey, this ain't about Owen at all. This is about your sister."

Margaret winced and set down her spoon. "I thought you were just trying to get me out of the house. If you tell me you're thinking seriously of getting romantically involved with Nori, I swear I'll scream the walls down."

"Why? Because sometimes I fall off the wagon? I paid that man cash money for the dog, Maggie. I got me a thirty-day token in my pocket from AA, and in a week, I'll have me two of them."

She hung her head, ashamed. "Joe, you're too good a man to endure the amount of heartbreak Nori can deal out."

"Heartbreak or nothing, she's good to look at."

"And about as fickle as this weather. Trust me. This would not be a healthy idea."

"Well, maybe not. But I sure can't stop thinking about her."

"No one can. Nori gets under your skin. Peter has measured every female he's ever met by his charismatic aunt, and I'll tell you, his mother can't win a single argument standing beside that blazing candlepower. I just hope Bonnie can erase a little of that wonder before she moves on."

"Oh, him and Bonnie are stuck together for a long while yet. If Verbena's predictions come true, you might get yourself a Navajo-Ponca mix daughter-in-law sometime."

"Well, there better not be any hurry on that."

He laughed. "Man, you mothers make a job out of worrying. Your boy's coming along good. Look how much firewood he split for you. You can probably go into next winter with that pile. Almost had to fall over dead before he could figure out when to stop chopping."

"I think he was chopping more than firewood, Joe. Owen's leaving. . . " She let the words trail off. "Never mind. You were about to say something about Nori?"

"Here's the thing, Maggie. I think you need to make up with your sister. Have her come for another visit."

"Nori once a year is about all I can take."

"Ah, you probably blame her when you stub your toe." He paused a minute, then said in a softer voice, "Owen just had to go, Maggie. So he went."

"Do you know the real reason he had to leave?"

Joe frowned. "Well, we been to some meetings. I can't say nothing because they make you promise you won't talk about what's said there outside of it."

Frustrated, she wanted to tell Joe that it was stupid, if they both knew, why couldn't they could talk openly? But to do so would be a betrayal of friendship neither one of them was willing to make, and further, it meant he really was gone. "Tell me he'll be okay. That's all I want to know."

Joe pushed his plate away and smiled at one of the pretty waitresses, but his smile faded the second the girl passed them. "Got no good old Indian wisdom for you there, Maggie. Wish I did. I think he'll make it, wherever he is, cause he's been doing this a long while. Or if he wants to call it in, he'll do that, deal with whatever happens."

"But he'll never be back, will he?"

"I don't know. Time passes different for everyone, don't it? Especially me—when I don't take my medicines time don't follow no clock. You need to get busy, that's all. Before you know it, it'll be spring, and you can work on planting a garden to grow some tomatoes. Start them seeds now. Your sister, when she comes to visit, she can help you eat them. Hey, maybe we can put together a glasshouse, for growing 'em in the cold. How's that sound?"

It wasn't the answer she was seeking. But Joe would talk to her when it was the right time. "The subarctics Rabbott's carries don't have much taste to them," she said. "Let's look through the Burpee catalog at the library."

Echo was nowhere in the house when they returned. Joe stayed, helping Margaret search every room, open each closet, listen hard for any telltale sounds that might give her hiding place away.

"Nowhere," she said when they met again in the kitchen. "Now what?"

"Let's start looking outside."

"It's cold and dark—where would she go?"

"I don't know. She likes razzing that old ewe pretty fine. Let's try looking there."

The slushy fence line was quiet, Ruby lying down in the shelter near her feeding trough. RedBow followed them into the barn, hoping a second dinner was in the offing of all this human activity, pestering Joe by sticking his long nose into his back and neck. "Throw that gluepot a quarter flake," Joe said. "He's about to drive me to drinking blowing down my shirt like that."

Maggie separated the flake into a thin snack that would make the horse happy. In her mind's eye she was unable to shut out seeing Owen's hands performing this same task countless times. He was everywhere in this barn, from the tack he'd left behind to the diminishing stacks of baled hay, and that was one reason she'd avoided spending any length of time here. "Looks like I need to order more hay," she said absently.

"I can get you better price calling my cousin Lester," Joe said. "Them guys down to Feed and Tack see you walk in, the price'll skyrocket." He shook his head. "Sorry, don't see skinny girl dog nowhere in this barn. Maybe she run off."

"Don't say that. Peter will kill me. I'd never forgive myself if something happened to her."

"Well, we ain't looked in the bunkhouse yet."

"How could she get inside the bunkhouse?"

"I don't know. Dogs are relative to Trickster, and that's one coyote sure don't follow the rules. I can go look by myself if you don't want to."

"No, two pair of eyes are better than one." Margaret came into the barn each night, tunneling her vision down to the task before her: hay into hungry horse. After a fashion that kind of vision worked. However, it wouldn't function so smoothly where he'd slept, played cards, or where he'd kissed her.

Joe was already cracking the door, and switching on the light, making brightness out of what had been totally dark for months. It was cold in here. When she heard the shuffling and mewing, Margaret understood that here was the one spot Echo felt peaceful enough to give birth to her babies—in the room where their father had lived. She and Joe listened hard and began searching anyplace that looked likely. They pulled the stripped bed away from the wall, opened the cupboard underneath the tiny sink. He'd left behind some clothing in the cardboard box— but then, traveling light, you didn't need much. Stacked against the wall was that thrift-shop painting, and next to it, a low box of clean rags he used for cleaning tack. A few had spilled out onto the floor, and that was where they found her—curled up into a nest of clean rags, just the tip of her brown tail visible behind the painting. Margaret tilted the frame back and Echo looked up at her, traces of bewilderment apparent beneath the instinctive pull of motherhood.

"Joe," she called softly. "Over here."

She'd managed by herself. Two white puppies with crimped ears lay at her side. One, sturdy and fat, already nursed. The other pup was much smaller, skinnier—a runt—still squirming around, trying blindly to find its way to the milk. With one finger Joe pushed it, an inch at a time, until it found Echo's teat. In the bloody toweling to the left of the dogs, Margaret found a third puppy, its protective sac torn open, but the body inside unmoving. "Oh, Echo," she said, feeling her own memory of that same kind of stillness revive. She touched the dead pup, its perfect little body, all that promise, wasted. Would feeding Echo more food earlier have helped it survive? Covering it with one of the clean rags, she turned her attention back to the living.

"Good girl," she said to Echo. Her tail thumped in response. "What a wonderful mother you are. You found the safest place for your babies. You are such a brave girl."

Joe squatted down on his heels. "Same way some lambs are born dark, them heeler dogs are born white. Later they turn a color, but you can't tell for awhile yet whether they'll be red or blue. I sure like the look of that big one. Hope it's a female. I sure do need me some female company."

Oblivious to their words, exhausted from her efforts, Margaret saw that Echo had decided it was safe now to go to sleep.

Blue Rodeo

The moon has her porches turned to face the light,
but the deep part of her house is in darkness.

AUTHOR UNKNOWN

▊ 19 ▊

SUMMER WAS ON ITS WAY OUT AGAIN, THE DAYS GROWING shorter, the wind growing more teeth with every gust that blew through. During the two years she'd lived in the Starr farmhouse, Margaret Yearwood had learned several lessons. If you wanted to grow summer tomatoes, you'd best do it under fine-gauge screen, or all you ended up accomplishing was feeding the grasshoppers. By September you'd better have five cords of dry firewood stacked within walking distance of the front door, unless you wanted to pay ten times what it was worth after the first snow fell. And snow didn't know the names of the seasons, it was just as likely to surprise you in the fall as it was in late spring.

In California fall had been a kind of idealistic agreement you entered into: The stores set out clothing it was still too hot to wear; you bought them anyway. The beach traffic let up a little, so you could walk along the shore to get some exercise, turn your dog loose to play in the waves when no one was looking, maybe not even get a ticket. You knew fall had arrived when your teenager started sleeping through his alarm and had to be kicked in the butt to make his bus, and, like most things in life, you took it on faith that his destination *was* the bus, then school, and not some Tijuana fiasco that would reorder his future with a permanent, swift jolt. But it seemed like as soon as you found a shelf on which to set your faith, things changed; wasn't that true, and then you had to work harder at believing what you took for granted than you did at anything, which was not unlike trudging through a Blue Dog winter with only two dogs for company.

Here in this high country, you could smell winter coming, the sheer freight-train determinedness of it, not the same as in Margaret's childhood Massachusetts, where a shiver now and then caught her unaware, and damp red-and-yellowing leaves underfoot revealed the first ice crystals when kicked away. The smell of snow from the north blew in the kitchen window one day, and as you shut the window, you knew fall would be gone in another heartbeat. In Blue Dog the change was gradual, but honest if you paid attention. One day the yellow flowers dropped their petals all at once, scattering pollen to the wind in the belief that come next summer, they would find a field. Insects spun cocoons, farmers baled hay after harvest—and weather was at the root of everything, as irrepressibly responsible for comfort and pain as human desire, or at least that was how she remembered it, those late summer days leading into winter, back when she believed she was loved by Owen Garrett.

She remembered that first swim they'd taken together, a long time before he'd left. The aspens were turning, the leaves shimmering silver and gold in the late sun. How afraid she was to let him touch her, and how, once he had touched her, he never pushed or expected it was his right. There was never any hurry to making love, yet it seemed like whenever they did, she felt as desperate and rushed as a teenager. The pleasure they mined from each other's bodies now seemed solemn. Just recalling it held the power to make her feel ageless. Owen had been the gentle half of their lovemaking; it was she who grasped a little too tightly, pushed for more, couldn't seem to ever get enough of him to feel full and satisfied, as if the physical part of her sensed the transient in him. Every time Owen seemed to linger deliberately, taking great pains to make sure there wasn't an inch left to her skin that wasn't singing. But sex aside, their collective laughter was the best part of their relationship. In the river that night, hers had been a nervous laughter, in her marrow still a good Catholic girl at forty, afraid of being caught outside without her clothes. Then it turned damp and chilly. No matter how close they hugged, they couldn't get comfortable and reluctantly agreed to go for their clothes. But before they left the water, made that long dash from the river to the bunkhouse, Owen had looked up at the darkening sky and said, "Fall's coming."

Maybe from the first moment she'd seen him, deep down, she'd known he was already traveling a path heading away from her life, that her iron bedstead and kitchen were only the briefest interlude, some kind of proving ground where she could learn whatever she needed—how to make peace with Peter, forgive her sister, make the final break free from Ray before she returned to her California life. In a way it had almost worked. Peter came home his first summer after Riverwall. He never would be easy at making friends, but he cut the grass back where it was long, ate dinner with her the nights he could bear to be apart from Bonnie, and was kind enough not to ask when she was going to start painting again. He also got up each morning to feed and ride the horse Owen had left behind. He looked great on that horse.

Dr. Kennedy from Riverwall had talked the powers that be into bending the rules for Peter and Bonnie to take summer classes at San Juan College in Farmington. It was only a humanities survey, but Peter was holding his own. After his year with the Hidalgos, he boarded full-time at Riverwall. He claimed his roommate wasn't a "total geek": He seemed to be getting along.

These days there was nothing coming out of her paintbrush except stray sable hairs. When she finally picked up her drawing things, it was to put them into a box and to get them out of the way. Sometimes she drove out to Shiprock and sat in the shadows of *Tse Bida'hi*, seeing the art there, and trying to resolve the giant bird the *Diné* believed had deliberately grounded itself with cooling rock that had plugged an ancient volcano's throat, sparing this land. For all her education, theory, and research, she knew Verbena was right—painting came from those twin pockets of light and dark found in the heart or it came not at all. When a part-time job in the Blue Dog library became available, Margaret shut her heart's eyes, shelved books, and ignored the bristles altogether.

Several times a day she found herself swiping at her eyes, but tears were for other women. Like a river, Owen had said, strong and treacherous in places, still and murky in others, the good Lord alone knows what grows on those river bottoms.

Maybe Owen Garrett was the only surviving true gentleman left on the face of the planet, and the only way he knew to exit his complicated life here gracefully was to simply tip his hat and go. In the back of her mind one sliver of doubt remained. What if she hadn't mattered? Well, the seasoned Margaret Yearwood had to admit that wallowing in what-ifs was too comfortable, like baking cookies on the pretense that they were all for Peter, chocolate smells hooking their perfume into your nostrils, knowing it was just a matter of time before you gave in to self-pity and gorged.

Through those ridiculous faxes her sister thought made better sense than letters, she and Nori had butted their heads together enough times that they'd made a kind of mutual peace. She loved her sister but had come to recognize that what she felt was love only in the oddest way. They didn't go about teaching each other female wisdom, as came naturally to Verbena Youngcloud, or helping each other out over hard times the way Margaret could depend on Joe Yazzi to find her a decent price on hay midwinter. As sisters she and Nori had never been easy with any of their emotions, least of all with loving each other. But that went way back—from her mother on down to the baby girl Margaret had birthed stillborn. These tall females were suspicious of the world around them, lacking balance, yet determined to grit their teeth and endure. They never wanted to let anyone see them in other than their Sunday best, but neither of them went to church anymore—unlike Peter, who would sit through an hour of anything if it meant a chance to rub thighs with Bonnie Tsosie.

Margaret had gotten sick this spring. A bad cough she couldn't shake. With each new prescription of antibiotics, the doctor kept warning her if she didn't rest and take care of herself it could go into pneumonia. In the bottom lobe of her left lung, it felt like there was a tiny balled-up wad of cellophane, a rustling that crinkled like leftover Christmas wrapping paper with every breath. Finally she drove out to Joe Yazzi's and let him make her tea.

"This thing in your lungs, Maggie. Better find a way to let them tears come on out or you won't get well, I'm telling you."

But how did you let go when you had no clue where the knots began?

Joe had asked to fill in at Rabbott's, and this week anyway, his truck was running. "Let me tell you a story," he said as he mixed the herbs for her drink. "That legend of Blue Dog Owen told you? I heard different. In this story Blue Dog was a regular mutt, living out near Great Kiva in Aztec. You been there?"

"I've driven by."

"We'll go sometime. It's a holy place. Nobody's lived there for hundreds of years, so they turn it into a big tourist thing to make a few dollars the Indians sure won't never see. And the way the story goes, right around the twenties this skinny dog shows up, won't leave for nothing, all the tourist people coming in wanting to adopt him. A few even take him home. Dog run back to the Kiva every time, just waiting there outside the ruins, waiting on something. There's this young ranger kind of dude working there, fairly handsome for a white man, taking money, telling them tourists how Anasazi used to live, showing them grinding stones, walking 'em through rooms they used to live in. Ranger dude brings some dog food, kind of partners up with old Blue Dog.

"Then one night he meets this woman in a bar, and she's just moved to town. Good-looking woman, maybe even a little bit like your bullheaded sister. They have few beers or whatever, and he take this woman out with him to Kiva, figures he'll get her down in the great room, out of the heat, on account of summer's extra warm, she'll be feeling cool and holy, and think taking off her clothes, doing what comes natural will be a real good idea. So he takes her there, and it's one of them nights when the moon's face is full up in Father Sky, you can see it shining through hole in the ceiling, moonlight all over the place, big helping medicine when it comes to making love.

"But before he can get this woman to let him touch her in the right places, this big old shaft of light falls on her body and Sha! Before you know it, she ain't a woman no more, she's a dog, and she leaps out of the Kiva through that ceiling hole and runs off with the other one."

Margaret took the packet of herbs Joe offered. "Is that the end of the story?"

"Not hardly. Well, his friends notice the old ranger dude moping around, not doing his jobs so good anymore, they kid him about it, call him Hangdog, Mister Blue, stuff like that until man goes a little crazy and moves away to get free of the teasing. He's a lazy white man, though, and only goes one town away, here, in Blue Dog, and can't find no work on account of his laziness. People see him always walking around downtown talking to himself. Pretty soon he's famous, and people start calling the town that place where old Blue Dog hangs out."

She sipped her tea, which in the time it had taken Joe to tell the story had lost its warmth and tasted like tepid sage. "Joe, that is a pretty lame tale, even for you."

He smiled, the silver tooth just showing its tip. "Maggie, the truth is, there ain't no one legend. You make up whatever story works good for you when you need it. It can be one of them sad stories where old ladies go to twisting hankies, or it can be the big old windy kind I like to spin. Some things happen you can't do nothing about, but mostly it's your choice and you can do a little something, even if it ain't no more than make a cup of tea."

On Thursday nights they were regular dining partners. Enchiladas and salsa so hot sometimes her lips felt blistered, but in a good way, as if shocking her taste buds awake. Sometimes they looked across the table at each other, and Margaret couldn't speak for the loss that bound them. But nothing held Joe's tongue for very long. "You know, like Verbena said, our people believe that only by remembering and talking about someone do you set them free. Got new twin lambs out of them ewes of his. Little black babies going to turn snow white. Come take a look, you can see his work in them."

She shook her head no. "They'll just get sold off for meat at Blue Dog Days. I don't want to fall in love again."

Joe whistled for his dog, and the half blue heeler–half mutt came immediately to his side. "Blue Dog," he said, addressing the animal though Maggie had the feeling Joe was speaking only to her. "Think it might be time to get me a few cattles again. I hear them beef ads on radio. People quit eating red meat again, can always practice my roping. Come to Blue Dog Days, Maggie. Watch the dancing."

This year Peter and Bonnie were involved in Blue Dog Days, Bonnie with her family heading up the sing, and Peter dancing alongside Joe, the whitest man in the circle. He looked handsome, dressed in the shells and metal beads Bonnie'd fashioned for his wrists and ankles. They made a music he could not hear but had to feel as they rattled against his ankles and wrists. Margaret stood for awhile on the sidewalk outside Rabbott's, where the same vendor who offered her the silver beads the first year again showed them proudly, this time for twenty dollars more.

What do I need silver-tooled beads for? Maggie said to herself, but tried them on anyway, felt their weight and chill metal warm against her breastbone. She dug in her pocketbook, handed the woman her money, and suddenly they were hers, for no other reason than she held something she could fasten around her neck.

She waved to Peter and wandered down Main Street where the singers were running instrument checks. Bonnie's brothers were good boys, proud of their guitars and their abilities. They played their way through a few of the expected numbers, and

Margaret half listened, not really buying the enthusiasm they threw into the country music numbers currently gracing the charts, songs that in her estimation had been played into the ground long before this summer. She checked on the children dressed up as their favorite books for the library's entry in the parade. Smiling faces peered out from circles cut into the oversized cardboard. The tallest kid was representing Gary Paulsen's *Canyons*, and the smallest, the classic *Goodnight Moon*. Everyone's spines set straight, she turned and headed for the booth where Verbena and Minnie Youngcloud were busy frying up the bread. She'd lost her taste for it, but customers stood three and four deep, feet tapping in impatience, dollars sticking out of their fists.

"Need a hand?"

Minnie pushed her glasses up her nose. They were spattered with grease, as was her apron front, advertising Rabbott's Hardware, the only place to go for home improvement. "Maggie! Good to see you. You want to take change or fill up the napkin dispensers?"

"Both. Just show me where everything is."

She collected quarters and separated oily dollars, clipping the nozzle tops off honey bears, wiping small sticky faces, and still found time to admire the youngest dancers' costumes. A little envy was natural—when people born into this much poverty and prejudice banded together and danced, kept their customs, responded to all that with art—how could you not want to belong? Sometimes she wondered if she should look for another town, a place she might fit in better. But she knew as well as she knew her own breathing, she wasn't leaving the town of Blue Dog, if only for one more chance at that brief season when the wildflowers blossomed in fecund fury, turning dry ground and scrub into a sea of waving yellow.

She sold bread to a few of the rodeo boys, decked out in chaps in hot pink and aqua as well as the traditional brown calfhide. Polite to the bone, they always said, "Ma'am," tipped their hats, and kept their language clean. They had his walk, that prideless bowlegged swagger that came from years of wrapping your legs around horseflesh. She shivered, missing him, and accepted Minnie's offer of an old Disneyland sweatshirt. Silver beads on top of Mickey Mouse, her hair tied back in a knot, and smelling of frybread grease. The cover of *Vogue* had to be right around the corner.

After a few hours it got dark, and they started lighting the arena and stage. Bonnie's brothers played on, dauntless under the darkening sky. They had Bonnie onstage with them, tapping a tambourine against her leg. My boy Peter's sleeping with that girl, Margaret knew, and under her fear of the complications that accompanied first love, she tried only to be happy for him. Now Bonnie was going to the microphone, and Margaret stepped away from the booth to better hear what she was saying.

She was singing. Low and slightly off-key, eyes shut. Peter caught up to his mother and touched her shoulder. In her deeply focused state, she almost shook him off.

"Tell me what she's singing," he said.

Margaret had never heard the song before but knew instantly that although Bonnie might not have been the singer to make the song famous, she was the writer to give it life.

> *"You always were a dreamer, you chased your dreams so long*
> *you always were a renegade, living hard and strong*
> *and when this old world wasn't big enough*
> *you had to carry on*
> *so strike up the band in heaven, boy*
> *give us all a song*
>
> *from the blue rodeo*
> *all the horses are white, the trophies are gold,*
> *come on shoot us a star, play some guitar*
> *so we can find where you are in the blue rodeo*
>
> *Perfect sky is up above, the sun shines off a wing*
> *God in all his wisdom, boy, he thought of everything*
> *He gave his gift for us to share, to have but never own*

and when we've given it back a hundredfold
He lets us come back home

to the blue rodeo
the horses are white, the trophies are gold
come on shoot us a star, play some guitar
so we can find where you are in the blue rodeo

Now the silence is deafening from the music that we don't hear
but the sound that echoes in our hearts
now falls on more worthy ears

from the blue rodeo
the horses are white, the trophies are gold
come on, shoot us a star, play some electric guitar
so we can find where you are in the blue rodeo
we'll try to find where you are in the blue rodeo. . . ."

Peter's requests and his persistent hand signing were like mosquitoes buzzing. Margaret signed woodenly, giving him what he asked for. *Blue,* the letter *B* held vertically, shaking. *Rodeo?* She improvised for the sign she didn't know: *horse,* the two-fingered nod over her right ear; *celebration,* the palm clap and swirl of index fingers on each hand up into the air. What she couldn't do was face him and put her heart into it, like you were supposed to, the way Bonnie was doing, whether she hit the notes or missed them.

Bonnie's song made her recall every moment of Owen Garrett in her life, the brief wonder of feeling and returning faithful love, and how it felt to have it severed. She wished she'd run down the highway after him, even if it meant she was reduced to visiting him in jail, one weekend a month.

When the song ended, Peter ran off to Bonnie, who was blinking her way back to earth, surrounded by applause. This town loved her. Their faith in their children never faltered. Margaret pulled up Minnie's sweatshirt, wiped her face, and went to

watch the rodeo cowboys mistreat their animals in hopes of winning a massive silver belt buckle. Buckles, she thought. That was
the one thing she'd change about Bonnie's song, not gold trophies, but gold buckles to replace the silver. Goddamn every single one of them for their good looks, their ability to pour into
worn jeans and bright shirts the myth of an eternally western
man, out to conquer wild prairie and skirt, not necessarily in that
exact order. The young girls loped in to cavalcade, balancing flags
in special cups attached alongside their stirrups. They rode as if
fixed to their horses, carousel ponies, all glittering silver bits and
bridle decorations, flowing blond manes to match their horses,
equally fearless.

The first event was steer wrestling, and Margaret cheered
inwardly every time the cowboys lost and the steer trotted off
proudly, horns held high, to be ushered through the chute. Next
came the team-ropers, and she brightened, remembering Joe and
Owen's entry that first year, when he'd explained how he and Joe
rode with their entry numbers turned upside down, just for
sport, not to compete for prize money. Of course, now she knew
why: He was a good roper, but he couldn't have afforded to win.
Sooner or later someone would want to take his picture, publish
it in a newspaper, and then someone might recognize him. A hus-
band-and-wife team won this time—people she didn't know.
Dave Rabbott fell off his pinto mare and dented his new hat, and
the crowd tittered softly at his outrage. Maggie was the only one
he told about missing Owen. *Two years he worked for me, never
took so much as a quarter or borrowed against his pay. Like a son to
me, Margaret. If there was a problem, why didn't he say so? I just don't
get it.*

She hated the bronc riding, where they cinched the horses
around the testicles with those mean straps to make sure they'd
buck high. She bought a Coke and drank it over by the library.
She came back to watch the bull-riders and cheer on the bulls,
and because she was curious to see who was foolish enough to try
this suicide endeavor in hopes of winning five hundred dollars.
Assured a full day's work, the paramedics were lined up behind

the arena, stuffing Navajo tacos into their mouths, waiting to be called. Three sour-looking cowboys got tossed and rolled to safety; a fourth made eight seconds but got hung up in his grip, and the clowns earned their salary, freeing him before he lost any fingers. He was a college boy, well known in town, and the crowd was distracted while the paramedics set aside dinner to tend his injured hand. She watched, too, almost missing the cowboy who came out of the chute next, riding Crankshaft, a gray Brahman with one dark eye. The rider had his hat parked down his forehead, covering his features. He was thin, older than the others, determined enough that he did not look up at the crowd cockily, which seemed to be so many riders' downfall. He had a left-handed grip and kept his right hand aloft, as was the custom, while he spurred and rocked his legs like you were supposed to, not to *hurt* the animal but in order to fully impress the judges. The announcer began to narrate: "Ladies and gentlemen, it's a crying shame we don't have television instant replay here in Blue Dog, cause I think we're lookin' at the ride of the night, a seventy-nine if I'm any judge of bull-riding. Entry form states his name as Bob Williams out of Durango, Colorado, but he sure enough don't look like no Willy Bob to me. . . . Who is this mysterious stranger?"

His number was 53, and it was right side up. He dismounted his bull, which, as a final protest, bucked high and twisted, causing the crowd to ooh and aah, but Margaret only saw the rider's hands, the bandanna tied to his belt loop, and the cattleman's crease in a very worn Resistol hat as he hopped the arena fence. Her heart tripped inside her chest as she struggled to see him making his way through the crowd to the money window, and she broke into a run to catch up to him.

"Collected his money and took off toward the parking lot," the lady at the winnings table said.

Bootprints, pawprints, hoofprints, steamy buns of horse manure marked the dirt where the trucks and trailers were parked. He was there, bent over and packing his gear in the truck bed, already heading to the next rodeo, another five hundred dollars to be won. He looked at her and smiled, as if she might be part of his good luck for the evening. "Hey there, honey."

"Nice ride," she told him, and walked away.

It was the way your heart worked sometimes, making your eyes play tricks on you because every organ wanted desperately to believe those things that came true in movies and good books.

That night she lay awake in her own house. Two rooms away she could hear the unmistakable sounds of her son and Bonnie Tsosie making love. She started at first, fought the urge to flip on lights, make accusations, give them advice they hadn't asked for and she didn't really believe in. This was still her house, and they needed to respect that. But they were smart kids, they knew about the condom business, they were seventeen, and they were in love. Only two days earlier she had sat with Bonnie at her own kitchen table, braiding her thick black hair into plaits in a way her own would never go, listening to the girl's dreams for college and a way off the reservation, only long enough that she could return armed with enough education to make a difference. "If I can study to become a nurse, I can make sure kids get their shots," Bonnie said, signing her words automatically.

Margaret turned her face so Bonnie would see her speak. She tapped the letter D on her wrist. "Try for a doctor, Bonnie. Go as far as you can, and don't let anything stand in your way."

Bonnie smiled, and Margaret knew if it wasn't Peter who would crimp those goals into compromise, it would probably be some other boy.

Now Echo and her errant son wanted out. They were scratching at the bedroom door in the moonlight. "Okay already," Margaret said, and took them down the back steps.

She slipped on her boots near the door, and walked across the empty pastures in her nightgown. Old Ruby, the yellow, nearly toothless eating machine, stood like a puddle of light near the fence. Joe wanted to take her to Verbena's, where Minnie would look after her, but Margaret couldn't let him. It was worth grinding Ruby's feed when she pictured the pasture empty. Beyond the ewe the bunkhouse was dark as solid rock. She shut her eyes and heard Echo rustling around in the weeds behind her. It had been hard to think of a name for the runt. Dinky seemed appropriate but too ordinary. When she finally bought a television and VCR to fill up her endless evenings, she found that Blue Dog's video inventory consisted mostly of horror movies and early westerns. The clerk who recommended John Wayne's *The Cowboys* swore it was a classic, that if she didn't like it, she could have her two dollars back. "Little budgers," that was what Wayne had called the young boys he hired to replace his men, the kids he tried to teach the rough art of cowboying. They were always disappointing him, nearly running off cliffs, getting into hilarious mischief. Hopeful's son had in his short life run up a similar résumé, including a dinner of acrylic paints, so Budger it was. When Budger began barking Margaret called out, "Hush," though she knew even if Peter and Bonnie's hearing were fully restored by some sudden miracle, they were so lost in each other they couldn't have been disturbed by the half-heeler's yapping. She followed the barking down the road toward the mailbox. For a moment she swore she saw a man. Standing there in her nightgown and cowboy boots, she thought about going back for the rifle Joe had given her and taught her to use, but this wasn't California, it was Blue Dog, a small town, where every stranger passing through was a potential friend. She put purpose into her step and went to claim her dogs.

It wasn't a man, it was a coyote. They stood twenty feet from each other, still enough that she could see the hair on the animal's ruff lift in the wind. He was well fed, coming up from the river from a drink, probably. Her eyes adjusted to the dark, and she noticed something she hadn't seen before. The coyote was missing a front leg. "Get out of here," she called out to him, in a deep, low voice that masked her fear and feigned strength, clapping her hands before one of the neighbors could come shoot him. "Go on!"

The coyote took her suggestion and ran away, that funny soundless hopping lope she hadn't seen in so long she'd nearly forgotten how it went.

In her mind's eye, she could see another face—thinner, bearded, but familiar. Wherever he was he set his left hand on the horn of his saddle, leaned into it, smiled as he tipped the rim of his black hat. He was safe somewhere, and wasn't that what mattered, what it all came down to, what made legends worth remembering, telling to your children?

In that moment Margaret Yearwood believed in so many things it wasn't enough to call it religion: she believed in the infinite wisdom there was to balancing the ingredients of human life, in the necessity of grief and its partner, joy; in a time to heed the urge of recklessness and then admit a need for restraint; in hello and goodbye; and sometimes, if you were lucky, or very forgiving, hello again.

20

HIS MOTHER WAS PAINTING AGAIN. HUGE CANVASES THAT BORE no resemblance to the detailed nature paintings she'd labored over those first few months she lived here, like the one of Shiprock Monument he had framed above his bed. It was still about animals, but as far as Peter could make out, animals that were neither of this world nor fully of the dream world where he sometimes envisioned them. These creatures were caught somewhere in between, their wings clipped, eyes blinded, limbs malformed. The coolest ones were the six-foot-tall crazy-colored dogs leaping and soaring outward from the canvas, scaring him, thrilling him. Peter knew without any art critic's two-bit review they were her best stuff. They cut to the chase; they had *cojones*. On those, she didn't even bother to paint in the background, just left it stark white, didn't bother cleaning up the handprints or smudges from moving the canvas. Sometimes he woke up in the middle of the night to get a drink of water, and she was already downstairs at work, a single lamp shining on the canvas, her hand the only living thing visible out of the shadow.

He stood in the doorway watching her, trying to imagine what it felt like to have that kind of desire move through you, noticing how she couldn't seem to squeeze the paint out fast enough to give the dogs space to run. She'd paint three hours, then sleep in until noon the next day to recover. He tried not to make much noise.

When Mrs. Youngcloud dropped by for a visit, she walked around those canvases and nodded, saying, "Good work," then embraced his mother sadly, as if she knew the world those paintings came from, but wasn't about to encourage anything by saying so aloud.

She would never do anything *really* crazy, but there were times he felt like he had to keep an eye on her, act up a little, push limits to remind her she had other reasons to make dinner than just a son being home for the summer.

Kennedy's bullshit aside, turning seventeen wasn't any easier than being fifteen or sixteen. Oh, there were corners you turned with relief. His half-sister's christening, where he and his father had to shake hands, be "men," and Peter had to look at that baby and realize he was no longer the only child in his father's life. She wasn't totally ugly. He sent her birthday cards, stuffed animals Bonnie loved to help him pick out. Bonnie Tsosie had saved his life. When they took off their clothes and touched each other, he understood why adults did the things they did. It was all there, right there under your hands, in your faces, the spaces you fit each other into and around. When she did what he liked most— something that had nothing to do with sex—spoke his name aloud, it didn't matter that he couldn't hear her. Her compromise made a space that was all theirs, not of the deaf world, where he still got some of the signs wrong, and not of the hearing one he could never go back to. If he had come to any understanding in the time since his illness, it was that he would always be caught somewhere between those two worlds, but it didn't have to be by himself.

Otherwise his life felt regular, like one giant waiting game where you harnessed your restlessness and sat through classes for credits. The things they tried to teach you didn't always get sucked into the sponge, but he when he needed those facts, he'd find out he'd learned more than he thought. If you piled up enough credits, they let you go off to college. San Juan was like a trial run, but real college, that was more like waiting for the one bus that never came. He'd look up from his textbooks and there would be Bonnie, signing to him, "Ten more months, Washington, D.C.!" and he'd nod his fist, yes, yes, but he still couldn't see over the horizon to Gallaudet University just yet.

Riding the horse helped. Feeling Red's responsiveness to his leg cues, cutting through woods where his ancestors had once lived, had made their way though bad weather and famine, leaving bits of flaked rock and pottery behind—that helped pass the time. Horses didn't care if you were deaf or hearing; they cared how light your touch was, if you remembered to check their feet for stones or thought to put the sliced green apples into the bucket underneath the oats for a surprise. If you stroked them softly, said their names over and over, what happened was your anger filtered away, and even better, they looked forward to your visits. If deafness was a penalty, Peter guessed RedBow was one reward.

He was waiting for another thing besides college, and growing up. He was waiting for the right time to tell his mother something he'd known all along but felt move into his heart only recently, charge into the chambers with an urgency as real as and wonderful as sound. It was something "John Wayne" had said— whatever his real name was, he wasn't a liar. A man didn't leave behind a horse this good, not willingly. After riding Red all summer, Peter knew. It was a matter of time, of clearing a path through some heavy-duty crap, maybe. But in two and a half years, he'd learned a new way of hearing—that what passed through your heart amounted to a different kind of hearing, a sound you could believe in and trust. This whole thing—her being sad, painting demented dogs on the canvas, the longing it seemed like she never could fill—all that was as temporary a thing as those weeks he'd slept on in the coma, until Echo barked loudly, insisting he come home. No matter what the doctors said, he knew he'd heard her, and that the ears sprouting from your head were no match for those in your heart. His mother's own dogs were barking. She had to listen, and she had to believe.

If not before the first snow, then soon after. Peter Sweetwater might be deaf for good, but O-w-e-n Garrett was coming back.